TWO DRAGONS

Also by Octavia Randolph

Sidroc the Dane

The Circle of Ceridwen

Ceridwen of Kilton

The Claiming

The Hall of Tyr

Tindr

Silver Hammer, Golden Cross

Wildswept

For Me Fate Wove This

The Circle of Ceridwen Cookery Book(let)

Light, Descending

The Tale of Melkorka: A Novella

Ride: A Novella

BOOK NINE

THE CIRCLE OF CERIDWEN SAGA

TWO DRAGONS

OCTAVIA RANDOLPH

PYEWACKET PRESS

Two Dragons is the ninth book in
The Circle of Ceridwen Saga by Octavia Randolph

ISBN Softcover: 978-1-942044-34-5
ISBN Hardcover: 978-1-942044-35-2

Book cover design by DesignforBooks.com. Photo credits: Castle, iStockphoto©vcstimeless; landscape photography, photo-manipulation, Anglo-Saxon manuscript design (inspired by Sutton Hoo gold belt buckle) and dragon illustration (inspired by Historia Regum Britanniae manuscript depicting two dragons) by Michael Rohani. Latin by Octavia Randolph. Maps by Michael Rohani.

Pyewacket Press

The Circle of Ceridwen Saga employs British spellings, alternate spellings, archaic words, and oftentimes unusual verb to subject placement. This is intentional. A Glossary of Terms will be found at the end of the novel.

For Beth Altchek, who cures elf-shot, and
Libby Williams, who tames fire-drakes

CONTENTS

LIST OF CHARACTERS

Ceric, son of Ceridwen and Gyric,
grandson of Godwulf of Kilton

Worr, the horse-thegn of Kilton, pledged man of Ceric

Edwin, Ceric's younger brother, Lord of Kilton in Wessex

Edgyth, Lady of Kilton, widow of Godwin,
mother by adoption to Edwin

Dunnere, priest of Kilton

Begu, a woman of Kilton

Eorconbeald, captain of Edwin's body-guard

Hrald, son of Ælfwyn and Sidroc, Jarl of the
Danish keep of Four Stones in Lindisse

Yrling, son of Ceridwen and Sidroc

Ælfwyn, Lady of Four Stones, mother to Hrald,
widowed of Yrling; marriage dissolved with Sidroc

Burginde, companion and nurse to Ælfwyn

Bork, an orphan boy, taken in by Hrald

Ealhswith, daughter to Ælfwyn

Eanflad, youngest sister to Ælfwyn

Jari, a warrior of Four Stones, chief body-guard to Hrald

Kjeld, second in command at Four

Stones, and body-guard to Hrald

Sigewif, Abbess of Oundle

Bova, consecrated nun and brewster at Oundle

Asberg, brother-in-law to Ælfwyn, in command at the fortress of Turcesig

Æthelthryth, sister of Ælfwyn, wed to Asberg

Raedwulf, Bailiff of Defenas in Wessex

Æthelred, Ealdorman and Lord of Mercia, son-in-law to King Ælfred

Æthelflaed, Lady of Mercia, daughter of Ælfred and wife to Æthelred

Pega of Mercia, ward of Æthelflaed

Mealla, companion to Pega, a maid of Éireann

Haward, a young Danish war-chief

Wilgot, the priest of Four Stones

Tilbert, steward of Geornaham, under the protection of Four Stones

Dagmar, daughter of the late Guthrum, King of the Danes in Angle-land

Vigmund, a Danish warrior, former body-guard of Guthrum

Heligo, King of Dane-mark

Haesten, a war-chief of the Danes

Ceridwen, Mistress of the hall Tyrsborg on the island of Gotland, wife to Sidroc

Eirian, daughter of Ceridwen and Sidroc

Sidroc the Dane, formerly Jarl of South Lindisse

Tindr, a bow hunter, and Šeará, his Sámi wife

Rodiaud, youngest daughter of Ceridwen and Sidroc

Eskil, a warrior of the Svear

Gunnvor, cook at Tyrsborg, and **Helga**, serving woman

Rannveig, a brewster on Gotland, mother of Tindr

Gudfrid, cook at Rannveig's brew-house

Berse, weapon-smith on Gotland

Hrald, father of Sidroc, and **Stenhild**, his Gotlandic wife

Gwydden, a Welsh priest, correspondent of Dunnere

Dwynwen, a noble maid of Ceredigion, in Wales

Elidon, King of Ceredigion in Wales, uncle to Dwynwen

Luned, a woman of Wales

TWO DRAGONS MAPS

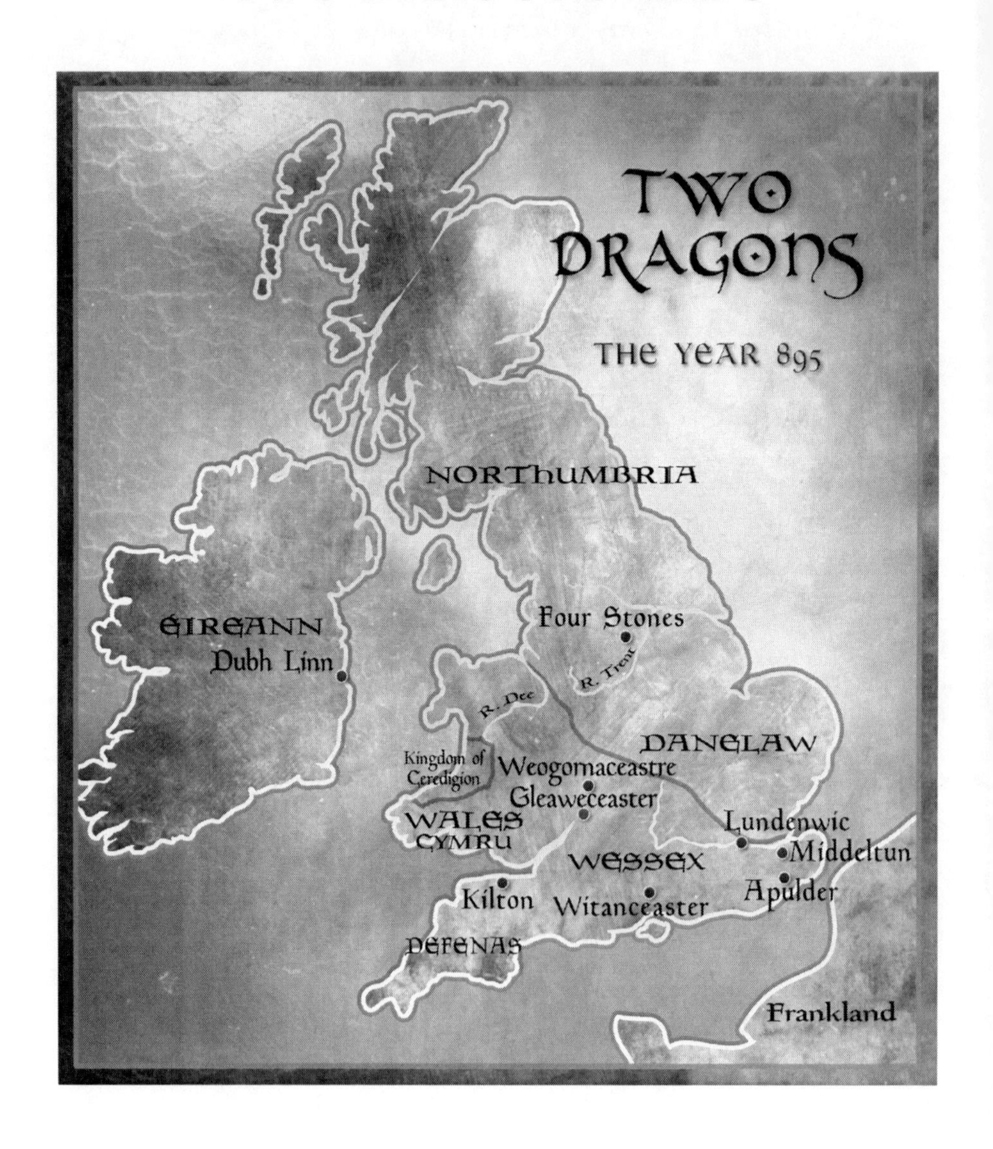

TWO DRAGONS
THE YEAR 895
Land of the Sámi
Land of the Sámi
Norse
Uppsala
Svear
Land of the Rus
Gotland
Tyrsborg
Viborg
Danes
Öland
Ribe
Skania
Prus
Pomerani
Four Stones
Polanie
Wessex
Kilton
Frankland

TWO DRAGONS

Chapter The First

THE GREEN MAN OF KILTON

Kilton in Wessex

Late Summer The Year 895

CERIC lived as a wild man in the forests of Kilton.

He had walked from the crowded chantry in which his grandmother Modwynn, Lady of Kilton, lay under her pall, shrouded and ready to be lowered within the earth under a slab of stone. He had walked out, and gone on walking. He had passed through the hall yards, nearly deserted in this time of great grieving, then through the palisade gate, which was quickly opened for him. Free of its protective barrier, he gained the road, and trod on.

His feet had hewn to an almost undeviating line from those gates, a straight path which left the road at the orchards, and continued on through the pear and apple trees. Fruit, still largely unripe, hung in clusters from those trees. He did not turn his head to regard them as he moved forward. Here were the limits of the orchards. The forest loomed before him, a wall of green. He saw these things, took them in enough for his body's response to them. He pushed his way through the undergrowth and scrub beneath the trees, where mature leaves were even now feeling the withdrawal of their life's fluids. Soon they too would drop.

He went on, forging a track where there was scarcely one, planting his feet where the slender paws of foxes had padded. His face was slapped by leaves snapping back from the branches he pushed through. His hair was pulled, his tunic and leggings raked by twig and thorn, yet he felt it not. It was sound he was aware of. As he moved, the scrape and rustle of engulfing verdure surrounded him. He pushed deeper in. The birds of the forest, which if not in the full throat of their Spring carolling and nesting, yet made themselves known to each other, calling, hidden deep in the expanses of the still-sheltering trees. They made note of the intruder. Their chirps and snatches of song replaced the mournful chanting of the priest Dunnere, the ringing of the tiny and shrill bells from the altar, and the muffled sobs of those who had stood with Ceric inside the chantry.

He stopped still within a small clearing and let the birds speak. They were all that filled his ears. He felt his own animal heart begin to calm, his breathing slow, the clenched jaw release. He stood a long time, then pressed on.

Mosses were thick under his booted feet, the brown rocks covered with bright lichens. A tiny brook appeared, a rill snaking its way through a fringe of marsh woundwort, the watercourse pierced by nodding green spikes of arrowhead. He stared at it, the water glinting under the patches of sunlight escaping the trees high overhead. Kneeling, he dipped his hand to it, and carried a dripping and faulty handful to his dry mouth. He lowered his head and dropped his face to its coldness, that he might fully drink.

Then he slept, lying on his back amidst the ferns. His sleep was deep and heavy, stirring only when the Sun was dropping low and the air already chill. He lifted his head, blinking at the greenery in which he lay. He let his head fall back, and stared at the dark undersides of the leaves above him until his eyes again closed.

He spent all night there, by dawn sleepless and shivering from cold. He lay curled in his own arms, his cheek pressed against damp moss. The twittering of a bird, quite near, made him open his eyes. He lifted his head enough to see a redstart splashing in the rill before him, slapping its tail and ducking its beak as it bathed.

He was wet from the dew which had settled on him, and stiff from the clenched position of his sleep. He rose to his hands and knees, an act that made the redstart take wing. His mouth was again dry, and he drank deeply of the brook.

Sitting back on his heels, he studied the water in its swift but narrow channel, saw damselflies drop and lift above it. The Sun moved over his head, and clouds cast him in shadow. A sound reached his ears, that of a brass horn, far distant. It blew and ceased, blew and ceased, a purposeful and distinct call.

Ceric, he thought. They are calling Ceric. The elder son of the hall.

He turned his head from side to side, as if looking for himself.

He sat listening, and not moving. The horn fell silent.

His eyes dropped to the bracken of the forest floor. He cocked his head, taking in the sweep of the ferns' strong and arching spines, letting his eyes rest upon minute droplets of dew which glittered along their serrated edges. He plucked at some moss and placed it in his mouth, a green and woolly taste. Almost within his grasp grew a wild rose, its petals long fallen, leaving behind firm ripe hips. Looking upon them, he stood and moved to the rose where it clambered along the trunk of a declining oak. He stood, slowly pulling off the swollen orbs, and chewed them one by one. He ate several, and again lowered his face to the cool water, to clear his mouth of the sharpness of the gritty seeds. He slept.

When he awoke again the Sun was lowering and the air already chill. He sat up and looked about him at the enclosing trees. There was a broad pine, its heavy boughs low to the ground. He went to it, placed his hand upon the red and rough bark of the nearest bough. His other hand went to his seax, which he drew. He cut four thick and spreading boughs, their long needles dense enough to trap some of his bodily warmth when he pulled them over himself that night.

Ceric slept once more at the side of the small rill, the murmur of its flowing water barely sounding above his own breathing. He was still cold, but the pine needles spared him from the dew fall. Their resinous scent filled his nostrils.

Calling night birds awoke him, late-departing nightjars and the low and solemn hooting of an owl. At dawn he lay staring up into the grey sky revealed through the trees above. He pushed aside his night's prickly bedclothes, his hands sticky from the sap which had run from the severed ends of the pine. Standing, he turned slowly in the trampled ferns. A horn sounded, the same call he had heard the day before, a call for Ceric. He began to walk towards the sound.

The horn ceased, as did his footfall towards it. He stood still, his eyes fixed along the slight track before him, then turned and headed back to the rill.

He spent the day stretched out upon, and then under, the pine boughs he had cut. He lay gazing upon the action of the water as it wound along the tiny brook, opening his eyes wider when any bird dropped down to drink. Before it grew dark he pulled more of the drying rosehips and chewed them, their tartness filling his mouth and making it water. In the morning he again heard the horn. Rising to the summons, he began to make his way along the track, following the sound. He pushed his way along. As he grew closer he heard a new sound. A bird was singing as well, almost as soon as the horn ceased sounding, a blackbird. He knew that call. Again the horn blew, clear and insistent, calling for Ceric, or announcing him.

He kept coming, drawing nearer. It grew louder. A horn, calling for Ceric. The call of a blackbird, after.

Following the funeral Mass for Modwynn, Lady of Kilton, the horse-thegn thereof had spent an anxious night in the bower house where Ceric had lately stayed. Worr was disappointed in his hope; Ceric did not return. Worr had then ridden out, skirting the perimeter of the wood ringing the southern boundary of Kilton's common pastures. A cowherd told of having seen the elder son of the hall, entering the trees the prior day. The slight path could only be discerned by one as skilled at tracking as Worr, and had brought him to more and larger trails, those used by deer. Worr had whistled then, that blackbird call he and Ceric had used for years. He stayed a long while, in hope of an answering whistle, which did not come.

The horse-thegn retraced his steps, pulled himself upon his waiting mare, and travelling in nearly a straight line, reached the palisade wall of Kilton. Lady Edgyth met him at the gate. It was clear she had been watching for him, and her gentle face, already worn with sorrow, could not conceal the depths of her concern.

He swung off his mount and dipped his head in respect to her.

"Nothing?" Her single word was more hope than question.

"I may have found a track he made. A cowherd pointed it out to me; he watched Ceric walk into the trees, past the orchards."

Some light flickered in Edgyth's eyes, and her hands rose, as if in hope he might have more to tell.

"Right now I will gather a few things, his mantle, some food, a blanket, so if he stays another night in the open he might have them."

Her parted lips asked the question her eyes were also asking.

"There is no knowing when he might return to us," he conceded. They began moving deeper into the work yard, nearer those private dwellings of the family of Kilton, and the bower house intended for Ceric as a married man.

"I will take a horn as well," Worr continued, "that he might hear my call."

Edgyth was nodding agreement to all he said. "Yes. He will be hungered. And cold."

Edwin, the young Lord of Kilton, was now stepping from the door of the hall. He looked at Worr, returning alone, and at the pale cheek of his mother Edgyth. He came to them, falling in at his mother's side as they gained the bower house door.

Edgyth had locked it after Worr had ridden off that morning; the sword of Ceric, once borne by her father-in-law Godwulf, hung on a wooden peg by the bed. It was not only its golden hilt and trim that made the blade of incalculable worth. It was heirloom of two Kingdoms, Mercia and Wessex; two great Kings, Offa and Æthelwulf; and heirloom both of Godwulf, Lord of Kilton and his Lady-wife, Modwynn. It was this last who had carefully reserved the weapon for Ceric, and it was from her lap it had been awarded to him, at his sword-bearing ceremony, his symbel, years ago.

Edgyth was now Lady of Kilton, and she unlocked the door. Ceric had not locked it behind him when he had gone to the funeral Mass for his grandmother Modwynn. She and Worr had found that second key lying upon a chest later that mournful day. From the day he had been granted it Ceric had always kept it carefully, secreted in the slit within his belt. On that day he had left it, and all else, behind. She had given the key to Edwin.

Ceric's fine mantle of heavy green wool was hanging from a peg near his abandoned sword. Worr went to it, while Edgyth crossed to the large wooden chest on the other side of the dragon-crowned bed and began pulling forth tunics, leggings, a fur-trimmed hood, and other clothing. Worr was now at work with the leathern packs, still upon the broad planks of the oak floor. They were those he and Ceric had returned with, and he saw they had not yet been gone through or unpacked. This alone concerned Worr. Ceric had been taught, by both Cadmar and by himself, to take care of his kit, both on the road and upon his return. This entailed sorting through the contents, removing those things in need of cleaning or repair. Ceric had always taken care in doing so. These packs were untouched.

Edgyth had laid the clothing she selected on the coverlet of the dragon bed. Her eyes rose a moment to the bedpost nearest her. This bed and its watchful dragons had once been her own. Godwin had it made for their wedding, and in it she had passed from maiden to wife. In it she had also bled away many a stillborn babe. She turned from it to Worr.

"I will go to the kitchen yard, and fill a bag with food."

Edwin now spoke. He had been watching both Worr and his mother at their work, watching and wondering at the wisdom of their actions.

"Is it not better to let his hunger drive him back?"

Worr rose from where he crouched. The horse-thegn was possessed of a natural steadiness of nature, but the stresses he had been under these past few weeks made it hard to mask his own concern for Ceric.

"To force a runaway child home, yes. But this – this is different."

"Such might drive him back to the hall," Edwin posited.

Worr gave answer. "Or kill him."

The horse-thegn waited a moment before going on. "Ceric has been forced to live from the land before, granted with more kit and with companions. It is his fitness to do so now I think of. A man can live in the wilds, if he has skill and desire to survive. It is this last I fear for."

There was more than a note of urgency in Edgyth's response. "We must do whatever we can to keep him alive, and strong," she proffered. She was looking at her son as she said this, looking at him and anxiously awaiting a sign of his accord. Edwin lifted a hand in a gesture of helplessness, but gave a nod.

Worr filled a leathern saddle bag with the clothes. They made ready to leave the small house. Edgyth paused to look at the spear leaning against the wall. Ceric was in the forest, where walking could be arduous. "His father always used a spear to aid his walking," she remembered aloud. The moment she said it she knew her error. Worr did not wince, but he shook off the suggestion with a quick movement of his head. It was a spear Ceric had used to kill Ashild.

"He can cut a staff, if he wants one," Worr answered.

The horse-thegn remounted his mare and returned to the forest face. He carried two leathern bags, one packed with freshly baked loaves of wheaten bread, a pottery crock of soft cheese, and many hard-cooked eggs in their shells. He took no meat, not wanting to attract by scent the attention of scavenging beasts, large or small; and chose with Edgyth those food stuffs that would not soon spoil. The bread would harden in a day, but could still be eaten. The second bag held those items of clothing Edgyth had retrieved from the wooden chest, along with Ceric's warm mantle, two blankets, and two linen towels. Worr had also placed within it the flint and iron striker from Ceric's kit. Tinder was abundant in any wood; dried moss, the down of birds' nests, brown pine needles, all these would catch and hold a thrown spark.

Neither pack was burdensomely heavy, but hampered as he was, Worr's transit through the slapping branches and undergrowth of the fox trail was far slower than it had been the first time. When he reached the larger deer trails he chose the one which ran most closely to that he had begun on. Ceric had seemed to take a nearly unswerving route from Kilton's gates, and Worr guessed he might have continued to do so. He forged ahead until the trail opened into a clearing. A downed ash tree lay there, part of what had formed the tiny glade, as its fall had also taken down a number of smaller trees, some crushed almost to splinters beneath the great bulk of the aged ash. The trunk of the ash was still sound, though, and Worr lowered the two packs upon it. There they sat above the forest floor, and were easy to see. He took the small brass horn from his waist and lifted it to his lips, blowing out the signal which both announced, and called for, Ceric of Kilton. Its two rising notes were startling in the quiet of the small glade. When he paused, Worr noticed that even the whirring insects had fallen silent before the bellowing of the horn. He sounded the call again and again, in the hope that wherever Ceric might be, he might heed it.

Then he waited. A lost man following a sounding horn must hear it repeated at intervals, that he might correct his course as he moved ahead. A good woodsman would hear such a signal, sight upon a tree before him in its direction, and at once sight a further tree beyond that, to keep him upon a true course. Worr waited, scanning the trees for any sign of human approach, straining his own ears to hear an answering whistle. Neither came.

He sounded the horn again, in another long sequence of calls, and again waited. The natural stillness of the glade gave relief from the ringing horn blasts he had sounded, and soon a few birds, seemingly undisturbed by the noise he had made, twittered and called over his head. Worr stood, alert, and hopeful. He gave at last a low and heaving sigh, and with a final look at the packs he had carried in, quitted the place.

Worr returned early next morning, hoping against hope that when he reached the ash glade he would find Ceric there. He did not. The packs remained, undisturbed by man or beast. He had brought fresh loaves, fearing this, and added these to the food pack. He took horn in hand and began the call for Ceric. His efforts yielded nothing.

Worr gave thought. Ceric had now been gone from the hall three days. The funeral Mass for Modwynn was held in the morning, with the sacrament offered, and few if any would have broken their fast before partaking of the holy sacrament. Worr knew Ceric had not. That meant Ceric had not eaten for three days, save what he could forage in a wood growing increasingly fallow. The orchards of Kilton offered apples and pears, but he would need to leave the shelter of the trees to gather any. Worr did not think it likely Ceric would. Fruit grew wild in the forest, late berries as well, and if chanced upon could fill an empty belly, if not satisfy the craving for greater sustenance.

On the morrow Worr returned. He had spent the night wondering if he should forge deeper within the forest, or remain where he had established his supply point. He decided on the latter. If Ceric had heard him, he may have gauged where and how far was the glade Worr summoned him from, and remaining there brought Ceric closer to the forest edge. The track out was now worn by Worr's traversing, giving Ceric an easy path to follow back.

The hope Worr held was one thing, the reality he faced, another. The horse-thegn came supplied with two large and heavy packs, enough kit to enable a fit man to survive, and survive well, in the wild. Within were two more blankets, a large cowhide ground cloth, two sheep-skins, the cooking kit from Ceric's packs, with small soap-stone pot, iron griddle, toasting forks, spoons and bowls of wood, and the wooden cup he used upon the road. Some of this was battered and dented or gouged from the hard useage Ceric had subjected it to. Worr wanted them just the same, shaking his head at the better, newer pieces offered by the kitchen folk.

Edgyth, at his side as Worr gathered and packed these things, nodded in understanding. "Those things he will recall using; things which are his," she murmured.

They packed small bags of wheat kernels, barley, and oats. Worr gathered barbed fishing hooks, and line of animal sinew; also netting for the building of a weir. Mindful of how Ceric had eschewed the use of one on their way back to Kilton, Worr hesitated in adding a small tent, then relented and did so.

He again sounded the horn. In the silence between blasts, he whistled out the blackbird call he and Ceric used to signal each other's approach. The stillness after his whistled summons was far more poignant than that which hung in the air following his horn blasts.

The next day Worr returned. The days had been warm for after harvest-tide, still blest with Sun, though the nights were increasingly chill. This morning dawned with a lowering sky that grew no brighter, and the dampness of the air and briskness of the breeze made Worr pull his own mantle the tighter about him. Yet entering the glade, a spark of hope flared up in the horse-thegn's breast. The packs had been opened, and he saw upon examining their contents, certain things taken. They had not been ripped by an animal; there had been discernment in what had been chosen. The bag of wheat kernels was gone, as was the soapstone cooking pot. The flint was gone, though the iron striker remained. Worr considered this; a man could easily use the back of his seax to strike a spark. Bread, and a few eggs were gone; not all, but some. Other things had been taken out, seemingly held or looked at, and left behind upon the broad surface of the ash trunk.

Ceric was near; Worr was certain. On the remote chance some forest traveller had found his way to this glade, he would have likely availed himself of most, if not all, of the unexpected bounty. Worr thought again. What if some prayerful woodland watcher, such as Cadmar had been, had come across these packs? He may have praised Divine Providence for His provision, and in his human need, taken the bare minimum required for bodily survival. Worr shook his head, not wanting to accept this. Ceric must be near; this must be Ceric who had heard his summons, found his way to the glade, and taken the few things he had carried off.

He blew the brass horn with renewed energy, and true hope. Between blasts he whistled the blackbird call. But no returning call answered his, and Ceric did not emerge from the trees.

Ceric had followed the summoning horn to a small, yet open glade, one dominated by a fallen ash. He saw the light of the glade before he entered therein, a pearly grey sky admitted through the gap left by the vast crown of the fallen tree. The broad trunk was just before him, and on it perched several leathern packs. He stood looking at them, then moved to the first. He unlaced the thongs which held the mouth of the bag together. Within were loaves; several of them. He took the first, and holding it in both hands, set his teeth to its brown crust. The smell and savour of it made his dry mouth water. He tore off a chunk with his front teeth, chewing through the crunch of hardened crust, pressing the tender inner crumb against his mouth. It took no more than two swallows to feel his body's response to sudden nourishment. His hands, which had been near to trembling as he drew the laces of the pack free, now steadied. He stood there, tearing the bread with his teeth, tasting wheat and yeast and salt and even the water with which it had been formed. He tasted fire as well, that hot bed of charcoaled hardwood which had been raked aside on the oven floor so this loaf might brown and bake. He tasted the powdery ashes, clinging still to the bottom of the crust he gnawed.

There were several loaves inside the pack, and beneath them a leathern drawstring pouch into which he fished his fingers. Eggs. He pulled one out, squeezed it in his fist to crack the shell, and rubbed it between his palms, freeing much of the sharp fragments. He bit, breaking through the firm encasing white into a yolk deep yellow and creamy. The depth of its flavour, the sheer richness of the golden yolk, was a jolt to mouth and taste buds. Small as it was, he took the egg in three bites, unable to do more.

He gave pause, staring at the packs, his body in a heightened state, his hands, now at his sides, gently clenching and unclenching as if seeking direction. He went to the second pack, which was unlaced, but densely packed. A mass of fabric was there, deep green wool trimmed with the golden fur of fox. He pulled it out. A mantle, a long one. He swung it over his shoulders. He had been chilled. Now with one swing of his arms the thick wool shut out the cool breeze wafting through the glade. Going to the third pack he found cooking gear. He pulled out a small and heavy cooking pot, a spoon, a wooden bowl. A tiny wooden box, holding a sharp piece of flint and a steel striker. Studying these, he took the flint and left striker and box behind. Small hempen bags of some grain were there; they were sewn shut, but he took one and placed it in the pot. Then he returned to the first bag, took out two more loaves, and several eggs, and laid them also inside the pot.

A bird chirped, a wood warbler, making Ceric look up into the trees. He spotted the bird, perched on one of the dead ash branches now rising from a sharp angle over the decaying trunk. It made him aware that he was being watched. Ceric picked up the soapstone pot and began making his way back to the brook.

When he reached it he crossed over the rill in a single broad step. He had not done so before. The tiny brook had served as some kind of boundary. No longer. Not many steps in he found a hollowed-out oak. One old tree had given food. This one could provide shelter. The space within its walls was broad enough for a man to curl up in. One side of its broken trunk was rotted almost to the ground, making it easy to step into. He set down the cooking pot and did so. The inside walls of the trunk were dark with decay, but still thicker than a man's extended hand. Fungi hung in places within, just as they did on the bark still covering parts of the oak. He looked up. Blasted as it was, the tree lived, and a stunted but leafy canopy stretched above his head. He returned to the rill, leapt over it, gathered up the pine boughs he had cut. In a broad armful he carried them to the hollow oak, laying them on its floor of brown and spongy wood dust.

That night, with a semblance of shelter over his head, and something finally in his belly, the night-mare came for him. Since entering the forest he had slept like one dead, senselessly, without dream or memory when he awoke. Now he bolted upright in the dark. It was a dream he knew, of a warrior running on a field of battle amongst the broken bodies of men and horses. He saw the warrior pick up a spear, and watched him aim at a man's back. He flung the spear. It sailed with untrue slowness through the air. The figure the spear sought turned around. It was a woman, a young woman, and she opened her mouth in horror as she saw both spear, and then, looking beyond, he who had thrown it.

Worr returned to the ash glade next morning, to see nothing more had been taken. He had brought fresh bread and cheese with him, and set the leathern bag holding them upon the trunk. Emboldened by the fact the packs had been opened, he waited for Ceric to appear, sounding the horn, whistling the blackbird call, and then, instead of leaving, remaining within the glade. He stood a long time, hoping for the rustle of an approaching man. None came. The next day was no different. The new pack lay unopened. Worr began to truly fear. Had Ceric come just once, taken the scant supplies he carried off, and now fallen to some misadventure in the wood? He had taken the cooking pot and a small sack of wheat, and nothing would have given Worr more comfort than the smell of the boiling kernels. Ceric could not long sustain himself with so little, and the fact that he seemingly rationed himself so severely added to his friend's anxious unknowing.

The third day though, brought its own reward. When the horse-thegn stepped into the glade he startled several birds arrived before him. Ceric had visited here. He had been here and purposefully left food for the forest beasts, for Worr looked upon two hunks of bread threaded through barren tree branches, where the birds might feast. And Ceric had taken more food for himself, the rest of the eggs, another of the fresher loaves, a cured cheese. It gave Worr hope that he could provide for some of Ceric's bodily needs, for it was growing cold. Today in addition to fresh food he also brought the comb from the bower house. Worr left it on the tree trunk, in open view. Other than the towels the Lady Edgyth had packed he had not brought anything of a more personal nature. But the comb, sitting on a shelf in the bower house next the silver disc mirror, suggested itself. Worr hazarded blowing the brass horn, following its ringing blast with the call of the blackbird. Then he waited, with renewed resolution. He thought Ceric might appear, and would not leave until he did.

As Worr waited he watched the birds return to fluttering about the stale bread, perching with their clawed feet and pecking at the bounty. He imagined Ceric digging a hole in the crumb and threading the loaves there. It was a conscious act, this sharing, one that gave Worr heart.

Worr stayed a long time, leaning against a young hornbeam unscathed by the old ash tree's fall. He remained silent, and almost motionless. The birds had pecked and torn the bread so that it fell in uneven lumps to the lichens underfoot. Sated, they made off. Worr did not. From afar he began to hear the unmistakable crunch of human footfall through drying leaves, the brush and swing of branches as they parted to make way. Worr trained his eyes in the direction from which these sounds arose. They came steadily nearer. At last the branches of some alders trembled. A man appeared, hands first, reaching forward to push the leaves away. It was Ceric, dishevelled, but certainly him. He was looking not at the hornbeam, but at the branches on which he had left the bread. His eyes dropped, seeing the remains of the crusts on the forest floor. Worr did not speak, only waited for Ceric to discover him. He did, his eyes shifting up and then over to where Worr waited. Ceric's head jerked back, his mouth opening. He was already turning to flee when Worr called out his name. Worr could see the green woollen mantle about his shoulders. Then he was gone.

Worr had to fight the impulse to go after Ceric, to bodily tackle him and arrest him in his flight. The look in the haunted eyes which had met his own stopped him. He might do greater harm in pursuit. But at least he had seen him; knew that he lived.

Edgyth wept tears of relief when he told her. The watchmen on the palisade wall knew to send word to her at once when the horse-thegn approached. Absorbed as she was each day in the running of the hall, she would leave any task to meet Worr as he rode through the gates. She knew by his face there was hopeful news to impart, but they held their words until they were within the bower house. Edwin had joined them, and Worr faced them both with his news.

"I have seen him," he began.

Edgyth crossed herself, murmuring a fervent prayer of thanksgiving to Heaven as she did so. She held her clasped hands high, near her heart, and blinked away the tears welling in her eyes. None of them had been truly certain it was Ceric availing himself of the supplies Worr carried in; now they knew.

"And – ?" Edwin could not hide his impatience for further report.

"He turned and ran as soon as he spotted me."

Edwin swallowed back the oath forming on his lips.

Worr looked at Lady Edgyth. "He had done something, between my visit yesterday and today. He took stale bread and hung it in the trees, for the birds. They were eating it when I arrived. And when Ceric stepped into the glade, it was them he looked for. When he saw me, I spoke his name. But he fled."

"He fled," Edwin repeated. His eyes dropped to the planks of the floor, and then rose to latch on those of the horse-thegn. "And you did not go after him?"

Worr had fought that urge to do so, and understood why Edwin questioned him. But Edwin had not been there to see his brother.

"I would have done more harm than good," Worr said simply.

Edwin sighed and gave a shake of his head.

"We give thanks he lives," his mother said. "And great thanks to you, Worr, for your patience in this."

"We must catch him, somehow," Edwin said next.

Edgyth turned to her son. Edwin spoke almost as if Ceric were a felon, an escaped thief, or other criminal. Worr was silent, but his eyes met those of the Lady of Kilton. They were, all three, worn with the strain of so much loss and grief. The Lady's gently parted lips seemed to silently implore the horse-thegn to answer the young Lord. Worr did.

"This is no trap we are setting, Edwin. The stakes are too high."

Edwin could not disguise his frustration, expressed in a challenge to the older man. "Would you leave him to die in the forest?"

Worr took a breath. "He will not die. He has already shown that he will accept some of what is brought him – his mantle, some cooking kit, a bare modicum of food-stuff. A man bent on death would do none of this."

And, thought Worr, he has his seax. A man who wished to truly die could make short end of life with that.

"If we force him to return – capture him – we may crush whatever will he has to go on living."

Edgyth spoke now, the soft voice almost questioning, as if she thought aloud. "The birds he fed . . . he showed concern for them; he gave them bread." Her thoughts travelled back over the years, to her time spent at the abbey where she had sought and received great succour. She turned now to face her son.

"There is meaning in this. At Glastunburh we had men come to us, shattered from war. Some could not speak. Others had fearsome dreams. They were listless, or sometimes lashing out with violence at those caring for them. It is an affliction of the mind, which prayer and bodily work can help.

"Such men the Abbot would place in the gardens, straightaway; place tools in their hands, instead of the weapons they had lived by.

"We saw it on the women's side too. Women who had been ravished, who had seen their husbands and children be slaughtered. The Abbess would set them to work, caring for something, chicks or goslings, it mattered not how small.

"Ceric sharing his bread with these birds . . . it is not far from this."

Edwin felt near to snorting in derision. But Edgyth's eyes had turned to Worr, who nodded in agreement. Edwin took this in. He might be Lord of Kilton, but the man and woman before him each had more than twice his years. Their own spheres of authority were considerable, and he needed them both. His mother ran the hall, and presided also over the village and its folk. With Cadmar dead, Worr had assumed much of the role of the old warrior-monk. And now that Ceric had run off, Edwin was alone. The two he faced watched him bite back his anger in the face of their concerns. He must concede.

"What will you do now," he asked the horse-thegn.

"Take him more kit," came the reply.

The first camp Ceric had made was nought but a depression in the ferns. The hollowed-out oak became his second. Oak leaves take long to fall, and though they shriveled and browned above his head, held firm. They kept the dew from him, and much of the rain. The oak was shelter, an enclosure which open as it was, did not confine him. He slept within at night, and sometimes retreated to it in the middle of the day. Some days he would cross the rill and lie again where he had slept the first few nights; the sky was more open there, and afternoon Sun might strike and warm him.

He lived as a feral cat did, sleeping, resting with eyes narrowed to slits as he studied a leaf or a blade of grass before him, closing them to sleep again, rising to feed himself. His senses, deprived of ordinary comforts, scaled exquisite heights. He could watch with entranced attention a single ant, burdened with a precious piece of leaf litter as it struggled across twigs and stones on its ordained path. The thronging dawn chorus of singing birds resolved itself into the unique warbling calls and challenges of nuthatches and bramblings. His sense of smell, something he had rarely given notice to, filled his head. Lying upon the earth he would breathe deep of herbs and grasses and leaf mould, pine sap and rotting logs.

He knew who he was. He was not sure why he now lived in a forest; this was a fact he could not trace to its source. He knew Worr, and that Worr had seen him. He would awaken in the dark, knowing he had wept in his sleep, and feeling, as awareness rose, that he was somewhere on the road in Anglia. I must get back to Kilton, home to my grandmother, he thought. I will start home now, home to my grandmother. She will help me.

When dawn came he never did.

Picking up stones to form a fire-ring, his body and mind were aware of picking up the same to set upon the hastily shrouded body of Cadmar. It was a bodily memory as much as one in the mind. Cadmar is there in a forest, he would remind himself, Cadmar who had lived years in the forest. His mortal remains now nourish the trees under which he lies. Ceric would look up from within the oak in which he lay, almost not knowing if he himself lived.

One day when he walked to the ash glade, he found a bow and many arrows there. He looked at them, but did not take them. The tent, tied in its parts with cords of leather, he also neglected.

Small sacks of grain he took, and using his seax and the sharp-edged flint, cast sparks into a nest of tinder formed by floss and browned pine needles. He dipped water from the rill, and boiled the wheat, or barley, or rye kernels in kind. He plucked mature leaves of ground elder, lamb's lettuce, red mints, wild parsley, and purslane, pot-herbs which when on the road with other men were gathered to enrich the scant portions of their simmering browis. He saw such things and acted. It was as if his body knew how to keep itself alive, without thought or consideration.

Sleep, so fugitive in his final days at Kilton, became his refuge. Yet the night-mare pursued him. Often it was the single scarifying dream of running on that field of battle, flinging the spear, watching the horrified face of the woman as it drove for her breast. He would startle awake, a scream trapped in his throat, unable to again sleep until purging tears wrung him dry.

As terrible as they were, his dreams brought him closest to his old self. The galloping night-mare carried him to the edge of sanity.

Once the night-mare seduced him with darkly soft caresses. He dreamt of being in a dim and enclosed space, illumined by a single cresset. The golden light fell aslant and from above, as if it were on a table, and he on the floor. In his embrace he held a woman, feeling with every particle of his being her lush strength as they possessed each other. First she was beneath him, then above him, their bodies moving together. He was grasping her, holding her to him, rooted in her. His mouth was upon hers, the remembered scent of her hair, of hay and horses and lavender blossom all about him. He was suffused, subsumed, awash in the fulfillment of his long and fervent desire. Its potency was too great. The night-mare reared, tossing him off, abandoning him. He awakened, the bliss of their union dissolving into utter desolation.

Ashild, he choked out. Ashild.

Chapter the Second

THE LOST WAY

WORR made careful note of what Ceric availed himself of, and what he eschewed. Ceric had taken fish hooks and sinew line, and Worr wondered if he had found water deep enough to fish. He had taken plaited hempen line, suitable for a season of use if woven as a fishing weir. Worr had no way to know if he had used it as such. Ceric had not taken his wooden comb, which Worr had left upon the trunk, and after many days Worr placed it with new items he carried in, tweezers and shears. Ceric showed no interest. The tent went unused, the bow and arrows ignored. Once Worr brought a jug of mead, which went untouched.

Ceric would take the small sacks of kernels of grain, a few loaves, cheeses and eggs. Considering this, Worr realised it was not much more than he had subsisted upon in the field with Prince Eadward. It was as if Ceric were back there, in the days leading up to the battle in which Ashild fell.

He had claimed to Edwin that Ceric would not die, but now it was Blót, that time when all animals unlikely to survive the coming cold were slaughtered. Winter was coming, and soon. He secretly feared his friend's ability to survive it. Should Ceric die of exposure it would be upon Worr's head, and upon his soul.

On the Eve of St Martin's Edwin told Worr he would go with him next day into the forest. Worr could not demur; this was after all the Lord of Kilton.

They rode early to the edge of the forest with Edwin's chief body-guard Eorconbeald. It was said that on this day the warrior-saint Martin let loose Winter from the half of his cloak remaining after he had divided it with a freezing beggar. Indeed, the morning was fittingly cold and gray. Their mounts paced through a rime of frost tipping the longer grasses beneath the now-barren orchard trees. Eorconbeald remained with the horses as the two set off. Worr shouldered the small pack filled with fresh food: loaves, more eggs from the dwindling store the hens were laying, a cabbage, apples. The horse-thegn went first, forging through a trackway which at its beginning looked scarcely travelled to Edwin. Only when it opened up to the former deer paths was it readily discernible. Yet when more leaves fell, these trackways, losing the definition the parted foliage provided, would become little more than a maze of slightly bruised lichens, or stones which might have had the moss scuffed from them by the passage of human feet.

They reached the ash glade. Edwin came up alongside Worr as he lowered the new food pack to the trunk. The Lord of Kilton's eyes fell on the line of packs, opened and unopened, arrayed there. So many; and his brother had taken hardly anything. He stood in silence as Worr unhooked the small brass horn from his belt, held it to his lips, and began to blow the summons.

The blast shattered the forest stillness. Worr repeated the call, then lowered the horn and whistled. They waited.

Worr again lifted the horn, again blew the summons, a ringing demand for the elder son of the hall.

Edwin scanned the circle of trees about the glade; most had dropped their leaves and he could see a fair distance. No motion, no sound, answered that summons. From the tail of his eye Edwin saw Worr take a breath, as he too studied the trees before him.

Of a sudden Edwin was filled with a kind of sharp anger; almost rage. The silence mocked him, mocked them both. Worr was now the senior-most warrior-thegn of Kilton, and he was spending part of each and every day here in this wood, carrying in food, patiently standing and hoping for a glimpse of Ceric, attempting to cajole his brother to return to the hall and his responsibilities. Worr had far more important things to do; he should be serving him, Edwin – and Kilton. It must come to an end. Ceric had been gone long weeks, and it was growing cold. And Edwin was afraid his brother would die out here.

Anger and fear both found voice in the young Lord's words, issued as a bellowing command into that silence.

"Ceric. You are my pledged man. I order you to come back! I order you. Ceric. Ceric!"

The violence of both words and tone made Worr turn to him. Edwin's eyes were fixed in a glare straight before him, his brows knitted at the empty and barren branches. The pale blue veins in his temple stood out, such was the concentration of effort in his demand.

His words echoed in Worr's ears. A memory arose, of similar words, similar anger, from a time almost lost in the mists of years. Worr was standing outside the bower house as a youth, and hearing Godwin shout much these same words to Gyric.

It was the day the Dane had arrived, and Gyric had insisted on riding out, unwilling to return even when Worr suggested they must, to prepare for the welcome meal that had been planned. He and Gyric had finally trotted back to a hall yard in the throes of final preparation for the feast. Worr had hastily changed his own clothes. Then, passing by the bower house where Gyric lived with Ceridwen, he heard Godwin's wrathful words.

Hearing Edwin's desperate orders to his brother, Worr felt an almost visceral pain, a twisting around his heart. His words tumbled out, a defence for he now absent.

"He is like a wounded animal. Do you curse a horse which has gone lame? You can curse the cause of the lameness, but the horse itself? No."

It caught Edwin up short, but only for a moment. Worr's directness surprised him, startled him in fact. But Edwin could not readily concede.

"He has a duty. To me, and to Kilton," he pressed.

I need him, he wished he could say. Grandmother and Cadmar are both gone. I need Ceric. Instead of saying this, he found new heat to utter his next words.

"He has his duty."

Worr only stared at him. The Lord of Kilton was in no position to accuse Ceric of shirking anything. The horse-thegn studied Edwin. Now there was real admonition in Worr's stern response. "Godwin was unjust to his brother Gyric. Unjust and unkind. Do not make the same mistake."

It was almost the last thing Edwin expected, Worr's mention of his father. This potent conjuring was matched by the tone of warning in the horse-thegn's voice. They made Edwin remember that this thegn had secret knowledge which he had imparted to him; they had a bond beyond that of thegn to Lord. Worr alone knew of his true parentage, at least here in Angle-land. It meant that Worr alone could confirm or deny this, should the fact ever be revealed. And Edwin was sure Worr knew things he did not; things he had not yet told him. The man was worthy not only of Edwin's full attention, but respect.

Edwin's eyes fell to the browned bracken.

Worr could almost guess by the changing expressions flickering over Edwin's face that the young man was thinking this; remembering himself as it were, and also, remembering Worr.

They stayed a while longer, in shared silence. Worr felt certain that if Ceric had heard his brother, it would have only driven him further afield. Edwin's ready acquiescence when the horse-thegn turned to leave showed that Edwin did as well. He felt a sense of embarrassment, even shame, but could not speak of it.

Edwin said nothing when his mother greeted them. The three of them walked through the crowded hall, its fire-pit ablaze against the cold, to the chilly treasure room; its braziers had gone out. The young Lord let the horse-thegn do the telling, without comment. Worr spoke only of his horn blasts and his unanswered whistled call, nothing more. Edgyth's hope had once more been dashed; she had nourished a vision of Ceric somehow sensing his brother was nigh, and of his returning with him. Both Edgyth and Worr left Edwin then, off to their myriad duties.

Edwin stood alone on the cold treasure room floor. His eyes were fixed on some unseen point beyond the confines of the room. He found himself walking to the stacked chests against the wall, those which Worr had once led him to. He pulled off the first two, set them on the table there by his bed. It was the third he opened. To do so he knelt down, just as he had the first time Worr had opened it before him.

He moved the protective sheepskin aside, and looked down upon his father's blackened ring-shirt. He saw again the slightly mashed places where it had received stout blows, and where fully broken rings had been snipped out and replaced. He put his hand upon those links, thinking of his knowledge. This was Godwin's, he was Godwin's true son. He thought now of riding by Eadward's side, thinking just that; and of how badly he had performed in that first test of his ability. He did not want to be like Godwin, yet he wanted to be just like the man.

That night, lying in bed with his wife in the small house in which he had been born, Worr gave long thought to the day. Wilgyfu had dropped off to sleep; with three small boys she was kept running all the day. Her smiles, and the laughter of his boys were constant reminder of his good fortune. It had taken Worr a long time to wed, but he had been blest in Wilgyfu. She was the daughter of a rich and powerful thegn, the Bailiff of Defenas, one who rode at the side and had the ear of King Ælfred. And young as she was, Wilgyfu had as much chosen Worr as he had chosen her. It was she who had smiled first at the Kilton Yuletide feast she was attending, and she, Raedwulf later told him, who had proclaimed to her father later that night that she had just met the man she would wed. Being named horse-thegn of the hall, taking

Wilgyfu to wife, and now bearing the sword and seat of Cadmar had been the three landmarks of his life.

His father Wiro had been horse-thegn before him. Worr had exceeded that good man's accomplishments, and in both awarded treasure and battle-gain Worr's winnings had far outstripped those of his father. In recent years he had re-built the house, fortifying it, making it larger and more commodious. He had set aside arms for his boys which would be the envy of the other youngsters when they began their training. And when she dressed for feasts, about Wilgyfu's lovely neck were draped choice plaited chains of silver, and one even of gold he had won for her. From father to son had been a rapid ascension, one predicated on skill and hard work.

Wiro's own father had been of ceorl stock, his family living in the village on a modest croft. Wiro had stood out as a spear-thrower in one of Godwulf's battles, and then shown a true affinity with horses. He was after some years named horse-thegn, and no longer slept within the hall, but was given a small timber house built against the palisade next to his charges. Worr was his eldest child and only son, and blest with his father's skill. Horses, and following the trails of wild animals through meadow and forest filled his boyhood days, that and dreams of one day serving as warrior to Godwulf.

To this end Worr had early presented himself to one of Lord Godwulf's body-guards, wishing to join a campaign which Kilton was about to undertake. The skirmishes with the invading Danes were then many, both in Wessex and in Mercia, and Godwulf was once again riding out to meet the threat.

Worr had already proven his ability as a sling-thrower, scattering birds which came to feast on Kilton's ripe fruit with a hail of tiny pebbles. Yet on this occasion he had not yet twelve Summers, and was sent back with a grin by one of the captains. It deterred him not. After his own chores were done, he would view the young thegns of Kilton at their practice as they drilled in open pasture-land. Much could be garnered, merely by careful watching. His steady presence there was how Worr came to the attention of Godwulf, who, noting the boy's keenness, gestured him forward.

"You are Wiro's boy," the old man nodded.

"Yes, my Lord," Worr offered, not a little surprised. This was the Lord himself addressing him, who knew who he was. There were so many young about the hall.

Godwulf studied Worr's face. The boy's eyes were deep and blue, and his Lord looked fully into them. "Would you be one of my warriors?"

It did not sound a jest, but a true and serious query. Worr's eyes widened, in surprise and in wonder.

"Yes, my Lord," he repeated, but this time with unmistakable resolve. He thought he might add more to his affirmation.

"I try to serve you now, my Lord. I am good with sling, and have saved many a ripe pear for Kilton's tables."

Godwulf must smile at this. "Few tasks matter as much as protecting our food stores," he noted. His mouth was still smiling but his voice carried a note of gravity. "I admire any man who understands that."

He looked around, and gestured to one of his captains.

"This is Wiro's son. Give him a spear, and start his training."

Worr had fourteen years that Summer. His life changed at once. Worr would sleep henceforth in the hall of Kilton, with the majority of the Lord's men. He would be given arms, and be taught to make his own shields, the iron bosses supplied by the weapon-smiths of the hall. Even as a sling-man, or a spear-man flinging light throwing spears, he would have a small share in any battle-gain that was won. Both groups of youths would be kept far from the action due to their size and inexperience, but in any successful outcome they would be rewarded. Worr would receive silver from the hand of Godwulf.

That night Worr did not sit with the rest of the children, but joined the youngest of the warriors at the nearer tables within the great hall of Kilton. It gave a fresh vantage point, and he felt he saw the hall anew. His eyes were filled by the brightness of the painted and many-hued walls, the carving of intertwined beasts and vines snaking their way up the timber columns and along the cross beams, the casements of precious glass held in place by narrow channels of lead. Crowded though it was, he could clearly espy the high table at the end of the hall, as it was set upon a dais above the level of the floor. He could see the grey hair and beard of Lord Godwulf, sitting in majesty at the centre of that table, and the tall and lovely woman, opulently garbed, who was his wife, Lady Modwynn, moving about it as she poured ale for the men and women who sat with them. Behind that table stood a door leading to the treasure room of Kilton.

To the right of Lord Godwulf sat his son Godwin, newly wed to the rich and gentle Edgyth, and next her, Godwin's younger brother Gyric. Also there was Dunnere the priest, who sat always at the left of Modwynn; and perched on a stool at one long end, Garrulf the scop. The rest of the benches around that table were taken up by Godwulf's most esteemed warriors, those who served as his personal body-guard. Godwin, next in line as Lord, had his favourite warrior Wulfstan, who sat at the high table as well.

The tables within the hall followed the route of the alcoves pocketing the walls. Those most in favour, the senior-most warriors, sat closest to the high table to the right. On the near left sat the men of Godwin, who already fronted his own war-band of thirty warriors pledged to him at his symbel, his sword-bearing ceremony. Behind these sat all the other warriors, those who had not yet earned that right to move up, and those who never would.

As a boy Worr had always liked horses, and being raised within the hall yards felt grateful to have ready access to them. Only the rich owned horses; none of the cottars in the village, even the most prosperous, kept a horse. Horses were for those who need travel long distances, and quickly. They also gave pleasure. From Worr's earliest childhood watching the thegns on horseback, exercising their mounts, racing against each other for sport, was a sight which filled him with wonder.

Learning to ride was required of all thegns, and Worr had a good seat and hands from a young age. He was fearless, yet gentle with the beasts, and had an innate quietness which helped calm the most skittish. The same acuteness of observation that made him good at tracking deer and boar helped him see when a horse was ailing. He noted first the drooped head and dulled eye which might presage colic, was quick to see a horse just beginning to favour a strained leg, and learnt which flick of the ear or shrill whinny might warn of a beast about to lash out at another with high hooves.

He had early interest in the breeding of better animals, and looking over those in the paddocks would ask of his father, who was this one's dam, and sire? And that one's? He studied their fine points and their flaws, then would do the same to their parents, that he might learn what results their match had brought to their offspring.

As a fighter Worr came through the ranks, from sling-thrower to spear-thrower. When they saw how tall he was growing, how broad of shoulder, his training to become a thegn began. Up until that point there was always doubt that any boy would be large enough, fit enough, and brave enough to make a good warrior in the hand-to-hand combat the shield-wall demanded. This was ever the goal, to take one's place in the shield-wall of a great war-chief. Some never progressed, and once that was made clear, if they were sons of thegns, must content themselves as archers or in the throwing of light spears. If they were ceorls, such young men resumed their farming lives. They would drill occasionally with the rest of the warriors to keep them fit, and their skills sharp. In times of real hazard they would be asked to march out and risk their lives with the thegns, but other than this their flocks and fields became their main concern, as it had been for generations out of mind for their grand-sires. Their chance for advancement was at an end. Not so for Worr.

When Worr had acquired enough fighting skills Lord Godwulf passed him on to the elder son of the hall, Godwin. It offered scant protection to Worr and the other young men, for as they struggled to perfect their skills they would in any encounter with the enemy be exposed to the greatest danger. They might attack first, serve as decoys, feint retreat, any stratagem to deflect the rapacious fury of the Danes from Godwulf and his direct body-guard. Godwin and his men served the same role in battle to Godwulf as did Prince Eadward to his own father, King Ælfred. Protect one's Lord, unstintingly, unthinkingly.

When his father Wiro died from wounds taken in a battle with the Danes, Godwulf named Worr as horse-thegn. The title was not hereditary; another worthy man good with horses could have been elevated to fill this role. But Worr had fully earned it, even at his young age. It was a signal honour, placing him in charge of every mount, pack-horse, and cart-horse of the hall. He was charged with not only making sure the animals were well trained and well-cared for, but for improving their bloodstock. It was Worr who now made determination of which mare should be bred to which stallion, which colts should be gelded, which horses could be culled and set aside to be offered for sale to passing merchants. And it was Worr who taught all those new to it to ride.

Worr had moved from that back table where he first supped as a recruit steadily forward, and now took a place amongst those at the high table.

His service expanded at the return of a blinded Gyric, guided back to Kilton from the edge of the grave by a maid of Mercia, Ceridwen. Worr was asked to now serve as body-guard and companion to Gyric, and save for those hours when the second son of Kilton was with his young wife, spent nearly every day at his side, riding with him, swimming with him, taking him out in one of the small boats launched from the bottom of the sea cliffs. They had ridden off on campaign together into Mercia, one led by Godwin. Worr served thus until Gyric died, carried off by the fever which felled so many that year, including the tiny daughter he shared with Ceridwen.

After this he served at Godwin's side. The elder son was Lord now, had been for some years, and his service was a demanding one. Godwin possessed a kind of daring that looked reckless but was actually fueled by calculation, that quick summing up of any foe's perceived ability and weakness.

Worr could remember Godwin's face contorting in fury as he plunged ahead in some encounter in which the men he fronted thought they had little chance of winning or even gaining ground. Worr, at his left, could feel his own shocked expression, and then his response to it: Move. Attack. You will only survive if you kill first.

Worr had his own natural gifts as a warrior, and did survive. He quickly gained Godwin's trust. The reward was not only arms, silver, and horses. He was also given the more disagreeable tasks to carry out. He had acted as assassin more than once at Godwin's behest. The killings might have been justified in law, but carried out secretly as they were, gave a furtive quality that resisted easy absolution at the hands of Dunnere the priest.

There was more. He did not like to think back to his few days on Gotland with Godwin. It shamed him to have been a part of it, for when Lady Ceridwen beseeched him, "Do not let him take me, Worr," he fully understood the root of her fear. If the Dane had not ordered him not to interfere, he did not think he could have stood by and witnessed that single combat, so fearful was he of its outcome. If Godwin had triumphed Worr would be forced to watch him lay claim to Ceridwen, who begged only to be allowed to remain in peace with her husband and children. Worr could have been placed in a position of defying his pledged Lord, should he attempt to deny him this woman he so wanted. His thoughts could never progress past this when he recalled that day, still fraught with shock and loss as they were. An attempt to stop his pledged Lord would have marked him a traitorous renegade; Godwin would have cause to try to kill him as well.

Instead he arrived back at Kilton with Godwin's weapons, an unexpected boon to the grieving family. Worr's thoughts drifted back to the sequence of events following Godwin's death. When Ceric was returned to Kilton after his year on Gotland, Worr became the boy's body-guard, but also friend. He had himself just wed Wilgyfu, and their first son had not yet been born.

Worr was proud of Ceric. Both boys had been deprived of their parents, but Ceric had lived through bloody episodes to be wished on no child, and had as well to come to grips with the fact that his younger brother, not he, had been named heir to Godwin and Kilton. Ceric had borne this well and without grudge, only questioning Worr about it once or twice while still a boy. Ceric could not know, and Worr hoped, might never know, the real reason Edwin had been chosen. His younger brother was the son by blood of Godwin, a secret which must ever be guarded as long as Lady Edgyth lived.

Edwin now wore Godwin's war-kit, all save the blackened ring-shirt preserved in the chest in the treasure room. Weapons were heirlooms, destined to be passed down. Worr, lying there next his sleeping wife, reflected on this with wry comprehension. He himself had been passed from hand to hand, from the direct yet distant service to Godwulf, to the intense and demanding one required for Gyric, and then as henchman to Godwin, a warrior he might admire but could not love. After this it was Ceric to whom he pledged, and now in Ceric's absence, Edwin whom he companioned, and also trained.

Worr had been valued for his abilities, but made to ally himself over and again from man to man in their best interests. It was the nature of service; he knew this. He had seen much of each man, and in the vault of his heart felt that Kilton could not remain great without Ceric.

Cold rains fell. The forest floor was sodden. Spiny conkers dropped from the horse chestnuts, spilling open their polished brown nuts upon the glistening moss. Most trees, stripped of their leaves by Winter's coming, stood mute and unclothed against the strong northerly gusts. The pines held their green-needled boughs out, affording brief shelter for bird and beast, but the hollowed-out oak in which Ceric had found refuge offered not enough. To the east of his oak stood a hard ridge of rock, a cliff face. Before the rains had fully darkened the shortening days Ceric moved his camp there. He kindled his fire near the stone expanse, with yet enough room for him to sit or lie between the fire and the wall, which reflected the thrown heat upon his back as well as warming his front. Worr had taught him this wood-craft when he was a boy. This, and many things he did seemingly without thought, served him well. As Winter's hard cold set in, he worked his way along the outcrop to a low cave, where his fire was sheltered from the harsh winds by thick walls of rock.

It was a longer walk to the ash glade and the food supplies left there, but to Ceric time was measured only by the rising and falling of the reluctant Sun.

Mindful of the icy drizzle of Yuletide and the snows to follow after, Worr had brought additional tanned hides to be used as makeshift cover. Slung between trees they could give shelter, and sat or slept upon as ground cloths, keep the body away from rising damp. Ceric had taken the hides, which heartened the horse-thegn, but never availed himself of the tent. Perhaps he had found a dry hollow, as appeared in the banks of deep streams, or had resorted to the caves which Worr had shown both Ceric and Edwin when they were boys. If the horse-thegn knew this was the case he would have known further ease of mind.

Dunnere came with Worr once, making his way through the dripping trees and into the glade. It was the Feast of St Birinus, that holy converter of Kings in Angle-land, and, the priest thought, an auspicious day to expel any forces of evil. He came armed with holy water and aspergillum of silver, with which he flung the blest water through the drizzle and about the glade, lest Ceric be possessed of a demon. The priest chanted prayers to which Worr attended, and crossed himself respectfully at their end; but he could not help but think the application of yet more droplets akin to offering water to a drowning man.

In the darkest ebb of Winter Ceric lost himself in the forest. His paths had been deliberate and slow, and though he had left no markers for himself, he had not failed to return to his respective camps when he went out foraging, nor to find his way back when he struck out for the ash glade and its waiting supplies. This morning he had come down from his rock shelter to replenish his firewood, which he stored in a shallow alcove in his cave where it could dry and be at hand. A light snow had fallen overnight, mantling the landscape, blurring and softening it. The wood axe left him by Worr was one of the things Ceric had taken from the glade, and it hung at his belt. The great heap of faggots he had gathered were tied upon his back. He had learnt to chop them not much longer than his shoulders were broad, lest they slow him too much with getting snagged on that living wood of the trees he passed through.

Perhaps it was his tiredness after this effort, or the quickly melting snow which altered the ground first in its presence and then absence, or the fact that his back was bent, and his eyes not fully scanning the dark trees and boulders before him, but after progressing some distance he did not come across either flowing rill nor hollow oak, two of the markers signalling the rightness of his path back to the cave beyond.

He stopped, looked about him. No bird sang; he was alone in the frosty silence. The sky was a featureless grey, with no glimmer of Sun. He knew not where he was, nor how long he had been walking.

Turning, he could see where he had come; snow enough was there to discern this. He followed, but his own tracks did not lead him to any landmark. He stood, staring dully at the trees surrounding him. The wind sloughed through sodden branches, shaking free the beaded drops. He had as yet eaten nothing that day, needing more wood to boil up his barley browis, for he had exhausted the remaining supply overnight in warming the corner of the shallow cave in which he slept. His boots were wet, the lower part of his leggings soaked through. His bare hands were chapped, and numb with cold.

Panic seized him, an animal panic that made his heart pound and chest too tight to draw full breath. Shrugging off the heavy burden laced to his back, he let the carefully gathered branches impede him no more. He began to run. The haft of the axe fastened to his belt slapped against his thigh, but his seax was secure in its sheath across his belly. The toggles on his leggings had long ceased to work as fasteners, so thin was he, and his two belts, pulled tight, were all that kept them on.

He ran, tripping over rime-whitened tree roots, and sliding on rocks made slick with rotted leaves. He fell, sprawling open-armed upon a hillock where moss and lichen lent scant cushion to the decaying tree roots they covered. He rolled on his back, panting under that blank and indifferent sky. His terror dropped away, to be replaced with a memory as clear and cold as was the water in the rill he drank from.

The girl Ashild was running after him and her brother Hrald in a wood. She tried to catch up to them, but they would not let her. She fell, her skirts tangled in vines and brambles, and struggled to stand. He had been running behind Hrald and stopped to look back at her. She was fighting off tears, but was now defiantly standing, holding her ground and with pointed thumbs, throwing a curse at him. It was the curse that years later she told him of: That you should lose your way. Well, he had done so, lost his way, and likely forever.

He could not be more lost if he were in the pit of Hell itself. Hell was the final destination, nothing leading out, all abiding there far beyond the reach of grace. He still lived and breathed, albeit worse than any animal. He felt himself already in Hell.

Ashild is dead, he thought. But I am the one who is a ghost.

Chapter the Third

INTO THE HANDS OF GOD

EDWIN and his mother Lady Edgyth were headed for the small keep at Sceaftesburh. This had been Modwynn's birth hall, and had passed to her directly at her parents' death. Modwynn had set it aside for her younger son, Gyric, as the place he and his wife would live. Yet Gyric returned blind to Kilton. He and his young wife Ceridwen must remain at the burh. Modwynn had instead passed Sceaftesburh into the hands of her cousin, Heahstan. The elder of Heahstan's sons now ruled there. A new son had been born to him and his wife, and Edwin and Edgyth rode to the babe's christening. It was nearing Winter's end, still cold, but the soil slowly warming under lengthening days.

Sceaftesburh was but two days away, secure in Kilton's sphere, and Edwin set out with a body-guard of fourteen men, including his two captains thereof, Eorconbeald and his second, Alwin. The men had their saddle bags with provisions. Edgyth sat in a light waggon, horse drawn for speed, with a team of two to better keep pace with the riders. The waggon was hooped, with an oiled tarpaulin for shelter lest it rained. They were nearing the end of a gladsome trip in which to welcome the child and lift a cup in the presence of kin.

The hall of Sceaftesburh sat in a narrow defile, hemmed by forest on one side and the deeply-cut banks of a meandering stream on the other. Both village and hall received their water from this source, the crofts, grain fields, and common pasturage stretching long from the palisade wall.

The road ran fast by the stream, with view of the hall cut off at times by forest growth. Before Edwin's party had gained sight of the first of the crofts, uncertain calls and cries filled the air. Edwin, flanked by Eorconbeald and Alvin, were in the lead, shields on their backs, and with glances at each, the three touched their horses with their heels to urge them forward.

A small group of spear-men were emerging from the wood on the left, a few on horseback but mostly on foot. They numbered eight or ten men, and those in the vanguard were in the act of kicking in the doors of the crofter's hut and store house which sat furthest from the hall of Sceaftesburh. The family so beset ran terrified towards folk afield, who looked up, gaping, from their labours before dropping hoe or plough-bat. The attackers let them run, intent on the sacks of grain they pulled from the storehouse, tossing the bags almost willy-nilly out the door to their brethren. Some of them fell and split open, their precious contents scattering on the damp soil of the croft.

Eorconbeald had his brass horn in hand in a moment and raised it to his lips, calling out alarm to the palisade in the distance. Edwin twisted in his saddle to gesture the rest of his men forward. As he did so a second group of the attackers appeared behind him, come from the wood. They were all on foot save two, and in equal if not larger numbers as those who now were ravening through the croft.

At once the three were cut off from the main body of Edwin's troop, and the waggon in which sat Edgyth. Edwin wheeled his horse about. He had no spear, only his sword. Eorconbeald was similarly armed; of the three of them only Alwin had this day taken up his spear. On their horses Edwin and Eorconbeald could not approach the spear-men; the longer reach of those weapons would make them and their horses an easy mark.

Edwin could see Edgyth's waggon down the road. About eight of his men had closed up around it.

What he also saw was the attackers had few animals, and had now been presented with many of them, tantalizingly near. Horses, saddled and ready to ride were ever a great prize. Beyond this was the light waggon, in which they might carry their plunder away at speed.

The choice for Edwin and his captain was to quit their horses and fight their way through on foot, with Alwin, still mounted, fronting their effort, or for all three to spur their mounts down the stream, back through its waters, to clamber up and join those attackers heading for the waggon.

Edgyth had been sitting on the waggon-board next to Balin, its driver. Balin was an older thegn, skilled in the driving of a team, and one who ofttimes had taken both she and Lady Modwynn afield. When Balin saw Edwin and his two chief men ride ahead, then heard the cries, he stood up, reins in hand, in alertness. He halted the team with the pull of his hands. It did not take long before he saw the unknown horsemen spilling out on the road ahead, and heard the winding of Eorconbeald's horn. Balin's progress with the Lady of Kilton had been paused in almost the tightest spot of the entire journey. If he could get free and turn their heads, he would lash the horses into a gallop while Edwin's horsemen kept those mounted of the attackers from pursuit.

"Lady," he said. Edgyth's fingers were even now clutching at the edge of the board upon which she sat. "Lie down in the waggon bed. Cover yourself with anything you can find. Do not move until I tell you otherwise. Do not look out."

Edgyth had barely time to do so. Balin was already shouting commands at his team, backing them up, trying to turn them in the narrow road. She felt the rear wheels begin to slip down the steep bank of the stream, swollen in its Winter flood, then the jerk of the horses pulling forward and out as Balin drove them. The furious jingling of harness hardware and the slap of leather on the horses' rumps mingled with his commands as he turned them. There was little of actual substance within that waggon with which she could protect herself once she had crawled over the wooden boards. A basket was there, a hamper with a few delicacies culled from Kilton's larders to present upon the christening table; the gift of a silver spoon and porridge dish to the babe; a leathern bag with her necessaries; the bedding she had slept on last night; and a few rough woollen blankets to place over one's lap in cold weather. She pulled bedding and blankets over herself now.

From without she could hear Edwin's voice in sharp command, and that of his captain as well, ordering their men. War-cries, fierce and unmistakable, rose along with the shouted orders of her son and his chief men. She heard screams of women, more distant, and again the hastily blown notes of a bronze horn, which she knew was sounded by Eorconbeald, calling for aid.

Edgyth, lying there as the waggon heaved and shuddered, took nothing up as weapon, not even the small knife she wore at her waist to cut her food. Her fingers rose to her forehead, made the sign of the cross, and lips moving, she commended herself into the hands of God. Modwynn had presented her daughter-in-law with a golden cross, centred with a garnet, which Edgyth wore every day. Its rounded arms were ever a comfort in her hand. Now Edgyth clutched it so firmly that she could feel the impress of the bezel of the red stone in her palm. She prayed. Her prayers were for her son and his men, fighting outside, that they might be preserved, and prevail. She asked that if all were lost and she were to be seized by the hands of the enemy, she might know the mercy of death at once, and instead be speedily delivered into the hands of God.

The waggon jostled without ceasing under her, and the snorting of the horses and sounds of Balin's efforts filled her ears. He had nearly turned the waggon, she was sure of it. Yells and oaths rose above the clang of steel as men fought upon the road. A spear sliced into the tarpaulin over her head, ripping it, its point clattering on the basket not far from where her head rested, the shaft still caught in the oiled fabric. Something hit the driver Balin; she heard him groan, and could feel the weight of his body toppling from the waggon board. By the harried snorting of the horses, and the tinkling of their hardware she knew men must be at the beasts' heads, trying to control them as they pawed and stamped. It was not the tongue of Angle-land they spoke.

Edwin, caught alone with his two captains, must respond with orders to them, either to charge forward and fight their way through, or plunge down the stream bank and make a run of it to join his other men. He looked, almost panicked, at Eorconbeald, who with a jerk of his head, indicated the latter. The captain led, kicking his unwilling beast down the steep bank, making of himself a shield to Edwin. The stream bed was littered with large round stones, unhappy footing for their horses, which at any moment might stagger with a crippling hurt to hoof or leg. Yet the beasts, well-conditioned as they were, held fast, and were urged up the slippery bank near to where the waggon sat, beset by the marauders.

Most of these were on foot, and Edwin and Eorconbeald leapt from their animals. Alwin went after two who were mounted, blocking their progress towards where the Lord of Kilton was taking hold of his shield and drawing his sword. Eorconbeald was at Edwin's side, and others of his men closed up about them. Edwin saw the body of Balin, perilously near the front waggon wheels as those of the foe wrestled for control of the team. He could not see his mother on the ground; she might still live, within the waggon itself.

"Lady Edgyth!" he yelled, rallying those of his men to protect she who that waggon had been carrying.

The attackers fought with desperate energy, battle-worn men hungered and in clothes too scant for the cold weather. None had helmets or ring-shirts, and in this alone were the men of Kilton and the invaders matched.

There was no one of them who gave orders or who the others provided cover to, but it was clear from their knives and the little they uttered they were Danes. Edwin, dressed as he was for a festive outing, a large silver pin fastening his fur-trimmed cloak, his father's good steel in his hand and belted across his belly, looked every bit the noble he was. His wealth made him immediate target for the spears bristling from the hands of the foe.

He and Eorconbeald found themselves confronted with three of the spear-men. A shield was also a weapon, and the young Lord of Kilton had been taught how to wield his by none less than Cadmar, Worr, and this man now at his side. The shields of the two were foremost in play, blocking the wrought iron spear points as they darted towards them, and with their bodkin-sharp bosses and broad surfaces striking back at unguarded shoulders. One of the Danes was armed only with a short throwing spear, allowing Edwin to move in the nearer. Eorconbeald worried the other two attackers, splitting his attentions between them, working for a way to reduce their numbers for an even pair off.

Edwin focussed on the Dane with the short spear. He felt a surge of triumph as he caught the man with a glancing blow of his sword edge to the head, then as the Dane recoiled, lunged in with his shield to topple him. The Dane's spear was still in his hand, but Edwin was in too close for him to bring it to bear. Edwin's sword sliced down upon the Dane's neck, nearly severing it. An issue of blood shot forth, bathing the Dane next the fallen man in hot gore.

It was exactly the opening Eorconbeald needed. He too had been sprayed with blood, and with his nostrils filled with that life fluid he held one Dane at bay with his shield as he taunted the second with the movement of his sword. He kept just without range of that second spear, challenging the two to break rank so one might come after him.

One did. The bloodied Dane moved forward, even sliding his hand back along the shaft of his spear to give it more reach. Longer reach meant less control, and Eorconbeald surprised the man by turning sharply to the side and leaping back. The Dane's spear followed, falling short and hitting the ground. Eorconbeald was upon it with his booted foot in an instant. He could not snap the point, but it was pulled from the Dane's hand. It gave Edwin free rein to step in for the kill.

As he did so the remaining Dane gave a mighty oath. He forsook Eorconbeald and came at Edwin, whose sword was lodged in the belly of the now fallen Dane. His spear swiped across the sword of Edwin, knocking it from his grasp. Edwin gave a roar and jumped back. From the tail of his eye he saw Alwin, still on his horse, poling men where they lay on the ground. Edwin's nearer men were fully engaged about him. If any saw he had been disarmed they would offer their own weapon.

It was Eorconbeald who did so. He flung his sword upon the ground at Edwin's feet, then snatched the Danish spear lying there.

Alwin was now off his horse and working his way with spear and shield towards them, joined by two others of his companions. The waggon holding his mother had taken a spear hit, and the body of Balin on the ground by the wheel had been joined by several others.

A yell behind him made Edwin, sword now in hand, whirl. A Dane was there, also brandishing a sword, one look telling Edwin it was fallen from the hand of Huna, his youngest thegn, now lying on the ground. Huna was three years younger than he; the sword was one Edwin had awarded him at his sword-bearing last year. Now it was in the hand of this marauder. This fact veiled Edwin's thoughts, clouding his mind behind his furrowed brow. The Dane grinned at him, turning the blade in his hand as if to show off his battle-gain.

Boast as he might of his prize, the Dane was unpractised in wielding of shield and sword together; he was a spear-man with a spear-man's skill. He could not long repel the punishing blows Edwin unleashed upon his shield. He left no chance for the man to try to bring the stolen sword into play. Edwin hammered away at the narrow iron rim of the shield, slashing at the leathern covering, battering the planks as they split and dropped. He would not allow this Dane a single blow with Huna's sword.

He downed the man with a slash at the torso, then kicked the sword from the Dane's unyielding grip. He would not die holding it. Edwin stood over the dying Dane, chest heaving for breath as he watched his life ebb. He must get to the waggon now and see if his mother still lived.

Then Edwin heard a yelp. It was Eorconbeald. Edwin turned to him. A spear-thrust had caught his captain from behind, in the shoulder of his shield arm. Eorconbeald had time to wheel around, but his shield arm, pierced high in the muscle, dropped away, opening his body to the oncoming thrust. The Dane he fought had no shield of his own, and with two hands made a drive of utmost power into the breast of Edwin's captain. Eorconbeald fell, straight down to his knees, face uplifted. He dropped to his side.

The Dane paused a moment over his handiwork. Edwin's mouth opened, yet no sound issued forth. His mind, crowded with thoughts of his mother's safety and the death of so young a companion as Huna, now emptied. A white-hot clarity overtook him.

The Dane who killed Eorconbeald had no shield; it lay in splintered fragments. Edwin came after him with his dead captain's sword in his right hand, and his own shield in his left. Both men were winded from effort, and one was enraged. Despite the strength the Dane could bring to bear with his spear held in both hands, Edwin advanced, blocking every thrust to his head with shield held high, then dropping it to cover any jab at forward knee. Eorconbeald's blade in his hand drove every move as it glinted under that noon light, as if the steel yearned to taste this Dane's blood.

The Dane, moving backward under the onslaught, tripped over the body of one of his brethren. He was able nonetheless to keep his spear foremost and pointed at Edwin. The Dane spied a shield, whole, intact, by the dead man's side, and went for it. Edwin charged. He purposely drove his shield onto the Dane's spear-point, fixing it in the linden plank beneath the boss. Before the Dane could free its point Edwin released his grip and shook the shield off. It fell, spear still lodged, to the ground. Edwin's left hand went to the seax strapped across his belly. He came with two blades drawn at the Dane, now disarmed and scrambling to fit the new shield on his arm.

He did not have the chance. Edwin lifted his sword to the height of his own face, angling the point of it down and above the Dane's collar-bone, fixing him there. The seax in Edwin's left came in from the side, above the Dane's right hip bone, squarely into the gut.

Edwin drew back, both blades bloodied. Alwin was at his side, Edwin's shield in hand. He had dropped his own to retrieve that of his Lord.

Calls and cries from the margin of the wood forced Edwin to lift his eyes from the carnage at his feet. The men of Sceaftesburh were now there, on horse and on foot, chasing down those few remaining Danes as they tried to seek shelter in the trees.

The attack was over. A few men groaned from injuries, but in such tight quarters the fury of the fighting had been such that few were left injured, yet alive. Two strides brought Edwin back to Eorconbeald's side. Dropping to his knees beside him, he placed his fingers on the man's neck, hoping that blood still coursed within. Nothing.

He looked up at Alwin. Eorconbeald had been the best of Edwin's men, peerless in skill. He had given up his weapon so that Edwin might have one.

The Lord of Kilton shook his head. The loss before him was too great to fully compass. He ran the naked blade upon his tunic arm, freeing it of Danish blood. The scabbard on his captain's left hip lay empty. Edwin held it as he returned the weapon within. He had downed two with it, including his captain's own killer, and the battle-gain from these men would go to Eorconbeald's mother at Kilton.

Edwin stood. Alwin had retrieved his sword and handed it to him. Still unsheathed in his fist he walked to the waggon, fearful of what he might find there.

He jumped upon the waggon board and looked within.

"Mother," he said.

So slight was Edgyth's form he barely saw the blankets within concealed a woman. She pushed herself up, white-faced, as he lay down his blade and extended his hand to her.

"You are safe, mother. They are dead. I will have you taken within the walls of Sceaftesburh. I must ride for Kilton, but will be back as soon as I may."

She clung to that hand, kissed it, and wet it with her tears. He thought of what lay outside and spoke.

"Sit here inside, mother," he instructed. She did not need to see the brown road streaked red with blood, the trusted Balin, dead, nor learn of the rest of their losses now. She needed care and rest and the tending of the women of Sceaftesburh.

As her waggon rattled on, driven by a man of that hall, Edwin and Alwin made ready to return to Kilton. Edwin sent his best rider back to Kilton, to ride at speed and tell of what had happened. His men stripped the bodies of those they had killed, and loaded those of Kilton across the backs of their horses. He wanted his thegns here, that they might rest, and serve as comfort to his mother and the hall they had meant to visit.

Next day he and Alwin were halfway through their journey to Kilton when Worr appeared. He was on his black mare, one as nimble as she was fast, and after hearing report of the attack from the man Edwin had sent, the horse-thegn had pressed her strongly onward. Worr slowed as he caught sight of those he sought. Ahead of him was a woeful train, a string of horses carrying the bodies of men. He saw Edwin, seemingly unhurt, riding next Alwin.

"Lady Edgyth," were the first words Worr uttered. His mare was tossing her head as he wheeled her around to them.

"Frightened, but unhurt," Edwin could say. He had in his hands the rein of a second horse, with a body slung over it. "But Eorconbeald – yes." Edwin need say no more.

The horse-thegn's eyes fell on the awe-ful burden. Eorconbeald's brown hair hung down past the stirrup, and the blood which had run down his arm to his fingers was dried and dark.

Edwin inclined his head to the other laden horses led by Alwin. He went on with his sorry report.

"And three more, fighting: Ewald, Hibald and Huna. And Balin as well." He had brought fourteen men, and lost five of them on his own land. Hibald and Huna were father and son.

Worr took this in, then spoke. "I sent extra men to guard our borders, and have watchers on both bluffs, scanning the sea."

Edwin gave a nod.

"Were they Welsh," Worr asked, "or of Haesten?"

"Danes, from their calls and oaths."

Worr gave thought. The whereabouts of the war-chief Haesten had gone unreported for some time. Since arriving by sea in great numbers, Haesten and his band had largely travelled by land, hitting randomly at villages and burhs seeking plunder, then moving from friendly keeps in Anglia, north to Jorvik, and as far west perhaps as Wales. He was, it was thought, ceaselessly on the move. This strike could have been made by his men, or those of any number of rival Danes, including some who once had counted themselves in Haesten's number.

They made the rest of the trip in near silence.

The sound of lamentation as they rode through the palisade was great. The thegn sent ahead had delivered the news of their losses. It had not seemed real until now. It was hard to countenance the shock of the young Lord leaving for a ceremony of promised joy, only to return with the bodies of those slain. Yet here was proof.

Tables were hastily placed upon their trestles, and the bodies carried into the hall and set thereon. Edwin's hand gestured one forward to the high table, which was never struck. It was that of Eorconbeald, that he might lie where he had long supped.

The men of Kilton who had stayed behind stood in sober attention, clenching their jaws in anger and in grief. Women young and old, and many children wept over the dead. Dunnere was there, praying aloud as he moved amongst the bodies, his murmured benedictions a hum below the wailing of the bereaved. Yet gratitude was voiced that Edgyth, Lady of Kilton, had been spared.

Alwin remained with the bodies, telling of the attack as he stood by the head of his lost captain. Edwin gestured Worr into the treasure room. He was road-weary, but the deeper exhaustion of the strain of such an action was foremost. Soon he must return to those mourning the dead, speak to them, and later give them silver for their loss. But now it was Worr he needed. A serving man brought them ale.

"One thing only proved a blessing," Edwin told the horse-thegn. "We met them just as they began their raid. They grabbed sacks of grain from a crofter's granary. They saw us, and wanted our waggon and horses even more than food. Our men closed up around it in defence.

This split their force. No crofters were I think, hurt; they fled. I will know more later."

They talked in depth, Edwin relating in vivid detail snatches of the attack as they rose in memory. Worr listened to the tale, disjointed at times, but ending with the loss of five good men. Eorconbeald was Worr's peer, and all were friends.

The silence that followed extended many minutes, as each man held to their own thoughts. It was Edwin who broke it.

"Worr – Eorconbeald." Edwin could not release the words rising in his throat; that this man had died protecting him. The weight of this truth pressed like a choking hand about his neck.

Worr gave the same answer he had often given.

"He died protecting Kilton. As he was pledged to do."

Edwin's eyes dropped, as did his voice.

"He gave me his sword. It was the second time he saved my life."

Worr had seen the first, when Eorconbeald and Alwin dragged him from the field of battle after Edwin's horse had been speared.

The losses, so sudden and so great, made little sense to Edwin. The attacking Danes had nearly all been killed. Grain had been spilled and wasted. And he had lost five men.

"We killed them, but neither of us won."

Worr gave a short and dry laugh. His own father had died of wounds sustained fighting in an indeterminate skirmish, under the banner of Godwulf of Kilton. He had seen many of his own companions die thus, under the flag of Godwin, and now Edwin. He must say what he could.

"It is often so. Rare are the times, even on a field of pitched battle, that one side can fully claim victory. I have seen leaders withdraw their troops, having gained the upper hand, to spare further losses. Perhaps only those left to plunder the bodies win." This grim reward, even if it be carried out by a carrion bird, was often all that marked the victor. There were few clear measures of success.

Still, Worr asked what he could.

"How many did you down?"

"Not as many as we could have, if we had been riding alone. We need protect the waggon. Fifteen or more. Their losses were far greater than ours, though they had more men, five-and twenty, perhaps." Edwin looked about him. "I will get a fresh horse, return, and know the full accounting."

From outside the closed door they heard renewed bouts of wailing. Each man drew breath.

"You did well, Edwin," Worr now told him. He meant it not as praise, but simple affirmation.

Edwin looked at him, and lowered his head.

Chapter the Fourth

YRLING

Four Stones, South Lindisse, Angle-land

SIDROC had been right. With three war-ships, Hrald and his men had no fear of attack. Several times on their sea journey from Gotland to Angle-land they spotted drekars, some of which rapidly came about to study them. In every instance they were dragon-ships plying the waters alone, and turned and fled before them. They passed through the narrow straits of Scania without threat or challenge, and made it to the trading port of Aros. As he had on the outbound voyage, Hrald stayed upon the largest of the ships, captained by their ship-master, the dwarfish Aszur. Thorvi the star-reader had by this time determined to sail on with his cousin Aszur, and in Aros they not only reprovisioned the ships, but took on six more men, so that when Hrald and his men landed at Saltfleet, Aszur might have enough crew to sail all three drekars up to his home port of Jorvik.

For young Yrling every day at sea brought its own adventure. To assist in furling and unfurling the heavy sail; to help handle the lines as the nimble craft swiftly came about; to sit on his own sea chest and try his hand at pushing the heavy oar through the air, into the water, and pulling back to free air, an act which left the boy with aching shoulders and reddened palms; all of this filled him with eagerness and satisfaction. He relished each demand. To sleep on the open deck with the heave and swell of the ship beneath him, to eat the cold provender offered, to be soaked and chilled when it rained; he took it all in stride. His best hours were standing in the prow, looking forward, and even better than this, standing next Aszur in the stern at the oak steering-oar, his hands also on that beam as Aszur guided the oar to make the safest and swiftest passage through the waves.

The shores of Lindisse came into sight nearly eight weeks after Hrald had left them. The vast island had filled the horizon for two days. Now the wooden pier of Saltfleet was before them. Hrald could not look at it when they sailed off. Now his eyes latched on to every landmark of the place. He had moved with Yrling to the prow of the lead ship, and the brothers stood there in silence, one returning home, the other seeing it for the first time. Men were gathering now on the pier their father had built, come out from the small buildings clustered at its end. Hrald put his two fore fingers to his mouth and let out a shrill whistle, as signal it was he. An answering whistle was accompanied by the waving of arms in welcome. Yrling absorbed it all with bright eyes, and waved back. As they neared the pier he spotted the scuttled drekars off to one side. To Hrald they were nought but a painful reminder of the actions leading up to the great battle in which he had lost his sister. Hrald told Yrling in but few words why those ships were there.

"But we should raise them," Yrling protested. If the wood-worm had not got thoroughly into the keel, such ships could be restored to service, he knew.

Hrald gave a shake of his head. "The men who landed them – they killed all my men here, all but one." It was no satisfaction that he who had captained them had been the first to die, when the men of Four Stones caught up to them. Hrald would like to burn the hulks to the waterline.

"But they are drekars – they cost much silver to build –"

"Too many died," Hrald answered. The finality of his tone made the boy drop his questions, that and the fact that Hrald was not looking at his brother but staring down at the water creaming alongside the sharp prow of the ship in which they sailed.

Almost at their arrival, three of the Saltfleet men were sent off to Four Stones, to fetch horses and waggon to return them all home. Hrald would not leave in advance of his men, but would wait until they might all arrive as one. As for Aszur, his ships refilled their water barrels from the well, and took their leave up the coast to Jorvik; they were not far now. Aszur grinned at Hrald in parting, showing fully the gold-wrapped tooth he sported. "If you seek passage again, seek Aszur," the man called. The ship-master looked with satisfaction at his new ship.

"That I will," Hrald promised.

The horses would not be brought to them until next day, and after Yrling had explored the few buildings comprising the outpost, he asked if he and Hrald might climb the bluff he could see a short distance up the coast. Hrald gave thought before answering, then nodded. They took two of the Saltfleet horses, and four of his men, also mounted, to accompany them. Yrling had already seen the horses which served the guards here, and exclaimed over their size. Being atop one was yet another excitement for the boy. Their escort split at the base of the bluff, two men remaining behind to watch, the other two on foot, trailing just behind Hrald and the youngster. They wandered the paths of that Fated hill, which gave a vantage over the empty coast from several points.

As they walked Yrling broke the silence with his question. It had dawned on him all at once, and his wonder was in his voice. "Is this the hill where father met the Idrisids?"

Hrald's own mind had been much occupied with this truth, yet he still felt surprise that Yrling had at once named the place. He could imagine his brother questioning his father about it, so keen was the boy to learn of his past adventures.

"It is," Hrald confirmed.

He went on to tell the story of the small silver coin which had been found here, a coin with writing on it like thread-work, in letters none could read, but Godwin of Kilton recognised. That small coin, and report of a strange ship with sails of dark red, gave a hint of the abductors, and the near-fruitlessness of any attempt to reclaim those who had vanished at their hands. As a boy Hrald had held that coin in his hand, feeling it was the only clue to his father's disappearance.

"Father beat them," Yrling pronounced, referring to the blue-clad slavers who had captured his parents. He had his hand on the grip of the knife Hrald had given him, almost as if ready to draw it for defence. "He and a lot of Danes," the boy added, in justice.

Hrald could only smile and nod, wondering what the boy really knew of the bloody battles their father had fought as he worked his way east to the Baltic. Hrald was grateful that today no ship, red-sailed or not, bobbed upon the waters beneath them.

When they returned the horses to Saltfleet's paddock Yrling jumped down, and almost staggered. He laughed aloud at getting his land-legs again, the absence of which the brief sojourn on horseback had reawakened. Even with the stops to reprovision the ships, his feet felt heavy yet uncertain beneath him, no longer shifting his weight to compensate for the heave and roll of the deck.

When the riders from Saltfleet arrived at Four Stones, that hall's Lady was there to meet them, along with Jari and Kjeld, left in joint command in Hrald's absence. Ælfwyn's anxious waiting was brought to an end even before the men had swung down to nod their heads to her; she read on their faces that all was well with her son. As they stood there Bork came out from the depths of the stable and took a place at Kjeld's side. Burginde also appeared, coming from the hall, and at once gauging that a party of men and horses would be starting for Saltfleet, made for the kitchen yard to have them gather provisions for a waggon.

Ælfwyn and Jari turned to each other with looks of shared gladness. She had a special word for Kjeld, who had, she thought, been of particular aid to Jari in dealing with the younger men of the hall. "I will not fail to tell Hrald of your service," she promised.

She now looked at Bork. "I am sure Mul will do the same for you, Bork, for the way you have cared for my son's horses." She turned and left them, eager to join

Burginde in the kitchen yard, there to plan with the bakers and cooks a welcome feast for the next night.

Kjeld was turning now to some of the men, to send them to bring mounts from the valley of horses to the hall, to be saddled and bridled. Bork clung to his side, almost touching him. His request sounded near to a desperate plea. "Please. May I bring the Jarl his bay?"

Kjeld looked down at the boy. It was true that the stableman Mul had entrusted the youngster with the personal care of Hrald's own animals, and the boy had repaid that trust in his meticulous care. Hrald had favoured Bork, not only taking him on a visit to Oundle, but also sitting with him several times a week over the small wax tablet he had given the boy, where he might learn to form letters. Kjeld was the first of Four Stones who had been placed in charge of Bork. Hrald had asked him to escort the boy, and the body of Bork's father, back to the hall. The youngster had reason to trust him. Bork stood before him, eyes starting, biting his lower lip in anticipation.

Kjeld looked at Jari. The Tyr-hand gave a nod, and his answer. "I will ride to Saltfleet, Kjeld. You remain here in command." He let Kjeld say the rest.

"You will go, and ride next to Jari. And you will lead the Jarl's horse, and give it to him, yourself."

Bork gave a nod of his own, a grave one, but his eyes danced. He turned to the dimness of the stable door, eager to ready the big horse, to give an extra shine to the leather of saddle and bridle, and silently naming the things he must pack, the sturdy wooden comb he used on the beast's black mane and tail, and the cloths he used to wipe him down. They would camp overnight, he knew, and he would have what he needed to keep the bay looking his best.

When both the Lady of the Hall and Bork had left, one of the Saltfleet men had further word for Kjeld. "We will need an extra horse. Hrald has brought a boy with him from Gotland, another son of Sidroc's."

A train of twenty mounted warriors leading an additional two-and-thirty horses reached Saltfleet next day. In their midst was a single ox-drawn waggon, not the two which had delivered the men here. One would suffice, for other than the nearly empty provision casks and the men's sea chests, the bulky trade goods Hrald's warriors had carried had been replaced in most instances by tiny pouches holding gemstones from the Ural Mountains and beyond.

They whistled their approach, and found their young Jarl and the rest of their brethren gathering at the mouth of the worn track before the port buildings. Some of the men on both sides were hooting and calling out greetings, and Hrald himself must smile at their approach. Jari was heading the file, and riding next to one of the Saltfleet men was Bork. A lead line to a bay stallion with black mane and a tail that swept the ground was tied to his saddle ring. As they reined to a stop Jari nodded at Bork, as signal. Bork grinned at Hrald, then jumped down from the horse which had carried him here. He untied the careful hitch he had made to the tie line, and placing his hand on the bay's thick neck, spoke to the horse, some word which made the beast slightly lower its fine head. The boy was now able to pull off the neck loop and return the lead to his own saddle. Bork placed his hand above the stallion's left leg. Without pulling the reins over the stallion's neck, he led the animal, with the lightest of touch, to Hrald.

It was only when Bork grew truly near to his Jarl did he see the boy standing at his side; so intent he had been on Hrald. But a boy was there, one his own age, perhaps, of sturdy build, with light brown hair which nearly grazed his shoulder. The boy stood alongside Hrald, legs slightly spread, his hand on a knife at his hip. It was a commanding, even aggressive pose, one a warrior would assume when unsure if who approached was friend or foe. Bork saw enough of the hilt the boy's hand covered to know it was that knife which Hrald had left wearing. As he came up before Hrald, Bork gave the strange boy a final last look. He himself was taller but much lighter bodied.

Now before Hrald, Bork had almost to fight the impulse to embrace him, so glad he was at his return. He might have tried, if the strange boy had not been there. Instead he did what he had asked to do, deliver his Jarl's favourite horse to him. The animal stopped as soon as Bork did, and Hrald regarded both stallion and boy.

"He looks well," Hrald told him, which forced a quick smile to Bork's lips.

Now he laid his hand upon Bork's shoulder, and spoke again. "As do you." Bork's smile deepened, not at the words, but at the touch which Hrald offered.

Hrald gave the boy a longer glance. Even after camping out overnight Bork was noticeably clean, and wearing a new tunic and leggings that Hrald could guess had come from the hands of the women in the weaving room. Indeed, he was correct in this. Hrald's mother, not wishing to add to the burden imposed on Mul's wife in caring for Bork, had been clothing the boy. Bork sported new brown boots upon his feet as well, not the outgrown pairs he had been given from Mul's sons.

Yrling, watching this, had much to take in. The horses of Saltfleet were big and well formed. This dark red stallion before him was the biggest and finest horse he had ever seen. And it followed the skinny boy with him as a trained hound would.

"Who are you," Yrling demanded. He did not know whether to speak in the tongue taught him by his mother, or in Norse, so he chose the former, as Hrald had.

"Bork," was all the skinny boy said.

"I am Yrling. I am Hrald's brother." This statement was no less than a bold assertion.

They had no time to say more, as Jari was now before Hrald, and had Yrling's full attention. Jari threw back his head and gave a laugh, then took Hrald in his arms in embrace.

Yrling knew he was staring but could not help it. His father was tall, as was Hrald. This man was tall as well, but so broad he looked near to a giant, one with ruddy-hued hair and beard. As his big hands reached around Hrald's back, Yrling saw the right, badly maimed from the lack of pointing and middle fingers.

The two had now parted, and the red-haired man looked at the youngster at Hrald's side.

Yrling in turn squinted up at this giant. "Are you Asberg?"

Jari gave another laugh. "Asberg is at Turcesig, far from here, and likely holding an ale cup. But you will meet him at Four Stones; word has been sent.

"My name is Jari. I have been your brother's bodyguard since he was younger than you."

Yrling's head gave a little snap. It meant something, meant a lot, that a boy was given a body-guard. It proved how important he was. Yrling did not then stop to think that Hrald as a boy needed such, as his own father was no longer there to protect him.

On the journey back to Four Stones, Bork trailed behind the waggon, with the final warriors at the end of the train. Hrald and Jari rode in front of the waggon in the centre of their ranks, with Hrald's young brother on his right. Bork could not hear Yrling at this distance, but whenever they might stop to water the horses or break to eat, he watched Yrling chattering away at either Jari or another of the men. Bork knew riding at the end of any rank and file of warriors to be an exposed position, and one of high responsibility. To bring up the rear was to bear the brunt of any overtaking assault from behind, and after watching the careful way in which the warriors around him turned their heads to scan down the road, he began to do the same. It did not entirely console him; he had somehow imagined himself riding next to Hrald on this return. He was gladdened to see his Jarl once more upon his fine beast, and proud of the animal's coat and condition. Jari had selected the horse Yrling would ride back, a black gelding, and a far better one than that which Bork was mounted upon. But then, he was only a stable-boy. Yrling was Hrald's brother.

As they approached the hall Hrald and Jari moved up to front the troop, with Yrling at Hrald's right. There was no such timber fortress as Four Stones on Gotland, at least none that Yrling knew of. He had in fact seen no settlement to rival the size of the village fronting it. The pounded clay road they took split the village in almost perfect halves. The folk thereof came out to line that road, and stood blinking up at them, and raising their hands in welcome. A stone pillar of some kind stood outside the palisade wall, a thick shaft rising from the ground, carved all over with figures, and ending near the top in an openwork circle of stone. Yrling could not look long at it, for the height of the timber palisade awed him, and the action of its gates swinging open to admit them seemed a noteworthy event in itself. A raft of men and women waited within, finely, even gaily attired, their faces wreathed in smiles. The hall was now before them, its base built up from stone, and topped by timber. The stable across from it was larger than the largest barn or stable he could imagine. And on the other side of this was a second hall, nearly as large as the main hall, where, he would learn, the younger, unwed men lived.

Hrald brought his horse to a stop. Of all the folk there, a group of women were foremost, and it was these Hrald regarded. One, who had long fair hair, held a toddling child in her arms.

"Who is that," Yrling asked, as they readied to dismount.

"My mother, the Lady of Four Stones. The boy is my sister Ashild's son."

Yrling knew Ashild had died on a battle field. He had forgotten she had left a small child behind.

The next moments were a confused whirl of embraces, uttered prayers of thanksgiving, and happy tears from the Lady and a girl, older than Yrling, who looked like her.

The little boy made a roaring sound when he saw Hrald; Yrling could see he was trying to say his older brother's name, and laughing at the sight of him.

"This is Yrling," Hrald was at last able to say. "He has come to see Four Stones."

At this the Lady gasped, and handed the child to the plump woman at her side. Yrling found himself caught up in her arms. She smelled like flowers, of a kind he did not know.

When she let him go, more tears were running down her cheeks. "You are as welcome as can be, Yrling," she told him. "Your mother and I came here together, many years ago."

Yrling nodded his head to her in respect, as a man should to a woman of high estate. He felt himself almost grown and wanted to be thought of as such. "Thank you, Lady," he said. He did not know what more to add, then recalled an important point. "We must sacrifice a cock or hen to Njord and Freyr, for our good crossing."

Hrald gave a little laugh. "I think the cockerel father and you offered on Gotland is enough."

That night, and each night after, Yrling sat at a table of older boys. He was not too old to sit at one of the many children's tables, but Hrald, mindful of Yrling's self assurance, placed him instead at the table where Gunnulf had once supped as a youth. These were boys mostly shy of their fifteenth Summer, and so not yet of sword-bearing age, but close. Yrling, at coming thirteen years, would be the youngest amongst them, and might find both friends and guides amongst the warriors' sons there.

Asberg and Æthelthryth had arrived just as the hall was filling, giving Yrling a chance to see all the key members of the hall together at the high table. He had already been brought before Wilgot the priest, and by the way Hrald's mother had presented him, understood that this dark-robed man was held in special esteem. The youngster had sometimes seen men dressed in long gowns walking amongst the stalls of the trading road. These were come from foreign ships, and he assumed Wilgot to be a trader in spices.

The boy was far too young to sleep in the second hall amongst the rowdy unwed warriors, and Jari made offer that Yrling stay with Inga and him. Their daughters were both wed, one living out at the valley of horses, and their small dwelling large enough to house a boy in one of the empty alcoves.

When all were assembling in the morning to break their fast, Asberg gestured Yrling to his side at the head table. "This red-haired blockhead tells me you want to know me," he said, tipping his head over to a grinning Jari. "Share my bench, son of Sidroc," Asberg invited. "We do not stand on such ceremony in the mornings, and I would know you."

"I want to train with you," were the first words from Yrling's lips.

The older man looked surprised. "You have been hearing tales," he surmised, with a grin of his own.

"Only that father says you are the best with a spear. And so I want to train with you. Can I?"

Asberg considered. "I live at Turcesig. But let us see what you can do, this morning. I will give you pointers, if I can. And then later, if Hrald allows, you can come and live with me at Turcesig a while." The older man looked over at Hrald, making Yrling do so as well.

"Can I go?" he asked his older brother.

Hrald gave a laugh. "You have not been invited yet. Asberg has the training of well over a hundred warriors to occupy him. He has captains to help him in this. If your skill is worthy of their attention, or his own, then it will be his choice."

After they had eaten, Asberg called out a few of the boys, both some of Yrling's size and age, and those older. There were eight of them Asberg led to the sparring ground, and he let no man nor woman watch, to keep the boys from that distraction. They were armed with just blunt-end shafts of ash, with no iron points. Such were not needed in practice, nor to judge a warrior's prowess in handling a spear. They had each brought their shields, Yrling running back to Jari's house for his, which he had hung in his alcove, but Asberg had them set these aside. They would begin without them, for shield-handling was an art in itself, and Asberg wished to see Yrling unimpeded by anything held in his left hand. And the lack of a shield meant that he could gauge the strength and skill the boy had in hands and arms, and his ability to block another shaft with his own.

This was to be a test, and as such Yrling would be taxed with challenges meant to expose his weaknesses. Asberg began by setting him against a boy his own size and age, one, who being raised within a fortified keep, and surrounded by warriors and with one as his father, had seen good spear-fighting from earliest childhood. To Asberg's pleasure Yrling quickly bested him, proving both quicker and cannier in where he aimed his blows. He then paired Yrling with an older boy, one taller and with longer reach. Yrling proved his father's son in this, for he sized his opponent up at once and struck first. Aggression was important in spear-play, for if from the first thrust you attacked the warrior you faced with relentless speed, you could at once begin to drive them back, ground hard to make up. A counter to this was the ease in which such a fighter could be made to tire, and it was the third boy Yrling faced who had learnt this, and kept himself, by dodges and feints, from the bruises Yrling's shaft could impose. One over-eager could wear himself out with needless show, while an older, more savvy warrior returned just enough to goad him on.

Asberg called a break then, so that Yrling might rest, and as the boy gulped water he dipped from the cask at the corner of the field, selected the boys to form two shield-walls. He wanted to see how Yrling would fight with his warrior brethren, and placed him in a line of three, with two larger and older boys flanking him. The boys slipped their left hands through the leathern loop on the inside of their wooden shields, to grasp the handle behind the iron boss in the centre of the disc. Yrling's shield he had painted himself, a zigzag of red, like a hot bolt of lightning, on a dark blue ground. He and his father had made the disc together, piecing together the boards, and his father and Tindr had formed and shaped the iron boss and rim encircling the disc.

Yrling's lack of experience now showed, and he took multiple hits to his shield, any one of which, if administered harder, would have knocked his shield askew, allowing an opening to permit a spear-point to dart in from left or right, hitting his upper body, disabling either shield or spear arm.

After a while Asberg stepped into the line facing that which Yrling fought in. After parrying a few spear-thrusts with the boys flanking Yrling, he knocked them down with forceful pokes to their shields. They laughed, and took advantage of the rest so granted to sit there, watching Asberg face this new boy alone. Likewise, those in the line Asberg had joined tailed off, so unneeded were their efforts now that he had stepped in to face Yrling.

Asberg used no shield, so able was he in his spear-handling. His quick wrists could turn the shaft to block any attempt at a touch the boy could offer.

"Do you tire?" he asked the panting boy. "You will need to fight many a battle when you feel you might drop. You will need to face men fresher than you, faster than you." He gave a sudden poke to Yrling's shield, which knocked him to the ground. "Also men older and slower than you," Asberg said, with a laugh.

Nothing deterred, Yrling leapt to his feet and came back at Asberg. His teeth were gritted and his ash pole darted with frenzied speed. Asberg, moving with calm ease, sidestepped each thrust, parrying every blow as if he knew exactly where Yrling meant to place it. Twice Yrling got close to making a hit, once on Asberg's forearm, another at his leading knee. This was enough to earn praise, and a call to an end of the sparring.

Yrling stood, both hands still clasped about the upright shaft, now planted on the ground. Despite the coolness of the morning, he felt red-faced and sweaty. The older man eyed him.

He could not help but be impressed. Yrling had been eager to show off his skill, which was for his young age, considerable. It was impossible not to take to the boy, who, the more Asberg looked at him, seemed to resemble, if not in person, then in spirit, his namesake. And in his spear-work this young Yrling possessed boldness and attack, which will put a man off. Much of fighting took place in the head.

"You fight like a Dane," Asberg judged.

Yrling blinked at him. Of course he did; he was his father's son.

"You are good alone. More than good. But you must be able to meet a line of warriors coming towards you, and work within your own line, giving and receiving protection while making the correct thrust. It is as much keeping your brothers alive as it is keeping yourself alive." Here Asberg gestured with the butt of his shaft to the boys watching. He fixed his eyes back on Yrling. "That is what we will work on."

After the welcome feast Hrald had that night asked his mother to join him in the treasure room. He presented the letter from Ceridwen, which she grasped in both hands, but saved to be read in her bower house. The second item was a bulky one. Within a bag of hemmed linen was a folded length of fabric. The room, lit by two oil cressets, was still dim, but her fingers told her it was silk. By the golden light of the lamps she could not be certain of its hue, but her son told her it was cobalt blue. She pulled it out and open, holding it up; it was well more than enough for the making of a gown.

"She told me father had traded for it, but she wanted you to have it, for the sake of your eyes," her son reported.

He could not help but smile, seeing his mother's astonished happiness.

"You safely returned – Yrling with you – a letter – and silk," she murmured. She shook her head in gentle wonderment.

As she readied herself for sleep in her bower house she read the letter, first to herself, and then aloud to Burginde. Ælfwyn wept, to read of Ceridwen's joy in hearing of Cerd. The boy was sound asleep in his alcove a few footsteps away, and Ælfwyn must draw back the heavy curtain and give the boy a kiss, from them both.

Burginde as she listened had been smoothing the gown her mistress had taken off. Her thoughts were now on another boy, he mentioned in the second part of Ceridwen's letter.

"Yrling," Burginde uttered. The youngster's appearance could not help but put her in mind of his namesake. Anyone could see the spunk the boy had, and the beginning of a natural sense of command which could be the legacy of both father and grand-uncle. His arrival could not help but remind her of the potential claimants to leadership here. Hrald was Jarl, and Sidroc's eldest son. But Yrling was also Sidroc's son. And perhaps with more claim than either, that toddling boy breathing the sleep of innocence was a direct heir from the Dane who had won this keep.

Ælfwyn had looked over to Burginde, awaiting her next words on Yrling.

"He be too big for a small island," the nurse conjectured.

Ælfwyn's brow had slightly furrowed at this judgement, which only increased at Burginde's next words.

"Likely too big for a big island, like this," she ended.

In the morning after all had broken their fast, the Lady of the hall asked Hrald, Yrling, Asberg and Æthelthryth to go to the treasure room with her. Burginde came as well, as did Hrald's younger sister, Ealhswith, who had charge of Cerd. It was Yrling's first peek at the room, and all could see he was eager to explore. The stacked rows of shields against the long wall, and the iron hoops holding excess spears were enough to excite his wonder, not to mention the trove of casks, chests, and boxes, and what they might hold. The wolfskin spread on the broad bed made his eyes widen; and as Asberg and Æthelthryth filed in he asked Hrald if they were the pelts of dogs, as he had no knowledge of wolves. Cerd meanwhile had run right to the stacks of shields, and Yrling would have followed and gladly looked over their painted faces with him, if Hrald had not with a movement of his head asked him to remain standing there at his side.

When all were gathered Ælfwyn smiled at Yrling.

"This will be a special day for you, Yrling," she began. "You will be born in Christ, and baptised into the Holy Church. Wilgot our priest is preparing the sacrament for you in his house." Ceridwen had given her leave in her letter to instruct the boy in the Christian faith, and she would not risk the child's soul a day longer than she need.

The Lady of the hall looked at her sister and brother-in-law. "And I ask you, Æthelthryth and Asberg, to serve as god-parents."

Yrling's head swiveled as he looked about him, and from face to face. The Lady's sister wore a delighted smile; Asberg looked at him with a slight grin.

"What is that," Yrling asked. His uncertainty was all too clear.

"A ceremony, to welcome you fully here to Four Stones, and into the Church," Ælfwyn answered.

Yrling looked up at his big brother. "It will be quick," was the best thing Hrald could think to say.

Ælfwyn felt need to say the next. "As Hrald says, it is quick," she promised. She did not mention that their father had agreed to baptism. It was, she knew, a mere condition to the Peace, and had not taken; for all his qualities Sidroc was never an adherent. Nor were Hrald and Ealhswith good examples, having been baptised as infants, as she had. But she thought of another exemplar she might use. "And it is no more than what Guthrum, the great King of the Danes here, had done. Also, every warrior here at Four Stones." She looked meaningfully at Asberg.

Yrling's eyes shifted as well to Asberg. He had submitted to baptism that he might wed the Lady's sister, and though he duly attended to Wilgot's preaching, and had allowed Æthelthryth a free hand in the churching of their boys, could not in truth testify to his heartfelt commitment. He had in fact been one of the men who had visited the Place of Offering a few years ago, with a fowl in a sack, and left that place without it.

For these reasons Asberg could offer Yrling no more than a wan smile of support.

The boy returned his eyes to the Lady's face.

"Why?" Yrling wanted to know.

Ælfwyn had ready answer.

"So that you may know God's mercy."

Yrling's face made it clear this meant nothing to him.

"So that after your death you might aspire to Heaven."

This he could make comment on. "I want a warrior's death," he told all, "and if I make a good one, I will be called to Asgard to the hall of Odin, or the hall of white-armed Freyja. There I will fight all day and feast all night."

Ælfwyn paused, and after taking a gentle breath, went on. "It might be good, would it not, to consider a third home, one in which all who have led upright and just lives can hope to win a place."

Yrling regarded her well. Her voice was kind and soft, but she had that patient look that he had seen often on his own mother's face.

Both of his parents had told him of the courtesy demanded of a guest. One must be alert to the host's customs, the need to comply to the best of one's ability to reasonable expectations. This was no different, and his brother Hrald was there nodding agreement and approval of what the Lady was telling him. Besides, if there was a third hall to go to, he might be able to take his pick. He did not like to think of the day of his death, not yet, but choice was ever a good thing in life, and it made sense it would continue to be, after it had ended.

He pulled himself up to his full height, put his hand on the hilt of his knife, and nodded. "I will do it," he said.

The ceremony, within the small house of Wilgot, was indeed brief, if mystifying. The man who looked like a spice merchant moved his hands above Yrling's head, speaking in some strange tongue which the boy's ears did not open to; like some of the traders Yrling had seen, he seemed to speak this tongue as well as that of Hrald's mother. At one point Asberg placed his hand on one of Yrling's shoulders, and the Lady's sister on his other. Wilgot had a silver vial of water, and a basin, and a tiny towel of white linen.

Yrling was asked to tilt his head back over the basin, while the man dribbled water over his forehead, muttering the whole time. Then Wilgot dabbed the water off with the towel, but smeared some kind of oil on his brow. Yrling raised his own hand to touch it, but the priest gave him a warning look, so he stopped.

"You may take off your tunic," the priest said to him next. Yrling blinked, but pulled it off. The man handed him one of white, and indicated that he slip it on, so he did. Then the priest tied a kind of sash about Yrling's waist, and knotted it, three times. "On the eighth day I shall unloose you. Arise now and walk Christ's path," he told him, though Yrling was already on his feet.

Then it was over. Everyone crowded around him, smiling, and the women hugged him, all but Ealhswith, who was shy.

"It will make sense later," Hrald told him, close to his ear so no one else heard. Yrling only nodded, in trust of his big brother's words.

Hrald's mother looked happiest of all, so happy there were tears in her eyes. She bent near him, to say, "You remind me of your mother. You favour her."

Yrling knew he scowled. It was dark-haired Eirian who looked like their father, not him.

"But I am strong, like my father!"

"I can see that, as well," she quickly answered.

Cerd had been in the arms of Burginde, as Ælfwyn had wanted every member of the family to witness this christening. He was getting to the age when he no longer liked being held, and the nurse had lowered him to the floor. Cerd had not often been in the priest's house, and now ran about its four corners, trying to pull himself up to peer over the edge of the work tables, and then climbed into a large carved chair, one conspicuously of quality make, far nicer than the simple bench and stools. It had been given to Wilgot after the departure of Hrald's wife, as the Jarl had not wished to see it in the hall.

The child jumped down from the cushioned seat, and running to the priest's single alcove, gave a solid slap with his small hand to the coverlet on the bed there. He ran back into the midst of those assembled, and craning his neck as he looked up, seemed to study their faces. Both Ælfwyn and Hrald were watching Cerd, and their eyes met in silent communion. It was almost as if he looked for someone, the mother who was not there.

That afternoon Yrling was wandering about the work yards, exploring. All knew who he was; even amongst the folk who did their eating in the kitchen yard or in their own small dwellings, word of the boy's arrival and his relationship to the Jarl was already known. Yrling had made a circuit of the place, glancing over the extensive fowl houses, stopping to watch an old man at work grinding down a butchery knife at a whetstone, standing back to count the number of cooks already labouring at the many work tables, chopping root vegetables and mincing cuts of pig. He headed back to the tall timber stable, just across the side door of the hall. The paddock attached to it was large, and a number of horses were within. One of them, standing at the back rail, caught and held his eye. The horse was not only white, but huge. Its bright coat shaded to a downy black at muzzle and fetlocks above its dark hooves, adding to its striking colouration. Hrald's big bay stallion was a beauty, but this white stallion was one exceeding even that.

The horse was standing alone by the rail, while a few others moved about in groups closer to the stable wall. Yrling had eyes only for the white, and without bothering to open the gate, climbed over it and leapt down into the paddock. Yrling knew horses, and headed not straight towards his target, but slightly aslant. The stallion wore but a halter. No matter, once he was upon his back, he could guide him with his weight and heels, and with his hands in the beast's mane, give further direction, as he held on.

As he made towards the stallion a figure emerged from the doorway which led from stable to paddock. It was the skinny boy, who had brought Hrald's bay to him at Saltfleet. Bork stepped out to confront the intruder in the paddock. It was Yrling who spoke first.

"Who are you," Yrling demanded, though he knew his name.

"I told you. Bork."

This did not seem sufficient for his challenger; Yrling's face did not change. Bork went on.

"I care for the Jarl's own horses. One day I will be his man. And serve in his body-guard." He paused, in justice to an unknown future. "If I am good enough," he ended.

Yrling considered him. He had seen enough of life here that he knew he had special standing, and could order someone like Bork around.

"I am Hrald's brother," he said again. "My father is his father. He was Jarl before Hrald."

Bork knew this, and had nothing he could say to these facts. Yrling now shifted his gaze to the white stallion and proclaimed, "I want to ride that horse."

Bork was quick in his answer.

"You cannot. No one rides him." He had taken a sudden step closer to Yrling, to underscore this.

Bork had spoken the truth. Since the body of Ashild had been lifted from his back, no one had ridden this stallion. Mul and Bork kept him in shape by running him from the end of a lead rope with the other horses wanting exercise.

"Why?" Yrling wanted to know. "He looks sound."

He studied the animal from afar, letting his eye rove over the deeply arched neck and its spill of white mane, the broad chest and well-set legs. The stallion's power was proclaimed in these, and in the heavily muscled rump from which the snowy tail streamed. A well-favoured beast could yet have unseen flaws. "Is he mean?"

Bork had ever been cautious about the horse, who though not ill-tempered, lacked the friendliness of Hrald's bay stallion.

Bork gave his head a shake.

"He is not mean. But he is the horse of Ashild of Four Stones."

Yrling took this in. He knew the fallen Ashild was the daughter of the famed war-chief for whom he had been named. It made him want to ride the horse even more.

He was well skilled in riding bareback. He could guide the horse to the mounting block within the paddock and pull himself on. He turned from Bork and made for the stallion. He did not get far. As Yrling was beginning to extend his hand to the cheek piece of the animal's halter, he was hit from behind. Bork was upon him, pulling him down and away from the beast.

They both yelled, and the stallion snorted, tossed its head, and shied away in prancing steps from the figures rolling on the ground. The horse was forgotten. Both boys were swinging, pounding on the other, switching places as first Bork and then Yrling had the advantage as they rolled in the mud and manure of the paddock.

Of a sudden Mul was there, and yanked both of them to their feet. He kept one hand on each of their shoulders, to separate them. He listened to both.

Mul's loyalty to the family of the hall stretched back to when he was no older than these boys he stared at, with their split lips and eyes which would soon blacken from the blows they had given each other. When she arrived here, the Lady of this place had fed him, given his desperate mother silver, and lifted all the village from wretchedness to hope. Ashild had been her firstborn, and Mul had loved the girl for her own love and skill with horses. When the white stallion had been brought as wooing gift to her, Mul had quietly ridden it first, to make sure it was well-mannered; he would let no harm come to Ashild by allowing her on an unruly animal. And this stallion had been the last horse she had ridden. No one had the right to him, none save the Jarl himself.

"Bork is right," he told Yrling, in no uncertain tone. "Do not touch the stallion. He belongs now to the Jarl, and no one rides him. Not even him. And it is Bork who has care of the Jarl's own horses. Not you."

Seeing the lip of the boy curl up, Mul gave further warning. "Do not try again, unless you want the Jarl to know."

He dismissed the boys, Bork back to the stable work bench, fashioning a new bridle, and Yrling to the hall. But

Hrald found out quickly enough, for he caught sight of Yrling as the youngster made for Jari's house, where his clothes were. The white tunic Yrling had been given by Wilgot at his baptism was now smeared with mud, and the bits of straw clinging to some stains gave proof of manure too. His tangled hair and bleeding lip told even more.

Hrald had no need to ask. He gestured his little brother around the corner of Jari's house, where they would be unobserved. Yrling started right in with his explanation, spluttering not a little at his surprise at how he had been treated by Bork, and further reprimanded by Mul.

Hrald listened. He had but one side of the tale, but knew Mul and Bork enough to imagine both words and actions. He summed up his judgement in the same words Mul had.

"Bork is right."

Yrling's answer was rooted in indignation.

"He is a stable boy!"

Hrald was swift to add to this. "He is training to be a warrior. Just as you are."

In answer Yrling kicked at the ground with his boot, rubbing his toe in the dirt.

His brother's next words were low and solemn. "He came here an orphan. His father and another man ambushed me on my way to Turcesig. They killed one of my men, and we killed them. It happened before the eyes of Bork. I brought him here, to live."

"He is a stable-hand," he repeated, though without the vehemence of his first claim.

Hrald shook his head at this assessment. "Yes. Bork cares for my horses, and lives with Mul's family." He fixed his eyes on his brother. "And what will you do to help me?" Before Yrling could answer Hrald went on. "But Bork also writes and reads. I have taught him myself."

"You taught him that?"

Yrling had already found the wax tablet his mother had packed for him, and had shoved it deep under his box bed in Jari's house. Now his brother was telling him of the importance of reading and writing, something he was teaching the skinny boy.

"Yes. He is smart. And not boastful." Hrald studied the boy before him. "Because of this he will one day serve as my man."

"I will be your second, one day!"

Hrald almost had need to give a rueful laugh. He did not have a true second, not here at Four Stones. His uncle had command at Turcesig, and Jari, though a faithful and formidable body-guard, was not a true second, nor did he wish to be. The closest one to being that might be Kjeld. Any war-chief's second must be able and eager, and a man his warriors would be glad to follow, if the chief himself were killed.

For answer he let his eyes drop to his brother's new baptismal shirt, now filthy. The white linen sash the priest had tied was all askew, the knot almost twisted round to rest at Yrling's side waist. That protruding knot was now as dirty as was the front and back of the tunic itself.

"That is an honour, to be earned. Now go, and ask Inga to wash your shirt, quickly, and dry it by a fire. Then put it back on. If my mother or Wilgot sees how you have dirtied it, they will be even less happy with you than I am."

As Hrald walked back he stopped to gaze upon Ashild's stallion, now again standing in solitary stillness against the back rail. It would have been easy to take him out to the valley of horses and release him to the mares, and Hrald had in fact taken him out a few times to cover mares of especial worth. But Hrald could not leave him there. He liked to look at the animal, know that he was there in the hall paddock. It was constant and welcome reminder of Ashild. He could not banish so fine an animal as this, not when looking at the beast gave him comfort.

Chapter the Fifth

OFFERINGS

"WHAT happened to your fingers?" Yrling asked Jari one forenoon.

The boy was out at the sparring ground, alone, throwing two light spears in turn at one of the targets there, an upright pole stuffed with straw the width of a man. Jari had emerged from one of the work sheds, and seeing the boy, came to him. Asberg had gone back to Turcesig, and Yrling made it clear by his devotion to practice that he wanted to be worthy of that warrior's training. Now the boy paused, one spear stuck in the straw dummy, the other held in his hand, and regarded the big man.

Jari drew a short breath. "Your father and I, and Asberg, fought under your grand-uncle, Yrling. My older brother Une was Yrling's second. Some men say I have the strength of an ox; Une had the strength of two. We had not been here in Angle-land long. We had lost our ships; they were stolen. Your father, I think, would have told you that, and how Dauðadagr's loss meant we were stranded. We were hungry, and had won almost nothing. We came across a monastery –"

"A what?"

"A place where holy men live together." He could tell the boy still did not understand. "Men like Wilgot, who spend the day working and praying."

"Oh." Yrling's face was still blank, but he was eager for Jari to go on. Jari hardly knew how to continue; they had laid waste to what he later knew was a sacred place. The bare outline would be enough.

"We stormed the place, and gorged ourselves on food. We could not stop and rest, for we knew these places were protected by local war-chiefs. And in fact, they came after us. Their warriors were good ones, but we surprised them, killed their leader first, and were able to overcome them.

"They had a swordsman; one of the best. He killed my brother Une in front of me, a blow to the head, and then came back and took my fingers as well as my sword out of my hand.

"It was your father who came up behind me, and Une's skeggox in hand, ran down the Saxon who had done this. He killed him with Une's own weapon, a fitting revenge. Then he returned to me, put my fallen sword in my left hand, named me a Tyr-hand, and made me stand up."

"Tyr is important to father," Yrling reflected.

Jari gave a low laugh. "As he is to me, from that day. But for different reasons."

"That is why you always ride or stand at Hrald's left," Yrling decided.

"Já," Jari confirmed, "since I hold my shield in my right hand, I can give him extra cover."

Yrling considered this. "You are a good body-guard," he judged, with real gravity.

Jari laughed again. "I have served as such for many years."

Yrling was silent a while, as his thoughts turned back to the action Jari had just described.

"My father. Did he kill many men?"

Jari nodded. He knew the boy meant in Sidroc's long career as a warrior. "Many. But it was not only that, and his kinship to Yrling, that made him Jarl here."

The boy's face bid him go on, and Jari did.

"He was not reckless. And he did not risk his men's lives for his own glory. Once he had enough, he wanted peace, and worked with the King of Wessex to keep it. Just as Guthrum had, who first made that Peace with Ælfred."

Yrling was again quiet, his eyes cast down in thought. He then lifted them to the big warrior. "I want to do what you did."

Jari stared back at him. "And end up as I did?" Here the man lifted his maimed hand before the boy's face, spreading the stumps and remaining fingers before him. "Or as my brother Une did, dead, his brain split open in the dust?"

Yrling winced, but Jari went on.

"He died before he could wed, have a son of his own, enjoy any of the treasure he had just won.

"We were hungry," Jari went on. "We had to fight. When your father came here, he had only a sword he had been given from Dauðadagr." He paused a moment, remembering. "Many of us who set out together died, before we took Four Stones."

This was just what his father had told Yrling, and he must nod, to hear it again.

Jari reflected in silence a long moment. The young did not know how precious life was; one valued it more the older one grew. But he thought he might say something to make the boy consider.

"Hrald has told me your father has earned much on Gotland, amassed silver and even gold. Inside the treasure room here are arms beyond counting; much silver as well. It belongs to your brother, who is Jarl. You will have your own share in this. Is this not enough?"

The boy seemed at a loss, yet he found words.

"I want to win my own."

"Your father won more than silver or arms. He won peace so the men who fought with him could live to enjoy it. We could bring our wives and sweethearts from Dane-mark to live with us here, and we did. We have sons of our own now, daughters too.

"These last years, more Danes have landed here, from Dane-mark and from Frankland, and tried to take what we had earlier bartered for, the lands we had settled. Some of us joined them. Others fought against them, as Four Stones did. Your brother would not break the Peace his father had made."

Jari was not sure the boy was attending, and Yrling's next words seemed to confirm this.

"Show me how to use the shield in my right hand. That could come in handy."

Despite his initial row with Bork, Yrling settled in quickly at Four Stones. He liked the constant activity, the ebb and flow of each day of assembly in the hall to eat, morning sparring practice for the many warriors, and afternoons when all were at the needful tasks of craft and animal raising. His first trip to the valley of horses occasioned a look of astonishment which Hrald took deep pleasure in. Anything that sparked Yrling's interest was something he doggedly pursued, and in his first days he spent a long watch upon the ramparts of the palisade, pacing its entire circuit, and looking out beyond the village and the countryside as if he scanned for approaching invaders. He shadowed one of the weapon-smiths until the brawny fellow relented and let him take a hand at working the heavy box-bellows feeding his fire, a favour to the man's weary son; and tailed the spear-maker a short distance outside the walls when he went out to cut the straight and round shafts he had coppiced, growing upright from the trunk of a sawn-down ash tree.

All of these men were Danes who had arrived here with his father and the Yrling he had been named for, and the younger men were their sons. There were as well other Danes who had journeyed here to win treasure, and made their way to Four Stones. Their native tongue was the Norse of Dane-mark. Yrling spoke a mixture of that Norse, from his father, and from all on Gotland he had learnt the distinct and different Gotlandic Norse. He spoke an admixture of both, which made some of the men grin at him. He said as a matter of course "Nai" instead of Nej, when he answered in the negative, and had different words for some common objects, horse, and sheep, and woodpecker, or neighbour, and other everyday things. Even the words for boy and girl were different.

All these men had learnt the tongue of Angle-land, and as it was that spoken by the Lady of Four Stones and her priest, it had served them well. It was the tongue native to the folk here, that which they still spoke, and to get around his odd use of Norse he began to use this tongue each day himself, as he often did when speaking at Tyrsborg.

Wilgot the priest spoke little Norse, and so it was good Yrling spoke the tongue of Angle-land, as each day he had to report to the priest's small house and listen to the stories he told. They were about a God who had no name but God, or sometimes, Our Father, and his son, who was a real man, one who knew strong magic but was killed like a thief. Yrling had as well to go to Wilgot's house with all the family of the hall once each week, and stand for a long time while the priest muttered in that same tongue he had used when he poured water over Yrling's head. Then they must go out to the tall stone pillar in the village and stand even longer, while Wilgot repeated much of this for the village folk.

Yrling now wore a silver cross about his neck, presented to him by Hrald's mother when Wilgot untied the knot in the sash around his waist. He had been told it was in remembrance of God's son, who had been hung up on a cross, and he had seen that a number of folk about the hall and yard wore such crosses, of bronze and silver. It was an amulet he knew, and as such might bring him good luck, so he wore it. And it was silver, and had value for that.

"A symbol of our Saviour's sacrifice for us," the Lady had told him.

Yrling thought about this. A sacrifice and an offering were much the same thing. You could offer food or drink or a live animal, or something else of value, like silver. He nodded.

When Yrling discovered the Place of Offering, he knew it at once for what it was. He went straight to Hrald, wanting his brother to come back with him. Hrald did, leaving his task of sorting through a pile of spear heads he had uncovered in a rarely opened cask in the treasure room. They walked through the kitchen yard together, and Yrling for the first time spotted the underground rivulet that came up to the surface near it, and then spilled out under the wooden palisade to a steep drop. He would explore where that came out later. Now they unbarred the oak door and walked through it together, as Yrling had just done. They walked along a path that grew marshy on either side, and then dried out as it rose. A huge beech grew there, its canopy of leaves still unfolding.

Before this was the trace of a trench, choked with weedy growth, but from which protruding bits of rusted iron could be seen. A burial mound of some size was to one side, and a few smaller ones as well, all overgrown with shrubby bushes and even a few small trees. By the trench was a rotted block of wood, which had once been carved. Pieces of it, full of wormholes and crusted with fungi, lay near the base, where they had toppled. The two brothers stood side by side, looking on this. Hrald remembered when there were upright poles on which to hang the bodies of fowl and piglets, closer to the heavens; he remembered too watching in secret his own father do so.

Only a few short years ago, when the comet had appeared and lingered in the sky, making night-time bright, certain men had come here to kill fowl in supplication; and again when Four Stones was threatened by attack. As with the first memory, Hrald kept this to himself.

Yrling pointed to the ruined carving. "Is this Freyr?"

Hrald exhaled and gave answer. "It was Odin, I think."

He tried to remember what he had been told about the carving.

"It was old, when father came here. But it still had paint; I remember that."

Yrling looked on it in silence. He turned to face the larger mound.

"Who is buried there? The Lord that Yrling killed to win this place?"

His brother shook his head. "Merewala was Christian; I think there was even a church within the walls, a small timber one." Hrald realized he had no idea where the fallen Lord had been buried. Or if he had been buried. Sometimes the bodies of the vanquished were merely dragged away to rot under the trees.

"So who is buried there?" Yrling asked. He had taken a step nearer the mound. "A good warrior, it is a big mound."

This Hrald knew. "His name was Toki. He was father's first cousin. I never knew him; he died before I was born." Hrald did not say how Toki had met his end.

"I want to make sacrifice here," Yrling said next.

Hrald took a breath. "We do not make sacrifice. Not here. We do so in our hearts, when we pray to God, and in our deeds, when we try to be good by not doing something we want to do."

Yrling had shifted his eyes to the beech tree. "There are things in the tree," he noticed. With the leaves still unfurling certain things could be descried; keys, rings of metal, and in one case, something that looked like a looped chain. Those things that were not dark red with rust were black with tarnish.

"Before the men became believers, they would leave Offering sometimes in that tree."

One day I will leave something there, Yrling thought. When I decide what I want to ask for in return.

The next day Yrling again walked to the Place of Offering. He had no particular reason for doing so, except to explore it more fully. He saw as soon as the ground began to rise that he was not alone. Bork was there, standing by one of the mounds beyond the big one. It was one he had not really noticed before, a little way off, and not nearly as overgrown as the others. Long grass had grown on it, but no bushes had taken root.

"Why are you here," Yrling asked, without thinking that the same could be asked of him.

"My father is here," Bork said. He opened his hands slightly, to the mound before him.

"If he died fighting he is in Asgard," Yrling said. He inclined his head to the mound. "Only his bones are here, after they burnt him. He will get new bones in Asgard," he added. He had never thought of this before, but it must be true. A man could not fight without bones to hold him up.

"He was not burnt," Bork returned. "Christians do not burn the dead. But my father could not be buried in the burial ground; he was not Christian."

"His body is there? They just buried him, not burnt him first?"

Bork nodded.

"He might be nowhere," Yrling considered. "Or with the hag Hel, in the land of shades."

Bork bristled. "He is not nowhere. He – he is in Asgard. Where he wants to be."

Yrling gave a shrug.

"Do you make Offering here," he asked Bork.

The boy shook his head. "I am Christian now. Like the Jarl. We do not make Offering."

It was Yrling's turn to get his hackles up. This stable-boy made it sound like he had some kinship with Hrald, when in fact it was he who was true kin.

While he was getting ready to refute this, Bork looked at the silver cross around his neck. "You are Christian too, now," he told him. "You cannot make Offering. It is a sin."

"I can do what I want," Yrling tossed back. He reached up and closed his hand round the small cross, and gave it a yank. The silver chain snapped. He strode to the canopy of the beech tree, the broken chain swinging from his fist. He pulled back his arm and flung the cross into the green boughs. "There," he said. "I made Offering."

Ælfwyn had sent word to Oundle of Hrald's return, and the arrival of the second son of Sidroc. She was keen for Abbess Sigewif to meet the boy, and as it was near to the time when she would join the Abbess in going over the Abbey's accounts, the timing was fortuitous. The weather was dry and steadily warming, presenting the prospect of a pleasant ride, and time enjoying Oundle's gardens. And both Ælfwyn and Hrald wished to visit the ledger stone under which Ashild lay.

When their rider returned with Sigewif's invitation, Hrald found his brother in the paddock, grooming the black gelding he had been given.

"In the morning we are going to Oundle, and will spend the night there," Hrald told the boy. He looked over the horse, which Yrling had indeed taken good care of. Having heard from his father how careful the first Yrling was with horses, it was a point of pride with him that he take full responsibility for the animal himself. "He is ready to go, now," his older brother said, with a nod of approval at the gelding. "But pack your kit tomorrow, and ready your horse for our stay."

Bork had appeared in the doorway, attentive to the Jarl's need for a horse. "I will want my bay in the morning," Hrald told him, and then added, "You are coming as well, Bork. Ask Mul to choose a horse for you."

Bork's sudden intake of breath signalled his surprise in going, even if it was only to care for their horses while they were there. But Hrald's next words to him told he was wanted for more than this.

"Bring your wax tablet, so you can show the Abbess your progress."

Bork straightened up even further, and bobbed his head, hard, at this prospect. He might be invited into the special room where the Abbess kept her books.

Yrling had watched in silence. He had been told this Abbess was a holy woman, like Wilgot was a holy man, except it was clear the Abbess was far more powerful than the priest, and in fact ruled an entire keep of her own, men and women both. Now Bork was coming too, and this woman wanted to see him. He had already been made to sit with Bork at a trestle table in the hall and work in his own wax tablet, while Hrald or the Lady spoke words which they were to impress into the shallow wax. He had seen from their first practice that Bork used a stylus of brass, which Hrald had told him had been his, while Yrling's own was one of wood, from Gotland.

Hrald now turned to Yrling. "Do not forget your own tablet," he said with a quick nod to his younger brother.

In the morning those making the trek assembled in the stable yard. Ælfwyn and Burginde would ride with Ealhswith and little Cerd in a waggon, along with the provisions they would bring. Jari was already horsed, and would head the thirty-man escort travelling with them. The horse Bork would ride was tied at the rail; Mul had selected an unusually good animal for him, a pale chestnut mare in need of a leg stretch. If the boys should race along the way she would be more than a match for Yrling's black gelding, Mul knew. Yrling himself was tying his pack onto his saddle ring when Ælfwyn neared him. His arms were extended, forming a gap between neck and collar. She did not see the silver chain of his cross there, around his bare neck.

"Yrling, your cross – did you remove it?" Her voice, as was usual, was mild, but tinged with surprise.

Yrling finished his knot as he thought out his answer. He had removed it, but not in the way the Lady was asking. He could not readily produce it, either, as when he flung it at the beech, it became caught in the leaves far above his head. The best way out was often the most direct, and he took it.

"I Offered it," he admitted. There was no trace of either boast or shame in his voice.

"Offered it?"

"It is in the beech tree, by that big mound, and the carving of Odin."

"Oh." Ælfwyn was enough taken aback that she could summon no more than this.

She composed herself. "Well. Perhaps we can get it down."

"No one must get it down," came Yrling's ready answer. "If the beech releases it, yes, it will fall. But it has been Offered, and must not be taken by anyone."

"Even by you, who placed it there?"

"It is not mine anymore. I gave it in Offering to the Gods."

Ælfwyn could only nod. She had a long way to go with the boy, as did Wilgot. Perhaps this visit with Sigewif would help.

"Well," she said again. She smiled, and in fact had almost to repress a sense of mirth, one she knew to be misplaced but could not help. "We will speak of this later."

She could not expect the boy's understanding to encompass much, not at this point; and other than his speedy baptism, she had been careful not to overwhelm him. There was already a great deal for him to absorb here, as it was.

They reached Oundle not long after the closing of the noon hour. Sext, the mid-day prayers, were ending, and Ælfwyn had the pleasure of seeing the Abbess leading the combined houses from the church as they processed out. The priests and monks continued on to their own hall and gardens, while Sigewif and Prioress Mildgyth stopped before them, smiles of welcome on their faces. When Yrling was presented, he gave the deep nod required. He lifted his head to see the steely grey eyes of the Abbess upon him. She studied him for a long moment, one which had the boy begin to twist his shoulders, as if ready to spring away. Then she smiled, and spoke.

"Yrling," she considered. "Your father – the Jarl's father – is a remarkable man."

Yrling did not know what to say about this, but gave a nod.

"The last time I saw him, he aided Oundle, greatly," she went on. "He and Hrald's sister were a formidable pair," she ended.

Yrling again had no answer, so only nodded. He did not need to respond, for Hrald now spoke. He had just spotted Bova, who being amongst the youngest of the professed, came last from the church.

"Have I leave to speak to Sister Bova?" he asked of the Abbess.

She smiled in permission, and Bova, having seen the newly arrived party, had stopped, her face lit with a smile of her own.

Hrald opened a pouch at his belt, and without speaking, held out its contents to the young nun. Her mouth opened, a soft gasp coming from it, one she hid behind her raised hand. There was the many-coloured necklace of glass beads the brewster had given her, her first day on Gotland. She had been both a child and a slave when these beads first rounded her neck, an act of welcome and kindness she never forgot.

"Rannveig says you must take it again as your own, so that now you will remember her," Hrald said, and could not hold back his own smile.

After the arrivals had refreshed themselves they met with Sigewif in her writing chamber. Cerd was too restless for such a visit, and Burginde marched with him out to the nuns' garden, where he might run his fill upon the gravelled paths. All others stepped within the Abbess' private realm. Bork filed in last, clutching his wooden wax tablet, the brass stylus held fast in his closed fist. The Abbess had something to share, something which time and circumstances had prevented her from doing so before. It was the leech-book of healing recipes the monks from Æthelinga had carried with them. With it they had delivered a letter from Ceric, destined for Hrald, which was sent on to him. Hrald had clear memory of his reading it, then finding Ashild, bathing Cerd in a copper basin by the washing shed. The sharpness of this recollection made it hard for him to look upon the small pages, so neatly lettered with materials and methods, riotously embellished with paintings of herbs, roots, and flowers used in the compounds they described.

To Bork the book was wondrous. Here were flowers and leaves he knew, fixed in ink and paint on the nearly translucent sheets of parchment. It was the same feeling sparked in him during his first visit here, when the Abbess had opened a book before him, pointed out the swirling dark lines, and told him these were words, captured upon the page.

"In exchange, the good brothers carried off an herbal of our own creating," Sigewif told them. The Abbess spoke modestly in the collective, though the work had been entirely of her hand, including the binding. "We pray it may serve Æthelinga, and the cause of Ælfred, its patron, in the relief of suffering, and give beauty and comfort to those healing instruments of God who study its pages."

Yrling glanced down at the narrow pages of the leech-book as the Abbess turned them. The cover was plain brown calfskin, and of no value, unlike the gemmed covers on a few of the books lying on the slanted table running between the window casements. Still, he thought of his mother at Tyrsborg. She had often times told Eirian and him about books and how precious they were. He shifted his gaze to those tomes arrayed on the table, aware that the family of Four Stones regarded them just as his mother would. Bork, that skinny stable-boy, was even gaping as he listened to what the Abbess was telling them about the writing and pictures in the volume she held.

Yrling, watching, felt outside of them, and their interest. He could not excuse himself by his being a boy, with better things on his mind, because Bork was a boy too, and Yrling could see from the faces of the Abbess and the Lady that they were pleased with Bork. It made him dislike the stable-boy even more.

What came next was even worse, as Yrling and Bork were made to sit at the long table in the middle of the room. At one end was stacked a short pile of trimmed parchment, weighted down, Sigewif told them, by a fabric bag filled with pellets of lead to keep them from warping. Alongside was a great number of odd-shaped parchment cuttings, for use as practice scraps. Tiny pots of ink were there as well, and in flat pottery trays, the long wing feathers of geese, sharp-bladed trimmers to cut the quill ends, and even small rags for cleaning and blotting. Their wax tablets would not be needed; they would be asked to work with ink.

"Let us try our hands at transcription," the Abbess was saying. "Ealhswith and Jarl Hrald will help guide you," she went on, gesturing that Ealhswith sit next to Yrling, and Hrald next to Bork. Yrling wanted to protest this assignment, but his brother was already swinging his long legs over the bench to take a seat by the stable-boy.

It was Bork's first time with quill and ink, and his face was all concentration as Hrald showed him how to make the five cuts in the firm quill of the feather, and how deeply to dip that point he had created into the tiny ink pot. His first scrapes across the smooth surface of burnished parchment were a revelation. The brass stylus the Jarl had entrusted him with was like a tiny ard which ploughed a furrow in the wax. The liquid ink lay dramatically atop, demanding to be looked at, worthy of effort to make the result graceful. Bork made a line, then pressed harder to make it thicker, then began pulling the quill across the bit of parchment in dark, scrolling, sinuous curls. His astonished pleasure at the result was only matched by the Abbess dictating a few words for the boys to write out, testing both spelling and legibility of result.

Yrling was not looking over at Bork's work; he was busy at his own. Even when Ealhswith tried a whispered suggestion, he ignored her. From a young age he had seen much practice in his wax tablet, and his mother had him and his sister work with quill and ink both on oddments of parchment and large pieces of birch bark that peeled from forest trees. He felt secure in his ability, and when the Abbess asked them to write their own names, the name of the Jarl of Four Stones, and the keep's name itself, Yrling did not hesitate. Only at her final request, that they write the name of Christ, did he need ponder. He had in fact been made to write this out at least twice by Wilgot, and now brushed the firm feathery plume of his goose feather against his brow, as if to stir that memory.

When they were done Sigewif regarded their efforts. They all did. Each boy had used four scraps of parchment for his work, and as many as they wanted for practise. Yrling saw with satisfaction that Bork had slightly misspelled his own name, using the runic symbol Odel instead of the letter o: BᛟRK. The Abbess was not so harsh.

"It gives the same sound," she reasoned aloud, and then took the quill from Bork's hand, re-dipped it, and wrote his name in firm rounded letters, correct vowel included. Bork was eager to do the same, grinning as he took the quill, and copied what she had done almost exactly.

Indeed, everything Bork had written down was good. He had never before handled a quill, nor dealt with the vagaries of ink, but none looking on would have guessed this from the result. He may have not had the spelling right, but in service to the Abbess' dictated names his hand showed natural facility, and was no mere griffonage. Yrling's spelling was better, his examples of the written word more than serviceable. It was when Sigewif turned to the last name they wrote that the stable-boy excelled. Yrling, after cudgeling his brain, attempted to write the word "Christus" which is how he best recalled the priest chanting it. Bork had drawn a complete picture. It was the outline of a fish, enclosing the letters ΙΧΘΥΣ.

The Abbess paused when she saw it; no one else knew what it said. She looked to Bork, and repeated, "Jesus Christ, Son of God, Saviour."

Hrald was now standing near Yrling, and lowered his head to speak by his ear. His tone could not hide his surprise nor admiration at the drawing, and he shared both with his younger brother. "It is nothing I taught him; Wilgot must have. I know it is an ancient tongue. He remembered all that, however he learnt it. The fish is one of the emblems of a Christian," he went on. Yrling had memory of the priest referring to Christ as a fisher of men.

Both boys were praised for their efforts, though Yrling felt it clear that Bork's work far outshone his own. He felt of two minds: fling that grey goose feather across the room, as far as he could make it sail, or work to make his own ability as good as that of the stable-boy. Just now Sigewif's next words relieved him of the need to do either.

"I think now the boys may be excused to the gardens, or work yards, as they like," the Abbess said. "And Ealhswith, I am sure you too would like to enjoy the flowers and herbs.

"Jarl Hrald, if you will remain here with your mother," she further invited.

"I have something I would share with you," Sigewif said when the three were alone. The firm lips did not quite form a smile, but there was a softness there, as if the Abbess smiled inwardly.

"I have begun to write a Life of Ashild. My purpose is to record her brief span upon this Earth, the veneration at her tomb, and make the task of documentation the easier."

Sigewif was expert at reading faces, and answered the Lady's puzzlement without prompting. "The future documentation of any miracles attributed to her," she clarified.

Ælfwyn drew a deep and steadying breath. "Miracles," she repeated. She looked at her son, who drew his own slow breath at these words.

Sigewif lifted her hand, and said firmly, "None have been verified; none even reported as such. But I know too well how stories will grow, how one's life can be misread, even misused."

The Lady nodded. Sigewif had been but a small child when her brother Edmund was killed, but she had witnessed his war-time death be deemed a martyrdom. A thought floated up through Ælfwyn's consciousness, one she had not before encountered, but now gave voice to.

"You lost your brother, twice," Ælfwyn said. Her words were softly spoken, but her look could not be more pointed, so deeply did she feel this sudden truth.

Sigewif, always so composed, looked for a moment shaken by this summation.

"Just so," she uttered. "First to the arrows of the Danes, then at the hands of those who claimed so many acts performed by him, and who told stories of his life which were not true."

They stood silent, reflecting, thinking on this.

Hrald gave thought to what it must have been for the Abbess, to live through first his Earthly loss, and then to have him claimed by so many others as object of emulation, and then veneration. He understood in a new way how tales of great heroes were forged, and at the cost of the real men behind those deeds which were repeated in mead-halls.

"In Ashild's case," the Abbess went on, "I think it wise to lay the course, now, for what her tale may become. We would not see her childhood re-written by those who never knew her, who would ascribe to her spiritual yearnings and proclivities we knew she never bore.

"My own brother's story – none who knew him in life could recognise him now, as Saint. And though he died in service of his people, how he would laugh at his being named that. Just as our Ashild would, if such an appellation ever be bestowed on her rebellious head. Yet she died no less in service of her folk than Edmund did."

They were all quiet a moment, until Sigewif returned to her musings. "Still, our spiritual paths do not end at death. I do accept the workings attributed to Edmund; I must. As far as Ashild, we do not know what journey she is on, and where God's grace may lead her."

Other than the gift of Cerd, and the blessing of her remaining children, nothing gave Ælfwyn greater comfort than this thought, that her eldest's life continued on, in spirit.

The Abbess gestured to her own writing desk, near the windowed wall. Upon its surface were several sheets of inked parchment, and Sigewif led them there. Her right hand, large, square of nail, a hand suggesting strength and capability, opened to the loose parchments. She looked from mother to son in turn, beginning, and then ending with the Lady of Four Stones.

"This is but a draft. I would like your approval, and correction where needed, as to the facts of Ashild's parentage, early years, and life."

Still standing, Ælfwyn began to scan the first parchment. She read aloud, so that Hrald might hear it as freshly as she. Her eyes fairly danced over the neatly inked lines, set down in the firm writing of the Abbess. Ashild's story actually began with Ælfwyn herself, she saw. This was an unspooling of her own life, before her. She lowered herself to the chair, and began reading of her own parents, and how her father Ælfsige had used her hand to forge a Peace with Yrling, Jarl of Four Stones. After brief mention of Yrling's death the thread was taken up with the destruction of Oundle and her rebuilding of it. The Abbess now made appearance in the report. Soon after the Lady of Four Stones commenced her efforts at Oundle, word travelled to the Bishop of Canterbury. Sigewif had been called to head the foundation which would again arise there.

It then went on to speak of Ælfwyn's first born. Ashild was described as a girl of vibrant energy and resource, undeterred by hardship, rarely bound by convention, yet steadfastly loyal in her affection for her family and all comprising Four Stones. Her act of heroism at Oundle was described in detail, as only an eye-witness to each moment of the unfolding action could provide. Ælfwyn here must slow her reading, her voice catching more than once as she followed the account. In simple and direct language Sigewif related the massing of the enemy Danes outside the very walls Ælfwyn had just entered, the threat of fire to destroy those walls and overrun the abbey, the pillage and rape that could have followed. The horror and fear these dangers occasioned were brought fully home. Placed in this landscape, what seemed a wilful act by a stubborn girl resolved into something far deeper. Ælfwyn, reading this, now realised her daughter's insistence to help defend the abbey as the touchstone of her young life. Ashild's part in riding out to protect the persons and property of Oundle had been more than symbolic. Her risking her life there made that life a part of

Oundle, and its history. Every warrior who fought that day did the same, but they were Hrald's men, and this was their duty. On that day the daughter of Four Stones claimed a larger life for herself, and in return, Oundle claimed her as its own.

One line made Ælfwyn slow the more. "Afterwards Ashild brushed off all praise, acting as did Judith for her people against Holofernes and his enemy forces, not from vainglory, but outwardly directed and inwardly compelled to act for the preservation of Oundle."

At the end of the passage, Ælfwyn took a long pause. Hrald too was silent, but he had been told in much greater detail of the action before Oundle's gates by his father and Asberg. His mother had been spared these details which Sigewif now recounted.

The Lady of Four Stones now lifted her head to the Abbess.

"You say nothing of your own acts of courage during the attack. Ashild told me, as did Asberg, and other of our men."

The Abbess gave a dismissive wave of her hand. "Words, only."

"It was not words to climb the parapet to challenge the invaders, and expose yourself to danger, and abuse."

Sigewif gave a short laugh. "I should be so fortunate to be granted death defending a house of God," she said. The movement of her hand urged Ælfwyn to go on with her reading.

She came now to the birth of Ashild's son. The Abbess had carefully fixed Cerd's birth in the liturgical calendar, anchoring what could be verified as early as possible in the recording of her life, and the life of her sole offspring.

"After a marriage celebrated for a single night, God's beneficence was made manifest in the arrival of a son, Cerd, born at the Feast of St Gregory the Great, the Year of Our Lord 894. The father of whom is Ceric of Kilton, the esteemed family of Wessex."

St Gregory was that Pope responsible for sending missionaries from Rome to Angle-land. He was revered for rekindling the Christian faith brought by the later men of the Caesars, which had fallen away under attack by the early Angles and Saxons, its spark kept alive only in Wales, and Iona. Ælfwyn was not certain that chilly Spring day on which Cerd was born to have been that exact date, but it was near enough. And she was of a sudden moved by the memory of the new-born babe's hand closing about the golden cross around his mother's neck. She read the line again, a marriage celebrated for a single night, making the birth almost a precious granting; the father of a notable family, Ceric of Kilton.

Written like this, the child was not the result of a lone and secret coupling between two young people destined to be parted forever next day, but a blessing ordained by God.

Ælfwyn read further. Nothing was incorrect, but all was presented in a certain clear and yet mellow light.

Ashild had died in support of her devout brother, Hrald, as he was fighting to maintain a Christian foothold in a land again overrun by the heathen. She was laid to rest after her funeral Mass in the church which had been raised by her mother. Thirty-three days following her entombment began the first visits from those wishing to offer prayers at her ledger stone. The main body of the text ended here, though there was room on the second parchment to continue.

Ælfwyn looked at the section heading which followed. It comprised a single line, "Workings attributed to" followed by a brief list of occurrences as reported to the Abbess. "Daughter relieved of distressing thoughts" read the first, followed by a date, and the name of the girl's mother. "Safe deliverance of child following the invocation of Ashild's name" read another. Ælfwyn knew these were close to intercessions, the deeds of the saints as they acted as intermediaries to God. Sigewif had not labeled any of these "miracles"; she had not gone that far, but she was compiling a dated and verifiable list of what she had been told.

"Interest in Ashild may wane within a few years," the Abbess concluded. "Or it may grow to full scale reverence. But it is as the hand-maidens of truth that we attempt to exert control over the narrative of her life, while we are able."

While Ælfwyn and the Abbess conferred about the Abbey's accounts, Hrald joined the rest of the family out amongst the gardens. Respectful of the nuns' privacy, Hrald headed past the church to the monks' side. Neither boy was there. Yrling had gone straight to the kitchen yard, where Jari and the rest of the escort were lounging on benches, Bova's fine ale in hand. But Bork had paused when they had emerged from the Abbess' writing chamber. He stood blinking in the bright sunlight, looking after Yrling who wordlessly left him to go after the warriors. Bork hesitated to do so, and dare not enter the garden, though the Abbess had seemed to invite him to it. So he slowly walked around the nuns' wall, past the monks' garden, to the paddock, where their horses were nodding their heads over the hay forked to them. He kept his eyes on the wall, lest the Jarl come around it. Hrald did, and spotted Bork, standing by his charges. Hrald gestured to him to come, and Bork found himself walking over the gravel pathways, granted as much freedom to enjoy the garden as was any esteemed visitor.

Burginde and Ealhswith had charge of Cerd on the nun's side, and Hrald could occasionally hear the boy's delighted whoops as he ran the pathways, followed by Burginde's shushing discouragement of such noise-making. Suddenly the boy appeared around the end of the tall fence dividing the garden into its two spheres.

"Hraaah!" he roared, spotting his uncle and running to him. Hrald had to laugh as he caught the child up. Ealhswith appeared on the boy's heels, but seeing him safely in Hrald's arms only smiled and went back to the sisters' side.

Then Yrling appeared. He had grown curious of what was keeping his brother, and came looking for him. Hrald had put Cerd down, and the boy had run to where Bork stood, and was now prattling at him, asking to be lifted to a trellis upon which beans were hanging.

Yrling came up to his brother, and looked down the path at Hrald's small nephew. The boy was no older than Rodiaud, but Yrling saw Cerd was rarely excluded from any activities important to the family, and thus, the hall. And Hrald treated the boy almost as a father would, he thought. To Yrling the child was practically still a babe, and a bothersome one at that. Yrling was much closer in kinship to Hrald than was this boy all fawned over.

"Where is his father," Yrling asked, a question so unexpected that it took Hrald a moment to answer.

"In Wessex. He had to return there."

"Maybe Cerd should go there too," Yrling began. He had caught himself before he continued with his thought, that now that the boy's mother was dead, he should be raised by his father.

Hrald guessed Yrling's unfinished argument, and answered it, in simple and sombre declaration.

"His grand-sire is Yrling who fought for, and won, the fortress of Four Stones."

He said no more than this; he had no need to.

Yrling stood silent as his brother's words sank in. The elder Yrling, that great war-chief, was this toddling boy's grand-sire, not his. His own grand-sire was Hrald, an old man who had won nothing but the hard life of a farmer and fisherman up the coast of Gotland; a man of humble mien he had yet to meet, but could imagine. Still, Yrling was his father's son, and Sidroc had been Jarl. And greatness often ran from uncle to nephew. The first Yrling had been his grand-uncle, and that was something. He told himself these things, aware that the little boy chattering to Bork was thrice favoured. Cerd was nephew to Hrald. And he was not only a direct heir of the great Yrling, but the son of Ashild, who all held in such regard no one was allowed to ride her horse.

That night Bork did not sleep in the stable bunk he had used on his first visit here. He was shown to an alcove in the monks' hall by a young male novice, as any guest would be. Yrling was placed just one alcove down, as if the boys were friends. In the morning Bork arose early to wipe down Hrald's bay, and comb mane and tail. When he appeared slightly late at the table where all the men broke their fast, Yrling remembered Hrald asking him what he would do to help him, knowing that Bork had been this day already at work on his brother's behalf.

In the morning before they departed the family of Four Stones approached the church of Oundle. Sister Bova was there to greet them, and pulled wide the stout oak door for their entry. Burginde had Cerd by the hand. The dimness within the church was just enough to excite the boy's curiosity, and he broke from the nurse and ran inside. Burginde hustled after, to find the boy standing in the middle of the nave, scanning. His eyes were snared by the single flower lying on the floor off to one side of the alter. He ran to it, snatched it up and threw it into the air, so that it fell almost upon the tall letters bearing his mother's name. Burginde was there a moment later. She scooped him up, turned on her heel, and carried the giggling boy out, all flailing arms and legs.

"The pup goes with me," she told the rest of the family as she passed them, making straight for the garden with her wriggling charge. Burginde had made a habit of referring to the boy this way, as a pup, for the way he growled when saying Hrald's name, like the offspring of a dog or a wolf. Cerd had, she thought, greeted his mother in his own way, the tiny booted feet scampering over where she lay sleeping. He had chortled out a mighty laugh as he had flung that flower up, a salutation Burginde knew Ashild would have smiled to hear.

Ealhswith had not visited the church since the day of her sister's burial. Although she passed over the threshold of the church at her mother's side, she paused there, while her mother, unknowing, continued on. Ælfwyn genuflected before the altar and then moved to Ashild's resting place, to its right. Upon the white slab lay a single flower. She knew Bova had been unfailing in her placing of herb, flower, or branch there each dawn.

Ealhswith also stood aside as her brother passed her. He stopped and looked, seeming to decide if he should leave his mother a moment alone at the broad ledger stone. His eyes were fixed on the corner where the Lady of Four Stones stood, hands clasped, looking down at Ashild's name inscribed in the bright expanse of stone. Behind his mother he saw Ashild's spear, mounted upright on the wall. Something else caught his eye. A ray of sunlight, freed from a passing cloud, fell through the window, glancing brilliant on a small casket of silver laid on the Mary altar. He went to it.

Hrald confronted the silver box. His mother had told him what this box now housed: his battle-flag, soaked with his sister's blood. On his sole visit to Oundle before his journeying to Gotland, the Abbess had not mentioned it to him; nor could he remember having seen it. Now that Hrald knew what the box held, he could not but go to it. He remembered the night Ashild had presented the flag to him, and his pleasure at her gift. He recalled pulling the sleeve she had sewn over the butt end of a spear. He saw himself hoisting it, then her taking it from him, waving it over their heads as they both laughed.

He had seen that flag, dark with Ashild's dried blood, tucked into the collar of her tunic, when Ceric rode in with her. He felt overcome at this last memory, and closed his eyes against it.

His thoughts progressed to Ceric, he who had ridden all night holding her body against his own. Here lay his wife, and out there in the garden ran his child. How was Ceric coping with his act, Hrald wondered. He thought of his own culpability in Ashild's death, and that she was even there on the field. What she had created for him, the battle-flag, was her undoing. Despite his youth and strength he felt at that moment powerless, impotent. He was fighting to protect his family, and let her get killed.

Ealhswith still remained, off to one side of the open door. She had in her arms the sheaf of flowers she brought from her mother's bower garden, carried in a crockery pot to keep them fresh. She stood now with the loose flowers in her arms, unable to move to that broad square under which Ashild lay.

She had always known she and her sister must part, and assumed that Ashild, being older, would leave first, gone to Kilton as wife to Ceric. But even that absence left the possibility of reunion, and either one of the sisters might journey to see the other. Ashild's journeying was at an end. And Ealhswith had no idea who she would be sent to in marriage.

Ælfwyn, having said a prayer over her eldest, looked up to see her youngest, still at the portal. She extended her arm to her, in welcome, gesturing her to come. Ealhswith did, and found that arm wrapped around her shoulders, and her mother's lips pressed against her temple. Ælfwyn said nothing, and gently let her arm drop, so that Ealhswith might give expression to her own prayer or reflection.

Ealhswith would not walk across the ledger stone, to lay the armful of flowers by or above Ashild's carved name. She seemed reluctant to move at all, and instead leant down and dropped the bouquet at the foot of the stone. As she straightened up, Ælfwyn saw her daughter's tear-streaked cheeks, and heard the sob the girl choked back. Her mother was speaking the first words of comfort to her when Ealhswith picked up her skirts, and rushed, almost running, to the door.

Hrald had seen this, and now came to stand by his mother. She placed her hand on his arm and gave a squeeze, but they stood together, wordlessly. Hrald looked down at his sister's grave, then across to the silver casket. There was so little of her left.

In the stable yard Jari and the rest of the men were waiting. The family said their thanks, and bid Abbess and Prioress fare-well. Hrald pulled himself up in the saddle; his mother and little sister were already seated in the waggon. Burginde was still afoot, Cerd in her arms, and the boy kicked and squawked to be let down. She did so, and the child ran a few steps nearer to Hrald's bay stallion. Cerd raised his arms to his uncle, wanting to be taken up on his saddle. "Horse," he cried out, in glee.

Hrald froze, and for more than an instant. The boy was grinning up at him, begging to be placed on the saddle. It was the last moment Ashild had with Cerd, that of holding him there upon her white horse, and then the kiss she gave him. They had all witnessed this, Burginde too. Now the nurse came, white-faced but smiling, and picked the boy up and passed him to his uncle's arms.

"He can ride with me, a little while," he agreed. It was what Ashild would do.

He looked at Yrling and Bork, on their horses and eager to begin. "Bring up the rear, with the other men," he told them, giving them their first real orders. Their faces showed both surprise and readiness to comply, and they wheeled their mounts around to the back of the massing riders.

After the broad gates closed behind them, Ealhswith began to cry. She turned her face into her mother's shoulder, and wept. "I want Ashild," she sobbed out.

Ælfwyn stroked her hair and back, and with whispered words of comfort tried to console her. Ealhswith's next words were quieter, yet heartfelt with rending urgency. They were uttered in even greater pain.

"I want to be Ashild," she cried. "And I cannot be."

Chapter the Sixth

THREE KINGDOMS

RAEDWULF, the Bailiff of Defenas, arrived at the borderlands of Four Stones with the single escort he had requested. Ælfred, King of Wessex, had given his bailiff a choice: a small ship which would coast around the expanse of this great island, stopping each night to rest ashore until it reached Saltfleet; or the overland journey on horseback. Raedwulf had chosen the latter. He left behind a Wessex which over Winter had been wracked by misfortune. It was not the predations of Haesten or other Danish war-bands, but rather a plague and murrain affecting cattle. Many beasts had died, and this Spring was seeing few calves and little milk. Pigs suffered as well, for the young piglets were weaned with whey from cheese-making, giving them a strong start in life, and now little was to be had. The spectre of a lean year was nothing the royal house wished to contemplate, yet with so many other hardships, it had come, and like all else, must be dealt with. Raedwulf had twice made journey to Mercia, there to buy cows and bulls from Æthelred's estates, and transport them to Wessex where they might begin to rebuild a severely depleted stock. His journey now had taken him further afield, and with much different intent.

Raedwulf rode with a young thegn, a quick and capable man of his own selection, from Ælfred's ranks. They carried little but the necessities for the road, and had but a single packhorse between them. As was common, the bailiff was entrusted not with goods to deliver, but information. Raedwulf was mounted on the black mare he often favoured; she was a thrifty traveller, fast and uncomplaining at his requests for sudden bursts of speed, and quiet amongst other horses. Like all who passed the tall stone cairns erected beside the roads, when they reached the border of Four Stones they were met by Hrald's watchmen, one of whom rode forward with them to the next checkpoint, where they collected a second escort, and then the next, where they picked up a third guard. Hrald's men on patrol knew the bailiff was of import enough to deserve such protection.

They approached the gates unannounced, save for the men on the ramparts whistling out the arrival of escorted visitors. Hrald was at that moment in the work yard, where a new saw-pit was being dug. The thick planks comprising the palisade wall encircling Four Stones needed regular replacement, and a second pit for the sawyers would speed the work. His Lady-mother was in the weaving room with Burginde and Ælfwyn's sister, Eanflad; Ealhswith was minding Cerd, playing with him in the sheltered confines of his mother's bower garden. Yrling was out at Turcesig, living in the hall there with Asberg and Æthelthryth.

Raedwulf's appearance was entirely unexpected; no word had been sent. Hrald left the digging work and came to greet whoever was behind the gate being swung open. As the bailiff rode in, he quit his mount as soon as he had reined her to a halt, as did the young thegn at his side. This placed them on the same respectful footing as their host. Mul and his two older sons took charge of the guests' three horses, as Bork opened the paddock gate for them.

Hrald recognised Raedwulf at once, and saw the bailiff begin to smile. This was no bearer of grim news. Hrald approached and threw his arms about the man. Ælfwyn emerged from the side door of the hall to see her son do so, and then see them step apart. Her own face underwent a transformation. Her hands lifted in happy startle. Raedwulf gave a nod to Hrald, and came to her, bowing his head in respect.

"Ælfwyn of Cirenceaster," he said in greeting. His tone was low, yet full of meaning, and the light in his eyes, unmistakable.

He looked to both mother and son, "Ælfred, King of Wessex, sends you God's greeting, and his own," he began.

So the King had a message, some request, or news.

They walked into the body of the hall, where Burginde was already leading a short procession of serving men and women with basins of warm water and towels, so that the men might wash their hands, and if they wished, faces, from the dust of the road. Ælfwyn passed Burginde her key, and the nurse emerged from the treasure room with the large silver bird ewer, soon to be filled with their best and freshest ale. With a nod Raedwulf dismissed the thegn at his side, to follow Burginde to the kitchen yard, where he would be given food and drink. Jarl, Lady, and bailiff stepped into the treasure room, where the three silver cups Burginde had fetched awaited them. They sat down, and Ælfwyn placed her hands upon the table, one folded upon the other. Upon the third finger of her right hand was the lapis-set gold band he had left her, the sight of which heartened him the more. It was almost all Raedwulf could do, not to cover those hands with one of his own. He glanced at her; her eyes were lowered. There was however, more colour in the pale and lovely face, colour he was glad to see. It was he who had brought that slight flush to her cheeks, and it heartened him.

Burginde was soon back, filled ewer in hand. She set the ewer down and stepped back a moment, and glanced at the bailiff with barely averted eyes. He must smile at her. In no way would he ask this woman, by word or look, to leave the room. She was privy to every dealing of the family, had aided Raedwulf in the past, and might do so again. Seeing his smile, Burginde retreated to her customary stool, not far from the bed.

"How was your journeying?" Hrald began.

"Without incident, something ever to be grateful for. Even without Worr, I now remember the several ways to avoid detection to your lands."

"I am glad to hear this."

"Wessex has suffered great loss of cattle this past Winter," the bailiff went on, "a plague amongst the beasts that has sent me off repeatedly to Mercia, whose animals remain sound. Journeying here I am glad to see the cattle of Anglia also hale."

Any such news was always sobering, not only for the hardship and loss suffered by Wessex, but the fear of contagion spreading. Both Hrald and his mother offered their condolences.

Even before this, the mention of Worr turned Hrald's face grave. "May I ask, have you word of Kilton?"

"I do," Raedwulf admitted. "As report, it is not a happy one. I arrived there, on the business of Wessex, the day after the death of Lady Modwynn, and in time for her funeral Mass."

Ælfwyn's gasp was not muffled by her hand, quickly lifted to her lips in shock and sorrow.

"I am sorry to bring you such tidings." He looked to the Lady, who seemed unable to speak. The tears welling in her eyes looked ready to spill down those cheeks he had just admired.

"Yes," he said to her. "It is a loss incalculable. She was a great woman, one admired by all."

Ælfwyn could not yet give voice to Ceridwen's hope, that Modwynn would prove a comfort to the grieving Ceric. And in fact the bailiff was just about to speak of him.

"What follows is of deep concern. Ceric has left the hall. I was there as he did so. He walked from the chantry of Kilton near the conclusion of the Lady's funeral Mass. He walked out, and, Worr learnt, into the forest."

"He has left the hall," Hrald repeated.

"He is living in the forests of Kilton. Worr has seen him, but rarely. He has sent word to me at Witanceaster. But Ceric will accept some food, and other supplies. He has been there now for over eight months."

"He has lived in the wood over Winter?" Hrald asked. He could not bring the words forming in his mind to his lips. His mother asked the question, voiced just above a whisper.

"He has gone mad?"

The response was the slightest nod of Raedwulf's head. "His mind is broken, Worr says."

"Not broken," murmured Ælfwyn, wishing to disallow so cruel a Fate.

The bailiff was well skilled in couching news in the best possible light. It was one of the arts of diplomacy. Here he was truth-teller only. Ceric was not living as a holy hermit, on a small and self-created croft of his own, growing vegetables and worshipping God. He was closer to an anchorite, a monk or nun who had shut themselves up in a tiny and isolated space but yet still anchored to a religious foundation which saw to their basic needs. But from the glimpses Worr had caught of him, Ceric did not, he thought, spend his days in prayer, nor his nights watching. He had become like the wild men of yore; not savage perhaps, but one who had cut himself off from hearth and home, kin and kine. Some such men were violent and dangerous to come upon or approach. Ceric seemed the opposite, he had accepted no weapons with which to down game for food, none but fishing line and hooks. Yet it seemed clear to all that a surfeit of grief had broken his mind.

"His self, whole again, is not irrecoverable," he answered Ælfwyn, just as gently. He went on, as if thinking aloud.

"There have been men and women who have gone mad, and through the Grace of God, or through some crisis which brought their distress to a head, allowed it to spend itself, and the afflicted could then resume a normal life. Such things have happened. It could happen here."

Ælfwyn seemed to cling to these words, nodding her head, and then adding, "Our gratitude to your son-in-law, Worr, is boundless."

Hrald's thoughts were only with Ceric. "I should go to him," he now said.

"That day will come, I am sure, when Ceric will be eager to see you," the bailiff assured him. He added, in a softer tone, "He will wish one day to return here to Four Stones – and to Oundle. But now I think we must do as Lady Edgyth of Kilton, and Edwin, its Lord, do, and allow Worr free rein in his attempt to reclaim Ceric."

Hrald nodded, mutely, but his mind kept working. Ælfwyn stood, to refill their cups. As she did she saw Burginde, quietly wiping her face with her apron, where tears had spilled at this news.

Hrald must know more. "How – how does he live?"

Raedwulf told what he could. "It is a rudimentary existence. There are shallow caves, Worr told me. As boys Ceric and Edwin visited them with him. When it grew cold, Worr believes Ceric took one for his own, and is living there now."

A silence settled amongst them, which the bailiff broke by lifting his cup again to his lips. He looked to Hrald.

"Worr is doing all he can, but the last message we had said that Ceric had not relented, and still lived as a wild man in the greenwood."

Ceric's devotion to Kilton, and to Wessex, was so great that abandoning his duty to both was emblem of profound distress. Hrald had desired more than once to shrug off the burdens of his Jarl-dom, but other than a few days' respite in Oundle's peace and his trip to Gotland, had never done so. Ceric was not Lord of Kilton, but Hrald considered his role as his younger brother's guide and support to be even more onerous. Yet he had never complained to his best friend of the many claims placed on him by Kilton or Wessex, claims he must meet without the rewards of Lordship.

Whatever emotions the bailiff was reading in Hrald's face, his next words attempted to address them. "Still, I hope you will take heart, that he is in Worr's keeping."

All Hrald and his mother could do was to nod in assent. Raedwulf would move next to the actual purpose of his visit.

"As vital as this news was to bring to you, as much as I am cheered to see you both hale and well, I must take up my role as messenger, from not one, but two royal houses.

"I am here at the behest of Ælfred, and of his daughter Æthelflaed of Mercia. Here for your sake, Hrald."

The heightened alertness of mother and son could not prepare them for the bailiff's next words.

"There is a woman Ælfred has identified, one who might serve as wife to you."

The mood had shifted so quickly that Hrald found himself drawing a deep breath.

Raedwulf went on. "She is a widow, and of uncommon attributes. I have seen her, several times at the hall of Weogornaceastre and at Gleaweceaster both, for she is the ward of Ælfred's daughter, Lady Æthelflaed, and travels with her from royal hall to hall."

Hrald could say nothing save the words he next uttered, though they be hardly louder than a whisper.

"Tell me more."

Raedwulf was well prepared to continue. He would begin with the potential bride herself. He had natural skills of observation, honed from many years of acting as the King's eyes and ears when apart from Ælfred, and had brought them all to bear when in the presence of the Lady of whom he spoke.

"Of her person, she is of slightly below average height for a woman, slender yet becomingly formed. Her hair yellow – " here the bailiff's eyes shifted to Hrald's mother – "perhaps a shade or two darker than that of your Lady-mother; quite long, falling beyond her waist. The eyes a greyish-blue – perhaps I might say, a smokey blue – features regular, skin unmarked, teeth small and fine. The overall impression is one of loveliness in face, and in form." A long pause followed, until he said the next.

"She may as yet be a maid."

Hrald gave a slight shake of his head; his face showed his confusion.

"You said she is widowed."

"That is true. But the union was made by proxy, as the Lord she wed could not travel. They had met under the aegis of the King, and the agreement struck not long after. He was killed shortly thereafter, and I am not certain the marriage was ever celebrated. Needless to say, the union was upheld, and at his death she became heir to certain lands, the rents of which bring in a sum worthy of a princess." Raedwulf slowed, and his voice dropped to add the next. "This is in addition to her own wealth."

The eyes of mother and son met. A union with this woman would certainly enrich Four Stones, in direct gain, and through alliance with the royal halls of both Mercia and Wessex. But Ælfwyn was most concerned with the prospective bride herself.

"And her manner?" she asked. She had leant forward during Raedwulf's description of the woman, which brought her, for a moment, even closer to him. He was glad to give her his next words.

"Demure. Becomingly demure."

The bailiff gave thought to his meeting, and parting, with the young woman. It forced a smile to his lips. He looked from Ælfwyn to her son, wishing to convey a detail he found of note. "She has a hound which follows her everywhere. And, I think, is her closest friend."

Hrald gave thought to this. Such a companion suggested a private life, even if lived amongst royal trappings. He spoke now. "Do you know her age?"

"She has seen less than eighteen Summers."

"Only that," Hrald returned. There was no hiding the wonder in his voice. "So she will be two or three years younger than me."

Raedwulf nodded. "Yes, younger, and I believe entirely unspoilt. The death of her husband would have been a cruel blow, yet I know from the King she has been treated with kindness throughout her life. She is a favourite of the Lady of the Mercians. That alone is great endorsement."

Ælfwyn considered this. The young woman they spoke of might be almost as a daughter to the royal hall of Mercia. Æthelflaed might have true affection, even love, for her ward, and might want her near, especially as she had but one child by birth, a daughter. She looked at the bailiff. "And the Lady of Mercia will let her go?"

"I need not tell you that Ælfred's wife is of the royal family of Mercia. Their daughter, the Lady Æthelflaed, has further strengthened that bond in wedding Æthelred, Ealdorman of Mercia, and its Lord. Mercia is as much in her blood as is Wessex, and she will do much to ensure its peace and prosperity. Likewise her commitment to this young Lady will encourage her to seek out the best match, for Mercia, and the Lady in question. An alliance with you here in Anglia would be greatly desired."

Raedwulf paused, summoning the memory of standing before the Lady Æthelflaed, and the indirect, sometimes aslant manner in which they broached topics of delicacy. Yet experience in such converse gave the bailiff a high degree of confidence, and he said so. "This was unspoken, but well understood."

Ælfwyn would ask a question. "Raedwulf – your own impression of the young Lady. What was it?"

"A deliberateness, one without calculation. A seriousness consonant with her station in life. Yet a deep gentleness, as well. I was, if I may admit without colouring your own judgement, quite favourably impressed."

The Lady of Four Stones gave thought. She would never risk her son entering into a union in which happiness might be elusive. For Hrald to be happy, his wife must be able to find happiness. This concern prompted her next question.

"Despite the tragic loss of her husband, could she . . . know joy?"

"I think she could find such."

The Lady of Four Stones drew breath. "May we know her name?"

Ælfwyn asked this while looking at her son to see if he wished to take this next step. They were asking Raedwulf to divulge the girl's identity and lineage, so that they might dismiss or pursue her. The fact that she was the ward of a kingdom which Danes had long ago conquered, and Ælfred had won back and re-established, made this as well a royal confidence.

"Of course," he answered, his pleasure clear. "She is Pega, daughter of Swithwulf."

"Swithwulf," repeated Ælfwyn, almost to herself. She looked to the bailiff, and then her son. "Son of Swithwine. I know the family; at least their name. Their hall was, I think, on the River Severn, a two days' ride or more from Cirenceaster. "

Raedwulf nodded, glad to smile his acknowledgement to her. Even having known of the family made the opportunity of alliance a nearer possibility.

"You are correct," he returned. "They are an old family of Weogornaceastre." He looked to Hrald, understanding that Ælfwyn had knowledge of the place. "It was a great town under the Caesars, and even now has walls and buildings of stone to be envied. Its wealth and importance continued under Mercian rule, and the Lady Pega's family had full share in it."

He thought a moment. "It is to be lamented that Swithwulf fell in a skirmish against Haesten's forces, a twelve-month after that Dane invaded."

Hrald's jaw could not but clench. Haesten again.

The three were silent a space, perhaps measuring what that war-lord had cost them all.

"So she has been father-less for nearly three years." This was Hrald, pondering aloud what it had meant to a young maid to be so left. "She has no brother?" he asked.

Raedwulf shook his head. "None. And the Lady Pega's mother had herself died, shortly before the loss of her father in battle."

"Thus Lady Æthelflaed assumed her ward-ship," Ælfwyn said, nodding her head at the young woman's good fortune to have so powerful a protector. Yet the Lady of the Mercians must be expecting great things from the girl. Mercia was a Kingdom once richer and more powerful than Wessex; here was a daughter of that old lineage.

"Pega," she mused aloud. "It is a lovely name, and a blessing to be called after a pearl, something of natural richness and beauty. And it is a joyful name, one that suggests happiness."

Hrald was also thoughtful, but his thoughts lay in another direction. "Her husband – he who was lately killed – of what hall was he?"

"Of the King's own," came Raedwulf's considered reply. "He was Beorhtwulf, an Ealdorman of Essex, a cousin once removed to Ælfred."

Essex was far to the east of Cirenceaster, and Ælfwyn had no knowledge of it, but Beorhtwulf had been kin to the King.

The bailiff picked up this thread in his next words. "The King had encouraged the union, one to which his daughter Æthelflaed agreed. Now, the young woman being disappointed of her husband due to his untimely death, both King and the Lady of the Mercians seek appropriate disposition of the Lady Pega and her wealth, to assure she is justly wed, and to greatest advantage."

The bailiff paused, and looked pointedly at the Jarl of Four Stones. "The first match was a good one. But to wed you, Hrald, would be a union to benefit three halls in three Kingdoms."

Both the young Jarl and his mother fell quiet. It was much to compass, and having trust in Raedwulf as they had, was something they must consider with the utmost gravity and purpose.

"She is possessed of immense wealth," he now told them. "Her treasure – it is an unusual one. I have glimpsed small quantities of it, things she wears about her person, the cup she drinks from. They are things perhaps from the age of the Caesars."

Hrald took this in. It added another layer of interest to her story. The Lady Pega's material wealth was not counted in chests of crude chopped up hack-silver and coins, snipped into halves and quarters to reduce their value to sheer weight, but things of taste and delicacy, things which mayhap had been fashioned long ago in the splendour of Rome. This had significance, and seemed to reflect well on her.

Ælfwyn had listened with utmost care to the bailiff's words; she must, both for the weight of their import, and for the love she bore the speaker. Yet, watching Raedwulf as he delivered these further tidings, she could barely suppress her smile. He was masterful in conveying such news, and the subtle manner in which he could impart not only information but actual sensations in his listeners made her breast swell with loving pride at his skill. It gave her a rich and secret joy. His ability and worth were well-known to the King he served, and now he used his talents in attempt to aid and bless her son, and by extension, herself.

Hrald had made his decision.

"What – what do we next do?"

Raedwulf gave thought. "In most instances the young woman would be brought to you. In this case, seeing that she is a royal ward, I think it best for you to travel to Lady Æthelflaed, for the girl is under her protection, and it is she you must win over."

"The Lady of the Mercians knows that we are Christian," Ælfwyn asked.

"Indeed," Raedwulf assured. "More than that, she is well aware of your benefactions to Oundle." His voice dropped. "And I might add, she is aware of Ashild."

Both mother and son drew breath. News of Ashild had reached even the royal courts of Mercia.

"She will have no objection to Hrald's visit?" Ælfwyn now posed.

The bailiff's answer was decisive. "None. I believe she welcomes it."

Hrald's eyes were the brighter for hearing this. Still, there was much he was unsure of.

"Should I travel without terms being worked out?"

"Yes, though I agree it is awkward. It is highly unusual for there to be no preliminary arrangement, but given the respective wealth of the two halls, I believe that much will depend on your actual interview with Lady Æthelflaed. I would advise travelling with a certain generous amount of treasure; this should allow you to return with the Lady Pega. Should you of course find her agreeable, and choose her."

"And the Lady Æthelflaed approve of me," Hrald returned. It would be like courting two women, he thought, with the elder holding sway.

Raedwulf had to nod in agreement.

"I will only caution that Lady Æthelflaed will not lightly surrender a girl so dear to her," the bailiff added.

Raedwulf spoke directly to Hrald now. "You will excuse my next query, but I have heard of your marriage to a daughter of Guthrum, and the dissolution of same. If I knew more of the circumstances it would be helpful in further presenting your suit."

The pause Hrald took was only long enough to gather his thoughts, that he might tell the sorry tale as simply as he might. He related it in outline, much as he had to his father on Gotland. The status of the union in Church law was important, and Hrald knew revealing this to be vital. "Wilgot declared the marriage dissolved, annulled, for it had been contracted under false premises."

Indeed, there were many reasons a marriage could be voided. If either party to a marriage did not give of their heart unreservedly, the union could be annulled. Hrald had discovered his wife being willingly kissed by another man. Such was not only grounds to sunder the union, but to attack and even kill the interloper, and without fear of legal redress. The young Jarl, much to his credit, had stayed his hand, something which made the bailiff look upon him even more advantageously.

Raedwulf listened, head inclined to one side, and at this conclusion, nodded gravely. "That is helpful. Thank you. The Lady Æthelflaed must learn this in private, for I do not know what she may have heard on her own, if anything. It is far better for her to hear this history from us."

Hrald nodded his agreement.

Raedwulf stood a moment, looking at each in turn. "I think Lady Æthelflaed will be well-disposed to you. She is already well-disposed to your mother, and to the hall."

Ælfwyn's hands had risen towards her face at these words, and a pink flush could be seen mantling her cheek at this praise.

Hrald looked to his mother and nodded at this confirmation. Her own long labour here had aided him in this pursuit.

Hrald took a breath, then looked first to his mother, then the bailiff.

"Yes. I will go," he decided.

Ælfwyn was the first to respond to this declaring. "Hrald, do you not wish to think on it?"

Saying this, she was aware of the duality of her own mind and heart. She would protect her son, yet could not help but place her trust in Raedwulf. But Hrald needed no such reflection.

"Mother, I need a wife. One who can begin to relieve you of the burden of this hall. If Raedwulf believes this a good match, I trust in that."

She squeezed his hand in agreement.

"Lady Æthelflaed," said the bailiff. "She will I think insist on the wedding there, at either the royal hall of Weogornaceastre or Gleaweceaster. Both are built upon the banks of the great River Severn, a full day's ride from the other."

Ælfwyn now understood Hrald could return to her a married man, his new wife at his side.

"What will the bride-price likely be?" Hrald asked next.

The bailiff gave the slightest movement of his shoulders, but his lips bowed in a smile. "It will be a great one." His next words were both considered, and sober. "Lady Æthelflaed is aware that you will be travelling a great distance, and with limited means of transport. In light of Mercia's need, a waggon filled with arms will serve you handsomely."

The starkness of this martial necessity stood in strong contrast to the higher, and happier thoughts the Lady and Jarl had been nourishing. Raedwulf now went on. "I would perhaps add any ornaments of silver which might delight either Lady, when revealed."

He pondered a moment, then added, "The Lady Pega – she will bring you gold."

"As soon as the horses are rested I must return to Witanceaster," Raedwulf told Hrald at table that night. "I will then travel to Mercia. I will meet you with the King's escort at the Caesar's road at the border of Mercia and Anglia, on the Feast of St Walpurga."

"A good time to travel," Hrald agreed, as it was a day full of promise. That feast heralded the coming of Summer, and was marked by revelry and bonfires. It was a fortnight away, enough for the preparation Hrald must make for his absence.

The meal was drawing to a close. The bailiff was sitting at Hrald's right, and Hrald's mother was at the Jarl's left, with Wilgot the priest next her. It had been a long day for all, but no more so than wearying days of travel had been for Raedwulf.

Once again the weaving room on the partial upper floor of the hall had been given over to serve as the bailiff's own chamber; for the few days of his stay Eanflad and Ealhswith would sleep in the house of Jari and Inga. His packs were up there now, awaiting him. Notwithstanding the demands of his journey, Raedwulf was able to cast a meaningful glance to the Lady of the hall, whose time at table was very much being taken up by the priest.

Ælfwyn stood, a little abruptly, as Raedwulf and Hrald began to rise, and made her apologies to Wilgot;

she must be certain their esteemed guest would be made comfortable for the night. While Hrald was speaking with Jari by the door of the treasure room, she neared the bailiff.

She was just close enough that he might make his hushed request, in a tone near to a whisper.

"May I come to you?"

She brought her head the closer, almost as if she had not caught his words, for the noise of the hall. "There is little I want more," she murmured in return.

He had tightened his lips so that his smile would not show; but she saw it in his eyes. "Shall I await Burginde tonight?" he asked, hopeful that it would be this soon.

She nodded, and moved off.

After the silver cups were returned to the treasure room, and those of bronze washed and numbered and laid away in their locked chests in the kitchen passage, Ælfwyn followed Burginde to the bower house. The nurse had already relieved the serving girl who stayed with Cerd while he slept, and now parted the red woollen curtains of the boy's alcove and scooped up the sleeping child.

"The pup goes to Inga's with me," she declared. "'Tis nothing to tell her he's fretful with dreams, and you need your rest. 'Twill be but a moment till I return, to ready you, then fetch the bailiff."

Indeed, the nurse had already set the copper tub upon the floor, ready to receive steaming water from the cooking-ring, and well water from the kitchen yard. Ælfwyn's comb, silver looking-disc, and vials of scented oils also awaited her mistress.

With Cerd safely tucked away, and Burginde returned, the task of arraying Ælfwyn began. After the bath came the combing of her long and straight hair, pale as moonlight by the light of the cressets, and application of scent to her throat and wrists. Ælfwyn selected rose, for the very reason that it was a pink bud of that blossom that Raedwulf had once plucked to keep her in memory.

The ablutions complete, Ælfwyn spoke of their preparations. "I feel almost a bride," she confided, as Burginde helped her pull her shift over her head.

"You be as pretty as one," her nurse quipped. She could not help but grin. "Though what lies before you be far better than any bridal night."

The hall had long been quiet when Burginde reentered it. She made her way sure-footed in the dimness, gaining the wooden stairs, carefully stepping over the one that creaked, and then up to the weaving room, where the gap under the door showed a cresset still burnt. She gave the smallest of taps. The door opened almost at once under the hand of the bailiff. Soul of discretion as she was, Burginde signalled nothing but the smallest curtsy. Raedwulf extinguished the cresset and followed her down.

She led him through the kitchen passage, past men asleep in their alcoves. They passed the limits of the kitchen yard, where the heaped charcoal of the cooking-ring fires had been banked and glowed a dull orange. No Moon swam in the sky, but Burginde's firm step was unfaltering. He followed her to the boundary of the beech hedge enclosing the bower garden, and then within, to the door itself. She left him there, as wordlessly, and respectfully, as she had proved escort.

Raedwulf tapped at the door, the light from its edge telling him it was slightly ajar. He brought his mouth close to that edge, and spoke.

"Ælfwyn of Cirenceaster," he beckoned. He laid his palm on the door and pushed.

She named stood in the middle of the floor. Her hands, clasped at her waist as he entered, opened to him in welcome. He shut and bolted the door, then granted himself a moment to merely look.

She wore nought but a shift, the linen of a thinness so fine that her slender form was clearly outlined by the light of the cresset glowing on the table behind her. She looked every vision he might have dreamt of, with an allure demanding possession.

Her naked outline spurred him to cross the floor in two strides. His arms reached to enfold her, pressing her against his chest. After the first kiss, he swept her up, carrying her to her waiting bed.

This time their love-making was of a different character. His initial and commanding act, of bodily lifting her to lay her upon her bed, was as startling to her as it was thrilling. It was harbinger of far more. Their first night of tender union had been well-reviewed in both minds, remembered in every detail, reflected upon, savoured, something to almost be held in the hand like an amulet or cherished keepsake, which brought comfort each time one's seeking fingers returned to it. This second night, fuelled by recollection of the delights of the first, and freed from any reserve or shyness on Ælfwyn's part, was given up to shared, and exquisite passion. They knew the bliss that comes only with full trust. Despite the urgings of desire, this was a rapture that placed the interests of the beloved above one's own, granting each access to that inner realm of loving shelter and surrender.

Once again, Raedwulf would not allow himself the fullest expression of his own pleasure while still in her embrace. It was wrenching, both in body and in heart, but he could not risk a result which later, when they were truly wed, would be so deeply welcomed by them both.

He pulled away, and she gasped, then hid her face upon his chest as he laid back, his own breathing still heavy. His arm came up around her. She lifted her face to him. Tears had formed in her eyes. She pressed herself closely to him and closed her fingers around a lock of his dark and wavy hair. She whispered by his ear, "I yearn for you – all of you."

He gave an answering exhalation before he spoke. "That time may soon be coming, my dearest love," he told her. "If Hrald is accepted by Lady Æthelflaed, and finds Pega to his liking, it may be sooner than either one of us could have hoped."

"Yes, yes," she breathed in hopeful agreement, and moved back to look at him. Then she made a sound, almost a sigh, one of recognition of what this would mean. She shook her head. "But to leave him, leave Four Stones . . ."

"It is much to forgo," he agreed.

"But to know he is well wed," she offered.

"And that I shall be taking you to my own hall, back to Wessex and so much you have been parted from."

She kissed him then, almost unable to hear more, to dream of a life she once thought within her grasp with this good man. That, and so much more, had been crushed with the death of Ashild, and now was once again seemingly within reach. It made her speak of her daughter.

"Our first night together," she began, "was also the first night Ashild and Ceric knew each other. Their only night, as it turned out."

This had been her secret, that both mother and daughter knew love that night, one she must share with the man she had given herself to.

"That a child resulted . . ." he answered. There was gentle wonder in his voice at this granting.

"Yes. An immense blessing. And Abbess Sigewif and Wilgot both proclaim Cerd a child of marriage." Her voice dropped the lower. "She was buried with the gold ring he had placed on her hand, after her death."

They were quiet. She also wore a gold ring given by a man, but the hour was not yet here when he could name her wife, nor she call him husband. This thought went unspoken, but felt shared, for Raedwulf brought her right hand to his lips and kissed that ring.

The day – and now night – had been full; there was much to recount, and to share. She spoke of the happy tidings he had ridden to deliver.

"The hope that Hrald might wed the Lady Pega," she recalled. "We have you to thank for that."

The bailiff demurred with a shake of his head, but did not mask his smile. "I had offered it as suggestion to the King, yes," he admitted. "But it was solely Ælfred who endorsed it, allowing me to bring the possibility to Æthelflaed, who readily embraced it." He paused a moment in reflection. "To do so without knowing of what mind Hrald – or indeed you – were, was a boldness I hope to be excused of."

She smiled back. Given the distances and difficulty of travel, he had taken the chance that an opportunity to unite with the royal houses of both Mercia and Wessex would be a welcome surprise. And he had been right.

"Neither of us had dreamt of such a possibility," she answered. "It is one more proof of your concern for this hall." She must kiss him once more at this.

"And of my regard for its Lady," he added, as their lips parted.

He turned on his side, studying her face, watching it change to a deeper thoughtfulness.

"Hrald said something which struck me," she began. "It was his saying, near the end of your telling us all this, that he needed a wife. Not wanted; needed. And not even for his own sake, but for mine, to relieve me of the duties of the hall.

"I welcomed his willingness, but his reason saddened me," she went on. Her next words were uttered quite slowly, as if reluctant to give shape to them. "It has been more than two years since the end of his brief marriage. Yet I wonder if he has in any way recovered.

"That loss, of a woman he prized, was followed a few short months later by Ashild's death. Both young women left us abruptly, with no warning. His sister's loss is something we must accustom ourselves to, each day. I know Hrald does. But Dagmar . . . I fear her betrayal wounded him in ways beyond his knowing."

Raedwulf's responsive sigh was not only for Hrald, but his own younger self. He had seen Ælfwyn as a maid of seventeen in the hall of her father Ælfsige, and loved her. He had been forced to watch her, over the course of the following days, give her heart to the second son of the great hall of Kilton. Nothing overt in the actions of either Ælfsige's daughter nor Gyric betrayed them, but

Raedwulf, unable to take his eyes from her, saw it all. His attachment to her was one that shadowed the rest of his days, a hopeless attachment until sent here by Ælfred as emissary. This history, acute and personal as it was, made him say the next.

"Perhaps it is not the betrayal that he mourns, but the regard he bore for her."

The insight made her drop her head. His meaning held sudden and deep resonance. She could only pray that young Pega could heal this wound. Disaster could be followed by joy. All good was possible; she had seen it in her own life, and was living it now. She took one of his hands in her own as she spoke.

"The heart is an infinite chamber. This I have learnt. And there is no bar to entry, even when we think it locked."

Chapter the Seventh

SEEK FURTHER AFIELD

Kilton in Wessex

The Year 896

WINTER in Wessex had been mild, but Spring was cruel. The grave cattle sickness that had impacted much of Wessex so dreadfully was no less severe at Kilton. Some kind of plague went through the beasts, felling even the strongest amongst them, leaving them unable first to eat and then to rise. Those deemed unfit to weather the Winter had been, as always, slaughtered before the cold, their meat smoked or brined and set away. But many beasts of proven soundness, which both cottars and the hall of Kilton depended upon to pull ploughs and draw waggons, now sickened and died, along with the milk cows. It meant for early planting that men and women must break up the soil by hand with ard or hoe, and depend on dray horses granted by the hall to pull the ploughs. Great loss that it was, the village folk were forbidden to partake of any of that downed flesh; thegns went and roped the bodies of the cattle where they dropped, and hauled them out on horseback to the field where the mid-Summer fire was kindled, and burnt them to prevent the sickness from spreading. The pressure on the food reserves of the hall was great, for few cows meant little milk, no butter, and no beef.

The large granaries of Kilton kept grain from year to year, replenishing the store of oats, barley, and rye as needed, and that had been doled out against hunger. All had straitened rations, even within the hall, and none knew famine. But the lack of butter and cheese, the glory of Spring-time, was sorely felt by all.

It was not only Kilton which was so afflicted; word had been carried from neighbouring burhs that the loss of cattle was widespread throughout the Kingdom. Only a few burhs had been spared, but by the time the murrain had burnt itself out, there remained so small a stock of sound beasts that demand for fresh animals with which to rebuild herds was great. It was thus that Edwin, Lord of Kilton, must face the burgeoning Spring-tide, with hunger, cruelly arrayed in budding leaf and blossom, staring him in the face.

Ceric was not there to aid him, but still in his forest fastness. His grandmother Modwynn, with her graceful wisdom and wide circle of contacts, was no longer here to advise him as to which hall to apply to for relief. He knew from Worr's letters to his father-in-law Raedwulf at Witanceaster that the plague was felt even there. But word was brought to Edwin from another source, the priest Dunnere, which gave hope. Dunnere, through correspondence with a brother priest in his home Kingdom of Ceredigion in Wales, could report the sickness had not reached there. Nor, the letter had on good account, had it in the equally near Mercia.

Edwin determined that he would send to Æthelred in Mercia, to see if he could procure forty or fifty head of cattle, and drive them back. Edwin had never met the Lord of that place, but his brother had stood in his presence, and even taken part in Æthelred's failed attack on the Danish fortress on the River Lyge. That was connection enough. He sent two riders to Mercia to ask if beasts might be had. If so, he would come himself, soon after. The riders returned in a few days with a welcome, and affirming, answer. Their cattle had not been afflicted. Edwin was bidden to come and buy what he might from the royal herd kept near Gleaweceaster.

So the Lord of Kilton set out. Worr could not go with him; he must remain at Kilton to aid Edgyth and look after Ceric. Edwin was in secret glad of this. He wanted to go unaided by any advisor, wanted to prove that he was up to the task of this important purchase. Most of all he looked forward to entering the precincts of Kilton fronting a herd of milk cows, stout oxen, and two or three good bulls with which to rebuild their stock. It would be potent demonstration that he could provide for his folk, something he felt strong need of, for his own sake.

To meet the Lord of Mercia in one of his royal halls took on a lustre almost matching the hope that he might speedily end his folk's lack of cattle. He rode out with a body-guard of thirty. He felt free from his elders, fronting his men by himself. Many, granted, were experienced warriors twice his age, but there was no counsellor amongst them; he would perform this transaction himself. He had one supply waggon, and the lead drover of the hall's cattle to help him make his selection. Those most skilled with the dairy cows were ever women, and bringing one along was impractical, but the eldest son of one was here, eager to make his mother proud with his choice of milkers.

His journeying, in mid Spring, was slowed by mud, but luckily no further rain fell upon the road. It took two full days to reach Gleaweceaster. They were met at the Mercian border by a six-man escort sent by Æthelred, an unexpected courtesy which seemed to bode well for the success of his mission. The town was walled by stone; the work of the Caesars he knew; and Kilton's oaken palisade seemed primitive and feeble by contrast. He was received briefly but graciously by a steward in the timber hall of Gleaweceaster, and that night seated at the high table to the right of Æthelred. The table was long and crowded; he could not well see either Æthelred nor his Lady, Æthelflaed. He and his men were given their own housing, a small hall to themselves, and told that on the morrow following the Sabbath Mass he would be brought before Lord Æthelred.

The service next day was a splendid one, and the church a cathedral. Edwin had never entered so impressive a church. The robes of the priests officiating were encrusted with fine thread work of silver and gold, which caught the gleam of candle-light as they swept before the altar. When they turned their backs to the nave and raised their arms, one could be dazzled by such display. Edwin noted it, gauging the wealth in precious wire, and the hours of labour of skilled needlewomen in producing it, but his mind quickly reverted to more compelling thoughts.

Something else had caught his eye, and that was the entrance, just before the service commenced, of Lady Æthelflaed, or rather, one member of her train. That noblewoman, wearing a broad filet of gold about her brow, had been ushered in amongst a small crowd of richly dressed women, both young and old; also a little girl at Æthelflaed's right. The young woman at the immediate left of Æthelflaed was of uncommon looks. She did not look kin to the Lady of Mercia, though the affection between them was evident. This companion of the Lady was fair without being pallid, delicate in bone without seeming fragile, and had, when she turned her face where Edwin could see it fully, a look of intelligence about her eyes. It was not an easy face to forget. The Lord of Kilton vowed to learn more.

In late afternoon the steward came and brought him to Æthelred. They sat in some kind of private chamber of the Lord's; not treasure room Edwin saw, as it held no casks nor chests, but rather a space fitted up simply yet amply for conversation, the study of books or charts, or even private dining. As large as the hall was, Edwin was still impressed by this, and took it as no small honour that he had been received here, and alone, by the Lord. Edwin had not seen him at Mass, and now had ample occasion to study him.

Though he was son-in-law to the King, Æthelred must be close in age to Ælfred himself. His hair, uncommonly long for an older man, flowed past his shoulders. It was now more grey than brown. He was broad of chest, not overly tall, and opulently dressed. His tunic of sky blue was covered at neckline, hem, and sleeves in many-coloured threadwork, and from around his neck dangled a heavy linked chain of gold. Edwin wondered if this festive wear was to greet the Lord of Kilton, or if the man always dressed thus. The red-dyed leather of his shoes suggested the latter.

They began their parley. As he had neared Gleaweceaster Edwin had ridden past herds of grazing cattle, many with calves at their sides. The drover and dairyman he had brought from Kilton had been afield early with the Lord's own cattle-men, and had made their selection from amongst them. They numbered five and forty beasts. Though the Lord of Kilton was in no position to bargain, the Lord of Mercia would not press his advantage. He had too often to call upon the troops of Wessex to defend the land its King had named him Lord and Ealdorman over. After Lord Æthelred presented his price, and Edwin had agreed to it, Æthelred called for ale.

When the first swallow of foaming ale was tasted, Æthelred surprised Edwin by his next words.

"Your brother Ceric," he began. "Have you good report?"

Edwin was taken aback; the look of concern on the face of the Lord of Mercia, and the directness of his query could only be rooted in knowledge of how things transpired at Kilton. He was holding the silver cup by its foot, and now looked into its depths.

"He is still . . . away, my Lord," Edwin managed.

Æthelred grunted. "A bad business. And such a valued arm. Ælfred has special concern for him, I know."

"The King is his god-father," was all Edwin could respond. Of course Ceric had come to the attention of the King; he had always been watching him, since birth.

And what report has Ælfred had of me, he wondered. That at my first engagement I was thrown from my horse and carried off by my body-guards before I could draw my sword. Would that the King had heard instead of our defence outside Sceaftesburh, where I killed three and avenged my downed captain . . .

The Lord of Mercia's following words did not better the situation. "He left a son in Anglia," he recalled.

He gazed directly at Edwin, a piercing look that seemed to presage a command. "You must get the boy," he advised, clearly speaking of Cerd. He took another swallow of ale. "And you yourself must wed. You are an Ealdorman. You are not too young to begin thinking of futurity."

Edwin was relieved the conversation had veered away from Ceric and his son, two things he felt he had no control over, regardless of Æthelred's airy mentioning of them. He could answer this last heartfeltly, and did so.

"I do, my Lord. I do think of it."

It seemed an apt time to mention the young woman he had noticed in the cathedral.

"This morning at Mass your Lady was with a maid, one with yellow hair, who remained at her left."

Æthelred's chin bobbed once. "Ah. Yes. Pega."

Edwin watched the smile spread over the Lord of Mercia's face. "You aim high, which is only just." He seemed to study anew the young man before him. "She is the daughter of the late Swithwulf. But . . . I fear you come to dip your oar into that river too late."

"She is wed?"

"She is as good as wed, I should say. But it is in the hands of my wife. And her father, the King."

It was all the Lord of Mercia offered. Edwin did not know what to say, save for the next. "Have I leave to speak to your Lady?"

Æthelred gave a laugh. "She is more occupied than I with all her many interests, but I will make sure she calls for you before you depart."

This sounded less than hopeful, and when Edwin received the summons late in the day, he could not help but bolster his confidence by reminding himself that Kilton was the second richest burh in Wessex, and he its Lord.

He was shown to another chamber within the great hall, not dissimilar to that where he had met Æthelred, but this one of decided female character. It had even a loom set against the wall, one whose warp was half-full of densely packed cream-coloured weft. Several women were with the Lady Æthelflaed, companions, attendants, or relations, Edwin could not be certain; only that she was well-chaperoned and he, well-watched. He quickly saw the young woman who had caught his eye was not present; this gave some relief, and the ladies attendant on Æthelflaed were careful to move to a table in the further reaches of the admittedly small chamber, and occupy themselves with hand-work.

Æthelflaed was standing near the entrance door when he arrived, and remained standing, signalling to him how brief their meeting was to be. Now so close to her, he was surprised at her youth. But then, he reminded himself, she could not be old, given that her father, though now grey of hair, was not an old man. The Lady Æthelflaed had been wed over a decade to Æthelred, in years nearly a score older than she. There was little prettiness about her; she was far from homely, but her attractiveness was one of enterprise and intellect. This showed at once in her eyes, which addressed him without boldness and yet, he felt certain, had quickly assessed him.

Her hair was almost wholly covered by her veil-like headdress, but at the hairline it showed a soft brown. Edwin noticed her clothing; he could not help but do so, after the impression her husband's show had made. His wife dressed much as his own mother Edgyth would, in a kind of sober richness. Her gown was of a green so dark he thought it at first black; only when she moved to where a ray of sunlight struck her skirts did he discern its true, deep forest shade. She still wore her golden brow-band, as befit a woman both a princess and the chief Lady of a sub-Kingdom. She was in sum far more Queenly than her husband was King-like.

He bowed his head deeply to her. He could not see if she had made any reciprocal movement herself, and lifted his gaze to meet hers.

"My Lord," she began, in a tone more welcoming than he expected. Her next words told him why. "Your father Gyric was a favoured companion to my own; this I know." She went on. "And your mother Ceridwen is a woman who the King recalls, and esteems."

He thought of that secret he knew of his mother, which she before him of course could not.

"And your brother," the Lady went on, "is god-son to the King."

He nodded, less fully, but respectfully still. This listing of the close connections between the royal family and his own had him feel at a disadvantage, almost at a loss. He was not named therein; only his parents and older brother.

Æthelflaed now went on to the present. "My Lord has told me that you have inquired after the Lady Pega."

"I have, my Lady. I admit his answer was not hopeful to my interest."

It was her turn to nod. "I regret it must be so. Your awareness of my ward does honour to her, and it grieves me to tell you that she is spoken for."

Though cautioned by Æthelred, Edwin was taken aback. This was an outright rejection, without even the chance to present his suit.

"Is the decision final?"

Æthelflaed allowed her eyes to again meet those of the young man. Pega had become dear to her, and she wanted the girl's happiness. The granting of her hand was hers to give. Kilton was rich, a favoured burh in her father's Kingdom. Its Lord, young as he was, showed promise of growing into an impressive man. The bonds between her own family and his hall had been ever strong. Such a union would bring an exchange of treasure, yes. But it would do nothing to further her pressing goal of consolidating the Mercian Kingdom against additional incursion by the Danes. Her mother had been a noblewoman of Mercia. Æthelflaed felt this calling in her blood, to restore the great Kingdom of Mercia, or at least keep it from further diminution.

Kilton's attractions, and that of its Lord, could not compete with what could be gained by coupling with East Anglia. She must reserve such a prize for its highest use. Pega too would want this, if she should ever learn of her guardian's decision. The Lady of Mercia had not yet met Hrald of Four Stones, but based on the opinion of her father and that of Raedwulf his bailiff, she had already set Pega aside for him. Union with Four Stones would provide a foothold, and a powerful one, in the heart of Anglia.

Raedwulf had told her Hrald had been briefly wed to one of Guthrum's daughters, the man who had nearly toppled Wessex. That marriage had proved unsuccessful, but could have been fraught with danger. How much better that he now wed a Mercian woman, and not be either pressed or goaded by an ambitious wife – as Dagmar might have proved – to reconquer Mercia, or join with Haesten and again attack Wessex.

She would not be swayed.

"I regret to say it is."

It would be wholly improper for him to inquire the name of the fortunate suitor, but it was all he could do to quell his desire to do so. He would learn in due time, he knew. He said that which was expected.

"I wish her every happiness."

His awkwardness grew moment by moment, until she sensed it and said the next.

"Should there be any change in status, you will hear of it, I assure you."

Edwin found himself blinking. Lord of Kilton as he was, it was hard to be told he was the option of default. "I thank you, My Lady," was all he could answer.

All the long ride home his thoughts kept returning to this interview. He considered which great hall of Wessex was his rival. The Lord of Wedmor had lost his son in action with Eadward and Ceric, but he had a younger; and Edwin wondered if he could be the preferred suitor. There was so much he could not know. He was returning, much lighter in purse, with the cattle he sought, but the plod home lacked glory. The horse he was now astride was a good animal, but he did not like it as well as that stallion which had been killed. Denied the presence of Ceric or Worr the slog was largely solitary, making loud the creak of his leather saddle. At one point, weary of the ride, the endless lowing of the cattle before him, and his own fruitless imaginings, he laughed aloud at the fact that he had never found himself close enough to the maid to even know if his attraction to her was real. He knew nothing of Lady Pega, save he was not good enough for her.

It was some recompense that the entry into Kilton was all Edwin might have hoped. His folk were massed along the road to see the cattle being driven by, and cheered his name in grateful welcome. The gates of the hall yards were thrown wide, and as Edwin rode through he saw that even Dunnere the priest was there, employed in the act of blessing the thirsty beasts as they lumbered in. Herded by the drovers the beasts milled, heads nodding, ears flapping, in the broad stable yard.

Edwin's mother, eyes shining with loving pride, was smiling, and Worr came to his stirrup to greet him. While Edwin was still mounted, Dunnere raised his voice above the tumult of kine. He offered prayers for their health, and for those which would be breeding animals, for their soon increase. Now the delivered beasts would be sorted in the hall yards, and parcelled out to hall, village, and more distant hamlets. After a few words together with his returning Lord, Worr took charge of this.

Edwin found himself inside the hall, washing face and hands at the offered basin, and then gesturing both Lady Edgyth and Dunnere into the treasure room to take refreshment. He must tell of his time in Gleaweceaster; his mother would wish to hear all, and considering what had occurred, he wanted Dunnere there as well. With both his grandmother and Cadmar gone, Dunnere was now the closest advisor he had, and he thought, in many ways the most disinterested. Over a cup of mead he spoke of his reception at the royal hall, of the Mass in the cathedral, and of seeing a maid he wished to know more of.

"After Æthelred and I struck our bargain, I was able to inquire of her. Her name is Pega. She is the special ward of Lady Æthelflaed, and I spoke to her of the girl. But she has been set aside, for another suitor."

This occasioned a lengthy pause, one broken by his mother. Kilton's wealth and repute was such that marriage at the highest level was expected. Lady Edgyth worked hard to keep her tone hopeful.

"I am sure the Lord and Lady of Mercia, having seen you, will now hold you in thought when another worthy maid is brought to their attention."

Edwin's glum nod served as answer. Again, silence reigned.

There was something else of import Edwin had not shared, and it was Lord Æthelred's advice about Cerd, the simple dictate, "You must get the boy." If Ceric did not come back soon, Edwin might be forced to do just that. He did not want to speak of his brother now, and kept his silence.

Dunnere's thoughts toward a bride had not been quelled. He leant forward at the table they were seated around and looked first to Lady Edgyth and then to Edwin. "Mercia. Wessex. It is not only these in which an advantageous union can be made. Why not seek further afield?"

He had their attention, and he went on. "I speak of my homeland – Cymru. Wales."

"Wales," Edwin repeated. The priest might as well have named Dane-mark. "We have fought them plenty of times, and many different of their Kings and Princes."

Indeed, the native speakers of that tongue were united solely by this. The Welsh lived under many rapidly shifting small Kingdoms, some of fabled wealth, and all of known ferocity.

Dunnere turned to Edgyth.

"As you know, my Lady, there are brother priests to whom I write, and in more than one of the Welsh courts. Let me apply to them, and see what suggestion may result."

She looked to her son, who nodded.

"Yes, please do so," she answered.

Edwin considered. The Kings and Princes of Wales had fought both against and with the Danes. Their interests were their own, and seemingly ever-changing. But certain Kingdoms enjoyed more stability than others, and had warranted Ælfred's trust.

Priests and monks, nuns too, were often privy to power. Dunnere had indeed kept up correspondence with his brethren in his homeland; all knew that. Anything of strategic importance the priest would pass along to the King, but he might inquire of certain Welsh Princes who sought alliance not with the Danes, but with Wessex. And there were those disaffected war-chiefs, who had not been dealt fairly with by Haesten and his followers. These were leaders looking for firm alliance with whomever might emerge the victorious and dominant power. With Haesten gone to ground, this was Wessex. Such might be eager to send a daughter, heaped with treasure, to Kilton.

Still, the idea of a Welsh bride was utterly novel to Edwin, and the priest read this.

"Their loyalties are fierce ones," the priest acknowledged. "They are an insular people."

Edwin's brow furrowed. "Yes, and one of their own tongue, which I cannot speak."

Dunnere said something in Welsh, and then repeated it. "It is an ancient tongue, one spoken on this island far longer than that in which we now speak," he reminded.

"There is a priest, Gwydden by name, in the coastal Kingdom of Ceredigion, from whence I hail. He is one who sits at the table of the King, a monarch desirous of peace, and desirous also of influence."

"Ceredigion," Edwin repeated. It was one of several small Kingdoms in that land, and though he could not recall hearing of it before, the name conjured another to his ears. With Edgyth who had raised him here, he felt almost disloyal in his next words, but say them he must. "Like the name of my birth-mother, Ceridwen?" he asked.

She had always said she was half-Welsh, which gave Ceric and him a quarter of that blood. It was a realization he did not often consider, one that in its remoteness to his identity with Kilton he did not want to acknowledge or accept.

The priest nodded. "It is named for one Ceridig, made King of that place more than three hundred years ago." The priest thought a moment. "Such names are not unusual in the Welsh tongue," he allowed.

"Ceric said our mother was named for a Goddess. She told him that; he recalls it."

"It is regrettable that upon her late baptism your mother had not received a Christian name," Dunnere murmured.

Edwin looked surprised. "It was also a family name; at least in part, as her father was a Mercian named Cerd, a war-chief of some wealth and repute."

Dunnere, who kept careful record of all the family of Kilton, knew all this, yet Edwin felt he was of a sudden defending his absent mother.

Edwin paused before he said the next. "She had a right to her name."

Dunnere gave another nod. He was not going to fault the brothers of the distant priory by the River Dee who had taken a fatherless child in and tried to raise her to an upright life, blessing her with the gift of catechism and equipping her with the tools of reading and writing which would have made of her an honoured servant of God, or at least a dutiful and capable wife and mother. The Lady Ceridwen, while fulfilling her most vital charge of providing male heirs for Kilton, had otherwise in Dunnere's eyes proved a disappointment to the hall.

Edwin must ask the next. "And if there were Princess or suitable woman there, would such a maid be Christian?"

The priest's eyes lifted Heavenward, not in exasperation, but in acknowledgment of Divine Providence. He answered.

"Indeed, she would almost certainly be." The faintest of smiles crossed the thin lips of the priest. "The folk of Wales knew and kept to the true God long before the Angles and Saxons washed up on these shores. Caesar's men came to despoil Wales of her silver and gold, and enslaved its folk to mine it for Rome. But later the Word of God was brought by the men of the Caesars, and took firm root in Cymru's rich and ready soil. Churches, monasteries, and convents arose. Through God's mercy the holy men and women thereof kept the flame flickering through every privation and hardship. When Rome itself fell to the barbarian horde, it was Wales – and the monks of Iona – who held aloft the flame."

Edwin, now suitably educated and not a little chastened, could only nod. Dunnere returned to practical issues.

"But even if a woman of your choice were not Christian, there is speedy remedy. I will be with you, of course. She could be baptised at once. As for the difficulty of the Welsh tongue, young people quickly adopt a speech foreign to them. Neither would be true impediment to your union."

Edgyth looked again to her son. He exhaled a breath he did not know he had been holding. Then he nodded assent to the priest. There was nought to lose, Edwin thought, and possibly much to gain. A Welsh girl as his wife seemed as foreign as one from Frankland, but the Kings of Wessex had made wives amongst them. So might he, from Cymru.

The next night Edwin rode to visit Begu. He had not taken time to tell her he was heading for Mercia. He had meant to, but his preparations took more effort than he had allowed. Thus he had been away from her door, and bed, for two weeks.

Edwin wanted to see her for his own sake. Beyond this, he was now truly in mind that he must wed, and might do so soon. Ceric had made it clear that once he did, he must renounce Begu. But as he made his way by moonlight to her door, anticipating the pleasures he would find in her arms made him wonder if that would be possible. These were heedless pleasures as well, unlike that of being husband to a lawful wife. No responsibility hinged upon him, only that he bring her silver.

The tiny house, shaggy as a haystack under its thick roof, was dark. He tapped at the back door as he always did, and whispered her name. He heard a low sound of acknowledgment, then of movement. He knew she was moving from bed to fire-pit, and lighting a cresset from a flame carried on the tips of a few straws. She pulled the door open, blinking, her mouth beginning to form a smile, her shoulders wrapped in a shawl which she held tight in one hand at her breast.

Once within her door, she clung to him, happy just to see he was hale. He kissed her, and at once began unbuckling his seax belt, and pulling off his tunic.

"I rode to Mercia, to buy cattle," he told her. "As soon as the cows are bred, three of them will be brought here to the hamlet, to help rebuild your stock."

There had been a total of twelve cows amongst her neighbours; nine of them had died in the cattle plague. Her own milk needs were slight; she kept no cow, and amongst her seven sheep were good milking ewes, the rich milk of which she could turn to cheese. For butter she bartered what she needed with her neighbours. Three healthy animals would aid greatly in their want, and she murmured thanks at the news of this coming boon for them all.

Edwin spoke little more. As much as she yearned to know, she did not ask about Ceric; it was not seemly. She must wait until he volunteered his report, and certainly not until after they were done in her bed. She could not summon Ceric there, while she was trying to welcome Edwin fully.

He pulled off the rest of his clothes. Entering her snug house with its banked fire was a happy return to this private pleasure. He took a moment to glance around him. Between his gifts and those of Ceric, everything she valued was from their hands. Even the tabby cat curled up on the cushion on a stool had been given by his brother. Yet entering the place he felt it wholly of her, and now, of him. The herbal smell of the flowers and plants which hung drying in a corner from a rafter surrounded them, and was trigger enough. The two bronze cups they drank from were even set upon the small table; he wondered if they were always ready for him. Most nights he waited until afterwards to take mead with her, and this would be one of them. Her bed was heaped with cushions and still warm from her rising, and he went to it.

Edwin rarely spoke during their time entwined in bed. No man save her husband had ever whispered endearments to her during the act. But Ceric had ways to wordlessly convey his pleasure, and she thought, affection for her, when he spent nights with her. And they had sometimes laughed together, in a way that was nearly as sweet as words. With Edwin she had none of this, but was content still to have him here, and see him well. She felt at times a pang of tenderness for him, and for his striving to serve his folk. She saw his pride in having brought the cattle, and made much of it, for he needed much.

When they lay quiet he finally spoke of his brother. "There has been no change with Ceric," was all he offered.

Her muffled response was indistinct, and she feared to ask any pointed question. He had before told her that the horse-thegn Worr went out into the wood nearly every day to call for Ceric. Edwin thought it none of her affair, she knew, and the few things she learnt must suffice. Worr was a good man; she had seen this herself, and if it be within his power would let no harm befall the elder son of Kilton. She must wait, and patiently, as they all must.

To turn their minds away from the lost Ceric, she made request.

"Tell me of Mercia," she invited.

He turned on his belly and propped himself up on his elbows. "I went to Gleaweceaster," he began. "It is a great town, with buildings of stone. I dealt directly with Æthelred, the Lord. The beasts I bought were from his own herds. I feasted in a hall almost twice the size of Kilton. And I met his Lady-wife, the daughter of Ælfred. Her name is Æthelflaed. I went to Mass in a huge stone church."

And he added in thought only, I saw a maid I could have wed. But she is Fated for another.

His silence seemed to signal the end of the telling. She rose, pulled on her shift, and brought forth the crock of mead and a dipper of copper with which to fill their cups. He sat up on the side of the bed, and they drank. It was custom that they toast the other, as was only proper with all who shared drink, by briefly locking eyes and lifting their cups. This time Begu looked different to Edwin.

He again heard Ceric's voice telling him, "She will serve you well until you are wed, and then you must leave off with her."

Edwin had accepted that then, nodding his head to it. But now, having enjoyed her bed for so long, he knew the doing so would prove far more difficult. So what, if after his marriage he kept seeing her? He was doing Begu a service. She relied on his silver, he told himself, not wanting to imagine how much she had in store beneath her floor board. He could only think of her need for him, and his want of her.

They lay back down. She turned to him, her hand upon his bare chest, her face nestled next his shoulder. He found his own hand rising to cover hers. Another thought emerged, one far more troubling. Ceric would return to the hall; Edwin knew he would. His brother now had no wife, and might not wed for a long time. What if on his return, he wanted Begu back? Edwin felt his mouth working in the dark, trying to form answer to this. He would not give her up. No, he would not give Begu up.

Chapter the Eighth

PEGA OF MERCIA

Mercia

HRALD had determined on an escort of forty warriors to see him to Mercia. It was enough men to protect the treasure he carried, but not so many to be burdensome to supply either along the route from their own waggons, or for their hosts when they arrived at the hall of the Lord and Lady of Mercia. Jari was along; he had missed the trip to Gotland, and Hrald wanted him on this one. The old Tyr-hand was long-skilled as a quartermaster, and besides being the chief of Hrald's body-guard, would be in charge of the men at their destination. Asberg must remain at Turcesig, Hrald decided, which meant that Kjeld would command Four Stones. The man was but a few years older than Hrald, but had earned his confidence, and that of Asberg and Jari. There was also the fact that the Lady of the hall liked and trusted Kjeld. None had forgotten that it was he Ælfwyn had sent to fetch Abbess Sigewif on the day Ashild had been returned home.

While still on Hrald's own land, the troop could ride as quickly and in as much confidence as two heavily laden waggons would allow. Past this, they moved with greater caution and a few detours around roads upon which they might be most readily discerned. Their progress was nonetheless good. The late Spring rains were mild and slowed them but little, and there were days of bright and brilliant Sun which warmed them, harbinger of the season to come.

The ride to the Mercian border took four days, the last on a stone road built by the Caesars, a road recalled from earlier forays by a few of the older men amongst their number. Hrald had Raedwulf's map, carefully inked and landmarks shown, to consult. Approaching the point at which he might expect to see the bailiff's men, Hrald was struck by the import of what he now undertook. Should he be successful, he might be returning with a bride.

They found a distinct border marking, not a stone cairn, but two stout tripods of peeled logs which flanked the paved way. These were taller than a man, and well set into the dark brown soil on either side of the stone road. Grasses and shrubs had been scythed around them, making them easy to spot even at a distance. Here was a border of Kingdoms, Anglia to Mercia.

They neared it, seeing nought beyond that broad stone path than they did before, a mixed wood on either side of elder, hickory, and scrub oak. As they grew closer, a horn rang out.

Four thegns of Mercia, green serpent pennons springing from their saddle cantles, rode forth from the shrubby margin. Soon Hrald and his men were at the camp where the Bailiff of Defenas awaited them. "Well met," he greeted Hrald. "The Lord and Lady of Mercia are at the nearer of their royal halls, that at Weogornaceastre. They will be expecting us."

In as long as it took to strike that camp, all were on their way south to Weogornaceastre. They reached its limits two days later, on the afternoon of the sixth day out.

The town sat on the eastern bank of the River Severn, near the great Forest of Dean. As they approached, the ricks of the charcoal makers were much in evidence, as the hardwood of Dean furnished a seemingly endless supply for the braziers and cook-fires of the large and prosperous burh. The Severn, serpentine and sinuous, wound about it, defining and even naming the settlement, as people of the winding river. Growing nearer it was the palisade that caught and held Hrald's eye.

The protective wall they rode towards was not of upright timbers trenched into the soil. It was carefully dressed stone, massively broad and high.

"Stone," Hrald found himself uttering aloud.

The bailiff answered this, with no little awe in his own voice. "The men of Rome have never been surpassed at building. You will see more wonders," he promised.

Hrald scanned the vast length of the stone wall. In the few places where age or assault had breached it, it had been infilled, not with planks of wood, but entire peeled tree trunks set upright, scarcely less stout a barrier than the stone itself.

They rode through that wall in ranks of four, such was the breadth of the gates they entered. Four of Æthelred's thegns fronted them, followed by Raedwulf and Hrald. Behind them was Jari, the three thegns of Wessex the bailiff had with him, and then the body of Hrald's men.

Within was an entire town, bustling with folk of every class of life, turning to see who had been admitted. Hrald felt himself gawking and tried not to. Amongst the numberless timber buildings were many of carefully wrought stone. As they wended their way to the heart of the burh, he saw at least four churches built thereof. Such wealth staggered him.

There were in East Anglia a few buildings of stone; the new church at Oundle was one of them. But he had seen others, some in ruins, others in use as mills, houses, or even barns. Here were many stone buildings, some new, others, like the walls, of obvious antiquity. Certain of the roads and walkways were also of stone, paved with round cobbles and cut blocks. Shallow depressions ran the length of them, gutters carrying waste water away.

Raedwulf noted Hrald's reaction, and spoke. "Weogornaceastre is the work of the long-ago Caesars. We look upon what they left behind, and what the Mercians have built upon. One day you will travel to Lundenwic, and find much more than even this."

One of the stone churches the bailiff named to Hrald as being the Cathedral of St Peter and St Paul. It sat close to an inner palisade, the gates of which were open. The royal hall was just within. Once inside the inner precinct, they quitted their horses. The treasure-bearing waggon, its tarpaulin tightly laced, was pulled into an empty paddock and set under guard. Jari took charge of the supply waggon, now pulled alongside one of the stables, its horses freed to join those which had been ridden. He and the men of Four Stones would be lodged in a secondary hall, but take their meals in that great hall in which the Lord and Lady dined.

There was a separate small building set aside for the use of Lady Æthelflaed's father, large enough to accommodate the King and the key men of his body-guard. Raedwulf and Hrald were shown to it now. Its walls were half stone, half timber. It was hall in itself, complete with inner treasure room, and a score of alcoves flanking the fire-pit. Again, Hrald was forced to marvel. They stood not upon wood planking, nor even on blocks of stone of uniform size paving the area. The floor within this private hall was covered with elaborate pictures, made of small pieces of coloured stone, and Hrald could see, glass as well. Fantastic sea creatures in browns and reds rose from a body of water, conveyed in waving form by blue and white and grey squares. Perhaps it was the river without the walls these giant fish and monsters leapt from, while chubby infants sported upon their backs. Raedwulf had before seen this, but his pleasure in once more looking upon the scenes of blowing fish and swooping birds was clear.

This was not the only indulgence awaiting them. A large copper tub sat upon the floor, and the serving man told them he would carry in hot water so that they might bathe here, and forgo the bathing shed in the yard. At Four Stones this was a luxury only his mother enjoyed, in the comfort of her bower house. Hrald and Raedwulf were now offered the same.

They availed themselves of the bath, then dressed, as soon all would be called to the great hall to dine. Hrald took up the gift he had brought. The hall was already filling as they entered it, the trestles newly set up, benches scraping as men and women took their places. The hall was imposing in both the height of its walls and the loftiness this lent it. The Sun was far from setting, but even at night the lime-washing of the walls and the many torches projecting from walls and timber posts would have granted brightness. Their guide led them through the crowd towards the high table, and then the wall beyond it, in which were cut three doors. He stopped before that in the centre, rapped once, and opened it for them.

This was a kind of ante-chamber to another; perhaps to the treasure room itself. It was windowless; the sole illumination came from a pair of tapers set in low brass holders upon a table. The room was small and sparsely furnished, with the feel of a space used for the brief reception of guests. It might have no other purpose, other than granting access to the next room. It was empty when Hrald and Raedwulf were escorted in, but the inner door was soon opened, and the Lord and Lady of Mercia appeared. The Lord was not much taller than his wife, but broad of build, with long hair, well-marked with strands of grey, falling down his back. The Lady was in a gown of some dark stuff, the hue of which Hrald could not discern in the little light, but the hem, collar, and sleeves of it were trimmed with interlaced designs in silver wire, which gleamed in the candle-light as she moved. If possessed of no beauty, she was well-featured, her bearing and stance one of resilience, even strength. Even in the light of the tapers Hrald saw she had been given her father's eyes, sharp, clear, and blue.

Æthelred greeted Raedwulf with easy familiarity from their long years of acquaintanceship. Lady Æthelflaed too smiled upon the bailiff, and welcomed him with a warmth consonant with her prudent character. Her gaze then went to Hrald. He watched her eyes lift to take in his full height. He made a deep bow, as deep as the bailiff had himself given.

"Jarl Hrald," the Lady said, with surprising lightness. The quick, almost penetrating assessment of her eyes, paired with the gentle briskness of her tone, marked her as the possessor of a high intellect. "We welcome you. Time is short before our gathering to sup. On the morrow, we shall speak."

"I look forward to this, my Lady," Hrald answered.

She was much younger than he had imagined; he had thought of a motherly figure, but in fact Æthelflaed had only seven-and-twenty Summers. Despite the cordiality of the welcome, she had a commanding air about her. Need it she must, to aid in the rule of a land as large as Mercia, even halved, as it now was.

Hrald glanced down at what he held. "I have a gift for you, from my mother Ælfwyn, the Lady of Four Stones."

"Ælfwyn of Cirenceaster," said the Lady, calling her by how she was first known, just as the bailiff often did. "I thank you for carrying it to me."

He stepped forward and laid the bundle upon the waxed surface of the table. She unfolded the flap of linen and drew out a bolt of vibrant blue silk. Near-Queen as she was, her eyes widened. She lay her hand upon it. "What wondrous stuff," she told him.

For a moment Hrald was carried back to his own hall, when Ceric had arrived after a long absence. He bore gifts for the family of Four Stones. One of them, in a bundle not unlike this one, was a gown of golden silk, which he brought for Ashild.

Hrald could not but be glad at Æthelflaed's reaction. His mother had insisted he bring the silk Ceridwen had sent her, saying that if it helped him to a happy match, they would both take joy in his so giving it. Even Æthelred, who, to judge by his deep red tunic, enjoyed fine clothing, was impressed at so well chosen a gift.

"Until our meeting," the Lady ended.

They left the ante-room, Lord and Lady first, and took their places at the high table. It ran, Hrald gauged, nearly twice the length of that at Four Stones. In the centre sat Æthelred and Æthelflaed, each flanked with a long row of men and women. Raedwulf and Hrald were seated to the right of Æthelred, a few places down from men who Hrald guessed were the head of his body-guard. The Lady's side of companions was in its way even more impressive, as no less than a Bishop sat at her left side, followed by two priests, and then a range of splendidly dressed men and women. The high table was lit by an equally long row of tapers, all others by many oil cressets. Their golden and flickering light lent a radiant lustre to the hall. The grandeur of the setting was such that Hrald could not help his sense of awe, and said so.

"Is it like Kilton?" he asked the bailiff.

Raedwulf looked about him, remembering. "Very much so. This hall is larger, but no more finely appointed."

Hrald blew out a short puff of breath in amazement.

Silver salvers, heaped high with food, were set before them, carried in by serving men. A quick glance told Hrald all at the high table dined thus; and the salver placed before Æthelred and Æthelflaed was hammered of gold. Even those at the far tables dined from salvers of bronze; there were none who ate from wood. At each place was set a square of linen fabric. Before Hrald could question Raedwulf the bailiff showed him its use, by spreading it across his lap. "A knee covering," he noted, prompting Hrald to do the same.

A pottery bowl of steaming browis, thick with chunks of meat, lay on Hrald's own salver, surrounded by a seeded loaf, and a mound of stewed apples studded with walnut halves. As Hrald considered his food the bailiff leant close, and spoke in his ear.

"The Lady Pega is there, in a gown of deep green," he murmured, with a bob of his chin to Æthelflaed's end of the table.

Hrald looked over. Her back was almost turned to him, for she had pivoted on her bench as a serving man brought her salver. Hrald saw a light head-wrap of some filmy stuff, given her wealth, silk perhaps. When she turned back, she swept her eyes down at the table to the Lord and Lady of Mercia, as if to ascertain if her patrons had yet begun eating. Seeing they had, she addressed her food.

She lifted a spoonful to her mouth, and then looked again at the other guests, a fuller assessment of who this night sat there. Her eyes skipped from face to face, careful not to catch the eye of any, but curious as to who joined them.

"Does she look for me," Hrald dared ask Raedwulf.

"She knows nothing of you," came his steady answer. "Lady Æthelflaed will, I am sure, wait, until she has herself approved of you before she mentions your suit."

Hrald's eyes went back to the young woman in green. "From here she is lovely, indeed," he admitted.

"I am glad," said Raedwulf. "Nor will she disappoint when you near her," he added.

The meal they enjoyed, though not a feast, was still to be remarked on. The first salver was followed by another, then a third. There were spices and herbs unknown to Hrald, crusted fillets of sturgeon from the River Severn, and smoked eels too from that life-giving current; plump cheeses with downy rinds which oozed when sliced open, and, being Spring, green peas in abundance, flecked with mint and glistening with butter. The bread was of special savour, white-crumbed, tender, made wholly from wheat, Hrald knew; an indulgence he gauged only the high table enjoyed. For drink there was cup after cup of brown and frothy ale, the first filled by the Lady Æthelflaed herself as she moved about the board, the following offered by the serving men in attendance. There was to Hrald a kind of quiet thrill and honour in having such a Lady smile at him as she tipped the silver ewer over his cup. This ewer was ever refilled by the serving woman who aided her, following her about. With the third salver, that of honeyed sweetmeats, mead was brought, its potency felt even after so rich a meal.

Jugglers came out, togged in bright costumes with fringed sleeves, tossing rings and balls into the air and catching them with unfailing ease; musicians too, with pipes, harp, cymbals, and drum. Hrald watched all this, and watched the Lady Pega as well. As the hall grew darker her face receded in ever deeper shadow, making him yearn for the morning, when he might meet her. When Lady Æthelflaed rose, and the denizens of the hall began to take themselves off for the final tasks of the night, he could not take his eyes from her young ward, noting as she picked up her dark skirts in her hands and made her way out a side door.

Hrald lay down in his alcove, the haze of food and drink not sufficient to still his mind when he considered the coming morning. Æthelflaed had smiled upon him when she filled his silver cup, was this signal of her approval? But he had seen her smile too on all there.

The summons came before noon for Hrald to attend on Lady Æthelflaed. He again dressed himself in fine clothes; his mother and Burginde had made him two new tunics and pairs of leggings. He chose a tunic of rich brown, over leggings of even deeper hue. "Should I have a second pair of new boots?" he had asked his mother.

"Unwanted show may be alien to her nature," she had answered. "She is, I think, her father's daughter, and a good steward of resources. Your newer pair of boots with their silver toggles which you wear at feasts will more than suffice." He thought of this now, fastening this pair.

The serving man led them to the hall. Near its door the bailiff spoke. "I leave you here. The Lady will wish to see you alone."

Hrald's eyebrows lifted.

"She is well disposed to you, fear not. But she will have her own queries to make. I will be easy to find when you come out."

Hrald followed the serving man through the hall. Serving folk moved about it, at work sweeping or replenishing oil cressets and rush torches. The wives of warriors were there as well, the women spinning, or weaving at several upright looms, as their young children played at their feet. The ladies noticed Hrald, and their chatter died away as they watched his progress through the hall. The man led Hrald to the door to the left of the ante-chamber they had entered last night, and gave a decided rap to its wood planks. Hrald heard a woman's voice in answer, and the servant opened the door.

It was neither treasure room nor armoury. Rather it was more like a bower or day room for Æthelflaed, and for her child, for there sitting at a low table, playing with a collection of wooden blocks, sat a small girl in a pale yellow gown. A serving woman, perhaps nurse to the child, was also in attendance, and sat with the girl.

The Lady herself was standing by a casement, looking out on the fine afternoon, and took a step towards Hrald as he made his bow. She lifted her hand to the girl.

"My daughter," she said with a smile. "I have made a point of having her with me at such times. She must learn statecraft from an early age, for she is our only child."

The smile was still upon her lips as she turned back to him, though its nature had changed from one of tenderness to one of shared knowledge.

"We will now speak of the purpose of your visit. My ward is Pega, daughter of Swithwulf of Weogornaceastre. She is of a lineage long and storied here in Mercia. The King of Wessex takes special interest in her. As do I."

Hrald was struck at the Lady naming her father thus; it was a needful formality, he guessed, as she addressed Hrald in her role as a co-ruler of a dependent Kingdom.

She went on. "Raedwulf of Defenas has told you of Pega's recent history. We seek to wed her to an estimable man, one fully deserving of her fortune and personal qualities. I am not unaware that you may be in need of a wife."

This directness was almost startling from a woman, but Hrald welcomed it. And he had seen, and been told enough in his life, to have some grasp of her own circumstances.

Æthelflaed had lived almost her entire life during a state of war, one in which her father was prime target. Her marriage to Æthelred was a strategic one, and she had fulfilled the role of peace-weaver between former rival Kingdoms admirably; fulfilled it, and exceeded it to become an active and talented co-ruler with her husband. If she had come of marriageable age during a time of sustained peace, she would have had far greater choice in who she might wed, and she and her parents consider only bloodlines, wealth, and attraction. She was not granted this luxury, and few men and women were. In unsettled times what mattered was finding a complementary family to serve as bulwark and buttress, one which shared the same ends, even if it be no more than the thwarting of a common enemy.

"The King has had dealings with your father, direct dealings," she went on, "and told me of his meeting with you. He believes you to be a worthy man. Of Four Stones we hear only good report. But my interest in my ward is deeply personal. I care for her happiness."

She paused then, to make her request. "I invite you to tell me of your first marriage."

Hrald gave a nod of his head. She had been more than frank and deserved nothing less in return.

"Her name was Dagmar, a daughter of Guthrum with a wife named Bodil. I was more than happy with her. One day I returned to the hall to find her with another man, an old lover of hers, a Dane, who had served with Guthrum, and had returned to Dane-mark. I sundered the union then and there, before witnesses. She left my hall, taking all she had brought with her. I returned the dowry to her guardian." He took his own pause here. "It is my belief that she now lives in Dane-mark, with the man."

He must add another important point. "Wilgot, the priest of Four Stones, declared the marriage annulled."

"I thank you," she answered, her eyes as thoughtful as her voice.

In the eyes of the Church, and the laws of Wessex and Mercia, it was as if this young Jarl had never wed. Annulment or not, Æthelflaed could read on his face that the episode had deeply marked him. The simplicity of his story, its avoidance of casting aspersions upon the woman, his even stating he had been happy with her, impressed his listener.

This woman he was forced to discard must have had fine points or the man before her would not have chosen her as wife. And he was half-Dane, ruling over Danish warriors and their offspring. His first wife, as daughter of the man who had brought Wessex to its knees, carried with her every potent attraction warrior blood can bear. She let her thoughts lift to the unhappy possibility that such a woman might have tried to turn Hrald away from his insistence in holding to the Peace her own father and Guthrum had so painfully wrought. Far better for him to wed a true daughter of Angle-land, one who held both its laws and holy faith as sacred.

Æthelflaed was near to affirming her decision. She turned slightly away from Hrald, ready for a final, if slight test. He had just imparted information to her; now she would convey some of her own. Hers, like his, was not without an element of self-interest.

"You are not alone in your consideration of my ward. A great family of Wessex has also inquired after her."

Hrald's chin moved back, as if dodging a blow. Others were after Lady Pega – how could they not. He fought the impulse to ask which man sought her. To calm himself he let his breath out, as slowly and as quietly as he could. If Raedwulf were here he would have parried this disclosure with subtle grace. Æthelflaed's keen eyes were again fixed upon him, and he guessed, reading correctly every expression on his face. He felt immediate pressure to at once ask for the hand of Lady Pega.

"I could hardly expect otherwise," he ventured. "Such a young woman will be highly sought after, by many suitors." He had to swallow, discreetly he hoped, in attempt to slow his words. "If I am granted leave to speak to her, I hope she will find Four Stones, and me, worth forswearing all others." He waited just a moment before he went on, addressing her as forthrightly as he knew how. "As I hope you will, Lady."

She smiled then, just briefly, but one not without encouragement.

"Pega knows I would present no man I did not endorse. Yet the decision will be hers."

The Lady of Mercia walked the few steps to the casement and looked out. Then her little girl came running over to her, prompting her to speak again.

"Pega is nearly as dear to me as this one," she admitted, opening her hand to her daughter. "I do not wish to lose her. Yet the King, Raedwulf, the acts of your mother; all recommend you to me. As you yourself do."

She turned to him and ended his suspense, "I will speak to Pega, tell her of you, and your suit. You may speak to her this afternoon, and will be called for. If she consents, she will be yours."

Hrald scarce knew how to respond. "I thank you, my Lady," he managed, as simple as it was sincere.

The Lady had moved on, and now made question. "And for her bride-price?"

"The second wagon – it is filled with spears, knives, and swords."

"You know too well of our needs," she answered.

"Raedwulf counselled me, Lady."

"And did well in doing so. Your weapons are more than welcome."

She gave a slight nod, one of dismissal.

He passed through the hall, scarcely seeing the movement of those within. As soon as he stepped out into the forecourt he spotted Raedwulf, awaiting him at a bench near the well.

"I may speak to her," Hrald said. "This afternoon."

The bailiff could not conceal his pleasure. "Did you speak of terms?"

Hrald realized he had not even inquired what dowry was attached to Lady Pega. He gave a short laugh at his own expense. "I told her the second waggon was full of arms, at your advice, and she answered they were more than welcome. But I asked no question of my own."

Such a direct query was hard to make, without father or uncle at the side of a young man to do the asking. Raedwulf had a near-perfect understanding of what the Lady Pega would have brought to her first marriage, and trusted that this treasure, never delivered, was intact and ear-marked for the Jarl of Four Stones.

"There will be time enough to learn her dowry," the bailiff advised. "Winning her is what matters, as Lady Æthelflaed made it more than clear to me the young lady will have equal say in her choice of husband."

"Equal – or more," Hrald mused aloud. His eyes lifted to the hall he had just quit. "She may be speaking to her now, telling her of me."

And of my failed first marriage, Hrald thought, but did not say.

Hrald went back to the King's dwelling to await his summons. He was alone there, for Raedwulf thought it wise to leave him to his own thoughts, and had besides dealings with Æthelred to address. Hrald drank a cup of ale, but found he could eat almost nothing of the food brought to him at the noon hour. Some time after this a rap sounded upon the door. He fairly leapt to his feet. It was the same serving man who had earlier escorted him, who now led him through the work yard on the side of the hall. Just as in Four Stones, the kitchen yard lay directly behind the hall, and also like Four Stones, a hedge of closely grown trees gave out to an enclosed and private garden.

It was not unlike a smaller version of the gardens at Oundle, with fruiting trees at the back, banks of roses which one might walk between and catch their fragrance, and beds of lavenders, green and purple sage, rosemary, mints, and other herbs chosen for their flavour, scent, or healing properties. It held no vegetables, as Oundle boasted, and in this was closer to his mother's bower garden, a place for pleasure. Tall hedges of boxwood served as screens from one portion of the garden to another; even one as tall as Hrald could not take in the full sweep of it in one glance. The paths were of river gravel, small well-rounded stones, which had been raked to set them in order. This struck Hrald, that here amongst the serving folk was one whose task it was to care even for the gravel pathways of this secluded place.

The first person he saw was not the Lady he sought, but another, for as he ventured deeper into the garden he came upon a young woman, kin or companion perhaps to the Lady he sought, sitting upon a bench. She had a workbasket at her feet, with wool roving and a charged spindle, but she sat composed, hands in her lap, as if awaiting him. She was striking in her own right, with high colouring, a long and straight nose, and peeking out from her head wrap, curling hair the colour of a male blackbird's wing. She stood and gave a quick curtsy, and with a solemn face, inclined her head to her left.

Hrald took the path indicated. The garden was divided into many small defined areas of herbs and flowers, fruiting canes of berry bushes, and trees. He found another bench, upon which sat the Lady Pega. She was garbed in a pale gown, its full skirts draped from her knees and resting upon the tips of her shoes, which were of green leather. Her gaze was lowered, and Hrald saw why, for lying off to one side of her bench was a dog of unusual size.

It was a coursing hound, Hrald knew, with long and straight legs well suited to running down large game. The fine coat was a silvery grey, the short fur tipped near white. It covered a lean body rippling with taut muscles. The muzzle was pointed, the ears small and set well back from dark and liquid eyes, already fastened on him. As soon as he began to approach, both woman and dog stood. The hound made no move towards him, but stood deliberately at her side.

"Lady Pega," he began. "I am Hrald."

She nodded, and smiled.

Lady Æthelflaed had told her nothing of his person; Pega knew the Lady would not wish to colour her own first impression with her opinions of the Jarl. She had shared only the facts of his life deemed relevant to this meeting. Now Pega saw this young Jarl was the man she had noticed sitting next the Bailiff of Defenas last night. She had at that meal no notion who sat with Raedwulf; so many appeared at the hall table for a night or two. But she had indeed marked this tall and lean man, with his dark hair. This then was Hrald of Four Stones, a name Pega had heard for the first time but a short while ago. The Lady, in naming him, had made it clear both she and her father endorsed this match. Then, with a kiss on Pega's brow, Lady Æthelflaed had told her she would not be wed against her wishes.

As Pega rose she fully saw how tall her suitor was. She must lift her chin slightly to look on his face. What met her eyes was a visage far more welcome than she might have hoped. Æthelflaed had told her he had fewer than five-and-twenty years, so she knew he was young. But now, in bright daylight and so near him, his handsomeness surprised her. He was not possessed of male beauty; his looks were too rugged for that, but the strong brow line, with straight and heavy brows, sat above dark blue eyes remarkable for their stillness as they looked back at her. His hair, abundant and nearly reaching his shoulders, was deep brown, yet with some few streaks of a golden shade where the Sun had most touched it. The skin was smooth and still unweathered, and only when he opened his eyes the wider was she aware of the beginnings of a few furrows in his brow. He had, she guessed, earned those. He had already dealt with, and overcome much, to be Jarl of such lands possessed by Four Stones.

Hrald, looking back at her, was aware of the import of this moment, each beholding the other for the first time. No woman had ever attracted him as much as the tall and dark Dagmar. Pega, fair and slight as she was, was utterly different. Yet he could see her loveliness; few men would not.

Her hair was the shade of the lightest honey, with little variation in hue amongst the long and smooth strands cascading to her waist. The tresses flowed from beneath her white head-wrap, one of translucent fineness. Her complexion was ivory, yet warm; a natural pink blush lay upon her round cheeks, and her lips were a deeper shade of that rosy hue. Her gown of soft blue fit her eyes; they were indeed a smokey blue, as the bailiff had named them. They were, Hrald saw, rather deeply set under the light brown brows, and lent a gravity to her expression. This gave a shaded, almost hooded quality to the bright iris; a near gem-like flash when she moved her eyes up to look at him. These grave eyes kept her from common prettiness, and hinted at unusual thoughtfulness.

"I am honoured to meet you," she answered, words entirely unexpected. Her voice was high and sweet, almost musical.

Hrald almost did not know what to do, and so spoke of her dog. It wore a broad and costly collar of blue-dyed leather set with square studs of silver, fitting against the silvery coat.

"That is a fine hound," he said. The beast was almost in front of her. "Also a protector," he observed. "Will he let me nearer?"

"Frost. Sit," she ordered, in a tone only slightly more commanding than her greeting to Hrald. The dog folded its haunches under its lean flanks. Hrald approached the animal, murmuring to it in a low voice. With its white-tipped grey coat, it was well-named, he thought, and striking in every degree. The nose leather and broad paws were black. The long tail gave a thump against the gravel, and the graceful head cocked to one side. He extended his hand, and the dog sniffed him. Hrald wrapped his palm up and over the hard slope of the beast's muzzle, and onto its head and ears, earning a contented chuffing snort from it. The animal leant in against that hand that stroked him, an action not lost on his mistress.

The bench she had risen from was a short one; should they sit down they would be quite close to each other, closer than was proper for those not kin. She seemed to see his uncertainty, and made offer.

"Shall we walk?" she invited.

They stepped off together. The hound needed no word from her, but took up his position at her right, pacing slowly as they walked, turning his head often to look at her, as if awaiting orders.

As Hrald took his first measured steps he was at once struck by the sensation of Pega at his side. Everything in fact seemed heightened in those initial steps together. The crunch of the gravel under his boots sounded impossibly loud. The paths were not broad, and her skirts touched his leg at times as she walked.

Hrald glanced at her as they moved forward. There was a spare and delicate charm about her lissome form. She was no taller, he thought, than his little sister Ealhswith had been at twelve years of age; but the feeling of standing by her side was quite distinct.

Despite her small stature, the Lady Pega looked possessed of a becoming and modest composure, undoubtedly abetted by her upbringing, and the recent years spent in the royal halls of Æthelred and Æthelflaed. He felt his own self-consciousness, and attributed her seeming ease to a long heritage of noble blood.

Hrald recalled the bailiff's description of her, detailing her form and face to him and his mother. He had been truthful in every particular, save one. Raedwulf had said the Lady's skin was unmarked. Yet plain upon her upper lip, off to one side of the nose, sat a small brown mole. It drew attention to the curvature of her deeply bowed upper lip, in a way that made Hrald want to smile. It was almost the lip of a small child, and added a child's grace to her beauty.

As he looked upon her, a word formed in his mind, one which might describe her: fetching. He turned this word over in his mind, aware he must take the lead, and speak.

"Lady Æthelflaed," he began. He said no more, uncertain how best to learn what Pega had been told.

"Yes," she picked up. "She has just told me of your journeying here." After a moment she went on, in seeming reassurance. "The Bailiff of Defenas is a trusted friend."

It was all she said, and perhaps, Hrald considered, all she could say.

"Tell me of your dog," Hrald countered.

She turned her head to the animal with a quick smile, and then back to Hrald. "He was a gift from my father."

"He has unusual devotion."

"My father was good with dogs. Frost was a pup he gave to me after my mother's death, to help keep me company."

She laid her hand upon the sleek head that had turned to look up at her at hearing his name. "Frost and I took to each other from the start, and father and I trained him together. He did most of the work, of course."

The wistful quality of her voice said as much as her words. Deep affection for her lost father was there. She went on, unprompted.

"Not long after Frost was grown, my father was killed, by Haesten's men."

Hrald had been told this by the bailiff, and the flash of anger he had felt again rose. It felt a cut through his own skin. The harm caused by that Dane was the last thing he wished to think or speak of, yet he must acknowledge her own deep loss. He gave utterance to it in one brief line. "A man who has caused too much sorrow."

Pega only nodded. She still had her small hand on the dog's smooth head, and gently pulled one of the folded ears as she spoke again. "Frost is thus memento of both my parents."

Her smile gave inkling of the comfort the dog gave her. The hound served as reminder of beloved lost kin, a reflection hinting at the depth of their daughter's heart.

"He is a worthy animal, in every way," Hrald returned. "He must be a fine coursing hound," he further offered.

"That, I think he would be. I have never taken him out. I scarcely ride," she admitted.

"Would you like to?" he found himself asking. "My hall, Four Stones, has many horses." As soon as these words fell from his mouth he realized he was as good as asking her to wed him, merely by offering her a mount. He blew out a short breath.

Her eyes were cast down for a moment. He was aware of the advantage he held. He had known about the Lady Pega for more than two weeks. If it were true she had just learnt of the reason for his visit, she had been granted no time to absorb it. Yet she answered, simply and unaffectedly.

"The Lady told me somewhat of your hall, though she herself has never visited. Raedwulf of course told her more, including your strength in animals, which she conveyed to me."

"You have spent your life in Mercia," he now said.

"Yes. But I have once travelled to Witanceaster, with Æthelred and Æthelflaed."

"Would it pain you, to live far from your home?" Once again he saw the implication of his words, but they were here together for one reason only, to see if they might suit each other.

Her lips parted, and she almost laughed. "That is a kind question, and one women are rarely asked. I thank you for it." The smile she gave him was earnest. She went on.

"I have been grateful indeed for the care I have received at the hand of Lady Æthelflaed. She has become almost as a second mother to me. Yet I had not long ago made ready to leave, and must remain ready to do so."

She had almost no knowledge of what he had been told of her, and thought she could offer something of her own assessment of herself.

"I was mistress of our hall after my mother's death, and ran it with the help of a steward. He remains there still, with his family, keeping all in good order. Its rents are wholly mine," she ended. "Mealla you have already seen," she went on, lifting her hand in the direction of where that young woman had been stationed. "She is my companion and serving-woman, and travels with me." She paused a further moment, then glanced at the hound, and with a shy smile, back to Hrald. "And Frost you have met."

It sounded a dutiful reporting to her ears, but given her youth, a man would want to know she was not entirely unskilled in the tasks she must take up as Lady of a hall.

She could think of little more she must add. Æthelflaed had told her that if she accepted Hrald, she need not bring a priest; Four Stones had one, and the family thereof was devout. She had added that Hrald's mother was well-regarded by the King, and a great benefactress to a nearby Abbey.

Hrald's response was prompted by Pega's openness in speaking of the duties she would assume if they wed.

"My mother is not old, but she has run Four Stones for many years. She will help you." He paused here, considering the tender youthfulness of this maid before him. He overcame his hesitancy to speak for another, and found himself saying the next. "And I know she will like you."

The awkwardness of this shared discourse could not hide Hrald's pleasure in Pega's words, and in her manner. Yet there was something he must broach. He wanted to address it now, so he could lay that ghost to rest.

"Perhaps Lady Æthelflaed told you: I have been wed. It did not end happily."

"Indeed," came her soft answer. "And I am sorry for that grief." She lowered her eyes to the gravel path they walked.

Having spoken of this, Hrald did not know how to best continue. He could not ask a woman he had just met to never deceive him; nor, for the same reason of their scant acquaintanceship, could he seek assurance she would want only him. She had been wed herself, however briefly, and he knew little of this. He searched for the right words, and as none were forthcoming, groped forward as best he could.

"If we wed," he put forth, "I would like to know that . . ."

She could guess his concern, and gave voice to it now. They stopped, and she looked at him. "That you would not be visited by the same sorrow."

There was both decision, and true gentleness in her tone. Her words, as softly spoken as they were, had been driven home. Though she had begun to avert her gaze to give him privacy, she still glimpsed the hurt which now glinted in his eyes. His first marriage had been a love match, she felt sure.

Another bench lay ahead, one no larger than that she had earlier quitted. Still, she went to it and sat down. Her hound sat at her free side, and then stretched forward upon the gravel path, long legs extended in front.

Pega smoothed her skirts with her hands, then with a nod of her head, bid Hrald to sit next her. She folded her hands in her lap and spoke.

"I was wed as well, to a man I had seen once, at a crowded feast in this hall. King Ælfred was in attendance. Lord Beorhtwulf smiled at me, but never did we speak, and never did I feel the touch of his hand." She paused a moment, as if in remembrance of that repast. "He was older, but not ill-favoured.

"Some days after the King had left with Beorhtwulf, a courier arrived from Ælfred with message for both Lady Æthelflaed and me. The messenger told us the King proposed the union; he asked it of us. The Lady thought on it, then looked at me. 'What say you,' she asked. 'As my father thinks it a good match.'

"I could say nothing but, 'Then I have faith in this.' In answer she kissed me, and sent message back with the rider, who was before us the entire time.

"Then we found Lord Beorhtwulf could not come to Weogornaceastre; he could not return. A sword was used in his place, and I laid my hand upon its hilt before the priest, and made my vows.

"He was due to come for me in less than a month. He did not live that long. The wedding was recognized in law, though no bridal-goods had been yet exchanged. As a sign of his goodness he had made over to me certain lands in Kent, perhaps intended for my morgen-gyfu, which he told his priest should be mine regardless of the outcome of the battle he rode to."

Hrald reflected on this report. The dead Beorhtwulf had indeed been a good man, but then, the King would not have marked him out to receive Pega's hand unless this had been so.

She paused. "He was one I hoped I could feel affection for. I was not granted the chance to find out." She drew a breath. "Nor was he," she added solemnly.

Her tone was lower, but warmer, with her next words. She was not smiling, and seemed instead to be risking some great truth to share.

"There is no prior claim on my heart, this I promise you." She glanced down to where she held her hands, then looked up at him from under still lowered lashes. "And I am a woman formed for one man, and one man only."

Hrald did not know if any colour had flooded his face, but he felt warmth and a kind of pressure in his head. He could ask her now, he was certain of it.

"You are pleasing to me, Lady," he began. "More pleasing than I could have hoped."

Now the tint of rose came more strongly into her own face, the pale pink flush of her cheeks spreading, but she lifted her light eyes to his.

He drew breath and made request. "May I take your hand?"

She lifted her right hand to him and murmured assent. "I offer it, freely."

She placed her hand in his open palm, a hand delicate and soft in his own, large and hardened by riding and fighting. The contrast was great, and one he liked. He looked at that small hand, and covered it with his other.

"Would you wed me, Lady Pega? Fate, and God, took our spouses from us. Perhaps we can find with each other that which was deprived us."

Her smile was grave, but warm. "Dame Fortune has not favoured us in our first matches," she agreed. "She has, I think, amends to make."

She had not quite answered him, and spent a moment looking up into his face. He was so big, and a warrior of repute, despite his youth. A maid her size felt even smaller next him, and she could well imagine fearing him.

Her eyes shifted a moment to her hound. Frost was big, but not fearsome, only protective. This young Jarl had been endorsed by Ælfred and approved by Lady Æthelflaed, whom she knew loved her. And Hrald's looks – the narrow but manly face, dark hair, and deep blue eyes – were pleasing to her, she could fully admit this.

As she paused the hound lifted his head and swung it around to her. Seeing all was well, he lowered it again, to rest between his front paws. It prompted her to answer.

"Frost likes you," she offered. A smile grew on those lips he had admired. "I like you, too.

"I will wed you, Jarl Hrald."

Chapter the Ninth

TO WIN A BRIDE

PEGA led Hrald to the day chamber of Lady Æthelflaed. That Lady had asked that if they accepted the other, they should appear before her together, so she might know at once.

Her answering smile was followed by a kiss for Pega, and surprising words. "My father arrives tomorrow, a visit he had planned to make to us. But it will give enough time to create wedding and bridal feast, on the overmorrow," she decided. "Bishop Edbert will bless your union."

The overmorrow, thought Hrald; the day after tomorrow. It was all to be accomplished with near-breathtaking speed. Hrald knew it might be so, but still found himself blinking as he considered it.

With Dagmar he had many days in which to get to know her, to walk and ride with her, to feel himself in her presence, and to imagine their life together. They had shared the touch of their hands, tentative kisses, and then once, in the treasure room, those of true passion. All this had happened before they had gone to Oundle and were wed. With Pega there would be none of this. They had not shared a single kiss. He would marry her in but two days, and that night take her to bed.

Lady Æthelflaed now spoke to them of that very night. The smile briefly lighting her countenance had passed, and her tone was formal, almost clipped. "I offer you my bower house, to live in until your departure," she said. "It is on the other side of the garden you walked," she added for Hrald's sake. "The King will use his dwelling here; the bailiff and his other men will stay with him."

She went on, eyes trained on Hrald. "When the King arrives, you may display the contents of your second waggon." The corners of her mouth began to bow into a smile, and her voice showed it. "We cannot deny my father this pleasure, of witnessing it." Her gaze shifted to her ward, then back to Hrald. "And you shall view the Lady Pega's dowry."

She turned to Pega. "We have much to prepare," she cautioned, but her tone was mild. Her next words were those of dismissal, for Hrald. "My Jarl. Until tonight, at table."

He could not so much as extend his hand to his betrothed. He nodded at them both, and left.

Raedwulf greeted his news with a deep yet quiet pleasure. It was no small service that the bailiff had wrought a union which had so much to benefit two Kingdoms, and serve to fortify their sole ally in that fragmented third Kingdom of Anglia. There was also Raedwulf's private satisfaction, of leading a young man he liked as well as Hrald to an auspicious match. And in the deepest chamber of his desires, the union brought renewed hope of his own, concerning Ælfwyn of Cirenceaster.

That night at table Jarl and bailiff again sat to Lord Æthelred's right. Pega was there, in her accustomed spot to Lady Æthelflaed's left, and they were able to glance at the other; nothing more.

The next morning at Sabbath Mass the impending bridal was announced by a priest. It occasioned a murmur of surprise, which Hrald shared, as he had not expected this. Yet those men near him, Raedwulf foremost, grinned at him. Pega was there, standing at the side of the Lady Æthelflaed by the Mary altar, but he could not see her face. He wondered if she had again flushed to hear her name called aloud, and linked with his.

Ælfred arrived later that day, and was met with all ceremony. As it was the Sabbath, the unveiling of the bride-price was put off until next morning, the day Hrald and Pega would wed. There must be a welcome feast tonight, but any within the inner precincts of the burh knew that the preparations for the bridal feast took precedence. Carts and waggons rattling in from the granaries and the banks of the River Severn made crowded the already teeming roads leading to the hall and its kitchen yards.

At the welcome feast Ælfred sat in a special high-backed carved chair, carried forth for him from one of the rooms behind the table. It was placed between those of his daughter and son-in-law, a symbolic and fitting placement for their kin and over-King. Raedwulf had before greeted Ælfred, and now, before the meal commenced, brought Hrald to him.

"Whether feasting hall or at that rough table at Saltfleet, we are well met," the King told Hrald. Tired as he looked, the King's eyes still crinkled in pleasure. "You have won a bride any King might covet." He looked now to the Lady of the Mercians. "Greater than that, you have won my daughter's approval, something even more rare."

Æthelflaed gave a short laugh at this, a sound Hrald had already learnt seldom issued from that Lady's throat.

There was great reassurance in the King's words, and though the bride-price Hrald carried with him had yet to be accepted, he thought so circumspect a man would never utter such without just cause.

Sabbath as it was, the evening's entertainment was of subdued nature. Lord and Lady kept a scop who travelled with them from hall to hall, one skilled in the plucking of the harp and relating of heroic ventures. But tonight, after the food had been cleared away, it was one of the priests who rose to address those assembled. Such often recounted the great stories of the Good Book, hoping not only to provide diversion, but to inspire. This cleric was a young man, strong voiced and confident in his skill. All attended on his words. The story, though well-known, was rife with danger, and set in a time of desperate battle. It was also perhaps uniquely suited to celebrate the distaff side, and thus apt for the gathering. Hrald listened, ale-cup in hand, as the priest spoke of a besieged people, and the stern and unbending foe assailing them. The priest had not yet mentioned the heroine's name when Hrald knew the tale for what it was, the story of a daring young woman. He found his eyes fastened on the priest's face, until the name dropped from his lips. Judith.

Hrald lowered his head, his eyes finding the bottom of his silver cup. As he began to close those eyes, he thought he glimpsed the dark blue-grey eyes of Ashild looking back at him.

The tale of courage overcoming oppression was well-known, and loaded with significance for all. But none within that hall, not even Raedwulf, could know how Judith's story had been applied to his lost sister. Was Hrald meant to somehow represent a benign Holofernes in this telling, and Pega, in accepting him, to signify a truce that ended not in destruction for one of them, but peace, for both? He was layering too much meaning into the story, he knew. He blinked at his own thoughts. It mattered not how deeply it affected him, he must listen without reaction. He forced his eyes up, first to the teller of the tale, and then, far more welcome, down the table to Pega. She sat, rapt it seemed, but when she glimpsed Hrald looking upon her, gave to him a smile so unaffected and sincere that she banished all unwelcome intrusions from his mind.

Here is my future, he thought. Throughout Judith's tale, and then the rousing story of the brass horns which summoned the fall of Jericho, he allowed his eyes to return to her.

That night Hrald again slept in that hall set aside for the monarch. Now it was full of his bodyguard. There was an inner room, in which the King, his bailiff, and two others of his guard slept. As he lay in his alcove awaiting sleep, Hrald's thoughts travelled far from the curtained confines of the bed.

The extended period of celibacy Hrald had known had not been easy. Young as he was, the urgings of his body were hard to ignore. He could have found amongst the village women of Four Stones willing partners to pleasure him. Much kept him from doing so. These were the expectations of his mother, and Wilgot, not to mention Burginde, privy to his sole transgression. A further bar was his fear of getting a child on a village girl, and the implications for his own lawful offspring. The greatest curb of all was his own proclivity. Now, faced with the prospect of a wife of such grace and sweetness as young

Pega, he could not but help imagine the act of love with her, an imagining that, lying there, made his body respond in tingling anticipation. On the morrow he would wed, and was become eager indeed for that hour when he would be alone with his bride. He had been chosen for this role, honour enough considering those who had interest in her as peace-weaver; but deeper than this was a sense of exultant triumph in winning her. The bar had been high-set; he had cleared it, and had carried off the prize of Pega's hand. All here seemed to wish their union well. He wanted joy on his wedding night. He had never glimpsed Lady Æthelflaed's bower, but began to imagine entering it now.

It was when he pictured their first night in the treasure room of Four Stones, with Pega awaiting him in his broad bed, that images of Dagmar flooded in. He squeezed his eyes closed, forcing them away.

In the morning there was no public display of the bride-price Hrald had brought. The waggon, its tarpaulins still tightly laced shut, was pushed into a large barn, and save Jari, only those directly concerned with its contents were present. These were Hrald, the King, Raedwulf, and the Lord and Lady of Mercia. The latter pair would receive the treasure, and then, the bailiff had told Hrald, would make offer of its choicest parts to Ælfred. Lady Pega, the young woman for whom all the contents of that heavy waggon were being exchanged, was not there to witness. Few brides did; it was unseemly to gaze upon such goods, and not unheard of that disputes and wrangling took place at this near-last moment of maidenhood. For his part, Hrald was glad she was not there, and was spared the crassness of being confronted with those weapons he had been asked to buy her hand with. Yet to underscore his role as Jarl he today wore full weaponry, both knife at his right hip and sword at his left.

Raedwulf took charge, unlacing the thick leathern thongs sealing the tarpaulin at the waggon's back. Jari and two of the King's body-guard pulled forward the chests. The barn doors were open, admitting the strong morning light, and an oil cresset secured in a bronze hanger was at the ready for closer inspection.

Hrald, standing by, fought back his concerns. He had scoured the treasure room, the armoury of Turcesig as well, for fine weaponry, but had no idea then that his offerings would be revealed before Ælfred himself. This was a match desired by both sides, but Hrald knew that if the family of the bride was not content with the bride-price, bargaining would ensue. He still had no idea what Pega's dowry contained, but Raedwulf's remembered words, "She will bring you gold," was assurance that his steel would be well met.

Hrald had loaded the waggon with the advice of both Asberg and Jari, with things of lesser value being presented first, and thus loaded last. The bailiff, standing within the waggon with Jari and the two thegns, was responsible for lifting the covers of chests, and prising the top from casks. Hrald remained on the planked floor of the barn, ready to describe the contents of each.

Spears in two bundles formed the first part of the treasure, with a broad swath of laced cowhide circling each bundle. The spear shafts had been grown from the coppiced ash trees of the forests of Turcesig, and each selected by Asberg. Their iron points had been hammered out by the weapon-smiths of both that fortress and Four Stones, and were of formidable length and sharpness.

"Three score finished spears," Hrald told those before him, as Jari and the thegns rotated the bundles on the waggon bed so they could be more fully seen. The whiteness of the unmarred ash made strong contrast with the black iron of the oiled heads. Jari lifted the lid of a wooden chest, holding shorter spear heads, ready to be fitted to throwing spears. "A further score of points, from my own store," said Hrald.

Two stout chests, leather covered, strapped with iron, were now heaved forward.

"Two chests of knives, with scabbards, fifty weapons in total," Hrald went on. The top of the nearest was opened, and Raedwulf pushed aside the protective sheep fleece. He drew out two of the blades and held them aloft as representative of their fellows. Now the second, nearly identical chest. "Nearly a score of seaxes." The bailiff's hand sought under the sheep skin and displayed one of these emblematic weapons of the Saxons. Hrald allowed his eyes to meet those of Raedwulf for this. It was both a meaningful and fraught relinquishment of fine steel. These angle-bladed knives were in effect being returned, for they had once been strapped on the bodies of Saxon warriors. Hrald thought he saw approval in the bailiff's steady gaze back at him.

Next came a small fitted box, as long as a man's forearm, fairly broad, but not deep. Raedwulf untied the thong holding the two pieces together, and tipped the lower portion forward so all could see. Within sat a pair of silver-chased stirrups, remarkable to look upon.

After this was a far deeper box. Raedwulf lifted the lid, and as his hands vanished within a jingling could be heard, suggestive of further horse fittings. It was not. He lifted out a rolled goat hide, then pulled from it a ring-shirt.

"Three ring-shirts, newly made," Hrald noted. The silence that had been held throughout this displaying of the bride-price was now broken by sudden inhalations of breath, and more than one appreciative murmur. Jari pulled the two others out, unfurling their weight, each in turn, and holding them up in his strong grasp. They were long enough to reach well below the hip, with sleeves extending to the wrist. The costly ring-tunics made great impress, which only grew when Hrald directed Raedwulf to an even deeper box. The bailiff lifted out a steel helmet, again unblemished, and shining even in the sheltered light of the barn entryway. It had cheek and nose guards, and a crest of steel running from brow to nape, suggestive of the bristled spine of a boar. "Three helmets," was all Hrald said of these. Their worth was such that no other words were needed.

"The casks now," Hrald instructed. There were two of them, of the kind used to store rainwater, but so heavily reinforced with strapping that only iron could be within. Jari claimed the first, clasping the cask by the top, and tipped it towards himself. With the help of a thegn he spun it slowly to the edge of the waggon. The bailiff slid his knife under the iron-banded wooden lid and forced it off.

"Forty swords from the armoury of Guthrum at Turcesig, and from my own treasure room," Hrald announced. He looked to Raedwulf. "There is one with a hood of blue," he told him. The bailiff pulled it forth. It had a small sack of bright fabric marking its hilt. He passed it, sack intact, to Hrald, who turned to Æthelred.

"It is the finest of them, my Lord," he said, and drawing off the sack, he handed it to him.

Hrald had personal acquaintance with this weapon. It was that wielded by Thorfast at their duel. Hrald's father had claimed it from that bloodied patch of ground by the Place of Offering, and walked with it in his hand at his son's side back to the hall. The sword had sat, sequestered from his other weapons, a long time in Hrald's keeping. He had no desire to use it; Thorfast had tried to kill him with it. Nor could Hrald imagine setting it aside for Siggerith, the little daughter Thorfast left behind. Yet the weapon had both high intrinsic and symbolic value. It had been Styrbjörn, Thorfast's second in command at Turcesig, who had told Hrald what he himself was about to share. But for these first few moments he kept silence, as Lord Æthelred held the weapon up in his fist, turning the blade in the shaft of clear morning light falling through the barn doorway.

They looked upon a sword of unusual length, as many Danes preferred; and pattern-welded, the steel blade rippling blue with countless waving lines from the many thin bars of iron it had been forged from. Silver wire had been hammered above and below the leather-wrapped grip, and the pommel and guards had deep channels, into which that metal also coiled.

Now Hrald spoke.

"It was once carried by Horick, King of Dane-mark."

Æthelred, eyes bright, accepted weapon and origin with a nod, then turned with it to his father-in-law. "My Lord," he said in turn, ceding it at once to the King.

"I thank you," Ælfred said to both men, then spent a significant moment with his eyes upon the blade. The sword of Horick was then set aside; perhaps not the last, Hrald imagined, of what he was presenting which might be then offered to the King.

The Jarl of Four Stones turned to a few items of luxury.

"There are now things for the hall," he said. The first was a paired gift, also taken from the store of Turcesig. A wooden box decorated with flowing borders of painted scrollwork revealed a tall silver beaker, such as used for the watering of strong wine. With it was a squat jug of silver to hold water. There was in the rounded sides of the jug an immediate sense of the jovial, as if the plump thing was pleased with itself for its part in well-earned conviviality.

"From Frankland," Hrald explained. "The beaker is marked within by lines. One pours in wine, and with the jug adds water to the desired strength." Wine was costly, and all could see that such added show in its measuring and serving amplified its importance.

Last to be displayed was housed in a square and flat box of wood. The object itself was slipped within a linen bag, which Jari drew off. He moved to the edge of the waggon, and lifted that inside over his head, outside the confines of the tarpaulin. It was a round plate, large enough to serve as salver for two, of silver so pure that when held aloft it looked a small Moon.

Throughout this presentation there was little reaction on the faces of those to whom the items were displayed. The Lady Æthelflaed kept her countenance as tranquil as that of the men surrounding her, though Hrald had glanced her way more than once, looking for sign of approval. This was but the first part of the exchange; Hrald must now view the bridal-goods the Lady Pega would bring with her. If both sides were satisfied, the agreement was made.

They left the barn under the watch of Jari and Ælfred's thegns, and proceeded across the stable yard to the hall. It was, in the fine weather, nearly deserted, but a few women stood weaving at tall looms against a side wall. The party progressed to the high table, and from thence to the door through which Hrald had passed for his private interview with Lady Æthelflaed. She lifted the key from the cluster of those at her waist, and they entered. Within stood two of Æthelred's body-guard, unmoving, one each on either side of the door. Though the ante-chamber was windowless, beeswax tapers flared upon the table. It had been empty save for those tapers when Hrald had first entered, and had placed the bolt of silk there.

Now it was crowded with items of glistening gold and shimmering silver. This, and much more of Lady Pega's dowry was revealed to him. Chests upon the floor stood open, inviting the gaze to fall upon the gleaming objects within. Coins, cups, and bowls of silver proclaimed their worth, and a casket filled with brightly coloured gemstones seemed to wink at those eyes now being filled by such spectacle of wealth. Hrald found himself holding his breath in sudden astonishment, aware that few walked the rounds of Midgard who had seen such wonders. No dragon, when they yet lived, had ever guarded so much in his lair, he thought.

He trained his eyes first upon the table. This was no ordinary treasure, as the bailiff had promised. It was not only the abundance of precious metal, but how it had been fashioned. Dominating the table top was a large bronze urn, dark green, wide mouthed and shapely. It could be lifted by a bail of heavy twisted metal, which looped into the rings on either side of the urn, and whose fastening ends formed the heads of snakes. It was of style and use totally unknown to Hrald, but served as remarkable anchor to all else spread before it. Spoons of silver, and some of gold, had been laid out before the urn, their shallow bowls glinting in the candle-light. An array of things which might be table ornaments, or objects meant as votary offerings, marched at the edge of the table. Some were figures of animals, great cats and horses and bulls, completely wrought in gold, upon whose backs small forms of men or boys were standing, or in the case of the bulls, shown springing from their horns. His eyes widened; he had not seen such work before.

"From the treasure vaults of Rome," the Lady told him. "They once ruled all the Earth. These things were brought here hundreds of years ago, and came at last into the family of Pega."

Hrald felt the urge to say something in acknowledgment of these unparalleled riches. He had presented the bride-price first, as he had been asked; and it was now up to him to state whether he found the dowry acceptable. He had not imagined so much precious metal, and must in truth admit Pega's dowry was of far greater value than he had reckoned. He did not know what, if anything, had been held back, to be offered only if needed; but suddenly the cold steel which made up the bulk of his offer seemed crude indeed, and possibly wanting. They too could ask for more weaponry, and he had nothing with him in reserve. He would have to send to Four Stones. But the speed with which the Lady of Mercia wished to accomplish this union gave him heart.

He turned to her, aware as never before of the power she wielded. Pega's hand, and this vast treasure, was hers to give.

"I am greatly pleased by the Lady Pega," he told her. "And pleased indeed by her dower."

It was his signal of acceptance; Lady Æthelflaed must meet, or reject it. The final words to formalize the agreement were left to her. She looked at him a long moment before speaking.

"Then I grant you her hand, Jarl Hrald."

Before he could speak she turned to a side table. A piece of linen was there, covering some unknown item, and she drew it off. It was a circle of rigid gold rod, with two large round terminal ends of the pure stuff, encrusted with tiny beads of gold.

Æthelflaed put the fingers of either hand on these knobs of gold, and they unlatched, in some hidden way. She lifted it up and carried it to Hrald, and made gesture that she would place it around his neck. He bowed his head that she might do so, and she refastened the latch. The knobs of gold sat upon his chest, just below the collarbone.

"I am courier, only," she told him, her lips forming a smile. "This was Swithwulf's, and has been in Pega's family many generations. It is not my gift, but hers. She wanted you to wear it today, and I expect, at all other high feasts in your future together."

He had never seen any ornament of gold as large. His hand went to it, fingering the fine beads of costly ore that covered the end spheres.

"Bishop Edbert has been to Rome, and seen such there in the treasuries," the Lady went on. "It is called in the tongue of the Caesars a torc, and was worn by the great war-chiefs of those they conquered, and adorned their idols, as well." She considered a moment, and added in a soft voice. "It is older than Rome itself."

Now it was given to Hrald, and by the young maid he would today wed. He had sudden insight into the depth of her family's ancient history. It was Pega's fore-fathers who had five hundred years ago conquered Weogornaceastre from the men of the Caesars. They had won a storied wealth, spanning back from time out of mind. These things must have been brought from Rome at the point of its greatest glory and power, by the war-chiefs who had built the massive stone walls encircling this burh.

Hrald returned to the King's dwelling to ready himself for his wedding. Raedwulf walked with him, the older man praising him for his coolness and measured responses. Hrald still wore the immense torc about his neck; carrying it in his hand would seem to slight so grand a gift. Yet he was conscious of all eyes upon him, only heightening his awareness of what he was about to undertake.

He removed the torc, his fingers finding the concealed latch which held the two orbs of gold closed. The neck ring could not be quickly set aside; he must hold the bright thing in his hands, studying it, and thinking on those men who had before worn it, and of she who had given it. Then he splashed his face with water, and drew on his new tunic of deep brown. It was that he had worn when he had met Pega, and he wished to appear before her in the clothes she had accepted him in.

He placed the torc back on, as tribute to his bride and her kin. One other item he added to his dress. He had with him his father's golden cuff, and he pressed it over his right wrist. He had brought it for two reasons. The first, to add it, if need be, to Pega's bride-price, and if not needed for that, to wear at these nuptials. He was thus wearing immense treasure in gold, at neck and wrist.

The Sun had passed its highest point and was arcing westward when he heard the chiming of the bells. They were of the near cathedral of St Peter and St Paul, where a stone tower housed three bright-voiced bronze bells. They rang out in happy confusion, their higher and lower tones far more festive than the single tolling of a solitary bell, as Hrald was used to.

He found Jari, and all of his men, awaiting him in the forecourt. Their grins made it clear all knew of the outcome, and as he greeted Jari he was told that the bailiff had alerted them to Hrald's success. Jari was dressed in his finest tunic and leggings, with the still red-tinged hair more carefully combed than was his wont. He fell in next to Hrald, and with his men behind them all made their way down the stone road to the cathedral. Plenty of curious town folk were massed there, alerted by the ringing bells of some special occasion, and these waited outside the closed door of the sanctuary. More joined them, those who were passing by on foot or trundling wains and stopped to see what gathering this was. They made way for Hrald, and he took up position before the oaken planks of the door, Jari at his side, his warriors off to his left. They stood under a fine Summer sky of blue, dotted with fleecy clouds, the air Sun-warmed, and with a slight breeze blowing.

The buzzing of the crowd did not drown out the pounding of Hrald's heart, and it was some relief to see the royal party appear, walking with measured step to meet him. Lady Pega walked at the heart of them, between the Lord and Lady of Mercia. King Ælfred was at his daughter's left. Raedwulf had resumed his place at the side of the King, and despite the practised gravity of his countenance, allowed himself a brief smile for the young Jarl. Trailing behind Pega was Mealla, gowned in deep red, a shade that made her black curls all the more arresting.

As they neared Hrald had a few moments to merely watch. He had not seen Pega all day, and not been alone in her company since their first meeting. She wore a gown of delicate hue, a shade close to that of her pale yellow hair. Her head-wrap provided great contrast, for it was a veil of some filmy stuff of deep blue, which gained in depth of colour where it gathered in folds about her face. What adorned that veil was unlike any ornament Hrald had seen.

Circling her brow was a filet of gold, so broad as to be nearly a crown. It was not a plain band, nor of woven or plaited golden wire, but instead made of pieced open work of leafy golden foliage, set with yellow, rose, and green gems springing forth like fruit where a cluster of golden leaves had been hammered. Around her neck hung a chain of gold affixed to a sparkling rose-hued gem, caught and held in a frame of gold. The pink stone was the size of a grape, but with the near clarity of glass. She looked a Queen, in every way. Only the gentleness of her manner and the modest averting of her eyes could give lie to this claim.

As Hrald was looking upon her, Pega kept her gaze demurely down, aware that the eyes of all were upon her. Bishop Edbert now appeared, resplendent in a green chasuble, silver-tipped crosier in hand, to stand at Lord Æthelred's side. He was come to bear witness, as all did; and, as legate of the Church, to bless, as only he could.

Pega took the few steps needed, from the protection of those who accompanied her, to the side of the man awaiting her. Hrald smiled upon her, and she made him glad by smiling back. He lifted his hand, which she took, and together they turned to face the assembled, her hand in his own.

It was these joined hands, and their shared vows, formed by the couple themselves, which made the hand-fast. Hrald would speak first. There were several whose names he wished to voice aloud, and he had given thought to what he would say. He took one long look at the maid at his side, and began.

"I, Hrald, Jarl of Four Stones, son of Sidroc, also Jarl, and Ælfwyn of Cirenceaster, take you Lady Pega to wife. With the offering of my hand I give my oath to uphold the Peace made by Guthrum and by Ælfred, King of Wessex, and affirmed by my father Sidroc. Before the King, and Edbert, Bishop, Lord Æthelred and Lady Æthelflaed and all before us I make my vow, to honour your body with my own."

Pega's vow was even more impressive. Just as Hrald's had been, it must be more than private promise. Their union was an act of statecraft, and need reflect the gravity of the expectations both bore. In a tone clear and strong, she gave solemn voice.

"I, Pega, daughter of Swithwulf and Ebbe, granddaughter of Swithwine, great-granddaughter of Wulfsten, great-grand niece to Offa, King of Mercia, builder of the Great Dyke, do before the eyes of God, of my King and my Bishop and of those who have offered succour and protection to me, take you Hrald, Jarl of Four Stones in East Anglia, as my wedded husband. I vow to be helpmeet in every dealing towards peace, and to raise our children in the path of the One True God. I wed you willingly, and with an open heart."

They held silence for a moment. Edbert lifted his hand in the air and intoned his blessing. A cheer arose. Hrald was aware of the broad door being opened behind them. He wanted to hold on to this moment, and to this maid's vow to him. Her words were as impressive as her lineage, and did honour to she who uttered them, and her illustrious kin. But it was not only the mention of her ancestors that struck Hrald, but also of descendants she hoped to bear with him. She was one link in the chain of life, and in her naming of coming offspring, she hoped to be a strong one, carrying forward the line. Yet it was her last few words which touched him most.

He gave the hand he held a squeeze, then relinquished it; no display of Earthly affection could follow them within. They would separate within for the Mass, Hrald to stand with the other men to the right of the altar, Pega with the women on the left.

It was during Mass that Hrald became acutely aware of the absence of his female kin. It was not only the delight he knew his mother and little sister would be taking in event and ceremony, but the fact that his older sister had not lived to welcome Pega.

This feeling was overtaken by another when, following the Mass, the bridal couple was led by Edbert to the vestry. There they signed their names before the King and the Lord and Lady of Mercia in not only the cathedral register, but a separate document meant for Witanceaster. There were two copies of a third document to sign as well; detailed inventories of bride-price and dowry, to serve as records for heirs, and in the unhappy event the union was sundered. These four documents Pega signed with a firm and clear hand, using the same expression of august rank she had spoken aloud: Pega, daughter of Swithwulf and Ebbe, granddaughter of Swithwine, great-granddaughter of Wulfsten, great-grand niece to Offa, King of Mercia.

Looking on this, and at her able facility with quill and ink, the memory surfaced of signing the parchment Abbess Sigewif had presented to him at Oundle. He had signed that first document just as he had signed this second: Hrald of Four Stones. Dagmar had then inscribed her own name, but hesitated long enough so that a drop of ink fell from the tip of the quill, forming a blot.

Before they reached the hall Pega was spirited from Hrald's side by Mealla. The two women went with Lady Æthelflaed towards the garden in which Hrald had met his bride. He knew the bower house given them was just beyond, and watched the pale yellow of Pega's gown retreat from view as she passed beyond the garden hedge.

Ale awaited him, and all others who now entered the hall. Serving men darted amongst the assembled, carrying jugs to fill the cups set upon a trestle as they filed in, and all raised a first swallow to their lips. Hrald stood flanked by Æthelred and Jari, his men behind him, with Ælfred and Raedwulf facing him, and the combined body-guards of King and Lord backing them. Cheers were offered up, raucous jests as well, as they awaited the women of the hall. Jari for one was ready to enjoy the occasion to the utmost. Relieved of his duties for the remainder of the day, he had a cup in each hand, the claw-like right grasping the bronze vessel as tightly as his left. The meal would be early today, to give a better start to the entertainments befitting a wedding of such import.

By and by the ladies of the hall, the wives and daughters of thegns first, began to join their menfolk. All had attired themselves in as festive arrayment as they owned, and hung with silver and with touches of gold as they were, filled the place with bright flashes of colour and the shimmering glint of metal. The men too were bedecked, and all who owned them sported a store of precious ore at wrist and neck. Ælfred wore a tunic of light blue, upon which ran broad trim of golden thread, and about his neck a chain of gold.

As the assembled were beginning to take their places at the tables, awaiting the arrival of Lady Æthelflaed and the Lady Pega, the King summoned Hrald to his side. Ælfred, Raedwulf next him, was standing behind the high table, not far from where they would soon sit.

Hrald approached and dipped his head, and Ælfred, gold cup in hand, nodded.

"No human effort can restore your sister to your hall," the King began. "May the hand of Pega return a degree of felicity, and even joy to its walls."

It was a measured speech. The King was not suggesting Pega was in any way reparation for Ashild's death at the hand of a man of Wessex, and Hrald did not wish to think of his marriage like this. It was nonetheless a powerful reminder of the new linkage between himself and the King. And Hrald, having seen the dowry Pega was carrying with her, could imagine what sacrifice it was to see it pass out of Mercia and into his keeping. Pega was to have been wed to Ælfred's kinsman in Kent, keeping her vast treasure close to the royal family. Instead the King was letting it go to Anglia, another land, and one with no ruler.

Hrald uttered his thanks, then found himself speaking of the gift Ælfred had sent to Oundle in Ashild's memory.

"The ivory casket you sent to Oundle," he began. "The nugget of gold within – Abbess Sigewif showed it to me. As benefaction to Oundle it will enable its continuance for many years. As tribute to my sister it will never be forgotten, by either the Abbess, me, or my mother."

The eyes of monarch and Jarl met. Ælfred raised his cup in wordless acknowledgment.

The Lady of Mercia now appeared, Lady Pega just after her, and red-clad Mealla following in their wake. A cheer went up at this appearance of the bride, one that brought a deep flush of colour to Pega's face. She smiled though, as she lifted her skirts to make her way through the throng.

This night Pega was placed directly to the left of Lady Æthelflaed, and Hrald next his bride, to her left. The bridal pair were thus flanked by the Lady of Mercia and Bishop Edbert, an honour underscoring Pega's importance, and the role Lady and Bishop had played in her newly wed estate.

The feast began as it ever did, with the ceremony of the Lady of the hall pouring out drink for those at the high table. Hrald watched as the silver beaker and jug he had presented her with were carried forth, and all watched Æthelflaed add water to the beaker. When she lifted her head she saw Hrald's eyes upon her, and his smile, which she returned. She had made use of his gift at once, and at his bridal feast.

It was Mercian wine they drank, pressed from the plump white grapes, milky-skinned, that grew in such abundance along the forest margins. That for Pega was poured into her own cup, one Hrald recalled Raedwulf mentioning for its odd beauty. Hrald saw at once it must be part of the ancient treasure from Rome. It was not only of gold, but was stemless, and flared from bottom to top. It was not large; indeed it seemed forged for one as small as she. She smiled at him as her fingers closed about it in a gesture both familiar and graceful. All raised their cups, and loud were the cries of blessing and ribald wishes for a fruitful union from those before them. A grinning Hrald and Pega then lifted their own cups, each to the other, and drank.

The food came, carried in by those serving men and women who had lined up with platters of small loaves, bowls of browis, and salvers ready laid with those dishes the cooks had laboured over the two days past. In almost profligate show that the cattle of Mercia had been spared the murrain visited upon them in other parts, two animals had been slaughtered for this feast. No part of either was wasted. A savoury broth was boiled from the bones, and that flesh still clinging to them. It gave richness to the browis, enlivened with rounds of young carrots and leeks. Thick cuts from flank and haunch had been tenderized in verjuice for the high table, and fried on fat-rich iron griddles. A sauce made of boiled strawberries was served over this, adding a touch of sweetness to the strong savour of the flesh. The cattle plague had abated in Wessex with the coming of warm weather, but even the King had not dined on so much meat as was now set before him.

The young geese were still too small to be of use as provender, but capons fattened quickly, and their succulent meat was minced with ground chestnuts and cooked egg yolks and then baked in deep pans, slices of which, dressed with a sauce of parsley and mint, adorned every salver. The River Severn was running to the brim with fish, and these featured in abundance in the making of fish pies encased in rich butter pastry, and the serving up of platters of delicate smoked eels.

Custard tarts, the milk soaked in elderflowers before baking, were served last. Upon their white faces had been sprinkled rose petals of pink and red, making fine contrast.

All this the new couple partook of, their first meal as man and wife. To eat from the same salver – as those who were wed did – they must not only sit together, but quite close. Hrald had not so much as kissed this girl. Now they were sitting side by side, their thighs touching.

When the last of the food was cleared away, jugglers in their rag-tag tunics hung with tiny bells tumbled out, tossing copper rings and leathern balls up over their heads, while others rapped upon a drum, played a reed flute, and a third chimed cymbals of brass. This was followed by the calling out of riddles by one of the men, each of which had at least two answers, one bawdy and the other polite. Throughout all, cups had been filled and refilled, at the high table with watered wine, in the rest of the hall strong ale, and now mead was brought out for all. Soon dice and counters would appear, and those whose purses felt a surfeit of silver would risk some upon their play.

Before this Lady Æthelflaed turned to Pega and spoke in her ear. The Lady began to rise, prompting Pega to lean close to Hrald.

"Mealla will come for you," she told him, her voice just heard above the noise of the hall. She rose and left before he could answer, but the colour upon her cheek said much.

The gaming began, and men and women moved from trestle to trestle to play or watch. Hrald did not, but remained at the table with the King, Æthelred, and Raedwulf. When Mealla appeared at his side he stood at once, giving his thanks to host and monarch, and then, with no little warmth in his own face, made his way from the crowded hall, which erupted in cheers at seeing him rise.

Outside the evening air met him with welcome coolness. Bishop Edbert, who had earlier excused himself, was just outside, and Hrald surprised to see him. The grey-haired prelate greeted him cordially, and fell in next him.

Both made their way through the yard and then bower garden, following Mealla through the ever-deepening dusk to the bower house where Pega awaited.

Some bower houses were round; this was square, built of timber, with a pitched roof. A guard stood outside the door, and knocked once upon it. The door was opened for them from within. The Bishop crossed the threshold, followed by the newly-wed Jarl. Hrald was forced to stop, so full was the scene before him.

The single room was almost brilliantly illuminated with tapers, and looked crowded with people. A table and two chairs stood against one wall, the trestle-top holding an array of flaming candles in footed bronze holders. A flagon of ale or wine was also upon the table, as were two cups, Pega's own, and one of silver similar to that he had drunk from at table. Two more tapers were set upon a washstand, flanking the basin set there. He saw a chest or two upon the floor, his own packs as well. A curtained alcove lay against another wall, but the bower house was dominated by its bed. It was not of any great breadth, but Hrald was relieved to see its length. The four corner posts rose as high as his head, stout wooden posts crowned with the carved heads of grimacing men. His bride awaited him in that bed, with Lady Æthelflaed and two serving women standing by the foot of it. A third serving woman remained by the door. Mealla, coming in last, went at once to join Lady Æthelflaed. The hound Frost was also within, standing at alert by the bedside, and cocked his head and looked at the two men who now entered. Pega was sitting up against a pile of pillows and cushions, bare-shouldered, the sheet pulled up under her arms. The lovely yellow hair, freed from any veil, draped across her shrouded bosom.

The contrast between the first bridal night Hrald had known and this was great. His first wife had been the daughter of a dead King, yet was destitute, and he had learnt, nearly friendless. Now he was in another country, Mercia, and had wed a woman who was as close to being a Princess of that land as one could be, without being daughter of a King. Pega's importance to Mercia, to Wessex, to the Holy Church, was again being demonstrated here, before him. He found himself drawing a deep breath. Many depended on this being a successful match.

Hrald had gone to stand by the bed; with the Bishop in attendance there would be a blessing, he knew. He did not know if he should take Pega's hand, and one glance down at her told him she might lose control of the sheet covering her bare breast if he did. So he stood next to her, and turned as best he could towards her and also Edbert. The Bishop began intoning a prayer in the tongue of Rome. He ended by raising his hands, to bless both of the bridal pair in turn.

A silence fell. Pega had her eyes cast devoutly downward, in deference to the Bishop, and the moment. Hrald was not unaware of what might be running through her thoughts. There she sat, her shoulders exposed, patently naked under the slight covering she held to her, before a high Churchman and the stranger she had wed. She looked to Hrald's eyes impossibly young and brave.

Lady Æthelflaed broke the stillness by moving briskly to her. She bent low and kissed her former ward upon her brow. She looked then at Hrald, a pointed look, but one which made the firm repose of her lips lift into a semblance of a smile. A moment later, those not the wedding couple left. Mealla was the last, remaining to impart a final kiss upon Pega. As the companion turned away from the bed, Hrald saw her own cheek was nearly as red as her gown. The black-haired one was no coarsened serving woman, worldly-wise and full of vulgar japes, but likely maid herself, despite the almost haughty pride with which she carried herself.

The door closed behind them. Hrald went and shot the iron bar across it.

Frost had stayed standing and at full attention, his eyes on his mistress in the bed. The house was strange to the beast, and the assemblage of so many persons, some of them scarcely known to his sensitive nose, must have taxed his understanding. Hrald himself did not feel completely comfortable, with the large dark eyes of the hound upon him. He wanted to reassure the animal, yet a twitch of the hound's lean shoulders told Hrald the dog was wary.

From his position at the door he addressed his bride, and not her dog. "Frost . . ." he began his question.

Pega's answer was soft and low. "He will only be alarmed if he thinks I am frightened," she told him.

It struck him. She was a maid and must be frightened. She had wed a man she had spoken to once, and this was her bridal night. He was about to speak of this when she gave a hushed command to her dog.

"Frost. Lie," she told him. The dog's whip-like tail gave a swish, and he swung his head about. He walked to the near corner, where a sheepskin was spread upon the floor planks. Having gained it, he turned twice, and folded his long legs beneath him, ready soon to sleep.

It gave Hrald time to consider. The room was glowing with burning tapers, all wafting a sweet smell of beeswax, but far too bright. His first act was to snuff out half of them. In those few moments the bower house was transformed from near glaring day to welcome dusk. After he had done this, he turned to see Pega, a smile if not upon her lips, then in her eyes. A chair was near, at the small table. He lifted the golden torc from round his neck, and pulled off his cuff of gold. He began to remove his clothing, knife belt first, and hung it on the chair back. As soon as his hands went to the buckle, Pega closed her eyes. They were not tightly shut; she let the lids merely fall, but it was enough to convey her modesty, and the strangeness of what was about to happen. He removed the rest of his clothing and went to her.

He could not help but think of his wedding night with Dagmar, as she lay there in bed and he pulled the covers back to gaze upon her naked form. This was nothing he thought he could do now with Pega, to expose her in that way. He lifted the sheet and light blanket just enough that he might enter. Her hair was spilling over her breast, but he caught a glimpse of one pink nipple, and a flash of the bare skin of her waist, and gentle curve of her hip. He moved his arm about her, to pull her closer.

She was trembling; he felt that. He began by giving her a kiss.

No man had ever kissed her save her father, who oftentimes kissed her brow. Her mother did the same, and kissed her cheek as well. She and Mealla kissed, often, upon the cheek. But now this man she had accepted as husband had placed his lips upon hers. He kissed her once, then again. The nearness of him, the largeness of his face and person, the sense that when he kissed her she held her breath; it was close to smothering. He kissed her a third time, the mouth more insistent. She did not know how to return such, and feared being unseemly. He swept her hair away from her face and chest, lifting her slightly so he might free her of it. The ease with which he did so served as reminder of his strength. He began kissing her brow, and followed with a series of light kisses along the side of her face to below her ear. She felt his hand upon her waist, then running the short distance up to find her breast. It made her gasp, and for a moment he pulled his mouth from her as if in surprise.

He had cupped his hand over her breast, and now moved his mouth to her chin, her throat, and down to the nipple he had been caressing. A shudder ran through her body, one she could not control, and it shamed her. It felt a mix of fear and of sensations subtle and new, something she could not describe as it swept, with warmth like a flushed cheek, over her body.

Hrald pulled her closer to him, his naked body pressing against her own. His mouth had left her breast, and was now kissing her lips. He needed nothing more to excite him, yet he felt her body give a start when the flesh on her belly came into contact with his readiness. She did not resist any of his caresses, but held herself so tightly, as if clenched in fright. He moved his hand down between their bodies, over her belly, to gently brush over the soft curls beneath it. He placed his hand between her thighs, not to force them apart, merely to caress the inside of that tender flesh.

He was not sure what to do. Delaying the act seemed no answer; in the morning they would be faced by well-wishers, and if they were not truly man and wife some might guess. And he wanted to allow himself to feel this attraction to her; his body was aroused and he wished to respond to his desire. Her eyes were still closed, and he wondered if she was, in this, distancing herself from him, and how he was touching her.

"You said you come with an open heart," he whispered to her. "I thank you for that." This made her open her eyes. A small and courageous smile lifted the corners of her lips. He kissed that sweet mouth once more and then went on. "I will be as gentle as I can."

Pega lifted her arms and put them around his neck. A tear glistened in each of her eyes; she felt it, but she smiled at him for his kindness.

Hrald turned his head for a moment, to where her dog lay in the corner of the room. The animal lifted his head in response. Hrald had almost to laugh at himself, checking the hound as he had, to see if it was alarmed.

Hrald lifted himself over her. She let her hands slip to his shoulders, holding that firm flesh there. Her left hand touched the scar upon his shoulder, and she moved it down to settle on the muscle beneath this. She lay looking up at him in the flickering golden light of the tapers.

He kept silence, and did not repeat the words he had uttered on his first bridal night. The act alone was enough, and they were already wed in the eyes of the Church, and in law. And he would not conjure any memory of that earlier bridal or wife, if he could help it.

Pega kept her eyes open, and upon Hrald; she felt less frightened that way, for he watched her face with a look of concern upon his own. He took care in holding his weight from her, as if she could be crushed beneath him. The sensation of parting her thighs, of the intense pressure of his body against hers, and then yes, of pain, sharp and hot, surprised her. Mealla was yet a maid, and knew only the prattle of the kitchen-women, and Lady Æthelflaed had told her nothing, despite being wed and a mother too. Yet these things would be hard to convey, Pega knew. She was only glad she was looking up at Hrald as he moved above her, for she saw his own eyes close, and felt the near-violent spasm of the climax of his pleasure, when his closed eyes squeezed tightly shut. He took a deep breath, and opened his eyes, and then lowered himself to kiss her mouth.

He rolled away from her, slowly, and she too drew breath. She felt torn, ripped, between her legs, and she closed them, wondering if she was bleeding as Mealla said she might. But she was not unhappy. He had turned on one shoulder, and now scooped her to his chest, so that her naked body was pressed upon his. One of his hands held her about her back, the other stroked her long hair. She reached her hand to his shoulder as she lay there, and clung to him.

"It will be better," he breathed in her ear.

She tightened her hand, and made her words resolute. "It was not bad," she breathed back, "It was just . . . not knowing . . ."

Hrald could feel the shake of her head, as if to deny the pain she had felt. He ran his fingers over her hair, smoothing it as it spilled across her narrow waist. "Yes," he said. "And now you do."

He heard the click of her hound's nails on the floor boards. Frost came and stood at the bed side, as if seeking assurance all was well. Pega put her hand out upon the animal's fine muzzle, and then pulled one of the ears as he was used to. Hrald too reached to the beast and gave him a solid pat, more than a little grateful not to have earned a growl. Sensing all was well, the hound gave a wide yawn, stretched out its two long front legs, and went back to the sheepskin in the corner.

In a while Hrald rose, naked, and went to the table. He poured some of the contents of the flagon into the two cups, and brought them to his new wife. She was sitting up, and again had pulled the linen sheet up around her. She kept her eyes lowered as he approached. He sat on the edge of the bed and watched her small hand wrap around her golden cup. He toasted her, wordlessly, and she lifted her cup in turn to him. It held mead, its potent sweetness fitting for a bridal night, and Hrald was glad for it. He drank his up. She took a mouthful of her own, and then, seeing his cup empty, passed the rest to him. He smiled and lifted the costly thing to his lips, draining it. He kissed her again, lightly, and on the mouth.

"All that you own is rare and precious," he told her.

Rare and precious, Pega silently repeated. One day I hope you shall say that of me, was her next thought.

Chapter the Tenth

THIS, AND NOTHING ELSE

HRALD fell into sleep quickly after the mead, to awaken later in the dark. Pega was asleep at his side, the small hands curled up close to her face, as a little child slept. The remaining tapers were but guttering stubs. It was their uncertain and wavering light that awakened him, perhaps, and he would make sure they burnt themselves out before he closed his eyes again. He could see the glint of gold upon the small table: Pega's cup, the terminal spheres of the torc, the curve of his father's hammered cuff. Pega too looked gold, pale gold, the purest kind, that without copper added to give it redness.

When he again awoke in the morning light, Pega still drowsed. Light was streaming in a narrow channel through the crack in the shutters covering the casement. After such a feast, few would be up and about early. Hrald pulled on his leggings, and went to one of his packs to retrieve his gift for her. The noise he made doing so awakened her, and she reached for her shift, there ready at the bottom of the bed. When his back was towards her she slipped from the bed and quickly pulled it on. He turned to her as the hem dropped down to her ankles. He smiled at her, and shy as she was, she smiled back.

He had a small lidded box in his hand, the size of his palm. She sat down on the bed, and he stood before her.

"My morgen-gyfu," he told her. He did not pass the box into her keeping, but instead went on, and named her formally in his granting. "I give you, Pega of Mercia, a tract of virgin forest extending between Four Stones and the Abbey of Oundle. It is nearly eight leagues in breadth, and twelve in length. I will have the deed drawn up as soon as we arrive. You will see one end of the forest when we visit the Abbey."

Her hands rose in pleasure at this gift of land. As of yet the tract, though great in size, was wholly untenanted, and he must tell her so; she could expect no rents from it.

"As Oundle grows, it could be of service to the Abbey." He paused, letting her consider what she might do with it.

"Also," he went on, "the hardwoods there are good for charcoal-making, to further fatten your purse." He could not help smiling as he said this; she was already so rich. "It is yours to do with as you like."

She smiled. "As Oundle grows," she pondered aloud.

"It will grow, if peace could return, and stay," he answered. "Abbess Sigewif is honoured for her rule. More monks and sisters would come and join her, but the village to support them all remains small. It needs defending now, and will need that until a greater peace descends upon the land."

She nodded her head. "I understand. I am happy with this gift. It gives my mind room to range. I will think of how best to use it."

He now turned to what he held in his hands.

"I have also – this."

He passed the box to her, and she set it in her lap and lifted off the lid. Within was a small bag of red fabric, silk she saw, from the sheen of it, and her fingertips told her this as well. It presaged an exceptional gift within. She set the box aside and tipped the bag out onto her lap. A long mass of fine silver chain flowed out. She could see it had two clasps, and at least four ends, and many places in which the tiny links were joined to other strands of silver.

She looked, all unknowing, up at Hrald's face.

"It is perhaps a piece of jewelry, for the entire body," he explained. He took two ends and held them up. "The neck, here – and this portion, I think, goes about the waist. My Uncle Asberg commands the garrison of Turcesig, and he found it in the treasury there."

As he held it up, she saw how it fell, a shimmering web of interlocked chains.

"I am not certain from whence it came," he went on. "Wilgot our priest thinks from far to the east, along the trackways by which silk comes."

"Thus the bag," she noted.

She stood up, and took the ends of the necklace portion in her hands.

"I will fasten it for you," he told her. She nodded, and he did so. The piece, now anchored at her neck, dropped down her body. He gestured her to turn, so he might work the clasp at her waist. He did so, and the silver strands fanned out across her torso over her linen shift, a webbing of glimmering silver.

She looked down at herself. "It is a wonder, and unlike anything else," she said.

"I am glad you like it. It is delicate, and suits you."

It laid gently over her breast, then draped down across her front. The small links flowed over every curve of her lissome form, and even though she wore her shift, seemed to call attention to what lay underneath. A looping section in the centre dropped even lower than the waist, to the hipline, as if calling attention to where her legs met. Seeing it now on a woman's form, he could not help but think of it worn alone, with nothing beneath it.

"I would like to see you wearing this, and nothing else," he thought aloud.

Her cheek turned crimson, so great was her discomfiture. It spread to Hrald. He had blurted out this wish. Pega's modesty and demure demeanour had been one of the things the bailiff had spoken highly of. Hrald turned his own face slightly away, as if to give Pega relief from his gaze. But he was glad her hands did not rise to her neck, to unfasten the piece.

Not long after came a tapping at the door. Frost went to it at once, with a soft whine of inquiry.

"It will be Mealla," Pega guessed.

Hrald pulled on his tunic, shot back the bar, and opened the door. The black-haired girl was there, with a serving woman. Mealla had a hefty jug of water from which steam still issued with which to wash, and the serving woman, a copper tray. Upon this were oaten cakes, broth of some kind, soft cheeses, and dried fruits. This all was carried in and placed upon the table. Her hands free, Mealla went to Pega and embraced her. The bride still wore the silver webbing, and Mealla stepped back and exclaimed over it.

"Part of my morgen-gyfu," Pega told her. Her face was still slightly flushed.

Mealla looked at Hrald, and cocked her head at him. "A handsome gift, my Lord," she said. "My Jarl, I should say," she corrected herself.

These were some of the few words Hrald had heard Mealla speak, and she did so in an accent distinct from Pega's. She showed no hesitation to address him directly.

He nodded at her, wondering about her place in his young bride's life.

Mealla's eyebrows lifted slightly as she looked back at him. "You are trying to guess who I am," she answered, in a light, and almost teasing tone. "I am no country-woman of this place, nor none other than my own island. I am of Dubh Linn, in Éireann."

She bobbed her head as if that were enough. "Here is water for washing, and cold in the jug." She opened her hand to a large jug on the floor by the washstand. "Please to sit and eat, and after, Jarl Hrald, the King requests your presence in his hall."

This first breaking of the fast as man and wife was spent largely in silence. Mealla had taken Frost out with her, and the room seemed empty indeed when they left. Pega felt shy, and unable to say much. Hrald could not help wondering why Ælfred wished to see him, or what the King might ask of him. After they had eaten Hrald finished his dressing, adding only his knife as weapon. He left behind the gold he had worn yesterday, and after a warm word to his bride, stepped out into the morning. Mealla was sitting on a bench not far away, and rose at once to join her mistress. Hrald walked through the empty garden and passed the kitchen yard. Folk who saw him nodded their heads, some of them grinning as they did so.

Two of the King's body-guard were stationed outside the door of the hall wherein he and Raedwulf had passed their first nights here. One opened the door for him. Ælfred sat at the table within, but any sign of an early meal had been cleared away. Raedwulf stood next the King, bent over some chart or document before them both upon the table. The bailiff straightened up and smiled at Hrald as he approached. The King gestured him nearer.

Ælfred gave a nod, and was more than direct in his question. "Jarl Hrald. The marriage has been celebrated?"

Hrald took a breath. "It has."

"Good," said the King, sparing Hrald from any further comment.

"I again congratulate you," Ælfred added. "My daughter would like you to remain a week. But she is aware of your need to return, and I think she would consent to fewer days, if your Lady-wife Pega agrees. Æthelflaed's concern is for her health and happiness."

Hrald gave thought. It was Lady Æthelflaed who had given him Pega, and he was correspondingly in her debt. Yet he wished to make a start for Lindisse as soon as was possible.

"My Lord, I arrived not knowing how long I might remain. Thanks to your daughter – and you – I leave with Pega as my wife. I am eager, yes, to bring her to Four Stones. And I know my mother will welcome her. If Lady Æthelflaed accepts Pega's decision, we will leave as soon as she feels ready."

These words seemed to content the King. And the young Jarl did honour to his new wife by leaving the decision in Pega's hands.

The next few days were ones of acquaintanceship for the couple. They began in near seclusion, walking alone in the bower garden, accompanied only by Frost. These were hours unmarked by any outside cares; the confines of the garden itself seemed to shelter their thoughts. Pega knew its paths and contents well, and took relish in pointing out special trees, flowers she favoured, and herbs, the scent or flavour of which she was partial to. Several times Hrald almost told her of his mother's garden, but decided each time to save it as a surprise for their arrival, when she might discover it herself, and with the Lady of Four Stones who had created it.

They went further afield next day, leaving the inner palisade. Pega wished to stop at the cathedral to offer a prayer, and Hrald watched as she went to the statue of St Mary and blest herself and lowered her head. In a burh as large as this, the edifice was rarely empty, and others stood in silent prayer as well, including a large number of nuns attached to the nearby convent. It made the act of prayer both communal, and private, Hrald thought. When they left the church Pega made bold to place her hand on Hrald's arm. "I will make a gift here," she told him, "to honour our union. And –" she hesitated.

"And?" he asked, quietly.

"To ask for coming children."

He placed his hand over hers, and gave it a squeeze.

They went on, up and down the stone-paved streets and smaller lanes laid with wooden boards, past stalls and workshops, and many houses. She knew the burhs of

Gleaweceaster and Weogornaceastre well; she had spent much time within both, as well as at her parents' hall, between them.

Hrald was more than impressed at the trading opportunities the River Severn provided. Trade goods flowed up and down on flat-bottomed barge boats, bushels of grain, casks of charcoal from the Forest of Dean, and more costly objects such as bundled fleeces or woven goods of wool and linen. The snaking river also opened the burh to attack by water-borne raiders, and the number of sentries and ward-towers he counted told him they were prepared at all times for Haesten or any other raiding party to make its appearance in their dragon-ships.

The hound Frost joined them on nearly all these forays, frisking ahead at times if distracted by some water fowl at the river margin, but more often pacing alongside his mistress. It made Hrald speak of their coming journey, which they were due to start on in two days.

"Will Frost be content to ride in a waggon with you?" he asked Pega. "He cannot walk the whole distance. It will take us six days to reach Four Stones."

"When we travelled to Witanceaster he oftentimes sat with me in the waggon," she told him. She remembered that trip. "And he is a good watch dog. The men on guard at night liked him for that."

As if he knew he was being spoken of, the dog crossed over behind Pega, and came up and pressed his nose into Hrald's hand. It made Hrald laugh, and give the animal a good scratch behind the ear.

Though the road home was always shorter, the week's rest Hrald's men and horses had enjoyed was needed for such a journey. His second waggon, having been emptied of the weaponry with which he had secured Pega's hand, was being filled with her bridal goods. This comprised not only her treasure in silver and gold, but a store of bed linens, pillows, blankets, and bronze and copper goods such as basins, pans, braziers, cressets, rush-light and taper holders. Two looms were being packed, and wound on wooden spools, all manner of coloured thread for fine needlework. A third waggon, gaily caparisoned, was coming, as gift from Lady Æthelflaed, along with the team of horses to pull it. It was smaller than Hrald's supply waggons, and as different in appearance as could be. The tarpaulin spanning its arches had been painted in large pointed lozenges of red, blue, and yellow. Into its wooden bed were being loaded chests of Pega's clothing, a chest housing Mealla's clothing and goods, and all the kit the young women would need to make of the waggon a comfortable home while on the road. Cowhides lined the floor, over which sheepskins had been laid. Featherbeds and pillows had been rolled tight, ready to be unfurled and fluffed for sleep. There was even a small lantern, inside which a taper might safely burn, as the thinly shaved slices of horn enclosing the flame cut off errant draughts.

Hrald had forty men with him, a huge number, yet he suddenly wished he could set out with at least another score. Sixty men would not be too many to protect both treasure and bride. He shared this with no one but Jari, who grunted his agreement in response. Still, supplying provisions for a large troop of men on the road was ever a difficulty, and he had needed sufficient number to remain both at the hall and the valley of horses.

Hrald was still thinking on this when he returned to Pega and Mealla, who were walking together in the bower garden. The two, one so fair as was Pega, the other black-haired, made a striking pair as they turned to him. Mealla was taller than Pega, with a certain wiry quickness to her movements, but nearly as slight as her mistress. Hrald knew nothing of Mealla's parentage, but Pega had told him enough of her own father that he found himself asking the next.

"Your father – did he teach you to handle a knife?"

Pega's lips parted in surprise. She wore a small knife at her waist, nearly all women did. Hers had a grip set with walrus ivory, and she used it at table every day. Her fingers moved to touch the pretty leathern sheath that held it.

Hrald went on. "Our escort is made of most of my best men, but along the road anything can happen. I know you have Frost," he added, with a glance at the great hound, "but have you been taught to defend yourself?" He would not say before her that the first to feel a spear or arrow would be an attacking dog, though he knew it to be true.

Mealla also wore a small knife. She ignored it now, and did not wait for Pega's answering words. Mealla's right hand vanished into a side seam in her skirts, then pulled out a formidable blade concealed there. It was a seax, and of surprising length.

"I have butchered a pig with this," she told Hrald, in a low voice. It may have been a simple admission of fact, but was delivered in a way to suggest it was the least she could do with the blade.

Hrald took her in. "You will be at her side, regardless," he summed.

"That I will," she answered. "We women of Éireann came down from battle-Goddesses. Some of us have not forgotten this."

That night Hrald and Pega were alone in the bower house, sitting at the small table. Before them was the map Raedwulf had drawn for Hrald that he might reach Weogornaceastre. Now they would use it for the trip back to Four Stones. After Hrald had traced the route with his finger, Pega looked up at her husband.

"Tell me of Ashild," she invited. Her voice was soft, and her eyes even softer.

He gave his head a shake, but followed this with a short laugh.

"If I do, I fear you will not like her." His eyes fell again on the parchment marking the home she had loved. "Ashild could be . . . difficult at times, hard to understand. Even for us." He searched for a single word to describe his sister. "She was headstrong."

Pega gave thought. "That is said of a horse which wishes to go its own way," she observed.

"Yes. As did Ashild. She wished to go her own way. She was quick in her mind, and strong in her body. If she determined to do something, she did it, without fail, and accepted the results of her actions as the price she paid."

"She sounds a woman of integrity." This was a thoughtful remark, thoughtfully uttered.

"Yes. I think all would say that of her, after thinking on it.

"Thank you for that," he added.

"She loved Cerd, her little boy," he went on, in low tone. "And he changed her, for the better. She knew it, and would laugh about it."

Pega smiled at this. "As the advent of children generally does, I think. A babe, though a beginning, is an end in itself, taking us out of ourselves, to this new life."

He looked at her, struck at this wisdom.

She saw this, and laughed. "You are only hearing the voice of my parents, coming through my own mouth now," she said in answer. "We were very close."

She went on, "When my mother died, my father told me, 'Hold in your memory, always, those parts of your mother you cherished. Think of all you admired in her. Enumerate them, reflect on them. Make those traits your own. This is the best way to honour our beloved dead.'"

She was quiet, then looked at him and smiled. "And I do the same now, for him."

The morning of departure Pega had a private farewell with Lady Æthelflaed in the hall. Hrald found himself speaking to the bailiff in the stable yard where his men were readying.

Raedwulf was more than candid. "I would I could return with you," he told Hrald. "But the King will be heading back to Witanceaster on the morrow. I will set out with him, then spend a few days at my hall in Defenas. After that I join him there." Raedwulf paused, and said the next with eyes lowered to mask any deeper meaning. "Please to give your mother my warm regards."

Hrald knew his debt to the bailiff was great, and said so. "It was you who thought of me for Pega. It is a match beyond my hopes, and you have my gratitude for it. Also that of my mother," he added.

Raedwulf nodded, unable to comment further on that Lady. But there was another female of Hrald's relation he must mention, moved in part by his memory of speaking of her with Lady Modwynn of Kilton. It might be some time before he was again in the young Jarl's presence, and he would broach the topic now.

"Ealhswith," the bailiff said. His pause alone was meaningful. "There will be men of Wessex eager to wed her. Rich thegns, ealdormen, sons of Lords. And Lords themselves. Do not promise her to any in Anglia without first sending word to Witanceaster. There may be a better offer, in Wessex, or here in Mercia."

That was all he said on the subject, and Hrald took it in. His little sister was possessed of sixteen years, and now the sole daughter of the hall. Great would be her dowry, and great the bride-price he could ask for her.

He nodded his assent. Ashild might have forged a lasting bond between Wessex and Anglia, and had not lived to do so. She may never, in fact, have done so, and Hrald had been forced to accept this. One day soon her younger sister could step into that role – that of peace-weaver between former enemies, now allies.

It seemed that every denizen of the hall gathered there in the forecourt to see them off. Foremost was King Ælfred, flanked by his daughter on one side and Æthelred on the other, with Raedwulf next to Lady Æthelflaed. Bishop Edbert was in attendance, blessing the massed men with the flinging of holy water; he had earlier gone to the bower house and anointed the brows of both Pega and Hrald. All were being sent to the Mercian border with an escort of ten men, and these led the way, followed by ten of Hrald's men, with Hrald and Jari fronting them. After this came the waggon in which Pega and Mealla rode, followed by another ten warriors. The waggon bearing the treasure came next, with its escort of ten, and then the supply waggon, with the remaining ten warriors bringing up the rear. They rolled out of the inner palisade to cheers and not a few tears from the womenfolk waving them off. Wending their way through the burh they attracted much attention, and a swarm of children and attentive onlookers followed them some distance out the palisade gates, from sheer excitement of watching the setting out of such a large and festive party. Frost, roused by so much activity, trotted by the side of Pega's waggon, snapping his fine head in the air to look about him, and uttering yips of joy.

The road demands its own discipline, one in which Hrald's men and the Mercian escort were well-versed. The men riding at the highest pitch of vigilance, up front and in the rear, were rested by changing position with those slotted between waggons. All were watchful, but those tasked with scanning ahead and frequently turning in the saddle to look behind were taxed the more. They stopped near mid-day at a water course that men and beasts might drink. Food was passed, the simplest of repasts, but the best they would enjoy, for loaves fresh that morning from the clay ovens of Weogornaceastre were smeared with butter from its dairy. The pause gave

Pega and Mealla the chance to walk about, and be free from the jostling of the waggon. They had their own food supplies, and their driver lowered a bench for them to sit upon, and with a basket perched between them took their meal in the open air. Hrald did not eat with them. On the road he must maintain the line between commander and husband. His bride and her companion would sleep in the waggon; Hrald camp with his men. At night Pega and Mealla closed up front and rear flaps of their waggon's gaily-painted tarpaulin, lacing it loosely shut for their slumber. Hrald and Jari shared a simple tent nearby, laid with cowhide on the ground. His other men did the same. These took but minutes to pull up, and did much to shelter them from night-falling dew or outright rain.

Pega was not completely denied Hrald's company, nor he, hers. He ofttimes paced his bay next to the waggon, talking with Pega, or at least by his near presence keeping company with her. He found himself more than once looking down at her to think, This is my wife. His thoughts then skipped to how quickly all had happened, and the treasure this girl was bringing him.

The bailiff of Defenas had conjured this match, and Ælfred and his daughter Æthelflaed had given the Lady Pega to Hrald. The King, it seemed to Hrald, endowed him with her treasure, the Lady of Mercia gave the maid herself. He and Four Stones were now linked to Wessex, and to Mercia, in ways unfathomable to him a month ago. What did it truly mean? What expectations were there, beyond that honouring of the old Peace between the Kingdoms he had ever held to? And what was Anglia now, but a shattered land of war-chiefs acting in their own interests? Would there ever be a King in Anglia again? None had risen to claim it. He could not guess what Ælfred might require of him.

Hrald only knew the King was staking much upon this union. He felt the weight of it without fully knowing the responsibilities. Now that he possessed Turcesig he may in fact have more men than any other war-leader in Anglia. No one was certain where Haesten was, and Agmund, Guthrum's son, had taken no real move to control more lands than what he possessed around Headleage, where his father's remains lay. What if Hrald was part of some larger plan of Ælfred's to exert more influence in Anglia, perhaps even to make Hrald King? He recoiled from the idea.

Then he glanced down at Pega, her head lowered, intent on her work of winding skeins of spun yarn into balls. How much had been placed on those slight shoulders, he reminded himself.

The fullest blossoming of Spring was before them, every day showing promise of Summer soon to come. Nearly every tree bore leaf, save for those walnuts they passed which held off from donning their thick dress of green. Wildflowers brightened the meadows they crossed, and dotted the forest margins they followed. Courting birds, and those already nesting, filled the mornings with their determined carolling, and wild bees intent on nectar rose and fell above the red clover blossoms. The soil was still cool, but the breeze was that warm wind of Spring, and few rode with mantles over their shoulders.

Four of their number cooked for all, at two fire-rings. One ring was dedicated to the griddling of crisp flat bread, mixed from chestnut meal, water, salt, and powdered hardwood ash to lift and lighten the dough. The second ring held cauldron and tripod for browis, boiled from spelt kernels and dried peas. As the men ever did upon the road, they gathered growing greens to freshen the pots, cutting cresses, mints, wild green onions, and dock. On their departure they had been given a store of boiled eggs, and these were meted out as a treat. A wooden bowl filled with flaky salt was set upon the cook-table, that all might roll their shelled egg therein.

They met none upon the roads and tracks they took. Any cowherd or goatherd ushering his charges would hide both himself and his animals on hearing the approach of so many riders. The jingling of bridle iron and creaking of the waggons could be heard far enough away to ensure that. But on the day before their arrival at Four Stones they met a troop of warriors, paused at a crossroads. These were upon a slight rise, and were enough in number that they did not turn at once and flee. Hrald did not need a warning whistle from one of his forward riders; he could see them himself.

He raised his hand and gave the signal to halt. All slowed to a stop. Hrald had been riding at the wheel of Pega's waggon, telling her more of Four Stones. Now he looked down at her and nodded. Her face had paled, and one hand had risen near her bosom, a hand which she then lowered as she composed herself. Mealla, who was sitting next her on the waggon board, rose and vanished into the body of the waggon a moment.

Jari moved slowly forward with Hrald. It gave them time to look these riders over. There were no archers amongst them, so they were out of range of a flown arrow. And the men were certainly Danes. They were armed, not fully, but enough to defend themselves, and do damage as they did.

Hrald called out.

"I am Hrald of Four Stones. Who are you?"

A pause was followed by a helmeted man riding forward.

"Hrald. It is Haward." The man in the saddle lifted his hand, as if in greeting.

Haward. Here was Thorfast's brother, who had been conspicuous in keeping out of Hrald's way since the disgrace of Haward's cousin Dagmar.

He was on Hrald's land, but a friend might pass without penalty. Hrald was not certain Haward was a friend.

"Where are you going?" Hrald's demand was that an over-lord might issue to a straying underling. Both question and tone assured the hearer that the truth was expected.

"I head to Geornaham."

Geornaham, thought Hrald. It was the hall from whence Yrling's first bride had hailed; he knew that much. The girl had not lived long, leaving Yrling the richer, and ready to wed Hrald's own mother, Ælfwyn of Cirenceaster. Geornaham was run by a steward, one designated by the dead girl's mother, and was under the protection of Four Stones. Yet other than paying some bushels of grain each year into Hrald's granary, it was free of other tribute to Four Stones.

"Why there?"

Haward, outwardly discomfited by the need to raise his voice to his interlocutor, rode forward and alone, checking with his hand the movement of a man who rode at his side.

He neared Hrald with as close to a smile on his face as he could muster. Jari, on Hrald's left, did not like Haward and made no effort to hide it.

As Haward reined his horse he drew breath. "Hrald," he began. "I head there, as I hear Tilbert's daughter is of marrying age."

Tilbert was the steward of Geornaham. Hrald had to pause. There was nothing to prevent Tilbert from marrying his daughter to any deemed worthy of her. Yet one point remained.

"I would like to have known of this," Hrald told him.

Haward was quick with his answer. "I would have told you. I tried. I went to Four Stones to consult with you. Kjeld told me you were gone."

Kjeld had also told Haward to do nothing until Hrald returned, but this he did not add.

Still, Hrald could see little amiss. And he himself had lately taken a wife. He could see Haward craning his neck towards the waggon which held Hrald's bride. The two young women in their gowns of red and pale blue could not help but catch the eye.

Hrald took pity. "I have myself just wed. Come and meet my wife, Lady Pega of Mercia."

They rode forward together to the bedecked waggon. Pega was smiling as they approached, clearly relieved it was a friend who had arrested their progress. Mealla was not so easily won over. She sat next Pega, her sheathed seax across her lap.

Hrald made the introduction, as brief as was proper. Haward's eye fell upon the string of lustrous pearls about the bride's neck. His cousin owned bronze brooches set each with four pearls; no woman wore a full string of them. This was some manner of Princess Hrald had wed.

After Haward and his men rode off, Pega asked about him.

Hrald's answer was brief. "He was cousin to the woman I wed," he told her, as if Dagmar were now dead.

Chapter the Eleventh

JARL AND WIFE

HRALD had sent a rider ahead that Four Stones might know of their arrival on the morrow. He looked forward to returning home, but gave some thought to the contrast between it and the royal burh of Weogornaceastre. The keep of Four Stones was crude indeed compared to the paved roads, stone walls, and impressive halls of Mercia. He had tried to prepare Pega for this, and could only hope the hall itself would not contrast unfavourably with that in which she had been raised.

As they neared the hall the watch-men rode out to greet them, alerted by the whistled calls of Hrald's return. The troop climbed a rise, following a reddish road of pounded clay. Around a final bend Four Stones appeared, the tall timber palisade fronted by its thriving village. All the folk thereof were abroad, and began to line the road dividing the village in two. The palisade gates were already opened, and even at a distance those approaching could see folk massing there to greet them. Hrald was riding next the waggon, telling Pega who awaited them. His gladness was in his voice as he picked out the figures and named them to her and Mealla.

"The woman in blue is my mother. Burginde is at her side, and the small boy in front of them is Cerd, Ashild's son. The maid with the yellow hair is my little sister, Ealhswith. Behind her is my aunt, Eanflad. Wilgot the priest is there, too," he added, spotting the man in his dark habit. "Standing to one side is Kjeld. I left command of Four Stones in his hands." He looked carefully at two others. "And my Uncle Asberg and his wife Æthelthryth are there, come from Turcesig to meet you." Hrald saw Yrling, hand on the hilt of the knife he had given him, awaiting him as well. "The boy with them is my brother Yrling from Gotland, who I told you of." Hrald noted the boy was unusually tidy. "He has combed his hair," he laughed, "for you."

Ælfwyn, watching the approach, saw the cheery waggon, and the large hound trotting at its wheel. The silver studs on the hound's collar flashed in the Sun; even the bride's dog was richly appointed.

Ælfwyn then had the pleasure of seeing the village folk raise both hands and voices in welcome to the new couple. The contrast between her own arrival as the bride of Yrling could have been no greater. Burginde squeezed her hand in silent acknowledgment of that long-ago day. The Lady of Four Stones blinked away the tears in her eyes, and placed her arm about her daughter. Ealhswith was almost trembling with alertness, eyes trained on the bright waggon.

The troop passed through the gates. Bork was standing with Mul and his sons at the mouth of the stable, all of them ready to take the reins of the lead horses. The boy stepped forward a little towards Hrald; it was his special charge to take the Jarl's mount. Hrald had told

Bork before he left that he went seeking a wife, and now here she was. The boy gave a glance at her. It must be the yellow-haired one, he thought; some kind of beads were hung about her neck. His first wife had made Hrald sad. Bork hoped this one would not need to be sent away.

Hrald dismounted, and gave Bork a smile and nod as he passed him the reins. He turned to help his bride from the waggon board. Kjeld had come up behind him, all grins. He had been watching the approach of the waggon as closely as any. The rider Hrald had sent ahead had told them of the bride, but had made no mention of the Lady's companion. Kjeld was there at the waggon board just after Hrald helped Pega down. He reached up and offered his hand to a young woman with a sharply defined nose and cascade of black curls. She accepted it long enough for him to steady her; then, when Kjeld held on to her hand a moment beyond, pulled it from him.

Hrald led Pega to his mother. His bride curtsied to Ælfwyn, and at once found herself caught up in her arms. What followed was a flurry of embraces, hearty welcomes, and exclamations of joy from all who greeted them. Cerd had bolted forward to Frost, who took a step back, and a moment later was licking the laughing boy's face. Yrling too had come to the big dog, and had put his hands on the animal's back, and was speaking to him, and laughing too at Cerd.

The welcome ale awaited within the hall, and all, hound included, began moving towards its open door. Kjeld remained, quickly choosing a few men who had stayed with him at Four Stones to stand guard before the waggons.

The black-haired girl had not joined her mistress in the hall. The horses which had pulled their waggon were now being unhitched, and she remained by the wheel. Kjeld approached her, but she spoke before he had the chance.

"I will stay with the Lady Pega's things, 'till they be carried in," she announced. Kjeld lifted his hand towards the four men now stationed at this watch. One was standing nearly behind her; the goods were well guarded. The girl lifted her eyes skyward, and did not move.

Kjeld turned and disappeared into the hall. He returned with message of the black-haired maid's own quarters.

"You will sleep up in the weaving room, with the Lady Ælfwyn's sister and daughter," Kjeld told her. "I can take you there now," he offered.

She seemed to consider. He tried to help her decide with his next words.

"Soon we will be carrying in your Lady's things, to the treasure room. You will want to help her there. Best for your things to go up, first."

She pursed her lips, but gave a quick bob of head in agreement. Then she began giving orders.

"That chest there," she told Kjeld, pointing into the depths of the waggon. "Those two bags. And that basket."

The chest was not large, he could see that. He looked again at the black-haired girl. "I will bring it myself," he told her.

Together they moved to the rear of the waggon. Kjeld unlaced the ties holding the flaps together. He pulled the chest to the edge of the waggon bed. One of the men standing guard there made to help him, but Kjeld waved him off. He took up the chest in both arms and said, "Follow me," to its owner.

It was heavier than Kjeld had thought, and he was glad that he could gain first the hall doorway and then the stairs up to the second floor as quickly as he did. The door to the weaving room was cracked open, and he walked within for the first time in his life. He had never been up here before; few men had.

He placed the chest down against the wall which held the windows. She had brought up the basket, but kept it in her grasp.

There were two looms set up against the other wall, one holding an almost completed length of undyed linen, the other wool of mid blue, just begun. A table, two chairs, and a bench stood by one end. Three narrow beds, two of which showed they were slept in by the accumulation of pillows and coverlets, occupied the rest of the room.

Kjeld turned from the chest to see the black-haired maid taking in the room.

"I am Kjeld," he told her.

She gave a bob of her chin. "The Jarl told me," was her laconic reply.

Kjeld paused, waiting for her to tell him her own name. She remained silent, her eyes sweeping the surroundings. She dressed as did Lady Ælfwyn and her daughter, in a long-sleeved gown; the deep red that this maid wore suited her. Her expression was hard for Kjeld to read, but the longer he looked at her the more he wished to look. Her skin was almost milk-white, her height enough to make her stand out. Her form was slender but not without an attractive swelling of bosom and hips. The curling black hair, scarce contained beneath her head-wrap of plain white linen, was uncommon enough that he wished to touch it.

He looked at her so long that she was forced to speak, and did so with no little decision.

"I cannot wed. I am companion to Lady Pega, and must remain dedicated to her."

It was a startling declaration, and one that presumed much on his part, but he would let that pass. Right now he would be as direct as she had been.

"Cannot wed? Or will not wed?" he asked.

"It matters not."

"It does. It might matter a great deal, to me."

Mealla let her lids fall over her eyes. They were, he saw, a kind of tawny brown, with almost a touch of gold in them. She opened them again to study him.

Kjeld's hair was that light brown of a fallen oak leaf. His eyes were between blue and green, and light enough so that one must look twice to see which hue they favoured. The jaw was firm and square, the skin of his cheeks just beginning to weather from Sun and wind. His nose was well-formed, with a natural bump just below the bridge. It ran in Kjeld's family, and in no way marred the balance of his features. It all added up to a face many maids would consider deserving of a second look. There was not beauty about Kjeld, but there was strength there, and a kind of fitness. He had held the keep in the Jarl's absence, and the thick chain of silver about his neck suggested it was not the first time he had been entrusted with an important task. And despite his being a savvy and practised warrior, there was still an openness to the man's countenance, a searching quality. He was looking at her now, intently so.

"You cannot use your service to the Lady as excuse," he told her. "Much the same is true for Hrald and me. I have thrown in my lot here at Four Stones, and been rewarded for it. But I can still wed, and live my life with the woman I want."

"Then you should do so." She smiled as she said this, as if it were a challenge.

"And what if I have just met her?"

Mealla would now be blunt.

"I am the child of rape. Perhaps by your own father. He was a raider, one of you East-men as you call yourselves in Dubh Linn. He killed my mother's husband and took her captive. She escaped, but not until she was got with child – me."

Kjeld felt need to defend himself. "Dubh Linn. Those were North-men; the men of Norway."

This little satisfied Mealla. There was no rancour in her voice, only pride.

"You are all scaff to me. None of you will conquer us in Éireann. The men of Rome never brought us to heel, and you East-men have plundered and raided and made Dubh Linn a centre for the trade goods you have stolen – nothing more."

"I am a Dane. My people hail from Laaland. And I was born here."

She pressed her lips together. "Then seek one like you, born here. And there are plenty of your own kind, to look at it," she snapped back, lifting her hand towards the window and what lay outside it. Indeed, a number of the women of the hall had moved through the stable yard when she was down there.

Kjeld dismissed this. "Yes. But none like you."

"Tsk!"

"Tell me of your name. I have not heard it before. Mealla, your Lady told me." He said the name slowly, trying it out.

"Ha! It means lightning, like what comes out of the sky and strikes you dead."

Kjeld nodded, then showed he could turn her story to his own account. "I have been near enough to lightning so that my hair stood up, and my whole body tingled. Looking at you, I feel the same as that."

She laughed aloud. "Then take care you do not get struck."

After Kjeld had brought up Mealla's goods, she came down with him to the hall. He watched her go to Lady Pega, and vanish with her and the Lady Ælfwyn into the treasure room. Hrald was still holding his silver cup, standing and talking with Asberg and Jari. But he left them to give a word of thanks to Kjeld for how well he had kept the fortress in his absence. Kjeld was glad to be thanked. But he was more interested in asking about Mealla.

"The dark-haired girl – " he began, inclining his head in the slightest tilt to the treasure room door. He stopped at that.

Hrald searched his face. "Oh," he finally said. He could not blame Kjeld for his fast work; Mealla was a fresh face and more than comely. Many of his men would be after her. "I know nothing of her," he must admit. "She told me she is of Dubh Linn."

Kjeld's heaved sigh said much. "She told me a bit more than that. She is not friendly to us." He paused a moment as he considered. "Yet she came here."

"She is in service to my wife; she must do so." Hrald had might as well go on and say it. "But she will have choice in who she weds."

"That is just it," Kjeld answered. "She says she will not wed."

"Ah. A vow to St Mary, perhaps," Hrald ventured, "to remain a maid all her life?"

Kjeld shrugged his shoulders. He did not understand such vows. Every woman should wed, if a good man wanted her.

"I will ask my wife about her. But I think you must act on your own."

Kjeld nodded. He knew black-haired Mealla would.

Within the treasure room Ælfwyn and Burginde were acquainting Pega and Mealla with its contents. The first sound Pega made upon entering was a gasp at the wolf-skin spread adorning the broad bed. She exclaimed over it, and Ælfwyn had the pleasure of telling her its history, and how Burginde had kept its existence a secret until her wedding night. The young woman's gladsome response made Burginde chuff with pleasure.

Pega's personal goods began to be carried in, a train of men, directed by Kjeld, hauling chest after chest of clothing and linens, deep casks of straw-wrapped pottery and glass ware, and countless leathern bags. The looms and sewing goods were carried up to the weaving room, but the greater bulk of what she brought would reside here. The room seemed suddenly too small, and Ælfwyn laughed happily at this fact. Ealhswith had joined them in their labours, and the five women worked side by side, Pega gratefully accepting the suggestions of her mother-in-law and Burginde of which chests might prove most useful where. Mealla was not afraid to pipe up with her own opinion, and when Pega's big copper bathing tub was carried in, was quick to suggest a place by both a wall and upright timber beam, from which a curtain could be easily extended.

Burginde and Mealla had naturally paired up in these tasks. When Burginde had first spotted Pega's companion, she thought, Well and good. This one came with her own woman, and able too the girl looked. Young she was, but so had Burginde herself been once. And Mealla had the kind of brisk efficiency dear to Burginde's heart.

She led Mealla to a large leather-covered chest at the foot of the bed. "Linens and towels here," she said, opening its lid. She let her eyes travel to the many newly arrived chests crowding the room. "Though I daresay you travel with a store of them.'

"That we do," Mealla agreed. "Some woven by Lady Æthelflaed herself. But a large hall can never have too many linens."

This was more than true. Lengths of linen were always needed, to be worked into tunics, shifts, towelling, bandages for wounds, and for those first and last garments of life, swaddling cloths and winding sheets. Mealla let her hand drop to the contents of the chest Burginde had opened for her.

"And these of yours –" Mealla's fingers went to a corner of a linen sheet – "are truly fine."

"Spun for them myself, I did, and woven by the Lady," Burginde answered, with a satisfied cluck. This black-haired girl was as sharp as a rook, and had already risen in the nurse's estimation.

Burginde took time to show Pega where Hrald's own clothing was stored, as now his wife would take charge of its making and mending. Watching them together Ælfwyn could see that Burginde had formed the same opinion of Pega as had she. The bride, despite her youth, had a sweet soberness about her, and a natural warmth towards all at Four Stones which was at once endearing. Pega had taken Ealhswith in her arms upon meeting her, bestowed a kiss, and called her sister. And both Pega and Mealla were by nature dressed in the style of the Saxons, just as the Lady of Four Stones was. Even this pleased Ælfwyn, though she hesitated to admit it to herself. It was a sign of the familiar.

"We will have more shelves built," Ælfwyn promised, looking at the wealth of small caskets of wood, bronze, and even silver Mealla was lifting from the depths of a heavily strapped trunk. They stood arrayed upon the table, hinting at what treasure of metal and gemstones might lie within.

They saw the contents of one sooner than they thought, for as Mealla placed another on the broad table face, she upset a smaller one. The hinged lid opened as it fell backwards, and Ealhswith, nearest to it, was quick enough to catch something shining before it dropped to the floor. She looked into her palm, at a silver pin of a running horse. The girl caught her breath at its loveliness.

"Do you like it?" Pega asked her.

Ealhswith nodded. It made her think of her sister, who so loved horses.

"Please to have it. I want you to."

Ealhswith nodded her head, unable to speak, at this kindness. She took it not so much for her own sake, but for Ashild's, who could not wear it.

The two embraced. Ælfwyn stood looking upon Pega and Ealhswith together, and knew there was but a year or two between them. Soon Ealhswith might be wed, and Ælfwyn only wished she would be welcomed thus in her new hall, and her own sweet nature valued.

"My clothing is here," Pega told them, moving to the largest chest. "Please help me to choose a gown for tonight," she invited her mother-in-law.

Together Pega and Mealla lifted the heavy lid. Just on top was a sack of plain linen. The puzzlement on Pega's face showed she did not expect it there. She pulled the linen free of what it hid. It was a bolt of silk, cobalt blue. She lifted it in her hands.

"How wonderful," she exclaimed. "Mealla and I packed this chest; I had no idea this had been placed here."

"Lady Æthelflaed," guessed Mealla, clearly as surprised as was Pega.

Ælfwyn almost laughed, so great was her delight. She pressed her lips together in her smile. "That is a rich, and loving gift," she said.

"Yes," Pega breathed. "And I give it to you. Please to accept it, Lady Ælfwyn, for the kindness with which you have received me. And also – for the gift of Hrald."

This last brought tears to Ælfwyn's eyes, and she leant forward and kissed Pega on her brow. "I know you shall be a blessing upon this hall," she told her. Her smile deepened as she began to tell of the gift.

"The silk – it was brought to me by Hrald, a gift from Gotland from my dearest friend Ceridwen. It was of such value that I insisted he take it to Lady Æthelflaed as his gift to her. And now she has given it to you, and it returns to Four Stones."

Pega gave a little shriek of happy laughter at the circular route the cloth had taken.

"I am glad I can make sure Ceridwen's gift ends as she intended – worn by you."

Ælfwyn's hands rose to her waist, and the cluster of keys tied there. Tonight would not be a bridal night; she and Burginde would not join Pega in the treasure room to prepare her. She was bride, and Lady of Four Stones, already.

"Here are your keys, Pega. Wear them in good health, and happiness, and for many years to come."

Pega tied them on to her waist sash. Once again Ælfwyn was aware of how much lighter she felt, having passed them to another. She murmured a silent prayer that Pega be the steward Hrald deserved, a prayer she felt little needed, given the girl's affection and thoughtfulness.

"Would you like to walk about now, see the kitchen yard, storehouses, brewing house, and all?" Ælfwyn now invited.

As she finished saying this, a knock was rapped upon the door, and Hrald walked in, leading a train of men carrying goods from the waggon of Pega's bridal treasure. She turned to him, and he saw the keys, already at her lithe waist. Her beaming smile said more than any words could.

Ealhswith had made the circuit of the work and cooking yards with her mother, Burginde, Pega, and Mealla, and had left Pega and her companion to rest in the treasure room. Ealhswith walked with her mother to the bower house. She could not help but wish well to Pega, who had greeted her so warmly, and in fact she still held the silver horse pin in her hand. Yet she was attempting to grasp the new union. She had liked Dagmar, who had been kind to her, spent time in her company, and whom she admired. Then Dagmar was gone. Not only gone, but forgotten, it seemed to Ealhswith. Dagmar's name was never spoken; all acted as if she had never lived with them.

It was an unexplored hurt, and to Ealhswith, largely unexplained as well. She had seen Ashild's anger towards Dagmar on the day of her dismissal, but her sister had said little other than the application of a few muttered epithets. Her mother had only told her that Dagmar had loved another man before she wed Hrald, and that it was best for all she be with that man.

Now Ealhswith felt moved to mention Hrald's discarded wife.

"Dagmar," she began, and then having named her hardly knew how to go on. She and her mother were nearing the bower house door. Ealhswith felt she must not bring this inside with her, and stopped. Indeed, her mother had slowed at the mention of the name.

Ælfwyn searched her daughter's face, and read the uncertainty there.

"Pega will not end as she did," she assured her youngest, taking her hand. Her son had chosen his first wife, selected her for the deep attraction she held for him, and had his heart broken for it. This was different, a measured choice, and Pega seemed more than worthy of it. She must try to convey her own confidence in her.

"Raedwulf is our friend, Ealhswith, he has proven so again and again." She need not say more than this, that the depth of their friendship was beyond the girl's ken. "He would not have proposed a wife for Hrald unless he believed she would be truly fitting in every way. I know you will welcome her in your heart, as she does, you."

As dusk fell it came time to assemble for the welcome feast. There would be no formal unveiling of the dowry before the hall; Hrald had seen and accepted the goods when Lady Æthelflaed presented them, and they were already stowed within the treasure room. Yet it was more than fitting that certain objects adorn the high table, in addition to the bride. With Ælfwyn's help Pega placed items of silver and even gold upon the table. Salvers and bowls of silver gleamed there, and a row of the small golden figures of bulls and horses and cats were lined up at the edge before the places Hrald and Pega would sit. The special chair he had made for Dagmar resided in the priest's house; he had not wished to see it at this table again. Ælfwyn could have brought a chair from the treasure room for Pega. Instead she surrendered her own; she could have the joiner make her another. But the one she had sat in since Hrald's birth was known as that of the Lady of the hall, and now this was Pega.

Hrald appeared wearing the gold torc, and Pega, the same browband of gold and gems which had graced her on her wedding day. She looked Queenly indeed in her browband, and her gown of lilac shade set off her flowing yellow hair, adding warmth to its hue. The keys at her waist were the final touch, telling all the new Lady of Four Stones stood before them. There were claps and cheers, and her round cheeks flushed as she smiled back.

Then Hrald stepped forward, into the better light thrown by the wall torches. His men fell silent, seeing the huge ring of gold about their Jarl's neck. A moment later the hall erupted in whistles and good-natured shouts. All eyes were upon Hrald, more so than ever. He grinned back, but felt, with so much show about him, like a target. Yet the torc was not only part of the dowry, but direct gift from his wife. He need not wear it often, but must do so this night. As they took their seats Jari did not help matters by his whispered crack, that he would never be off duty when Hrald wore it, so coveted was such a piece of gold.

Mealla was sitting at the women's table at Burginde's left, with Ealhswith at Burginde's right. Cerd, on the nurse's lap, at once crawled onto that of Mealla. Nothing daunted, the black-haired girl began tearing bread for the boy, and guiding his hand as he spooned browis into his mouth with her purloined spoon in his little clenched fist. Frost had been wandering the hall, garnering many admiring looks and being fed random bits tossed to his waiting jaws. After having made a round, he came back to his mistress, and lay down behind her, his back against the treasure room wall.

For Hrald, it felt a strange feast. There was the best and clearest ale filling their cups, and mead after that, and the food was of the same high standard the kitchen yard dependably provided at festive events. Yet Hrald wished it were over long before it was. He did not want a re-creation of his wedding night – not here, at Four Stones. He wished it tomorrow already, and their every-day life begun.

As the salvers were being cleared away he leant to Pega and spoke in her ear.

"Let us go in together." There was a slight thrill of urgency in these words, so that Pega read them as half-plea, and half-command.

"The hall will cheer and laugh when we do, but let them," Hrald went on. "It is not our bridal night, after all."

"Yes," she smiled. "It is not our bridal night. We are married folk."

In truth Hrald did not wish to enter the treasure room to find Pega awaiting him there. His memory was still too filled with the image of barring the door and turning to the bed where Dagmar lay.

Chapter the Twelfth

FLIGHT

Lindisse and Dane-mark

DAGMAR had been pulled up on the saddle behind her lover Vigmund by one of his strong arms, pulled up none too gently. He kicked his horse as only one angry with his circumstances does, and the beast snorted and tossed its head in both protest and surprise. The animal had been ridden at some speed to reach Four Stones, and now it and the packhorse tied to its saddle ring would be further pressed. The wide gates of the palisade wall sounded as if they had been snapped shut as soon as the tail of the second beast cleared, so fast was it secured behind them.

The Spring days had only begun to grow longer, and dusk came early, but Vigmund would not make camp until they had passed one of Four Stones' markers, so eager was he to be beyond the reach of the hall. Wet snow was falling, and he built a hasty shelter of a tanned cow hide slung between trees, with a second for ground cloth. They had almost nothing to eat. If his visit to Four Stones had gone as planned, the kitchen yard would have filled his food bags for his return. Bearing a wedding present from Guthrum's widow as he was, Vigmund should have been invited to spend a night there in the hall, feasting with the rest of the warriors, sitting amongst them, while looking at Dagmar seated at the high table. Instead, cast off with nothing but their lives and what he had with him, they shared what little remained, a hardened half loaf of bread. They did so in near silence.

Vigmund had said nothing to her as they rode off. Though she clasped him about his waist and at times laid her cheek against his back as she clung on, he regarded her not. He built a small fire, and when he banked it up in hope of some embers remaining until dawn, turned away from her. She too could scarcely speak; all that had occurred was of moment too great to put into words. She tried to nestle against him, both for warmth and in contrition. The blanket they shared was thin, and Dagmar had nought but her cloak for warmth. Even huddled together she trembled from cold, and something deeper. She could feel the tenseness of his back, a wall of anger against her. At one point in that first night she awakened, shivering, from the cold, and in her misery began to weep. She stifled her sobs, swallowing her tears lest Vigmund awake.

At dawn he turned to her. Their fire was out. The sky was smudged, over-clouded, and the morning air as cold as the night they had passed. Without a word of greeting, and with a face betraying no emotion, he reached under her cloak, pulled up her skirts, and pushed her on her back. He lifted himself between her legs, forcing them open with his knees, and worked the toggles at his waist, freeing himself from the upper portion of his leggings.

He lowered his hips to hers, holding himself up and away from her with his arms.

Love-making it was not, rather an act of pure possession. No beast in rut mounted a female as purposefully yet indifferently. It was worsened by the utter silence of Vigmund. He spoke not a word through the briefness of his taking of her. She reached her arms to him, tried to kiss him, pull him nearer so she might feel some tenderness. He would have none of it. When he pulled away he rolled over, then stood almost at once, leaving her there upon the ground.

Dagmar rose, shaking with cold and sorrow. She stood, disconsolately, looking at Vigmund's back. He began to move off, toward where the horses were hobbled. She felt unclean, her clothes rumpled and increasingly soiled, and she had no way to wash herself. They had nothing to eat, and she would have wept aloud but for her knowledge that she did not deserve the relief of tears.

Vigmund was hurt, hurt and angry, and she was the cause of it. She had wounded his pride as well. Through the months and years of exile he had still loved her, and his sudden reappearance had stunned her both by his living, and his plan to carry her off to Dane-mark. It was like Vigmund, this careful and yet daring plan. She could not tell him now she would have refused him. Once in his arms she had not had the time to give him yet another kiss, one of fare-well, and send him off alone. They had been discovered by Hrald, and Dagmar had been repudiated, there before Vigmund's eyes. A cast off wife was not nearly as exciting as one stolen. She knew this. The hurt to Hrald had been immense, a guilt which hung upon her and would always be hers. But she had compounded the confusion and grief she felt ten-fold by her begging of him, and of the Lady Ælfwyn, to take her back. Hrald had summed it perfectly in his words to Vigmund: Now she has been false to both of us.

Hrald, in surrendering her as he had, made it more than clear: She was not worth fighting over. And Hrald had dismissed Vigmund as unworthy of challenging. It gave her sudden insight into Hrald's character, which had a depth she had not before imagined in a war-chief. Whether it was the Church in him, or the way the Lady of the place had raised him, she felt with sudden and wrenching insight that she would not see his like again.

The day grew worse. When they stopped at mid-day she walked about in the biting cold, mutely gathering any twigs and small branches which looked dry enough to burn, just so they might warm themselves a while. As she was bending over, Vigmund came up behind her. He grasped her round the waist and pushed her to her hands and knees upon the cold soil. Wordlessly he pulled up her mantle and skirts. Still holding her with one hand, she felt his other fumble at the toggles on his leggings, then the press of his hot flesh between her thighs. He entered her in one great stroke, forcing her head almost to the wet ground she knelt upon. He grasped her about her naked hips and again used her in silence, just as a thrall woman would be used by her master. It shocked her, far more than the morning's act had. He had never been rough with her, and this felt a desire to humiliate. She bore it in silent submission, and made no effort after he was done to turn to him and seek comfort or affection. If he need punish her, she must accept it; she was wholly dependent on him now. He could ride away and leave her, and she would quickly die in these wilds if he did. But the fact that their first acts of intimacy after their long parting were those of near violence against her wrung her heart. She had been a maid when she first lay with Vigmund, and passionate though he was, he had not once behaved callously in their coupling, nor mistreated her. If this was to be her life going forward she knew she could not bear it. Yet this second act of dominance seemed to purge the bitterness from him, for when they stopped that night he placed his arm about her in attempt to warm her as they lay together.

He said nothing to her as he did so, but by the light of the fire that still flickered she could see him squeeze his eyes shut with a grimace, as if against the memory of how he had earlier abused her.

"It is you I love, Vigmund," she whispered. She did not want to say more than this; did not want to carry them back to the terrible scene in the treasure room of Four Stones.

It could not help but do so. Vigmund was silent, then gave a low and dismissive snort.

"Such a pure man, your young Jarl. No woman would be good enough, pure enough, for him."

She had closed her own eyes at these words, and lowered her chin to hide her face. Vigmund must abuse Hrald; he had no other way to frame a man who had so easily dismissed him. Her lost husband, almost ten years younger than the man in her arms, had some inner knowledge she felt Vigmund would never possess. She bit her lip, hard enough to hurt. She did not wish to think of Hrald; it was too painful to do so. Vigmund's next words made her lift her eyes to him.

"But you are good enough for me."

His mouth formed a smile, just before his lips met hers.

In the morning it was Vigmund, not Dagmar, who opened the wedding gift he had carried. Two well-wrought stemmed cups of silver lay within the fitted wooden box that housed them. She looked at them with an aching heart, then let her eyes shift to the fire. He handled the cups, almost weighing them in his hands, judging them for their value as precious metal, and seeing them not for what they were, emblem of a married couple, meant for a Jarl and his new wife.

'We will trade them for hack-silver at Ribe," he told her. He did not add that the silver so received would be hers. She was just grateful to be included in his plan. And indeed the cups would not have been with her now, save for his scheme to arrive at Four Stones under the pretense of carrying a gift from Helvi, Guthrum's last wife.

Later that day they found a farm from which to buy food, sheltering at a fire-pit within a house no larger than a hut. The browis and bread Dagmar brought to her lips had never held as much savour. The woman gave them ale as well, flavoured with dried chamomile heads, and its flowery scent carried the comfort of Summer with it. Vigmund drank two large tumblers of the brew, and when Dagmar smiled at his enjoyment he allowed her a smile of his own.

They slept by the banked coals of the fire in that hut, Dagmar thankful for the shelter of a roof over their heads.

They rode off with food bags replenished with grain, and a few shavings of smoked pig. They reached Headleage late the next day, but did not so much as enter its precincts. Vigmund's treasure was secreted where he had lately left it, in a hollow tree in the wood outside the burh. As much as Dagmar would have liked to see Inkera, she could not bear the thought of her half-sister's face when she admitted she had forsaken Hrald and Four Stones. More than this, she had no desire to see her mother Bodil, the cause of so much grief in her life.

His silver recovered, they camped the night in the wood, and in the morning began to make their way to the coast. Their goal was a point near Middeltun, another three days' ride. Vigmund knew a ship owned by Agmund would be making the crossing to Ribe within a fortnight, and there were others of the Danish leaders who sent ships with trade goods, and to ferry their womenfolk or valuable livestock between their homeland and Angle-land. The point of departure was nothing more than a shingle beach, one beyond the scrutiny of Ælfred's men who still sporadically patrolled the coast line. Agmund's ship was a knorr, a broad bottomed cargo ship, and they arrived at the place to find a man with a bull, also awaiting transport. Vigmund meant to bring his horses with him; they were both good animals, and he would not find their like in Dane-mark. It was worth his silver to take them there. When the ship appeared two days later the waiting party had swelled, two men with four rams having joined them. The knorr, which had coasted down from Jorvik, spent a day, filling its water casks from the nearby stream emptying into the Thames, and loading animals and fodder aboard. Prize bull and rams were penned with

Vigmund's mounts just behind the mast. The slack-tide came, that moment when the tide began to turn. Dagmar, watching its receding ripples, felt it one more step on a road of no return.

By the time she stepped on the ship to carry them to Dane-mark, they had been on the road ten days. Her clothing had suffered, and her hair was filthy. She had no warm water with which to wash. The crossing itself was cold, wet, and rough, and she and several of the men aboard were ill and retching. She was crammed into the prow much of the time, and the waves were such that she could not move about without holding the gunwale. The last two days were smoother, and the wind and warming Sun aided them. When they finally arrived at Ribe after five days at sea she was more wretched than she had ever felt, in body and in spirit. The complaining animals were released, and Vigmund led both horses and a numb Dagmar along the trading town's wood planked walks. He stabled the horses that they might be fully fed, and he and Dagmar nearly fell onto benches at a brew-house. He ate heartily, and she enough to revive, both thankful for abundant food after the privations of stale bread and salt fish on the sail.

They next stopped at a public wash-house and each bathed, then put on the cleanest of their soiled clothes. Vigmund walked the trading town, seeking out news, while Dagmar remained at the wash-house and scrubbed nearly all of their clothes. This she did herself, as she used to, back at Headleage when her mother could no longer afford a serving woman; rubbing soft lye soap into stains, soaking the garments in a tub of warm water, beating them with a wooden paddle against the sides of the tub, rinsing and wringing them out. Dried by the wash-house fires they took on the smell of smoke, but though wrinkled and slightly damp, were at last clean.

They slept that night at the guarded camp-ground of Ribe. In the morning after they had broken their fast with bread and butter they collected the horses and made their start. Their goal was the garrison of one Heligo, made King of Dane-mark by his own bloody hand the year prior. It lay at Viborg, a three day ride north over pine barrens. These passed without incident, save for the weariness of the road. Viborg was one of many fortresses in Dane-mark. Now it was in the hands of Heligo, who had made it his chief hall. It was from here that Vigmund had made his start back to Anglia, after proving himself with Heligo's men and being named one of his body-guard.

Approaching the fortress Dagmar's eyes opened wide. The timber palisade encircled a vast area. She saw no village without, but to the south and west of the palisade cultivated fields spread, with rows of grain, and tilled furrows of vegetables. Men and women moved and worked amongst this, all thralls. Dagmar knew them by the poverty of their clothing. Cream-coloured cattle wandered beyond this, tended by other figures.

The palisade gates were closed, yet she could see the roofs of many longhouses within. It was a camp of hundreds of warriors. Vigmund had whistled their approach, and then called out and spoke to one of the men on the parapet by the gates. The watch-man knew him as one of the King's personal guard, and let them in.

They quitted their horses. Vigmund led them to the centre of an array of longhouses, to where the King's hall stood. It was much like the rest, larger, but no more ornate.

This was not a settled burh, but an army encampment. There was no living green within the palisade walls, save for tufts of grass springing from the base of the timber walls of houses and barricades.

More slaves were here, and in plenty, the paucity of their clothes and gauntness of their forms attesting to their hard useage. These were at work in saw-pits, in chopping and stacking endless piles of firewood, and in trundling barrels and sacks about the yard. Yet Dagmar saw also a number of free women, the wives and daughters of the men who had thrown in with Heligo and had been rewarded by a life under him as King.

It was mid-day, the air warmer than early Spring often was, and as they neared the hall a group of men stopped where they had been walking and looked over at them. Dagmar saw one surely the King; he had suitable gold about his person in the form of a broad bracelet upon his thick wrist. Flanking him were two boys, neither yet of sword-bearing age. The men about him fanned out behind, shadowing him. The one with the bracelet drew breath.

"Vigmund," he said. "You return."

The King's eye, having taken in his body-guard, now fell on Dagmar. The speaker had seen upwards of forty Summers, she thought, and had long trailing brown moustaches fronting a shorter, and greying, beard. He was both tall and of powerful build, a man who had fought his way to the top.

Vigmund gave a nod. "With my wife. She is Dagmar, daughter of Guthrum."

"Aho! Guthrum!" Heligo looked at her more sharply. "We expect much of your sons, Dagmar, daughter of

Guthrum. May they fight next to my own, as Vigmund does with me."

Heligo moved on with his followers, and Vigmund unlashed the packs from their horses. Dagmar stood there, the leathern bags at her feet, while he vanished with the beasts round a corner. She attracted no little attention amongst the many men who loitered against the timber walls of the King's hall, and with the women who moved between longhouses with their babes on their hips, or laundry in baskets, headed to the wash-house. Tired as she felt Dagmar stood erect, rumpled but fairly clean, her bronze brooches set with pearls speaking for her.

When Vigmund returned they took up their packs, and entered the open door of Heligo's hall. It was dim within, having never been lime-washed, and the smallest of fires burnt at either end of the long and narrow fire-pit which ran down the centre of the hall. A babe was crying, and toddling children screeching. Vigmund led the way along the stones bordering the fire-pit, taking them close to the front of the hall. He stopped before one of the alcoves pocketing the walls. It was not far from the high table, fitting, for the King's body-guard must ever be at hand day or night. Dagmar saw a door behind the table which might lead to the private chamber of Heligo; perhaps it served as well as treasure-room.

The women sitting or standing at nearby alcoves looked up with curious eyes at the new arrival. Many had a babe at breast, or small children at their feet. Vigmund took charge by making a general announcement.

"This is my wife, Dagmar. She is the daughter of Guthrum, King of the Danes of Anglia." That said, he pulled back the thick wadmal curtaining the alcove he had stopped at.

Dagmar had a moment to nod at the staring women. Her face fell when she looked inside the cramped alcove. This was her new home. The straw heaped upon the box bed gave off a musty odour, and there was but one yellowed sheet, and a single thin pillow. She had no linen with her. These would have to do, until she could buy or make more. Vigmund heaved their packs upon the bed, and saw her furrowed brow. He asked "What?"

His tone was low, but Dagmar felt both accusation and scorn in the single word. This was her life now, and she must accept it.

"It will have to serve," he told her, "until I have men enough to make my own way." He need not say this; the sharpness of his look was chastisement enough.

She nodded her head, swallowed, and set about unpacking. Then he left her.

The first few weeks at Viborg were not easy. She was with Vigmund, this was true, but much had been forfeit. Her life had shrunk to fit the confines of Vigmund's role here. Instead of the broad bed of her marriage, with its three plush feather beds cushioning her body, plump pillows, and rare wolfskin spread, she now slept in that rude alcove meant for a single warrior. The box bed was scarcely fit for two, so narrow was it. As Vigmund must sleep where he could leap out at once if needed, she was wedged up against the rough timber wall as she slept. The sheet of coarse linen cast over the straw offered little protection against the sharp pokes of the dried stems. The treasure room of Four Stones with its thick oak walls and stout door was a haven of calm. Here, there was nought but the wadmal curtain screening them from the activity of the hall. And with no more than these drapes of wool separating the head and foot of the alcove, she heard every act of congress between the men and women at either end.

It took her a while to get her footing with the other women of the hall. She and they dressed alike, in the fashion of the Danes, yet they had been born here, and she in another land. Her accent was strange to their ears, and they teased her for it. She realised how poorly she spoke what she had always considered her native tongue. She did not know the words for certain things, and when she did speak, spoke differently enough that at times the women did not understand her, or feigned this. Her being Guthrum's daughter was at first remarked upon, then quickly forgotten. No one save Vigmund even knew she had also been a Jarl's wife.

And Vigmund was often gone. The fighting that had led to Heligo becoming King was largely over, but there were still hold-outs, and the extraction of taxes in the form of silver, grain, swine, and fish was ongoing. With the rest of Heligo's picked men Vigmund scoured the countryside, wringing additional goods from the folk thereof.

Vigmund had staked much to take sides with Heligo, and had as reward silver, weaponry, and added danger. Heligo and his massed men had captured the garrison, but more than a few of the longhouses of Viborg remained uninhabited. It suggested to Dagmar that Heligo's hold on the land was more tenuous than most who held themselves up as King. His army must be more numerous and better armed than that of his rivals, or he could quickly be deposed. And having won King-ship, he must continue to command his own men's loyalty. If not, the greater threat would come from within, and treachery dodge his footsteps, lurking in every shadow.

When at Viborg Heligo sat at the high table, and at his left side sat his chief wife. Dagmar's father had taken many wives, but only one at a time. Here the King had four women he called wife, each prettier than the last, and all, Dagmar thought, seething with jealousy at the others. The fourth wife looked no more than a girl to her eyes. The three others sat further away, but at the high table still, and though the eldest wife wore the best gems and sat at the King's side when they dined, it soon became clear that none of the women knew which he would summon into his private chamber with him on any given night. Heligo had a number of children with these women. The second wife had a babe at the breast, and the youngest, who looked to Dagmar scarcely old enough to bleed each month, was great with child.

Dagmar must cling to Vigmund; he was all she had. But she now realised how little she knew him. More than once Dagmar found herself wondering why as a young maid she had given herself to Vigmund. His beauty of course; the fact that he had smiled at her and sought her out. Yet she saw now she had been rash in her giving. She considered her life at Headleage. In the mornings before her mother began her daily drinking, she would sometimes speak to Dagmar of her prospects. Bodil had high hopes for her, and hinted that Guthrum must be planning to pair her with a man of wealth and property. This hope had proven false; her father never spoke to her of this, even when prompted by her mother. And in fact, by leaving his daughters nothing, he had blocked all paths to a good match. Here she was forced to close her eyes at the coming truth. It was only Hrald, who wanted her for what she was – or what he thought she was – who had given her such standing as to make her Lady of a great hall, as Four Stones was.

After that first terrible day on the road together, Vigmund did not again use his body as a weapon against her. Yet their love-making stood in stark contrast to what she had lately known. She was six months a wife to Hrald, months in which he regarded her face and body as a wonder. Regardless of how tentatively he first began as husband and lover, he soon found ways to arouse and satisfy her. This exchange gave him as much pleasure, seemingly, as he himself took in her.

This was lacking with Vigmund. At Headleage when they first knew each other, they would meet both in an unused granary, and a back stall in the mare's stable. Their trysts were brief, but sweet with the thrill she felt in surrendering herself to a man of such looks and standing in her father's guard. She would feel at times glimmers of deep pleasure on her own part, but these never were given time to develop into the full ecstatic expression which Hrald had learnt to give her. Now, lacking privacy, and with the urgency of their early trysts as the standard, Vigmund was almost perfunctory in his actions. She did not in any way feel able to express in whispered word or gestures her need for more. That would, she knew, bring Hrald to his mind. She could not risk a repeat of

Vigmund's initial punishment of her on the road, when he made it clear he must purge them both of the fact that another man had known her body. So she clung to him, kissing him, accepting what he gave. Of choice, she had no other.

She was more than aware, too, that the other women of the hall looked at Vigmund. He had a male beauty which would draw the eyes of most women, and had been made aware of his looks from a young age, both by maids, and by other men, who watched their sweethearts gaze upon him, and found it all too easy to take umbrage at his presence. His response had been to perfect his skills as a warrior, and studiously avoid entanglements with any women who his brethren might have prior call upon. Vigmund was ever mindful to return no smile, no sidewise glance, sent his way by a female admirer. The women of Viborg envied Dagmar her role as wife to so handsome a man, and she tried to take pride in this.

Heligo's first wife took special note of both her and Vigmund. Indeed, on nights when she had been left behind by Heligo, and the door to his private chamber had closed behind him and another of his wives, Dagmar had seen her gaze slip to Vigmund. Dagmar also became the target of this wife's attention. The woman looked at her through narrowed eyes, and at times singled Dagmar out to do her special laundry, as if she took satisfaction in having the daughter of a King serve her thus. The first time she did so, the memory of Lady Ælfwyn asking Burginde to wash her own soiled gown rose up before her. She quickly dismissed this; she must. Here at Viborg Dagmar did all she was told, silently and without complaint. Whether King's wife or her own or Vigmund's clothes, she scrubbed them herself, hanging them on lines in a side yard by turns muddy and dusty.

In the kitchen yard by the swine pens she once heard two thrall women of middle years speaking the tongue of Angle-land. The sense of the familiar drew her to them, but when they noticed her, they quieted, their eyes wide. She wished to speak to them but dared not. Thralls were not spoken to unless to give orders, and these were not hers to command. To approach them in any friendly guise would be to lower her own standing amongst those who would watch.

The months passed, Spring slipping into Summer. She saw things at Viborg she had never seen in Anglia, the treatment of thralls worse than she had ever heard of or witnessed. In Dane-mark they were no more than disposable property, with no hope of redeeming themselves through their labour, and none that they might be set free at their master's death; folk here had no belief that doing so might help their own chances at eternal salvation. They had no refuge in the Church, for it and its notions of mercy were unknown, save for the few brave souls who attempted preaching of God's goodness. Slaves were widespread through all of Angle-land, but laws governed their treatment, and convents and monasteries bought slaves and redeemed them, giving them a better life as serving folk within their confines. She looked at this country, which she had always considered her true home, with opened eyes. The view was not one that flattered.

She missed the religious observance of the Christians. This surprised her. The rhythm of the services, the chanting and song in which all took part, the confidence the priest Wilgot had in salvation and eventual reward for the faithful – there was a kind of comfort there, she saw, one conferred even in the droning of the cleric's voice. At Four Stones she had seen what succour their faith had given to Lady Ælfwyn, and to Hrald too, and it made her more attentive in the rituals they followed, the prayers they said, and the way they looked at their own place in the cosmos. Belief was not a matter of convenience or tactical expediency for them; it was real. Here, witnessing the blood sacrifices of pig, goat, or oxen she watched with shrouded eyes, recalling Wilgot naming such acts as the work of unthinking children who had not yet passed into full understanding before God. What did she believe, she wondered. She had learnt much about the faith in her months at Four Stones. One day pondering this she had the sudden thought that she was the woman taken in adultery. As in the original tale, her life had been spared, and that of her lover. Then she corrected herself. Vigmund had always been her husband; she must hold to this.

One morning when she stood in the work yard, shaking out their bed clothes to freshen them, her head-wrap askew, Vigmund approached from around another of the long houses. He paused, watching her shaking the straw dust from their blankets. He walked to her. His eyes dropped to her hands; they were reddened and chapped. His tone was more gentle than she had heard in a long while.

"It will not always be this way," he assured her.

Hope for their future life flared in her breast at this, and she waited for him to say more.

He did not answer at once. When Heligo sought King-ship, the best way for Vigmund to earn the greatest share of winnings was to put himself in the vanguard of any action, kill as many men, and the best armed of these, that he could. Much of what he took from their bodies would go to Heligo, but he would have what remained, and thus build up his own store of treasure. Now, with a grudging peace, his portion was smaller, a share of what he helped squeeze from unwilling farmers. He did not plan for it to go on much longer.

Vigmund lifted his chin to indicate the barracks that surrounded them. "When I have silver enough, we will leave."

"Where will we go?" she asked, in quiet wonder.

"I do not know," he answered. "Not here in Danemark. Somewhere where it is easier to make a start."

She only nodded. The last place he would return was Angle-land.

A feast was called. Heligo had ridden out with his warriors, and secured a final corner of Jutland, triumphing over a rival who had long vexed him. Oxen and pigs were slaughtered, and ale and wine too flowed. The day was hot, the revelry held outdoors next the kitchen yards. All sat upon benches carried from the longhouses, and at trestles too brought from within. Vigmund had returned with some choice treasure, not only arms in the way of knives and two swords, but a purse filled with hack-silver. He had as well been awarded some fine clothing ransacked from the hall of Heligo's late opponent, tunics of linen and of wool, and a mantle trimmed with broad strips of white-tinged badger pelts.

The day was too fine to retreat indoors after the meal, and drink continued to be poured. The many young, having eaten their fill, ran amongst the tables, ducking around the corners of the nearest longhouse to hide from each other, and hold their own play battles with wooden swords. Others tossed balls stitched from leather scraps. At the end of the table where Vigmund sat with Dagmar, a young mother bared her breast to her hungry babe. Her husband sat next her, grinning as he looked on.

Vigmund, cup in hand, watched all this. Then he turned to Dagmar, and with unexpected sharpness in his tone, confronted her.

"Are you barren?"

She was startled speechless. She shook her head, and shook words into her mouth.

"Nej," she said, denying this charge. Yet month after month, with Vigmund, then Hrald, then Vigmund again, she had not conceived. At times she thought she had caught a child; she felt different enough in body to suspect it. But then her Moon-flow came and passed, and the feeling was gone, flushed out of her with the clotted blood she washed from her linen pads.

Her mother had lost many babes early. Dagmar's advent was cause for rejoicing; it was the first babe she had brought to term. Bodil's inability to produce another, particularly a son, was one of the reasons she had been set aside by Guthrum. Now Dagmar had increasing cause to wonder if she had not the same malady, in even worse form, for she feared she lost her babes before they had ever truly settled in her womb.

"I will give you sons," she found herself saying. It was what Vigmund, and Heligo, expected of her.

The Summer had been hot, and now was nearing its end. Sand and loose soil oftentimes blew through the air, finding every chink in the timber walls of the long-house. Dagmar stood with some of the other wives in the laundry yard. The work yards were dusty enough, but the blowing sand soiled the damp clothes as they hung on the lines. All Dagmar could do was allow them to dry, then shake and snap them in the air, freeing them from the grit.

The fine particles stung her eyes, and entered her nose and ears. She squatted down at a bench before her, folding their bed sheets, rolling their towelling. Squatting helped relieve the pressure in the small of her back. Her Moon-flow was coming on; she could feel it. Once again she was not with child.

She heard distant noise over her head, distinct from the chatter of the women off to one side attending to their own wash. Dagmar stood to see numberless birds swirling far above in the cloudless sky. They flashed bright as their wings turned towards the Sun, then became dark curves again. She could not make out what kind they were, but she could hear their faint cries as they regrouped on their flight. She watched, head tipped back, the palms of her hands on her aching back as they circled, split, and circled again, free from all that concerned her in this yard. Then as one they moved off west. West towards Angle-land.

THE DRAGON-SHIP

Island of Gotland

CERIDWEN walked with her daughter Eirian along the trading road, their hand baskets hooked over their arms nearly full, and quite heavy. They had been on this fair morning to the potter's, and bought from her six new ceramic cups, and eight bowls. These were thick-walled, dull blue from the local clay, but each enlivened with tracery of yellow line work around rim and base. This new tableware had been nestled snugly in their baskets, packed in straw by the potter, that they might make the short trip up to Tyrsborg intact. As they walked from the workshop, Eirian made a jest.

"With Yrling gone these will last far longer," she predicted. Her brother was hard on the crockery, and was the cause of more chips and breakage than all of them together, she reckoned. Yet the moment she said it, the smile faded from Eirian's lips. As much as she envied his going, she missed her twin. And she saw her mother's face fall. She missed Yrling even more, and worried for his sake. She thought her mother was about to answer, when they saw one of the leather workers, and then the amber worker, stand up from behind their work benches in their respective stalls. Both men were squinting out towards open water, and Eirian and Ceridwen turned their heads to look as well.

A drekar, a dragon-ship, sail aloft and billowing, was driving steadily to the shingle beach to their right. Drekars often landed, but to trade, not to raid, and when they did, their sails were dropped or already furled. Such ships rowed gently to the pier, to tie up. This one was driving for the beach where it was easy to leap from both sides into the shallow water, leap and then attack. Ceridwen was aware of other trades folk now coming from their stalls and workshops. She had stopped in her tracks, as had Eirian. She thought she heard voices from those about her, but they were indistinct, almost garbled, over the sudden pounding of her heart, which seemed to have sent blood coursing through her head.

"Shall we run?" her daughter asked. Eirian's eyes were on the pier. The old men who sometimes idled in the Sun on the bench there, ready to catch a thrown line from a landing ship, had risen, and now hustled away. Both mother and daughter looked again to the dragon-ship.

Its sail was abruptly dropped; it had been sewn in alternating stripes of dark blue and white, and collapsed on itself like the folding wings of a moth. The drekar was close enough that they could see the men aboard, manning the oars to slow their approach as they beached. It would land between the last of the trading stalls and the road they need climb to reach the hall. Mother and daughter would be fully exposed as they tried to gain that hill.

Sidroc and Tindr were up there, working on the extension to the stable arising under their hands. Their cook Gunnvor and serving woman Helga were also there, the latter caring for little Rodiaud.

Ceridwen looked about them. They had never suffered attack, but she knew every stall and workshop kept at least one weapon. The men and women too of the trading road had dropped their morning's labour and were now standing before the small buildings housing their livelihoods, spears or long knives in hand. It had been years since Ceridwen had tied her father's seax to her waist; and all she and Eirian had were the smallest of table knives on their sashes.

She could not see Tyrsborg's roof from here, though her whole being yearned to it and the man there. She knew what he would tell her.

"We must stay here," Ceridwen breathed. Here at least they were amongst others, ready to defend themselves. They put down their baskets.

Up at Tyrsborg the work of wrestling the new timber framing of the stable wall into place was underway. Rodiaud, at three years of age, was oblivious to her father's labour, and was chasing Flekkr about the work yard. The girl was laughing, and the dog dodging behind benches and skirting the rain barrels as the two took turns running from the other. Then Rodiaud tripped, and went sprawling on the hard ground. Helga was there a moment later to scoop her up, Flekkr at her heels. The child had barely time to screw up her face to bawl when Helga, straightening up with her in her arms, saw the drekar below. The sudden squeeze she gave to Rodiaud was enough to make the girl forget her skinned knee, and she fell quiet. Helga did not, and turned her head to the stable behind her.

"Master! Master!"

A moment later Sidroc, hammer in hand, appeared from around the corner of the stable. He looked past Helga down the hill to the placid Baltic, and the dragon-ship which was approaching shore. He ran to Helga's side. Gunnvor had left her oven and joined the serving woman. Sidroc stood there, sweat beaded on his brow, and uttered an oath over the heads of the two women. His shield-maiden and his older daughter were down there, he knew, on the trading road. And the drekar would land between them and him.

He found voice and spoke to the women at his side. "Take Rodiaud and head into the forest. Go to Tindr and Ŝeará's house. Stay there until we come to get you."

Tindr, deaf though he was, seemed oftentimes to sense a sudden shift in circumstances. He appeared now, head cocked, from around the stable. Seeing what they looked at, he broke into a short run to join them.

The curved prow of the drekar surged forward on a low and foaming wave. The thick keel met the pebbles of the stony beach. The warriors aboard began readying to leap off. They were carrying their shields, which were always left aboard for men merely landing to trade or drink. Some of the men were helmeted, including the first man to leap down, who looked to be the captain amongst them. He turned his head, scanning the road and its warehouses and workshops. To Sidroc's eyes, he seemed to take note of the folk massed there, then dismiss them. The captain settled his gaze to his right, to the brew-house. Tindr's mother Rannveig was alone there, with her cook Gudfrid.

The jolt of energy springing from the pit of Sidroc's belly had yet to recede. He must arm himself, now, and go and meet these strangers.

Tindr had a bow and fletched arrows hanging here in the stable as well as at his forest roundhouse. He was already miming the act of pulling back a bow-string to Sidroc, who nodded. They parted, Tindr to the stable for his weapon, and Sidroc to the treasure room for his own. There, hanging on a wall peg was his sword in its leathern scabbard. His seax was already strapped on, and now he buckled on the sword belt. He opened a low chest upon the floor, pushed away the fleece, and fitted his helmet on his head. Then he took his shield of black and white painted swirls from the wall. Coming through the hall he chose the shortest of the spears he had stored there. It was a throwing spear, one he had carried from the deck of an Idrisid slave ship years ago. He stepped out into the day to see Gunnvor and Helga vanishing up the trail at the back of the kitchen yard, Rodiaud and Flekkr in tow.

He met up with Tindr, who had his filled quiver at his hip and his bow in hand. Sidroc must take a moment to sign to him his orders, telling him, "Do not let loose an arrow unless I tell you. If I do, shoot to kill." This last he gestured with the huntsman's own sign for a kill, a thumb thrust at the breast. Tindr nodded, his face as still as his ice-blue eyes.

A sound – low, sonorous, and compelling – reached Sidroc's ears. Someone along the trading road had taken up a curved horn made from that of a Gotland ewe, and was sounding it now as alarm.

Sidroc glanced up to the clear Gotlandic sky. The name of Tyr crossed his lips. Tyr was not only a warrior of utmost skill, but to Sidroc the God of Justice. It was Tyr that Sidroc had given himself to as a youth, trusting that God would help guide his actions as well as the sureness of his arm. He would once again need Tyr to face what awaited below.

The two men moved off together. They would be readily seen on the road, and so threaded their way through their neighbour's work yard and then along the back of Rannveig's house at the bottom of the hill. In doing so they lost sight of the landed ship and its men, but kept themselves hidden.

Sidroc and Tindr came around the back of Rannveig's small house, trusting she was within. They had clear view of her brewing shed and kitchen yard, and both were empty. They took up position behind the corner of the shed, giving on to the brew-house door. Sidroc, spear in hand, hazarded a peek around the corner towards the beach. He glimpsed the body of warriors making their way along the road and right to them. Their captain was fronting them, striding, his shield on his back, but his right hand clutching a spear. The man had two long yellow plaits dropping down from beneath his helmet.

Rannveig's brew-house was not yet open; its oiled fabric awnings unfurled to the low partition of its front wall. The door was closed. Yet the captain in front moved with decision towards it. He had nearly gained the door when a spear was flung from a nearby vantage point, flung from the hand of an unseen warrior. Its long point struck the wood of the door frame, the shaft vibrating with the force with which it had been thrown. It formed an abrupt barrier to the progress of the landing party, and came close enough to their captain to make him jump back.

He whirled, his own spear raised and ready, to face the man who stepped forward. The warrior who had thrown the weapon was of unusual height, and dark hair could be seen descending from beneath his helmet. The hand which had flung the spear with such strength was now resting upon the hilt of a long sword on his left hip, a sword he looked more than ready to draw. Yet the warrior fixed the captain with his dark eyes, then moved his gaze to the door to regard his work. The upright post serving as door frame had split, almost half its entire length. Still, its point was tightly lodged in the crevasse it had created.

The captain bristled, but held on to his spear. A second man, one with the spear-thrower, had stepped forward from behind the corner of the shed. He held a bow, arrow ready to be nocked. Other than that, no one moved.

The captain's declaration was couched in a grudging tone.

"I am come from Ivar, King of the Svear. I seek two men, Berse the blade-smith, and Sidroc the Dane."

The tall warrior he faced gave a laugh.

"The first is up at his forge, doubtless unrolling his ring-shirt in greeting. The second stands before you."

The captain pulled off his helmet. Sidroc stared at the man. Ten years had passed, but this was none other than the Svear raider and trader from whom they bought the flesh-slave Sparrow. Now he was a henchman for the King on the mainland to the west.

Sidroc pulled off his own helmet to better address the visitor. He used the same easy tone he had ever used with the man.

"Eskil. Your manners were better back then. At least I recall you being a good loser when it came to all I took from you over dice." Sidroc paused a moment before enumerating some of these losses. "The ball of crystal, the bolt of red silk, the bags of hack-silver . . ."

Eskil straightened up, little pleased at this reminder of being bettered so long ago. One of his men behind him made a guffaw, and Sidroc watched Eskil's jaw tighten at it.

Sidroc went on. "This visit will cost you more silver. Now you will have to pay Rannveig for the damage done to her door frame."

Eskil's hand had tightened around the shaft of his spear. He was under strict orders to incite no violence against these Gotlanders. Sidroc could guess as much, and ended on a more conciliatory note.

"Still, I think she will sell you ale."

In fact, Rannveig had appeared, Gudfrid at her side, from their house. Rannveig was armed with a poker, and the cook with her flaying knife. They had been watching from the slit in their closed shutters, saw both Sidroc and Tindr there, and decided it was time to make their appearance. The brewster knew that the offer of a deep cup of ale could diffuse many a tense situation, and was more than prepared to open up.

As the two women neared, Sidroc looked past Eskil and his men to the beached drekar. A few men would have been left aboard on watch; they always were, but now they were utterly outnumbered. Enough men and women were crowding the beach, weapons aloft, to swarm and destroy it, at whatever cost to themselves.

Sidroc glanced back to Eskil, and raised his hand to the beach. A mass of folk surrounded the drekar's prow. The men aboard were standing back, at the mast. Their spears were in their hands, but they too were under orders not to be aggressors.

"Ah," the Dane told Eskil. "But a bit of silver may not be all that you forfeit."

Every man with Eskil joined in looking back at the besieged ship. Sidroc presented one possibility. "My friends on the trading road have fire at the ready. Three or four oily torches would make short work of your fine dragon-ship."

A loud sigh escaped Sidroc's lips as he reflected on this Fate. "I have lost a ship, once. It is never good to be stranded. I know."

Eskil nearly gaped. The ship was his own, one of the reasons he had been given this mission. He had no desire to fight his way back to it.

Eskil looked at the brewster, then to Sidroc. He shrugged in the direction of the massed folk threatening his ship.

"Have them all come up, to hear what I come to tell."

"And for ale?" Sidroc prompted. He could barely suppress his grin.

Eskil huffed out his agreement. He had in fact a sum of silver from Ivar for just such purposes. Men gathered more willingly if ale was offered. He nodded.

"For ale," he conceded. He pointed to one of his men to go down and issue the directive.

At this Rannveig straightened up, and Gudfrid in tow, brushed past the captain. She paused at the spear buried in her door frame. She gave a sniff at the damage, then turned and gave Eskil a look as pointed as the iron tip.

As the brewster began rolling up the awnings a large man appeared, hustling along the road. He approached, and then passed Eskil's messenger, his face intent on the knot of men at Rannveig's door. It was Berse the blade-smith, shield on his back, kitted out in ring-shirt and helmet, and armed with spear and sword of his own forging. He was flanked by two younger men, his sons, as thin and wiry as Berse was bear-like. Like their father they also bore spears and shields, but instead of a fully-formed helmet, wore leather and iron war-caps upon their tousled heads.

Berse gained Sidroc's side, and looked from him to the newly landed Eskil. The blade-smith was winded from his effort, but there was no mistaking the brawn of his arms, nor the sureness of the hand holding his spear. Berse had once bought some good Frankish iron from this man before him, but knew that today trading was not Eskil's purpose.

Berse did not expect the Dane's next words.

"Ivar, the Uppsala King, is about to buy you ale, Berse."

Berse goggled at this unexpected news. But his attention shifted to the beach, and the movement there. As they watched the crowd about the dragon-ship funnel itself into a stream of folk heading for the brew-house, Sidroc was moved to again speak. This time he addressed the Svear.

"Eskil. You called for Berse and me by name. Why?"

The Svear's answer was direct enough. "Ivar sent three ships to Gotland, to bring word of his plan. I know the chief men on the eastern shores, and told him so."

Sidroc nodded. He had never sought fame, and cherished the quietness of his life on this island. Still, it was something to have been singled out in this way to the King of the Svear.

Down on the trading road, the lone warrior sent by Eskil had issued his captain's request. Even at this distance the folk he addressed could see the spear now projecting from the brew-house door jamb, though none had seen its flight. But they could plainly see Berse and Sidroc in converse with the captain, and determined the threat to be much the less than their growing curiosity.

Ceridwen, standing with a number of other women in the back of the crowd, gave Eirian's shoulders a squeeze of reassurance. Sidroc would not be standing there at Rannveig's door, helmet off, if there were danger, nor would he allow the others to be summoned up. She felt it safe to retrieve their baskets, and held hers gratefully, its weight helping to calm the too-fast beating of her heart. Here was the crockery they needed; this was reminder of the peace and safety they knew. How quickly that sense of safety had been dispelled by a single ship driving to shore. It made her bite her lip, thinking on this. She and Eirian moved forward with the rest, a low ripple of questioning wonder rising from their throats. Still, none who clutched weapons relinquished them, though spears were carried upright, and knives returned to their sheaths.

When all had gained the brew-house, the men crowded within. Rannveig and Gudfrid had been at work, passing out pitchers of ale to every table. Sidroc and Berse and a few other Gotlanders had remained standing, as had Eskil. The rest were seated. Eskil began to speak. The women of the trading road remained outside, but with the awnings up his words were clear.

"Ivar, King of the Svear, makes offer to you islanders," the captain began. "The free men of Gotland are to gather and form an Althing, in three days, to hear the terms. Those of you here are charged with the task of telling those who are not, so all may hear."

That was the message Eskil bore. Sidroc knew it was a summons, and no further details would be forthcoming until all were gathered. Sidroc lifted the pottery cup to his mouth and took another draught of ale, but let his eyes meet those of Eskil over the rim of his cup. Eskil's lifted a moment in confirmation. Nothing more could be said now.

The message, brief as it was, was not enough for Berse, and he was not afraid to say so.

"We will hear. Then we will vote, and see if we will accept those terms. Hearing is one thing, accepting another."

His words were met by affirming grunts and a few calls of "Gotland!"

Eskil scanned the men before him, ale cups in hand, proclaiming fidelity to their island, free of any King. He could guess the blade-smith, having taken a deep swallow of Rannveig's good ale, was just warming up.

Indeed, Berse was a good teller of tales, and no man was prouder of being a Gotlander than he. He would take a moment to expound on the long and memorable dealings of the island with the Kings of Uppsala, both to remind his fellows of the doughtiness of their forefathers, and to educate this arrogant Svear in his own history.

"You are not the first Svear to land on our shores," Berse declared. "We men of Gotland have not forgot that in every contest with the Kings of the Svear, we have won. And that it was rarely us, but those self-same Kings, who were the cause of fighting."

Berse took a meaningful pause, one long enough to take another swallow of ale, and allow those listening to do the same. He was about to invoke a hallowed name in the history of the Gotlanders.

"Avair Strabain was it, who made a lasting Peace with the King of Svear-land. His name marks him as scrawny of leg, but more than this, he was shrewd of purse. Aged in years was he, but wise in mind. It was Avair selected to go to Uppsala and deal with the King."

Those assembled nodded at this remembrance. It seemed a reckless undertaking, an aged and infirm man to venture thus. Berse did not add that which all Gotlanders knew, that Avair's prowess in business was such that before he sailed he had exacted the promise of not one but three wergilds for his efforts, one for himself, one for his son, and one for his wife, should he die.

"And deal he did. Never had such terms been worked with a warrior King! Avair's tongue was as silver as his legs were scrawny, for the King found himself accepting a mere three score marks of silver each year as tribute. In return the warriors of the Kings of Uppsala would be made ready to defend Gotland if needed, and the men of Gotland would come to that King's aid if warranted."

Berse must pause here to take another long draught of his ale. Rannveig and Gudfrid meanwhile had been threading their way with trays laden with filled ale cups amongst the women, for as Rannveig reasoned, a woman had a right to her thirst just as did any man.

Ceridwen and Eirian remained in the back of the women so assembled, but had moved to better see between the shoulders and heads of those taller than they. It gave Sidroc a chance to catch a glimpse of his wife. He let his eyes meet hers, and gave the slightest of nods in acknowledgment. That small gesture of assurance was enough. She felt her breath release, and gratefully took up the cup Gudfrid now offered from her tray.

Within the brew-house Berse's tale had come to an end. Eskil repeated the charge that all men gather three days hence at the place of Althing. This lay at the very middle point of the island, and less than a full day's ride from here. The men began talking amongst themselves, gauging how best to make the trip, and whether or not it might be worth it to carry along not only supplies, but goods to trade as well. Rannveig was back within the brew-house and waiting with calm expectancy; along with that poured out for Eskil's men she had served out more than four score cups of ale, and had the washing up to account for as well.

Sidroc watched Eskil as he moved to the brewster, purse in hand. They were coins Eskil drew forth, not hack, though they dropped, chiming, into the flat scale bowl countered by a tiny cube of lead just as chopped up jewellery would. Sidroc guessed this pouch was special, given directly by Ivar for this purpose, for the use of coins made good show. Rannveig would go through these tiny silver discs with care, he knew, plucking out any she thought of Angle-land as gift for his shield-maiden. She would also show him any coin new to her; such could be many, come from far to the east, marked with flowing writing like thread-work. Ivar's payment for her ale would tell something of what and where the current King of Uppsala had been dealing.

Sidroc walked to join the brewster as Eskil stood before her. He looked down at the bowl holding the coins, now perfectly balanced by the small cube of lead in the corresponding bowl.

"I thank you for the ale, Eskil," the Dane said. "Such fine drink helps all news go down the easier. Especially when we know not if the news be good or bad." He smiled, and inclined his head at the spear stuck in the door frame, and visible from where they stood. "Pulling out that shattered jamb will be thirsty work for the house-wright. Do not forget his labours as you pay Rannveig."

Sidroc watched in silence as the Svear drew yet more coins from the purse, dropping them onto the pile of tiny discs which lay shimmering there. Rannveig, who was used to a certain amount of wear and tear on her brewhouse, was more than grateful for the extra.

The men had risen and were dispersing, though Tindr stayed near Sidroc as long as he spoke to Eskil. There was a pause in speech and movement as Sidroc went to the door frame, and wrenched his spear from it. The three now walked out to where small groups of men and women stood talking over this summons. Berse was in the heart of one cluster, still boasting of Avair Strabain and the advantageous bargain he had struck with a long-ago King. Others of the men were planning to ready themselves to travel to inland farms where friends and kin lived, to bring them the news.

By the roadway and off to one side waited Ceridwen, her daughter at her side. She had not been close enough to Eskil to recall his face, but as he neared, his eyes made it clear he had not forgotten the wife of Sidroc. He had never any name other than this to give to her.

Walking as he was at the side of the big Dane, he could not make free of those eyes now, as much as he would have liked to, for at the woman's shoulder was a choice young maid, only doubling Eskil's pleasure in the looking. It was clear he fought against his desire to speak to the elder of the two, but with the eyes of the Dane upon her, all he did was nod. Still, he paused just before they reached the females, and asked of Sidroc a question.

"That girl you bought. Did she prove a good thrall?"

Before Sidroc could respond, his wife answered. The memory of standing on the pier and telling this Svear she wanted the starving and abused girl cowering aboard his dragon-ship had never left her.

"I bought her, and I freed her," she corrected. She spoke with resolve and not a little pride, and both men were compelled to turn to her. She made the most of her audience. "You did not recognise her worth, Eskil. She was later sent to Angle-land with gold, where she was received by a woman of great power and standing."

Eskil must look at her now; she had spoken, and his lips parted as he studied her. The hair dropping from under her linen head wrap was still a rich and ruddy chestnut. The lush fruitfulness of her form was just as he recalled. Upon her left wrist was the same silver disc bracelet he remembered her wearing. It must be a favoured piece of metal to so adorn her arm. She was a fine figure of a woman, fiery of eye and with a firmness of purpose none could mistake. He saw again how green those wide eyes were. Her words were a challenge to him, one with the Dane present he could not answer as he wished.

"Angle-land," Eskil repeated. "And with gold. Then I sold her too cheaply."

He gave a laugh, one at his own expense. In her beauty and mettle this woman before him was one most men would covet. What was she doing here, in the middle of the Baltic, when she could be adorning the hall of some high chieftain in Svear-land? He could say none of this to her, and so spoke to the Dane.

"I have not ventured to Angle-land. Your wife must be of there, so it would be worth the going." Eskil let his eyes flick down a moment, to the seax worn by Sidroc, the weapon of the Saxons. It made sense now, where he had won it, and won the woman.

As if aware he trod on ice too thin to hold his weight, the Svear shifted his focus to several of his men, calling out to them to ready the ship.

It gave Ceridwen the chance to pick up the basket she had again set down, signalling to Sidroc she and Eirian were ready to leave. They began to move off, but slowly, as she was loathe to miss anything which might be of value.

Sidroc had a final word for the Svear. "There is profit awaiting you, here on the trading road," he proposed, and named a few of the offerings. "Gotlandic wool, ready spun. Fleece. Beeswax tapers," he suggested. He tilted his head to where Berse still stood, deep in talk with a few men. "Not to mention prime blades, up there at his forge."

Eskil had to nod. "Good salt," the Svear remembered. "I will take a look before I sail, but must soon be off." He took in the short expanse of the trading road, then turned his eyes back to Sidroc.

"And I will see you on the third day hence," Eskil reminded.

Sidroc gave an affirming nod of his own. This was followed by a simple statement. "Whatever Ivar asks for, you know the answer is likely to be Nai."

Eskil laughed and nodded his head. "He thinks that, as well. But we were sent to remind Gotland of our near presence."

"Island folk are always fiercely their own," Sidroc pointed out.

The Svear shrugged. "Why do you care. You are no Gotlander."

"Only by choice," Sidroc answered. "This island is now my home. One I am always ready to defend."

The Svear's eyes shifted to the stony beach.

"There is nothing here but rock," he protested.

It was Sidroc's turn to laugh. "Já. Rock, and freedom."

They parted then. Ceridwen and Eirian had not gone far, and Sidroc and Tindr caught up. Tindr took the basket from Eirian, and the two went ahead, as the girl's parents lingered. Much had just happened on the shore, and at the brew-house, yet both were strangely silent. Ceridwen broke the stillness, as she generally did, though her tone was low.

"Do not say it," she began. "Do not say you wish I had not spoken to him."

Sidroc remained quiet long enough that she turned her head to him as they walked.

"I will not say it," he answered. "I did not think it," he added, meaningfully.

She must study him, to see if he repressed a smile. But his face was earnest. She watched him still as he went on.

"You gave him much to mull over. Now he thinks he lost out on a fine source of profit. The girl was of value, and he did indeed let her go cheaply. Or so he thinks.

"I could not have done better," he praised.

Now she could smile, and did so.

He shifted his spear from his hand to his shoulder. The unexpected summons returned as the pressing issue.

"And what matters now, lies ahead."

"What is it, do you think?" she questioned.

"One of two things: a need for silver, or war. And the first often leads to the second."

Once at Tyrsborg Eirian was sent to bring Gunnvor, Helga, and Rodiaud home. Sidroc and Tindr returned their weapons to safe keeping, and set about resuming their carpentry work. Ceridwen stood with them in the opened bay of the stable. New post holes had been dug in the stony soil, ready to receive the upright timbers. The men were about to hammer the tenon into the last piece of the top framework of the new wall before it was raised.

Sidroc's thoughts had continued on, even as he had again taken up his mallet. He was torn. He wanted Tindr to remain here, as safeguard to both households, but could not see how he could be left.

"Tindr can vote; he must come with me," he told her. "He will ride Yrling's horse." He was squatting down on the ground by the framework, and looked up at his wife. "You and the girls can stay with Šeará in her forest house; we will only be gone a night, two at most. Or you can go to Rannveig's, and stay together there."

Ceridwen gave her head a shake. "Šeará's house is far too small." Šeará, as a Sami, could not sleep under any roof save one into which her Goddesses had been invited.

"And Rannveig's would be crowded with us there. She does not like to leave her brewing shed, we all know this. But I will leave Rodiaud with Rannveig." She could say this last with confidence the child would be welcomed. Rannveig was as grandmother to Ceridwen's children, as much as she was to her own son's.

Ceridwen was not done. "Eirian and I will go with you."

Sidroc opened his mouth in protest, but she went on. "Whatever you men decide will affect we women. I want to be there to hear."

He nodded; it was fair enough. Before he could ask a question she went on, as if anticipating another objection.

"A waggon will slow you down; I know this. Eirian and I will ride as well. Between the four horses we can carry what kit we will need."

He considered this prospect. With an early start they would reach the meeting point later the same day. But once there, they must spend the night in the open.

"With no waggon, it will be rough, camping on the ground," he warned.

She had answer for this as well, one pulled from shared memory. "No more so than you and I have known together."

They had tramped weeks with all their gear on their shoulders and in their arms; this was true. And there was the faintest smile on her lips as she reminded him of this.

He need smile as well, thinking of their travels, the hardships they endured, and the fights they had had.

"Eirian as well?" he now asked. The girl had rarely slept away from the comforts of her own snug alcove.

Ceridwen nodded. “She must come, and for two reasons. Her own sake, to begin. We know she is growing restless. She must see more. And also, she must be seen.”

“Ah,” he said, in understanding.

The Althing was the main gathering at which families could show off their young. It was held every Summer. They did not always go, but when they did they would borrow a waggon from Ring up at the farm, and make it a three day outing. It would be some years before Eirian would wed, but it was not too early for a family seeking a good wife for their son to be made aware of her. Sidroc knew she would want to come. And Eirian was being brought up to consider matters and judge for herself, just as her mother always had. The brief outing would be good for her.

“Then you will come,” he agreed. Tindr and he were kneeling side by side now, fitting together the final mortice and tenon joint, pounding it in as it locked together. This achieved, he raised his face to her and must grin. “And I will get to see Eskil try not to look at you again.”

The night before they left, Sidroc, as was his custom, made a final check of the large iron box lock of Tyrsborg’s front door, and the smaller one on the hall’s side door, ascertaining both were latched. With both doors closed the hall was dim, though the glowing coals at one end of the fire-pit were banked up so that Helga and Gunnvor would have an easy time picking fire out of them for the kitchen-ring in the morning. Both women were in their alcoves, and after the labours of the day doubtless sound asleep. Sidroc's daughters lay sleeping in their own alcoves, head to head; though little Rodiaud sometimes climbed out of hers to crawl in with her older sister. The panels of heavy striped woollen wadmal curtaining their beds were pulled closed. He could just hear Rodiaud's soft sigh as he passed.

The last door Sidroc went to was that of the treasure room. This too had a wrought box lock, one which rarely saw its key. He lifted the latch and let himself in, then locked it from the inside using the key hanging on the wall. The room side of the door offered an iron bar as well. Such was the safety of the island that Sidroc had never occasion to slide that bar across the oaken planks.

It was nearly Summer; the days already long, and a soft light still illuminated the room from the sole window. He had no need for a cresset. His shield-maiden was there in bed, lying on her side. Her eyes were closed, but he was not certain if she slept. The tall head board with the spiral disc design he had carved into it loomed up against the wall behind her, the pale wood showing silver in the owl-light of waning day. Hanging above it from a leathern cord was the coarse and dark tuft he had cut from the auroch's mane, placed there as a talisman of manly potency. Beneath his feet, under two floorboards, were crockery jars of silver, and of gold. This hall, this room, held all he had battled for, bargained for, and won. The bargaining had been not only with folk through trade, but with the Gods, through dedication and his willingness to sacrifice for their favour. The battles had been countless, against countless men, most of whom he had triumphed over. There had been battles too with this woman, one of words waged over many years to win her.

He pulled off his clothing and slipped in next her. An indistinct sound crossed her lips, a murmur of greeting. In answer he spoke to her, a low whisper which made her open her eyes.

"Tonight we are in the bed I built for you," he began. "Tomorrow night we will sleep on the hard ground, with the stars over our heads, as you reminded me we did, so many years ago."

She was smiling at him now, her eyes crinkling at this memory. He went on, carrying them back fully to those early days of freedom.

"I recall you lying in the open, sleeping on your plush weaving, or within the tent we made, so close to me that I could hear your breathing. I remember every night, and how I could not reach to you and pull you near.

"Now I can, and will."

He did so, sliding one arm under her shoulder and pulling her atop him. Her left hand fell on his right thigh, and stayed a moment there. Under the warmth of her palm lay part of the scar running from above his knee to mid thigh. The tiny puncture marks tracking its path were those she had made, with needle and red silk thread. She could not feel them flanking the slightly raised tissue she had closed, only the long scar itself. He had been forced to kill a Lord of Kilton here in their stable yard, and before his death Godwin had exacted this price. The bloody contest had been waged over her, and she was left with silk thread, closing up the wound of a man who fought to the death for her.

Her palm moved up the length of his right thigh, lifting slightly as it brushed over the end of the scar. She let her hand continue up between his legs, until he caught his breath at her grasp of him.

Before their lips met, he opened his eyes, their faces nearly touching. "Daughter of Freyja," he named her in a whisper. "I will let nothing deprive us of this, and what we have built here at Tyrsborg."

THEIR OWN FOLK

THEY began their journey in sight of others, some in waggons, some on horseback, and many afoot. All took the side road branching off from that fronting the sea. The overland track led on a northwesterly route to the very centre of the island. But as those on foot lagged behind, and some with wains and waggons left to meet up with others on upland farms, they found themselves alone. No matter. The day was a fine one, dry, and for Ceridwen and Eirian, who had seen less of their home's landscape than Sidroc and Tindr, one full of interest.

They rode two by two, Ceridwen next Sidroc in front, Tindr and Eirian behind. The saddles of all four horses had packs tied to their saddle rings, bearing what they would need to make their camp at the place of Althing. Sidroc had considered what weaponry to bring, landing on that most simple for a rider, and most favoured by him for defence. His shield was slung upon his back, and at his left hip was strapped his sword, the sure sign of a warrior.

Tindr had his bow, and the leathern quiver holding a dozen goose-fletched arrows. The men were not the only of the small party who had armed. Ceridwen had taken her father's seax from the chest in which she stored it, and tied it at her waist. When she had worn it as a girl leaving the Priory she had done so, and now reclaimed it for this use. She had never worn it slung across her belly as a man would, and did not now. Its length at her side was enough, carrying her back to how she had set out before dawn on a cold late Winter morning, feeling herself protected by a knife she had no real notion of how to use. Before she had slipped the weapon on this morning she drew the blade out. There was the long chip in the edge, one which had always been there. Holding the grip in her hand had taken her for a moment back to being on the road with Gyric, and him asking her to use the seax against him. He was blind; she feared even lifting it up as he stood there. Yet he had stepped in and caught her raised hand, forcing it back over her head as the knife dropped from it. How easily a trained warrior had disarmed her. And with what care had he then shown her a better grip, taught her to use her own weight to upset an attacker, stressed the need for a single cut low on her attacker's body to buy her time so she could use her unencumbered speed to flee.

The thoughts of these two men, Cerd, who had left this weapon behind for her, and Gyric, who had shown her how to bring it to bear, had been strongly with her as she tied the worn sheath onto her sash. Sidroc was already out in the stable yard with Tindr and the horses, and when she emerged wearing it he took her in a moment, then nodded his approval.

These remembrances of two lost men lingered as they followed the northerly track. The steady rhythm of her pacing mare lulled her mind to deeper thoughts. They took her far from the Gotlandic grassland and bare alvar landscape they traversed. Her mind returned her again to

Angle-land, and to Wessex, and her two older sons there. She could not know how either fared, and no yearning of heart nor mind could carry her to their sides so she might learn. Each were destined to be warriors, like their fathers before them. Her eldest had paid the greatest price for his skill in arms. She must trust that he would come to terms with his act, and one day know peace.

Her lips parted in silent acknowledgment of the circle of births and deaths surrounding her. Fate was such that the seax of her father Cerd was today tied at her waist. Now she had a grandson, whose now-dead mother Ashild had bestowed that same name upon. She gave her head the slightest shake, one of wonder.

Of Edwin, anointed at fifteen Lord of Kilton, she knew so little, and could only seek comfort in those who had succoured him, the Ladies Edgyth and Modwynn, and the exemplars he had in men such as Worr and the lost Cadmar.

Her third son Yrling had not been raised to fight, yet in interest and aptitude the warrior's way seemed a clarion call. Sidroc would be glad to have him join in his trading ventures, yet Yrling must first explore that path his father, and the war-chief whose namesake he was, had chosen.

Ceridwen's mare tossed her head at a hare which ran in great leaping jumps off to one side. It roused her from the dim passage of her thoughts to the bright morning. She remembered another morning, one spent riding through grasslands with this man at her side, and being surprised by a vixen and her kits. It forced a smile to her lips, one Sidroc saw, and returned. She shifted enough in her saddle to look back at their daughter.

Eirian rode a pretty red bay gelding, one her father had selected for her before he had left to visit Four Stones. She had still not outgrown the animal, it was long-legged as she was, and would suit her as many years as she wished.

The girl had been more quiet than was usual, but smiled before her mother turned her eyes back to the road. She rode next Tindr, with whom she could converse with her hands, but both were holding reins. And Eirian saw that Tindr was watchful, as if he almost expected to come across warriors of the Svear on their way through the peaceful landscape. Eirian felt watchful as well. She too had seen her mother emerge from the hall wearing the old knife she owned. She saw it, and it gave her a slight shudder of fear that her mother had done so, but she did not ask for a larger knife herself. The one with which she cut her food was ever at her waist, and she did not want to think of it doing more than that when it was in her hand. Her father rode just ahead of her, and she trained her eyes on the curved face of the shield he bore on his back. The tight spirals of black and white swirls radiating from the iron boss captured her attention. One could almost get dizzy tracing the movement of them, she decided. What would it be like to face that shield advancing in battle, she wondered.

They stopped once, to water the horses at a spring which burbled from a low shelf of limestone. They all drank, the water of a clarity and sweetness few wells could offer. They had bread and cheese for the trek, boiled eggs as well, and a quantity of walnuts, ready shelled, with which to sustain themselves on the road. For tonight they had a section of smoked ham, from those many spotted pigs which Ring raised up at the farm, and dried peas as well as wheat kernels ready to be boiled up into browis once they made their camp.

As they neared the place others joined them, streaming in from various trails and paths to the broader and well tamped road leading to that land reserved for the Althing. It was after noon when they reined up, part of a vast crowd. As they had hoped, folk were there with victuals and drink for sale, including the local brewer, who had carted two wains full of crockery jugs of ale.

The tents of the King's men were being set up near the circle used by the Law-speaker. Not all of Ivar's messengers had yet come, but enough were there to make an impressive show of it. Today would be spent in arrival, setting up what slight camps those attending could, and in rest; Ivar's men would speak in the morning. In this it was much like a true Althing. Matters of law could only be discussed and debated under the clear light of day, as was just. These were generally settled upon the first full day of the gathering. The rest of the time was given up to trading, drinking, and strolling the campgrounds.

This assembly stood in sharp contrast to the yearly Althing, though, for this was one comprised of mostly men. Only men could vote; the same was true of the Althing, but those served both as law-giving and market fair. Whole families came, leaving their beasts and farm in the care of hired help or older children who did not mind missing it. This gathering, called in haste, and with only one purpose, to hear the proclamation of Ivar, the King in Uppsala, meant that most women remained at home, caring for farm and household. The mood of the gathering was markedly different, and even Eirian felt that at once.

While still entering the field they ran into Runulv and Ring. The brothers had come alone, yet together. With so many strangers about them it heartened Ceridwen to see trusted and familiar faces.

They claimed a camping spot amongst a pine grove, then surrendered their horses to local men, who with the aid of well spaced trees and many lengths of hempen line, formed a temporary paddock to receive them. The setting up of their modest camp came next. They had carried two rolls of oiled and waxed linen with them, light in weight but proof against damp. Sidroc and Tindr slung one between three trees to act as roof, while the second was unrolled as a ground cloth. The place of Althing had ample water from a broad rock-strewn stream, and Ceridwen and Eirian went to fetch water. As the cooking ring and kit was being set up Eirian went to work, walking beneath the trees, picking up twigs, pinecones, and sticks as kindling, with larger pieces of dead wood to fire the small cauldron Gunnvor had packed.

Runulv and Ring were not the only ones they met up with. Berse the weapon-smith had left a day early, rattling along the track in an ox cart pulled by two stout beasts. Within the covered bed he carried five swords, a score of spear points, and eleven long knives, all of his own forging. These had all been set aside to bring to the Althing in a few weeks, but as a good man of business he reasoned that with nearly every man of Gotland gathered to hear the proposal of the King of the Svear, a certain number of them might be placed into a fighting mood, and be moved then and there to part with some silver for a good weapon. He and his sons had set up just outside the circle where the law-speakers traditionally stood, and where he imagined Ivar's men would hold forth. He gauged that the look of his armaments would also remind them of the mettle of the men of this rocky island.

The Sun was skimming through the pine boughs as Ceridwen boiled up the browis. The four of them ate, sitting cross-legged on the oiled cloth. They had ale, carried from the brewer's waggons in their wooden travel cups, and as the day grew dimmer, all felt sleep grow near. Sparks jumped from their fire-ring when they prodded the coals, glowing specks of orange like the Sun's deeper descent to the west. Sidroc rose, and went out to walk the campground, stopping to speak to Berse and others. Tindr never enjoyed crowded spaces, and remained at their own camp. When Sidroc returned they all readied for sleep. The down-stuffed pillows which had been pressed flat and rolled to fit the saddle bags were shaken out and fluffed, and light wool blankets lay at the ready. They bent to enter under the covering oiled cloth.

Eirian slept between Ceridwen and Sidroc, with Tindr at Sidroc's back, their weapons between the two men. Before they closed their eyes, Sidroc gave a silent look over his daughter's still form to his wife. Their eyes met. They would sleep in the open again as they had so long ago, and as he had recalled to her last night. Then he smiled.

After they had broken their fast in the morning Ceridwen and Eirian took two small wooden pails and returned to the stream for more water. Many folk were there, doing the same. Threading their way back through the growing press of people clustering near the Law-speakers circle took care, lest they lose water through the sloshing of their pails. They had skirted safely around and were headed for the pine grove when Ceridwen stopped. Two men had turned in her direction. The elder of them had an unmistakable look. He was not gazing at her, but rather past her, but Eirian too made a sound of startled recognition. Heedless now of any sloshing Ceridwen stepped up to him.

"You are Hrald," she said, with true certainty. The man must have seen three score years, and was tall and gauntly lean. The hair, still thick, was entirely grey. The slightest stoop to his shoulders gave proof of years of labour. Ceridwen had never seen him, yet in face and form he was entirely familiar. His eyes, a deep blue, creased at her, not unkindly, yet in true surprise.

Those eyes now blinked at her, wondering how she knew him.

"I am Ceridwen, your son's wife," she told him. "Our campsite is not far. Sidroc will be glad to see you so soon."

The elder Hrald nodded in assent.

"This is our daughter, Eirian," Ceridwen went on. The girl made a little curtsy, her cheek colouring.

At last the old man spoke, with a gesture to the man at his side, one of middle age and sturdy build.

"This – this is Ottar, who lives with us," he answered.

Sidroc had gone to check on the horses, but as Ceridwen and Eirian led the way through the trees to their camp they saw Tindr at work, banking up the remaining coals in the fire ring lest they need them later. He looked up at their approach, and his face showed the same recognition as had that of the females of Tyrsborg.

"This is Tindr," Ceridwen explained. "He is deaf. He cares for our beasts, and hunts for us."

Tindr nodded to the two, then cocked his head at another approach.

It was Sidroc. Even though his father's back was to him, he knew the man for who he was. After their embrace, Sidroc spoke.

"I have never seen you here, at any Althing," he said.

His father nodded. "We do not often come. And," he looked behind him with a shrug, "there are so many folk who do."

"Já," admitted Sidroc. Unless you had planned to meet up with others at a certain place and time, it would be easy to miss them in the throngs.

"I am glad you did so now," Sidroc added. His father gave a solemn nod.

Sidroc repeated his promise. "And I will still come for you after the first grain harvest, so that you and Stenhild can visit Tyrsborg."

This drew a smile from the old man. He looked between Eirian and Tindr, and then spoke. "You have another son," the old man recalled.

"Ja," Sidroc confirmed. "Yrling. He is Eirian's twin. He left with Hrald, and if the Gods sent them fair winds, they are in Angle-land now, at the keep of Four Stones in Lindisse. But he will be back, and then you will meet."

For all the surety with which Sidroc spoke, he could not help but wonder what age his father might be when Yrling returned. But the old man nodded.

"We came by waggon," Hrald told them. "We have a crock of Stenhild's ale within," he added, with the slightest grin at his son.

It took no more prompting than this. Those of Tyrsborg took up their wooden cups and followed. Hrald and Ottar had stopped their ox cart on the western side of the Althing grounds, where they had arrived. The herbal tang of Stenhild's brew was unlike any Ceridwen had known, but just as Sidroc remembered from his visit to his father's snug seaside farm.

The Sun was lifting overhead; this far North it had been bright day for hours, and the time of assembly was near. A lur sounded, a deep and ponderous summoning issuing from the round opening of a wooden horn. It was time to gather.

A natural boundary had formed between the men Ivar had sent, and the folk of the island, who in short order surrounded them. The distance maintained was that customary and fitting at an Althing, but there was no doubt that those three Svear ship captains who had cruised the coast now faced some thousand wary Gotlandic men. More than a few women were there as well, standing at the sides of husbands or grown sons.

At a normal Althing, the Law-speaker stood upon a square slab of limestone, so all might see and hear him. This was brought to bear for the chief of Ivar's men, with Eskil and the third man standing atop benches. Each man had dressed with care, in clean tunic and leggings, and with hair carefully combed, a sign of respect not lost upon the islanders. The Svear were not afraid to show their wealth, for not only did each bear a fine sword and lavish scabbard, but each was adorned with heavy silver at their wrists, and about their necks, all save the chief man, who wore a chain of red-gold resting on his tunic. Yet elevated as they were, they were still encircled by Gotlanders. This cut them off from their own men who had journeyed with them from their ships. These remained nearer their tents, standing at alert and watching the masses.

It was forbidden to brandish any weapon at the Althing, but of carrying one there was no such stricture, and the men of Gotland had taken this to heart, for many had stopped by their campsites to take up their spear. Sidroc stood, sword at his side, with his father and Ottar, each of whom held a spear. Berse and the other men of the trading road found them, and moved with them up nearest the first row of men, as did all who hoped to speak. Berse wore not only a sword, but carried a spear as well, and had even his helmet upon his head. Tindr, bow on back and quiver at his hip, was careful to stay near Sidroc, masking his discomfort at the crowd, and helping make way for Ceridwen and Eirian behind them.

Of the three messengers from the Svear King, they stood closest to Eskil. As the noise of the crowd assembling began to die down, Sidroc watched Eskil scan the crowd, and then sweep his eyes forward to where he stood with the elder Hrald. Sure enough, the Svear did not hide his surprise at seeing what clearly was a second Dane, Sidroc's father, standing there. He shook his head slightly, taking this in, and Sidroc guessed Eskil was again wondering why this small island held such attraction.

The chief man raised his arms to signal his readiness to begin. He was a big man, as fair as Eskil himself, but showing many strands of silver in his full beard of yellow. He was well suited to his task, for his voice boomed out in clear and measured speech over the assembled.

"I am Ingifast. My words will be few. But take thought before you answer.

"Ivar, King in Uppsala, King of the Svear, bids the men of Gotland to accept him as their King."

The man had scarce formed the last of these words when the crowd erupted in howls of protest. Some of the Gotlanders thumped the butts of their spears against the hard ground, others took an active step toward Ingifast, prompting him to raise his arms for silence.

"Do not bypass the chance for greater protection. One day you may need it."

"Need it!" called a voice from opposite where Sidroc stood. He recognised it as coming from the brew-house owner at Paviken who had sold him and his son Hrald ale. The man was genial, and a good host, but there was fire in his words today. "The Gods have blest Gotland, allowing it to rise as it has in the middle of the sea. All sailors need us. You need us, all of you. Sailing back to the land of the Svear without fresh water – or ale – would be no pleasure."

Another shouted a question at the speaker. "Ivar bids us – what means that?"

"Já," a few cried out. "A demand? A threat?"

Ingifast took it in stride. He was ready with his answer, and ready too for the rebuke which he was sure would follow. "That the protection provided would be worth a trebled share of silver as tribute." He paused a moment before going on. "In return Ivar will garrison Gotland with two hundred men."

"To eat us out of house and home!"

"To tax our trade and skim our profits!"

Berse spoke now. There were few blade-makers on Gotland, and he was known as the best. He had also a sharp mind for trade, as most smiths possessed.

"A trebled share – " he looked down at his fingers as he worked the sum "– a yearly tribute of one hundred and eighty pieces of silver?"

The howls grew louder. Berse looked about him, nodding his head in satisfaction at the outrage. The smith spoke again, addressing Eskil, the only one of these men with whom he had prior dealings.

"Ivar demands we make ourselves as a holding to Uppsala. But our agreement is based on trust, and silver. Each year the sixty marks have been carried away without fail to Uppsala. What have we gained from it? Never have we made demand for help from any of the Svear Kings. If we take fish or grain to the lands ruled by the King of Uppsala, we land without toll. But here we charge no toll to any. Gotland is free to trade in.

"We will never surrender that!"

Hoots, whistles, and the clanging of knife blades on metal followed. Shrill jeers and oaths were flung like missiles at the three Svear. Still, the circle in which they stood was respected, and other than the slightest movement forward by a few Gotlandic men, no threatening action had been taken. Ceridwen had her arm around Eirian, and felt grateful for Tindr's near presence at their side.

Sidroc had travelled more widely than many there, and as an outsider could speak with a certain objective judgement. He had almost to smile at himself, seeing in what conflicted position the Gods had now placed him. He was being asked to align himself with the King of the Svear. Though born a Dane, his loyalty had foremost been to his own future. He took a step forward, turned his face away from the Svear, and began to speak to his fellows.

"I am a Dane by blood, but here by choice. Gotlanders are their own folk. We have no King, and trade fairly and freely with all comers. All recognise this. Dane, Svear, Rus, all from the Baltic rim and all from the west who venture to our shores acknowledge this. If this island bows its head to Ivar – or any King in Uppsala – we become a target for the Kings of other lands. We will cease being a free trading port, and a stop of respite on the long eastern journey to trade silk and spices and furs, and become a prize to be fought over.

"Whoever calls himself King of Dane-mark will look upon us as just that, a rich war prize."

Cries of protest against this Fate rang out, that of "Nai! Nai!" as this prospect sank in. He let the shouts die down, and turned to address the three Svear.

"I am a Dane," he repeated to them, "and have seen many men who called themselves King, both in Dane-mark, and in Angle-land. I have been here now a decade and more. Threats will not move the Gotlanders. They have no need of Kings. Ivar is new. Already his reach exceeds his grasp. His arm is not long enough to exact more from this island."

Ingifast would answer this. "Bold words, and proud ones," he conceded, fixing his eyes on he who had delivered them. "But Ivar is no common King. Not in my lifetime nor in that of my father have we had a King in Uppsala as skilled and cunning as he. He has many good men, with many good ships," he went on, nodding to the two Svear who stood with him, "and can do more than offer. He can take."

This threat, bald as it was, silenced the crowd for a long moment. Sidroc met Ingifast's eyes, and again spoke.

"The island is long," Sidroc reminded. "Our coasts extend great distances. Gotland is also narrow. Folk can travel at speed from east to west. We would find it easier to defend than you know." He looked now with singular gaze to Eskil. "And as you have already seen, we are unafraid to protect our shores."

A low murmur of muffled voices rippled through the crowd. Ingifast let it continue, then made his offer once more.

"What answer do you have for Ivar? Protection and strength, with his might behind you – "

He could not finish, for another from Paviken spoke up, one of the ship-builders there. That trading settlement had the most to lose from any change in the island's standing as point of free trade. He glanced at Sidroc before he began, to acknowledge his past words. "Or do we become a prime target for the sea raiders of Danemark, the Rus, and all others who now land to trade with us freely, and in peace?"

A cry of "Vote now! Vote now!" went up, prompting Ingifast to again raise his arms for silence. Yet he nodded his head to agree to this demand.

"Free men of Gotland, what say you? Those who accept Ivar's offer, say Já."

There was some shuffling, but almost no sound. A few voices were raised in the back, a few calls, of "Já."

Ingifast cocked his head to hear them, and then prepared to ask the second question.

Berse did it for him. "And those who would remain as we are, free and with no bonds to any King?"

A near-deafening roar of assent rose from the throats of the Gotlanders. Tindr, who had been carefully watching Sidroc, let out a honking call above the countless cries of "Já!"

Ingifast was not pleased, and the scowl on his face prefaced the stern warning to come. Once again he was preempted. One of the workers in sandstone from the far south of the island spoke up.

"We could come to Ivar himself, and tell him," he offered. The crowd shouted in laughing agreement, pounding the butts of their spears on the hard ground.

Ingifast would have the final word, and delivered it over the snickers of those before him. "One day Gotland will regret this," he warned.

He jumped down from the Law-speaker stone, and Eskil and the other man stepped from their benches. It was just as well the offer was a jest. All three knew Ivar did not need a mass of indignant islanders to add to his concerns; the man had his hands full with keeping his Jarls and other war-chiefs in line.

The crowd began to disperse, many heading to the waggons of the local brewers. A jubilant Berse had clapped Sidroc on the shoulder, and was now leading a group looking for ale. Ceridwen felt she could finally draw a deep breath, and she pressed a kiss on the brow of her daughter, who looked pale. Sidroc had turned to have a word with his father. Then he noticed Eskil, talking to Ingifast. The older man was shaking his head in dismay, and then turned to join the third Svear.

Sidroc raised his hand to Eskil, gesturing him near. The man came, with something near to a grin on his face.

"There was no surprise," Eskil admitted.

Sidroc only nodded, and considered he who stood before him. He would much rather have Eskil as an ally than enemy. After such a set back to the Svear, this might be the right time to mention his future.

"Luck has been with you to survive this long, Eskil," Sidroc noted. "I know. I reached your age still fighting, and gave thanks each day I survived. You, I think, are past that age where I determined to only trade, and not raid. You have thrown your lot in with this Ivar, which only means more fighting. Your hamingja could tire if you press her too much."

This was not a conversation the Svear imagined having with the Dane, and he found it hard to hide this fact. Caught so off-guard, he shrugged his shoulders in response.

"Have you a wife?" Sidroc questioned next.

Eskil rolled his eyes.

"I have had. Two. No longer."

The Dane gave a nod. He could imagine the type of frivolous woman this good-looking Svear had attracted in the halls of the war-lords he had served. He had a better option to propose.

"The Gotland women are unspoilt, and will keep you on a true path. They are hardworking, and hard-headed." Such a one was, Sidroc felt, just what Eskil needed. He went on, with further reason for the man to change his life.

"Much silver can be made here from trade. I am proof of that. You can risk your neck for this Ivar, or the next King of Uppsala, or the next, as you wish. Just know, there is another way."

Sidroc took him in. Eskil's best days as a fighting man were behind him, and he had gained enough to want to enjoy what he had won. Though not lucky at dice, the man was no fool. Gotland with its wealth needed savvy men, especially those of the Svear. Eskil would be an asset here, if he could resign himself to a quieter life. Sidroc was as much as offering one to him. But he must temper that offer.

"If you join us, you must set up on the western coast."

"The western coast," Eskil repeated.

"It is closer to the land of the Svear. You will want to trade with the King in Uppsala, will you not? You will reach him the faster from there. You might even settle near Paviken, through which all the richest trade runs," Sidroc reasoned.

Anyplace where you will be far from my shield-maiden, he told himself.

It was past High Summer's day. On upland farms the first sheaves of barley had been cut and stacked to dry. Sidroc set out across the island in a horse-drawn waggon from Ring's farm. He drove west, and north, to fetch his father and his wife to Tyrsborg. It was a day out, a day spent with them as they readied themselves, and another day back. At Tyrsborg Ceridwen had been busy with her own preparations. She planned a welcome feast for the arriving couple, one to which Rannveig, Gudfrid, and the expanded household of Tyrsborg would be present. It was, she felt, a boon that she, Eirian and Tindr had already met the old man. Now all that was left was to welcome them to their hall, where they might see their life and meet their friends here.

The waggon jingled up the hill, creaking as the two small bays pulled up before Tyrsborg. Ceridwen's herb garden outside the front door bloomed in hearty profusion, and the grape vine she had carefully tended arced along a wooden framework over the bench below. The vine's deeply cut leaves glowed green as the strong sunlight hit them. Clusters of grapes shown smokey red amongst them, soon to swell into purple ripeness.

Sidroc grinned from the waggon board, reins in hand. He grinned the more when he saw his shield-maiden had donned the gown of ember red he had bought her at the trading post of the Pomerani. She took it from its chest only once or twice a year, always for high occasions. About her neck was the thick braided silver chain he had won for her at dice, along with another prize, the small sphere of pure rock crystal in its silver setting. Adorned so with silver hanging upon her breast, and her silver disc bracelet on her wrist, she looked every bit the wife of a rich trader, and Lady of a fine hall.

Next Sidroc sat his father, and behind them, Stenhild, both wide-eyed at the loftiness of the steeply gabled roof of the hall. The stable, newly enlarged, was nearly as impressive to their eyes. Massive stacks of neatly laid firewood against the walls of both stable and hall told that the dwelling place was warm in the coldest of Winters. Their eyes fell on the fowl houses, and the fat cows kneeling in the grass beyond them; then completed a circuit to the stable paddock, holding four handsome horses which tossed their heads and nickered a greeting to the two harnessed who had brought them here.

The alcoves of Tyrsborg were thankfully deep; two could sleep comfortably within, and Ceridwen and Eirian had lavished care setting up that which would be shared by Hrald and Stenhild. The best sheet was placed upon the feather bed, and the down-filled comforter was encased also with smooth linen. Gunnvor was instructed to spare no expense in the welcoming feast, and sent to Ring for a suckling pig, which he returned dressed and ready for roasting. Rannveig arrived with a jug of the herbed ale favoured by Sidroc, one she brewed with parsley and thyme leaves. She also brought a jug of rosy-hued mead, in which the native berries known as salmbär had been mashed into the honey, lending both flavour and colour. Šeará and her young, in their deer-skin tunics and leggings, occasioned many admiring glances from Stenhild. Both she and Hrald had seen Sámi traders come to Paviken with furs and tusks, but they had not before seen a woman of that tribe, and Tindr's wife was striking in any setting. It was a lively evening, for Tindr and Šeará's little daughter, Jaské, close in age to Rodiaud and great friends, ran about with Flekkr until the girls collapsed in a sleepy heap in Eirian's alcove. Juoksa, their son of nine Summers, and nearly as quiet as his father, watched Eirian as she attended to the girls. Eirian had almost thirteen years, and was beginning to bud, while Juoksa looked the flaxen-haired boy he was. But a careful observer might note the boy's high regard for the elder daughter of Tyrsborg.

The old couple were treated as honoured guests, so much so that Stenhild seemed near to bewilderment. She had her best gown on, suspended from a pair of cleanly cast bronze shoulder brooches which Hrald had presented her with upon the birth of their lost child. Her hair had paled to a handsome silver, and she wore it neatly coiled under her best kerchief.

Both Hrald and Stenhild spent time merely gazing at the hall, the large stable, and the horses. All was splendid. Though dwarfed by a keep like Four Stones, Tyrsborg, with its two walls of stone and bright timber interior, felt almost the home of some High King, so modest was their own farm on the western coast. And here they knew unusual leisure. The stay of a few days took them from their own myriad tasks of field, beasts, and household. To be sure, Stenhild had brought her spindle, so that she might not know idle hands, but much of the time was content to rest on the bench in the small garden by the well, the ripening grapes twining on their framework over her head, as she looked upon the sea. Mother and daughter joined her in handwork, and with only a little prompting from a curious Eirian, Stenhild told the story of how she had met a young and awkward Hrald.

"When he walked away for good that Summer, I tried not to believe it. He had left before, walked back to Paviken, but then returned to me. But that last time, he was gone." Even after the passage of long decades she must look down at this remembrance.

Ceridwen leaned in then, her voice as soft as she could make it. "Yet you never married afterwards . . ."

The old women shook her head. "My husband did not return; Hrald knew he would not; said he was dead or taken by slavers far from Gotland. I raised my daughter as best I could, took in another widow who needed a home, and we grew enough to fill our bowls.

"Then, after years, Hrald walked back up the track to me. It was like seeing a ghost, a beloved one. He was worn, as thin as a stick, and troubled, but he fell into my arms."

She paused and looked to the oaken door of the hall. "It took him a long time to tell me of his sorrow; of the viper he had been forced to wed, and leaving behind children. His daughters he wept for, but his natural son, who that viper had ill-treated . . ."

She cleared her throat, a soft setting aside of the past. "When Sidroc and Hrald rode up to the farm, I knew the boy had finally found his father."

Her eyes gleamed with tears at this memory. She looked to the wife of that son, and spoke again. "And Sidroc – he forgave his father, without words."

Ceridwen was silent. She too had felt this forgiveness, one granted without questioning.

Stenhild had something more to add. "When Sidroc and his son left, Hrald wept and wept. It was joy and sorrow both, but mostly joy."

All three sat quietly. Ceridwen looked to her daughter, eyes gently cast down, a look that told her Eirian was deep in thought. It was good for the girl to hear such matters, to learn of the workings of men and women, and to hear that even the hardest challenges of life could be met, and that which had been wrongly done, undone.

In the same wise Sidroc had his own private time with his father. He had taken the elder Hrald down to the shingle beach on the day of arrival, and pointed out to him the drekar hauled up along past the herb garden of the brew-house. One afternoon when Stenhild was sitting with his shield-maiden and daughter, he stood with his father outside the paddock where the horses were turned out. They had spoken of the animals, and of the elder Yrling's chestnut mare. Both fell silent, and then the old man said, "Tell me of my brother's death."

Sidroc drew breath. They might step into the stable, or enter the hall, but did not. Such things must be told out of doors, Sidroc felt; no roof was high enough to contain what he must utter, and what his father must hear. Together they walked away from the hall, passing the females in the garden, down the hill, past the brew-house, and to the dragon-ship. Yrling had sold his prized mare as the final payment for this ship.

Dauðadagr stood open; Runulv took her out to keep her planking tight and sea-worthy, but the last time she had sailed was with Sidroc and the boy named for his uncle. Today, with his own son, the older brother of he who had built her circled the ship, the single quartz eye of the carved likeness of the god Odin following them as they did. Not far from that carving in the stern, fast by the slot which held the steering oar once held by Yrling, the two sat down upon the rounded rocks rising from the beach. They were sheltered from some of the wind there, but the breeze ruffled their hair, and carried the mineral scent of salt and limestone on it.

"My uncle died no ordinary death," Sidroc began. "It was a Fate whose strands the Norns spent long in twisting, though the final cut from Skuld came sudden.

"As I told you, Hrald's mother is a noblewoman, one from a keep called Cirenceaster. Yrling made many raids upon her father's lands; we captured slaves and took much grain from storehouses. Her father was beholden to the King of Wessex, but made a separate Peace with Yrling. Part of that was his daughter, Ælfwyn, who Yrling wed. The rest was great booty in the form of rich fabric, goods of bronze, silver, and even gold.

"We stopped our raids on Cirenceaster, but it was too far from Four Stones for Yrling to keep other Danes away. Word came of rival war-chiefs who wanted the place. Yrling felt it his; no one could have it but him, as he had already the daughter thereof and much of the treasure. We rode out after the attackers."

Sidroc must slow now. He had not told this story in many years, and never told it in as much detail as he did today, so far from that distant action. Over the span of years and hundreds of leagues it came rushing back at him.

"We were not alone in heading there. Before this Yrling had accepted a Saxon thegn as a prisoner at Four Stones, a man of one of the great families of the Kingdom of Wessex. A man who the Dane Hingvar had maimed by burning out his eyes."

Sidroc watched his father's hand lift toward his own eyes, in horror.

"Yrling took no part in the maiming," his son went on, "but accepted the man at Four Stones. This had become known to the prisoner's brother, who was Lord of his keep.

"Kilton," named Sidroc, in a low voice.

"This warrior – Kilton – had already caught Hingvar, and avenged his brother in blood. But he heard that Yrling was nearing Cirenceaster, and wanted him too."

Sidroc was looking out to sea as he told the next. "We rode out, Toki and I with Yrling, and most of our best men with us. The other Danes had got there first, and Cirenceaster was in flames. It was not long past dawn; we saw the fire far off, and spurred our horses onward. On foot we fought our way to the palisade, so Yrling could claim what he could. Then the warrior Kilton called out Yrling's name, looking for him.

"Kilton was – he was a good warrior; famed amongst his people. But he was become a Berserkr. He slashed his way through all before him, calling for Yrling. And Yrling answered.

"There was mist. The ground was wet." Sidroc's words slowed even more. "Men moved in a fog about us.

"Kilton and a few of his bodyguard reached us. Yrling was hot, both for the loss of the fortress of his wife, and at this warrior after him, gnashing his teeth and swearing oaths for his blood.

"Toki and I – we had our hands full with the bodyguard. But Yrling hardly . . . hardly had time to bring his sword to bear. Kilton was too good."

As if not to diminish the skilled warrior Yrling was, Sidroc must say the next. "To withstand a Berserkr – few men have been granted the favour of the Gods to do so."

Hrald was nodding his head, chin down. His boy had seen his own uncle be slaughtered, before him.

Now Sidroc must complete the tale, tell his father what he did not know. Of anything he might admit to his father, this act would be most painful to share.

"We could do nothing; the fortress was burning, and to fight two foes was beyond us. All was lost. We could save nothing but our lives."

He stopped here in his telling, not wanting to remember how near a thing that was. He had slashed down a few Saxon thegns, and Danes as well, to get to their horses, feeling nothing but Tyr's hand guiding him to his own survival. He had gathered what booty he could along the way.

"Toki." The name came out on a shallow breath. His father had turned to him, waiting for more. He had told the old man his cousin was dead, and now he must tell why.

"When Yrling fell, Toki ran."

The start from his father made him add more.

"Not in fear. He did not run in fear. He ran to return to Four Stones. What I did not know was why: to claim it for his own."

The old man's lips parted.

"Já. Toki had his followers, just as I had mine. With Yrling dead, he thought to reach Four Stones first, and make it, and all within it, his.

"I followed, with my own men, and those of Yrling. Toki went overland, and got there hours before me. It was dark, but torches flared from the ramparts. The palisade gates were closed against us, but the men on the ramparts knew it was me. I called out to those within to open up. Toki killed one of them for trying.

"But the gate was opened, nonetheless. Toki had told the men I was dead as well. Now they knew it was a lie. Like so many Toki told.

"There had been trouble between us before. This scar, yes, but something more. When Ælfwyn came to wed Yrling, she brought a maid with her. He and I had fought over her. I marked her for my own, and Yrling agreed, as Toki had his wife back in Jutland, and children too. The maid – she is my wife now. But she had left Four Stones before this, and Ælfwyn was alone.

"Toki came out. He had been drinking and was wild with it. He had no shield, but his sword in one hand, and his knife in the other. He lunged at me, challenged me directly with his sword. He said things – "

Sidroc must stop here. He would not repeat to his father's ear the old taunt his cousin had thrown at him the day he slashed his face, about Sidroc being the son of a thrall. Toki had repeated the slur that night.

"We fought. I flicked the sword from his hand, wanting him to stop. But it was not enough. His men, watching us – one by one they left his back, and came to stand with my own. He saw it and grew crazed, mad with rage. He had tried to cut my throat when we were boys, and tried it again.

"I killed him. With an oath on my lips I drove my blade home."

Sidroc's hand felt again the strength in that act, the firm resistance and then utter yield of Toki's chest to the power behind that point. His hand had clenched in the telling, and he worked to release the tension gathered within his balled fist.

He let a long breath out. To sit here now and tell of a night more than twenty years gone was nothing Sidroc had ever countenanced doing. Yet the man he told this to was brother to Yrling, and uncle to Toki. And he was father to he himself. No one was more fitting to bear witness to this tale than direct kin, and Sidroc had at last such a man to tell.

His father's eyes had widened. Hrald knew Toki was dead; Sidroc had told him it was he who carried him to his burial mound. What his boy had not told him was why Toki died.

The old man was silent. But he reached out his weathered hand and set it upon his son's knee.

"What I left you to," the old man murmured.

Sidroc's answer would refute this. He gave his head a shake. "Few men who choose the warrior's way have had a life as good as mine." He tilted his head up the hill towards Tyrsborg as further answer.

He wanted to finish the story of his cousin's end, so he might return to Yrling.

"Toki was burnt next day with all his weapons, and all his treasure. I laid it all upon him. I fired it, and stood there until he was ashes. One thing kept coming back to me as I watched. When Hlaupari grew old, he had fits. He was in pain, and ready to die. Toki offered to do it for me. I took Hlaupari's life myself, but Toki helped me bury him."

Hearing of Sidroc's childhood dog gave Hrald a start. From what Sidroc had earlier told him, Hrald's sister Signe and brother-in-law Ful had not in fact provided a good home for his son, and the hound had served perhaps as Sidroc's only friend.

"What I left you to," the old man repeated.

"Do not say that, father. No man can judge another in such cases. I did not." Sidroc looked away now, narrowing his eyes to the deep blue of the Baltic. The sea was crowned with a few shifting white caps, brilliant white in the strong Sun. He turned back to meet his father's eyes. "I was forced away from my hall, my wife, my children. I took it as sign that the Gods had offered me another way. Could I have returned? Já. Though I was sure it would have meant my death, and even war. But my return would have held some meaning for others, though it ended in my blood."

He added, almost as an afterthought, "I did avenge Yrling's death." He did not say how, or that he did so in the stable yard of his own hall here on Gotland.

Hrald nodded. "Yrling awaits you, with a cup of mead," was what he answered.

Sidroc went on.

"A child was born after his death, a girl, who was named Ashild."

The old man's eyes lit. "Ashild," he repeated. "Our mother." He let his eyes drop in remembrance.

Having named her now, Sidroc must tell of her Fate. "She was a true daughter of Freyja, in every way Yrling's equal. She died on a field of battle, going to aid my boy Hrald."

The elder Hrald must cover his eyes with his hand at this, as if he watched the awe-ful action play out before them. After a moment he cleared his throat, so he could speak.

"Then she too will greet you, cup in hand, when you reach Asgard."

Ceridwen and Stenhild walked down the hill one morning to Rannveig's for a visit. The old woman enjoyed her time in the brew-shed, sampling the different herb-infused blends Rannveig was wont to make in the Summer, and told of her own home-brewing. Eirian was eager to join them, and had donned the gown which Šeará had helped her decorate in Sámi patterns. A full hand-length of the skirt hem was bound with colourful ribbands which had been folded into zigzags, shaped into squares, and cut and formed into star-like patterns, each length of ribband made fast by stitching. Šeará was proud of what Eirian had done, and how diligently she had laboured. And the girl's admiration for Šeará was great; even Stenhild had seen it at the welcome feast.

Now Eirian, listening to Rannveig and Stenhild tell of their brewing, spoke up.

"I must learn to brew, as well."

The three women looked at her, nodding their approval, and Rannveig gave thought to Sparrow, who was not much older than Eirian when she taught her to brew.

"That is true," the brewster agreed. "All women should know how to brew for their household. Though," she added with a twinkle, "the farm you go to will be a large one, and you are sure to have help."

"And if I wed in another land," Eirian thought aloud, "I might have care of many more folk than I can brew for. You will give me some recipes, Rannveig. I will write them down; mother will help me, so I will have them. That way wherever I wed folk will know how good your ale is."

"You are a wise girl," Rannveig noted.

Eirian's gentle musing continued, saying aloud things that perhaps she had never quite fully thought of.

"I might go as a bride in Angle-land . . . or Wales . . ."

Her mother took a quiet breath. Such distances were hard for Ceridwen to compass, and she countered this with a smile at Eirian's gown. "Or perhaps you will go north, to Sámi country, and wed a chieftain there, and live amongst the ren-deer."

Eirian laughed in delight. "I did not think of that," she admitted, and then paused. She wrapped her arms around her narrow chest and gave a shiver. "It would be cold . . ."

All four females were silent a moment, thinking of the day this maid must leave her home to become a bride. Rannveig broke it by returning to the girl's initial request. "As soon as you are ready we will begin. I did not learn how to brew until I had nearly twice your years, and wish I had started younger. But you will learn from my mistakes, so you need not repeat them."

They all smiled at this promise, but Eirian's mother had a deeper thought: Would we could keep you from making our mistakes.

One night Ceridwen and Sidroc, Hrald and Stenhild at their sides, walked down the hill to the brew-house. On Summer nights folk gathered at Rannveig's in greater or smaller numbers depending on the demands of arriving and departing ships, or the care of upland farms with their needful rhythms of sowing, weeding, and reaping. Fellowship was found within the brew-house, and a free exchange of news, conjecture, and outright gossip to enliven the long evenings. Then there was the ale itself. Full-flowering Summer herbs and newly harvested grains provided Rannveig with much material with which to assay the flavouring of her brews. Beyond the drink, the expanse of sea to gaze upon outside her rolled up awnings seemed reward enough. But the place held another attraction, that of gaming.

Rannveig kept three or four wooden tæfl boards with their pieces, some carved of bone, half stained dark; others with pieces of stone, sorted by colour into two groups. She had also many sets of small knuckle joints of sheep for the game of bones. And men who favoured dice oftentimes carried them in the pouch at their belts. Sidroc was one of these, and had four dice of walrus ivory at his belt, as he thought his father might enjoy a game or two.

"Ottar and I play, of an evening," Hrald told him, speaking of that man who with his wife Runa helped him and Stenhild at their farm.

"Good. We will form a team, you and I against all comers." The boldness of this claim made the old man grin.

As the two couples walked it seemed broad daylight, yet the evening meal was long over, and the sky only now paling to a softer blue. Rannveig and Gudfrid greeted them heartily, and dipped up thick walled pottery cups brim-full. The four sat on two benches at the corners of a square table, savouring the creamy brightness of the brew. The Sun, still high but shifting across the sky, left a shimmering ladder of light in the dark blue of the sea.

Two men now entered, and Sidroc waved them over to meet Tyrsborg's guests. One was Ketil the rope maker. The second, younger man was his nephew Runulv, who sailed for Sidroc on his trading ventures. At gaming Sidroc had proven much the winner against each, especially Ketil, who in attempt to even the score, grew more daring as his cup grew empty.

After their words of greeting, Ketil and Runulv glanced over to a corner where two men were already at their dice-throwing.

"We are come to drink, and to play," Ketil announced. It was dice he meant, the only game Sidroc had interest in.

"Join us," Runulv invited. Indeed, he wished to be able to look at the old man, for rarely had the ship-captain seen a father and son more alike.

Sidroc began to rise in agreement, ale cup in hand. He gestured to his father to follow. "My father and me, against uncle and nephew," he proclaimed.

But Hrald shook his head.

"Nai, son. I will hamper you. We will play alone, and not in teams."

Sidroc was undeterred. "But you will let me put up your stake, since you have left your silver back at the hall," Sidroc said evenly. He would not let his father risk any scrap of silver he might have upon him.

The old man smiled in understanding, and nodded agreement. "Já, já, since my silver is at Tyrsborg. That is fair."

In truth when Hrald played with Ottar they never wagered; neither could be profligate with coin.

As the men began to move off Ceridwen turned to Stenhild. They may have been forsaken over tiny cubes of ivory, but could find their own fun.

"I play tæfl," Ceridwen offered. "Also counters."

Sidroc heard this, and turning his head, was quick to comment on this last.

"You do not want to challenge her at counters, Stenhild," he warned, "unless you have firm hold of your purse. She is hard to beat."

Ceridwen laughed, remembering how at a trading post on the southern shore of the Baltic she had attempted to teach him how to win at this simple game, which required sum-making and counting.

Stenhild laughed as well. "Tæfl then, I think." They would see which of them was better at capturing the King in the middle of the board.

"I play during Winter's Nights with my daughter," Stenhild went on, after Ceridwen returned with a board and playing stones. "Gudvi is, I think, a few years older than you. She was but a toddling child when Hrald first supped with us. It was his first night on Gotland." Stenhild cocked her head to one side, and smiled at the memory. "Gudvi was shy, and barely talking, but liked him. I recall her offering her bread, holding it out to him."

Both women were now smiling at this remembered gesture of their children.

"She had young of her own?" Ceridwen asked.

"Já, four, all hearty. Frigg has blest her. We see them twice each year. We go to them for Winter's Nights, and also Mid-Summer. They live up the coast, and inland. There are a raft of grandchildren living nearby, nine of them." The old women's eyes creased in pleasure.

"That is a blessing," Ceridwen agreed.

Stenhild nodded. "I see our lost daughter in them," she added, more quietly. She spoke of the single child she had born with Hrald, taken by fever.

Ceridwen touched her hand. "Já. I have lost a daughter, while she was teething. She will always be her own in my heart. Yet, what joy when Eirian, and then Rodiaud were born, to have a girl again."

They began setting up the pieces on the board. "Eirian," Stenhild asked, considering the girl who had impressed her. "What name is that? I have not heard it afore."

The girl's mother answered with a rueful smile. "It is of Wales. The place she spoke of travelling to."

Stenhild only nodded. "She has the wander-lust to travel, like a boy." She set the last piece in place. "But Rodiaud is of Gotland, through and through. Her, you will keep."

The men played, each placing small bits of silver to one side of the table as their opening wager. Runulv, good trader that he was, and knowing he would this night game, had brought a tiny scale set with him; they need not depend on Rannveig's larger one. Runulv was a skilled, if cautious player, making up for the reckless daring of his uncle. Each man was well-used to the ebb and flow of Sidroc's winning, used as well to his easy manner, which did not mask the look of determination in his eyes. Much to Sidroc's pleasure, his father held his own. He had no memory of playing dice with him as a boy; life was spare enough, and the woman Hrald had wed hard enough, to forbid such innocent triviality.

Berse entered, and saw Sidroc at dice. The Dane had taken so much silver from him that the blade-smith was always looking for a way to win. He was good-humoured about it, and on the few occasions he had bested Sidroc, had not gloated, but walked away with a sense of quiet self-satisfaction at his feat.

The pile of silver, both coin and hack, grew steadily. It was shifted from man to man as the cast of the dice and call of the numbers dictated, but spent more time at the side of Sidroc than the others. Any in the lead could call the game at any moment, but such was the growing excitement that none did. Still, the purses of Runulv and Ketil were growing light. It was Runulv who retired first, empty-handed, and unwilling to wager his last pieces of hack-silver. Ketil was next. Both remained at the table, steadily drawing on their ale, watching the action between the three still playing. Berse, late to the game, had wagered a large handful of coins to even the field. He was warrior enough to never discount any opponent, and did not look upon the old man at Sidroc's side as an inferior foe. Yet the steady surety with which Sidroc wagered and cast the dice kept his mind focused on beating him.

Then Hrald began to falter. His hamingja, his luck-spirit, was grown weary, and began to desert him. His own pile of winnings steadily shrunk, and three rounds later he had but two thin quarter pieces of silver coin left with which to wager.

At their own table the tæfl game was also coming to an end. Ceridwen found herself cornered by Stenhild, her men taken one by one, until she lost the King she was defending. She shook her head with a laugh.

"You are very good," Ceridwen praised.

"I have played all my life, which has been far longer than yours," Stenhild said.

"Let us have more ale, and we will talk," Ceridwen offered. She rose to see Rannveig coming from the table at which she usually stood or sat. She was headed not at them, but at the gaming men. Berse was at this point about to throw, with Hrald coming after. Berse's call was good; the pile went from Sidroc to him. Hrald had now to surrender one of his last quarter pieces of silver, leaving him with a single piece. It was his turn to throw.

Both women watched as Rannveig inserted herself between the two men, and held out her hand to Sidroc's father, open palm up, demanding the dice. The gesture was quick, but a sly smile played on her lips. Hrald raised his eyebrows, but could do nothing but oblige the brewster.

He passed the dice into her firm hand. She closed her fist around the ivory cubes and shook them. As they rattled in her grasp she called out "Six, or nine," as she threw them.

Any combination on the two dice that led to either number would make the throw the winner. The dice clattered to a stop. One had six dots, the other three.

Sidroc gaped. He had never in all these years seen Rannveig game with dice. Now she had made a perfect call her first time.

Rannveig reached down to the pile of silver, cupped it in her hand, and pulled it to the old man. Hrald, with the brewster's help, had won all this.

"Time to close," she announced, cheerily. This was met by feigned howls and laughter at her boldness. Nonetheless, Gudfrid stood ready at a crock to dip up another cup for all who still thirsted.

Sidroc refilled his own, then followed Rannveig to the table and her scale set, that he might settle his bill. He made sure he paid for Berse as well.

"How did you do that?" he asked.

She grinned. "My hamingja," she answered. But it was not only the prompting of the brewster's luck-spirit, for she went on.

"I have not stood here in this room for these many years watching the likes of you, without seeing something of how you win. No one had yet called those two numbers tonight. I knew they must come up."

As the four climbed the hill to Tyrsborg, Hrald turned to his son. Ceridwen and Stenhild walked ahead of them, under a sky through which stars were just beginning to dazzle.

The old man put his hand on his purse, now heavy at his belt. It held more silver than he had carried in many a year.

"Half of this is rightly yours," he told Sidroc. His voice was low; he did not wish the women to hear. "It was your stake I began with; I could not have played without it."

Sidroc glanced at his father, moving slowly forward at his side in the late dusk. Then he lifted his head to the bright wanderers in the sky, those stars so much brighter than the others.

"It was Rannveig made that final throw for you. But Rannveig has gold, and no interest in it."

Hrald had seen that himself; the brewster and her son Tindr and his wife lived a life of unusual content.

His son went on, as if he guessed at Hrald's thoughts.

"I too have gold, and though my interest in it is great, would not take a single piece of silver won by you."

Sidroc looked again at his father. "It was time for Fate to favour you," he suggested. It brought to mind Rannveig's claim that six and nine were bound to come up on those dice.

"Before you leave you and Stenhild might walk down the trading road, find some things of worth you might value," he went on. He wondered how long it had been since they had treated themselves to anything other than new tools or the most needful of necessities.

Hrald's step slowed further at this thought. He and Stenhild had taken a walk there with Ceridwen and Eirian the second day of their stay. The old couple had seen and admired much, all out of the realm of possibility for them.

He recalled the lengths of heavy woollen wadmal Stenhild had looked at, not even allowing herself to touch their surface. Their blankets and alcove curtains were thin, and such warm and heavy stuff took more wool than their small flock could yield.

Living with a good woman at his side was most of what Hrald had ever wanted. He had been granted that in Stenhild, as well the peace of a place like Gotland, and a farm they had worked for decades. Now the Gods had granted him his son back, a man who had made his way so surely that perhaps Hrald should heed his words.

"I will take Stenhild back there tomorrow," he decided aloud. He thought of the wadmal she had studied. Those bolts woven in stripes of red, yellow, and blue were more costly. He would see that Stenhild chose from such, as her eye had lingered longest on them. And he might just get them both one of those fine ox-horn combs, as well.

The seven day stay drew to its end, marked by another feast, one of fond farewell until next time. Sidroc drove the couple back across the island, spending the night at the farm where Ottar and his wife Runa welcomed them home. Hrald and Stenhild had many lengths of heavy woollens with them, and small gifts too for Ottar and Runa, gratefully received. This pair, younger by a score of years than Hrald and Stenhild, made it possible for the old couple to stay on at a farm they had built from ground up. Life for all four was sparse, the beauty of sea and landscape the only indulgence. Sidroc took it in, seeing it fully. Of the two milking cows, one was old, and likely growing dry, and the single pig they must barter for each year would not feed them much beyond the first Winter's Nights feast. The thatched roofs of house and barn called out for more packed sedge, and another hand to help with seasonal sowing and reaping would ease much labour. Sidroc had never forgotten how his father had worked at the farm back in Jutland. He was working thus still. Before he left, his son slid a fat pouch of silver under the pillow in the old couple's alcove.

Chapter the Fifteenth

NONE MORE FITTING

Four Stones in Lindisse

HRALD took Pega to Oundle the month after her arrival at Four Stones. His mother and sister came as well, and as Ælfwyn was as mother to Cerd, the boy must accompany her. Burginde and Mealla were there to rein in the boy's high spirits, as well as attend to their respective mistresses. Yrling was along, glad to be put in charge of the hound Frost, taking care he did not disturb the many Oundle cats at their mousing duties around granary and brew-house; and as had become the norm Bork joined, to care for the horses of the family. Jari and twenty men rounded out the party.

For Hrald, the purpose of the trip was twofold, that the Abbess Sigewif might meet his wife, and that both he and Pega visit the ledger-stone under which lay his sister Ashild. Ælfwyn had always matters to discuss with Sigewif, and in this case, aware that it would be the Abbess' first glimpse of Pega, wished to be there to see if her own warm feelings toward the girl were shared by her. Ealhswith would pass up no chance to visit Ashild's tomb, and also to see her grandmother, Sister Ælfleda, who for the duration of the stay of the family of Four Stones, was given dispensation to speak freely with them. Ealhswith had developed a close relationship with her grandmother, and visited Ashild's tomb alone, save for her company, and later went to Ælfleda's cell, so they might both pray and visit together.

Though all of her guests would dine together with her later, Sigewif received the Lady of Four Stones, her son, and his bride alone in her writing chamber. Pega, small, demure, and yet with smiling eyes, looked the tender young woman she was, yet returned the Abbess' greeting with grace. Clad in a gown of deep pink, and with a simple pin of gold at her neckline, she made fine contrast with Hrald, so tall, and dressed in dark blue. When invited to sign her name in the registry of the family of Four Stones kept by Oundle, Pega did so with calm ease, penning her full name and title, just as she had on the day she had wed: Pega, daughter of Swithwulf and Ebbe, granddaughter of Swithwine, great-granddaughter of Wulfsten, great-grand niece to Offa, King of Mercia.

After Hrald had signed, Sigewif turned to address the couple. Her face, one full of resolve and womanly strength, softened. She lifted her arms and placed a hand on each of their heads.

"I bless you, my children, in the name of Christ and our Holy Mother Mary. May your union be fruitful, and of long duration. And may you ever be a blessing to the other."

This benediction by so august a woman, deeply meaningful to both Hrald and Pega, seemed the final confirmation of their new estate. Pega had brought a sheaf of flowers to lay at Ashild's tomb, and they left now to do so. Passing out of the Abbess' chamber, they looked on the garden, where Mealla was chasing after Cerd as Burginde looked on, content to have younger legs run after the boy.

Ælfwyn and Sigewif were left alone.

"This one," the Abbess murmured.

"Yes," Ælfwyn agreed, unable to hide her smile. "This one."

"None lovelier," Sigewif judged. "None more fitting for a man such as Hrald."

Ælfwyn nodded her agreement. "Pega is more than any of us could have dreamt for him."

"How has she been received at the hall?" Sigewif inquired.

"Her simplicity and openness won the admiration of the entire folk," Ælfwyn could tell her. She thought of the single exception, one which she felt was being overcome. "Ealhswith has been slow to warm to Pega. She is, I know, still hurt and confused by the loss of the friendship she was building with Dagmar, and fearful of entrusting such feelings again. Yet Pega's kindnesses to her are so many that the girl is relenting in the face of such freely given affection." Ælfwyn considered her own words, and had more to add. "Their closeness in age helps, as well."

Within the church Pega stood at Hrald's side. They were still a moment as they paused just inside the door, so that Pega might take in the sweep of the edifice. It had stood for less than twenty years, and new as it was, the stone had still that brightness of the quarry about it. Pega could see the statues to be old, and thus the more precious, salvaged from some earlier church and set here. Hrald lifted his hand, drawing her eyes to the sprig of greenery upon the stone floor to the right of the altar. Hrald led her to his sister's grave.

Pega laid the flowers at the foot of the stone, then stood and crossed herself. The single cornflower lying across Ashild's name must have been placed by the nun Bova, who she looked forward to meeting. Then Pega noticed the spear, bolted upright in the corner. She turned to her husband.

"It is Ashild's. She carried it on the day of her death." His own eyes went to it, and then he finished, "Abbess Sigewif had it mounted there. It is what – visitors touch."

He had mentioned to Pega that women and girls had been making a kind of pilgrimage here, to lay flowers at the tomb of Ashild. Just as I have done, she reminded herself. Yet I have everything, and need ask for nothing.

They passed to the Lady Altar; the statue of St Mary was such that one could not enter the church without approaching it. Pega knew the gems draping neck and wrists of the statue to be those given by her mother-in-law. They were indeed splendid. Pega and Hrald stood before the statue, and then her hand gestured to the fine silver box at the base.

Hrald could not today tell her what that silver casket held, the blood-soaked raven banner his sister had made for him. He answered more simply. "The box is also gift of my mother."

They made reverence to the altar, and stepped out into the afternoon sunlight.

Once outside, the garden, at this time of High Summer, beckoned. Pega slipped her arm into Hrald's and they set foot upon the broad gravel paths. They were flanked by beds of creeping thymes, rosemary, lavenders of every shade, sage, caraway, nightshade, and varying mints too numerous to count. The day was warm and the aroma as they moved by these herbs lifted in the air around them. Mounding flowers of monkshood, oxlip, rue, and towers of foxgloves and columbines nodded in the sunlight.

Pega was drawn to that same quadrant which Hrald had retreated to on the Winter day he arrived here, bereft of his wife and his hopes. It had been a morning made the more bitter, not so much by the cold and wet, as by the breaking of his heart. The space he wandered had been writhen and ragged. Now it was filled with blossoming flowers, roses tumbling, heavy with scent, from their supports of twined sticks and wooden trellises. He could do nothing but let himself be led there, so Pega could enjoy it. He tried to see it anew, through her eyes.

Pega paused in their transit, and clung the firmer to his arm. She must tell him, and there was no more beautiful spot than here.

"Sigewif's words," she recalled softly. "I think . . . the union is already fruitful," she whispered.

He looked down at her shining eyes. It was all she said, but her words struck home. She was with child. It had not been two full months since they were wed.

He could not speak; it was a moment in which everything changed, a new order imposed on the landscape of his life.

She went on, hoping she had not spoken too soon. "I am not certain yet . . . but I feel it to be so . . . "

The wistful look in her eyes, the hope in her voice as she gazed up at him awakened him to the moment. He bent to kiss her.

"I am happy," he told her, as of course he knew he must be.

It took him a while to say more, so she went on. "I think our child will come at Candlemas," naming that late Winter cross-quarter day, when the season would be half over, and begin to lean towards Spring.

He closed his hand over hers where it lay threaded through his arm. He felt surprise, though this was what he had wed for.

They spent the night at Oundle, and could not do so as man and wife. Pega stayed with Ealhswith on the nun's side in a cell given them, while Hrald and his men slept in alcoves in the monks' hall. It was the only thing Pega regretted of the trip. She wished she could be in Hrald's arms now, and whisper to him again about the babe to come, and her hopes for it. In such a setting she felt sure that he would hold her close, and tell her that he loved her.

When they pulled into the gates of Four Stones, Kjeld was there to meet them. After greeting his Jarl he was quick to meet Mealla at the back of the waggon.

"I missed you," were his first words. She was reaching into the waggon bed to retrieve her leathern pack.

"I was gone a night," came the prim response.

"The night is when I miss you most," he answered. He could not hold back his grin.

His look was such she could hardly feign insult, and must smile as well.

"You are not Churched," she said of a sudden, as if throwing some obstacle in the path of his desire.

He was taken aback. "I was baptised," he protested.

"Pish. A mere sprinkling of water, and the receiving of a white tunic leaves you far from being Christian."

Kjeld must pause at this. This maid from Éireann had been here long enough to form opinions, which she seemed never to be in short supply of. And she was sharp in what she noticed, and recalled. Kjeld felt she had discerned a great deal through those snapping eyes. One was the general laxity of belief amongst his brothers, despite the presence of a priest. Few men in their ranks were as devout as Hrald. The story had gone round, after his duel with Thorfast, that it was his calling upon the Christian God that made him the victor. This carried weight with the men, though it may not have made them more diligent in their prayers. All stood at the preaching cross each Sabbath; they were commanded to; but how receptive their ears were to the stories of Wilgot – well, each man must gauge that for himself.

"You can have our son sprinkled as soon as he is born," he promised.

"Our son!" she answered, in cool affront. "You move very quickly."

A man needs to, he told himself. Surrounded as they were with many of the escort looking on at their exchange he could think nothing else. It had been clear from the day of Mealla's arrival that he wanted her. Given that he was now second in command, it would take a bold man amongst them to make a move towards the woman after that. It was unfair to Mealla, but advantageous to him.

Mealla had in fact been thinking of children on the ride home. She had noticed certain things about Pega which made her suspect the coming of a babe. The possibility of the expansion of her duties made her change the subject, so close was it to Kjeld's own way of thinking.

Kjeld tried another tack. "Why was it right for Lady Pega to wed the Jarl, if your feelings are so strong against us?"

"'Twas right for her. She is like unto a princess, and her task is to weave peace. Besides, she had no choice. Or, I should say, her only choice was to say no to this one man. If she had, the Lady Æthelflaed would have found another."

"But you do have choice. Full choice."

"That I do. But how can I care for Lady Pega, if I need care for a man?"

Mealla, whose gaze could be bold at times, now assessed his clothing from top to bottom. She had already ascertained that Kjeld had no female kin. The state of his clothing certainly showed this, with the frayed hem of his tunic, and leggings almost out at the knees, and calling out for patches, if not a new pair.

Before he could answer this challenge, she completed her sweep of his person. "Your beard is scraggly. And your hair wants cutting." Arms full, she turned and made for the hall.

Jari had been within hearing distance and now passed close to Kjeld's shoulder. "A good sign, that. At least she knows what you look like."

A day later Pega was alone with her mother-in-law in the treasure room, sorting linen. Hrald's bride felt compelled to speak.

"I think I am with child."

It was softly spoken, but the smile on Pega's lips told of great joy.

"Pega! Happy news, indeed!" Ælfwyn's arm came round the girl, and she kissed her cheek. "Does Hrald know?"

She gave a nod. "I told him. In the garden at Oundle."

That was two days ago. Ælfwyn was glad to hear she had told her husband first, yet struck by the fact that he had not come to her with Pega to share the news. It surprised her; she and Hrald were so close. When he had been courting Dagmar she felt he had confided nearly everything to her. It made her fear some misgiving in him now. Still, Ælfwyn would let nothing dim her current joy.

Her eyes lifted as she counted, then beamed at Pega. "The month of Candlemas, that time of seed-sprouting." Now she laughed. "And lambing!"

That night when Pega and Hrald were together in the treasure room, preparing for the evening meal, Pega opened a chest which she knew held rarely used table ware. To one side was a flat wooden box, one which might hold a small silver plate. She opened it. On a lining of linen dyed blue lay a circlet of gold, sized as a filet for a women's brow. Hrald was standing at the table, sliding a favoured bronze buckle onto a new leathern belt. He looked over at her exclamation.

She carried it, box and all to him.

"It was Ashild's," he told her. He had not been certain where his mother had placed it following his sister's death. "An award for her service defending the foundation of Oundle."

"You gave it?"

He nodded. Pega could not fully read the expression that crossed his face as he did so; a mix of warm recollection, yet shadowed with grief.

She touched the gold, and looking down at it spoke again. "We will set it aside, for our daughter."

This kindness moved him, and he said so.

"You are always kind, and thinking of others."

She smiled, set down the box, and stepped closer. "I am thinking of you." She drew a small breath and went on. "I love you."

Hrald heard the words. He gave a slight nod of his head. His eyes and mouth showed bewilderment, even confusion.

Pega was watching his face. Was it a nod of acceptance, a returning nod of agreement? She could not know. Its full meaning could not be read in his simple gesture. His eyes closed briefly, in pleasure perhaps of hearing it, but his lips moved not in answer. Yet he kissed her.

Hrald was in the stable looking over a new bridle which Bork had fashioned. The boy had skill at all hand work, this was more proof of it, and the smooth and even edges of the cut leather, the careful puncturing of the buckle holes, and the long reins with symmetrical knotted ends spoke for the care Bork had taken. He had part in even the tanning of the cowhide, and the deep rich brown of the oak leaf stain colouring the new bridle made it a worthy embellishment to the beauty of Hrald's dark bay stallion. Hrald's words of praise for Bork's efforts were returned by the boy's highly coloured cheek.

Cerd's laughter and the snorting of a hound made them turn their heads. Cerd had ventured into the stable with his uncle, and had tucked himself into an empty stall, where he was trying without success to ride Frost like a pony. Burginde arrived to collect the boy, and Pega appeared as well. Burginde was picking the straw out of Cerd's hair as the dog circled both of them. With a whoop Cerd broke away from the nurse and took off across the stable yard. Frost, in equal high spirits, ran with him, turning his fine head in the air and yipping in excitement. Burginde followed after, her scolding, half-hearted as it was, only making Cerd laugh the more.

Pega too laughed. "Frost is having great fun with him; I never knew how good he was with children." This would be an asset in future, and she smiled up at Hrald.

He gave thought to how short a span a dog's life was, and how much Frost meant to Pega. "He should sire pups," he suggested, as they watched the dog race about the yard, as if out of joy of feeling his long legs fly over the ground.

"We will be sending a waggon to Jorvik soon," he went on. "My men will ask after a worthy bitch there."

"That would be fine," she agreed.

"I could try my hand at training them to flush birds," he told her, remembering his visit to Ring's farm on Gotland and the flushing hounds he raised.

It was with this prospect of a future happy pastime that Pega returned to the hall. She was now four months along with child, and the morning retching she had known was largely passed. She felt and looked rosy. Burginde made much of her, forcing eggs and cheeses upon her so she might gain flesh for the leaner months to come, and Ælfwyn could not look at her daughter-in-law without beaming.

In the afternoon Pega came down from her upstairs sewing to the treasure room. Hrald was there, seated at the table, an array of six swords and an equal number of knives fanned out before him. She knew he was judging them, comparing their qualities, and knew as well these weapons were destined to be given as rich reward to his men for future service.

She kissed his brow as she passed him, and went to where their clothing was stored. She had arrived at Four Stones with a vast store of woven but unworked linen, and with Ælfwyn was sewing up swaddling cloths, sheets for the cradle, and even tiny caps for the infant's head. She drew out what she needed to take up to the weaving room; the light was always best there and the table ready for the laying out and cutting of fabric. She smiled at Hrald over the lid of a second chest, one belonging to him, into which Burginde and Mealla had laid certain heavier weight linen, meant for men's tunics. She wanted to make a new one for Hrald, and selected a long piece and placed it with the rest to carry up and show to Ælfwyn.

Lifting it revealed a tiny square box of wood, set in the corner of the chest. She held it in one hand, and opened the hinged lid with the other. Something small of fabric lay within. Her fingers went to it. It was a ribband of red, which had been coiled up, and set within this small container. The plain austerity of the box contrasted with the careful way in which the ribband had been coiled. She let it unspool in her fingers. It was a length of ribband such as she herself used to fasten the plait she made of her hair each night.

Small as it was, if it had been used as she used her own, it was of an intimate nature. It had significance, or would not have been preserved like this.

It was then Hrald glanced up. He saw what she held, and looked stricken.

He stood up so abruptly that the chair he had been sitting in tipped over backward. It clattered on the wooden floor, the sound quickly dying away, as he kept staring at her. He said nothing, but his face clouded with surprise and deep hurt, a look Pega had never seen. It was enough to make her hastily beg his pardon. She carefully rewound the ribband, placed it in its box, and laid it back in the chest.

She gathered the linens she had set aside and went up to the weaving room. Ælfwyn was there, but Burginde and Mealla were off with other tasks. Pega felt she could say nothing in front of Ealhswith and Eanflad, and with a look invited her mother-in-law to rise and follow her. They stepped into the drying room across the narrow hall from the weaving room. Pega was shaken from Hrald's reaction, and Ælfwyn read the trouble on her pretty face.

"I found a bit of red ribband in the treasure room, the kind a woman might use to tie her hair at night. It was carefully preserved, coiled in a tiny wooden box. I think Hrald had saved it. When he saw I had it in my hand, he looked – " she could not even describe it. "I put it away, and asked his pardon."

Her deeply set eyes looked shrouded, even pained, as they searched Ælfwyn's face.

"Was it perhaps Ashild's?"

Ælfwyn could answer this. "Ashild used no ribband to tie her hair."

Pega cast her eyes down. "Then it must have been . . ."

"Dagmar," Ælfwyn said for her. "Yes. I am sorry. It must have been hers. I had no idea he saved it. She took everything she brought with her, and the few things left behind, which he had made for her, he gave away. Please do not let it trouble you," she ended, while feeling troubled herself. It was a small memento he had put aside. Yet it was his strong reaction to its discovery that mattered, she knew. She laid her hand on the girl's arm in reassurance.

"Yes," Pega agreed, almost too willingly. "Yes."

That night Pega, who always fell asleep so readily, lay down knowing sleep would not find her. When Hrald snuffed out the last cresset and joined her in bed, she turned to him as she ever did, and he placed his arm about her. But she did not whisper good night, nor could she hide the hurt in her voice.

"The day we wed . . . that night you thanked me for saying, as we stood before all, that I came to you with an open heart. But you have not done the same."

It was true; Hrald knew it. Pega was entirely lovable; yet he felt he did not love her. His heart was somehow closed against her.

There had been only one he had loved, and she was far away, in Dane-mark, and wed to another. Dagmar had cruelly wounded him, yet he craved her, she who hurt him so badly. He could not hate Dagmar, but he hated himself for feeling this way.

He thought of his father now. Hrald had known for some time that Sidroc had not loved his mother. He had held her in regard, treated her with respect, but Hrald guessed she knew he had never loved her. His father could not love Ælfwyn; his heart had been taken by another. Just as his own had.

Now his father had lived for well over a decade with the woman he had loved since he was a young man, but could not have. Such could never happen to Hrald. Ceridwen was a worthy woman, widowed, and Sidroc did not see himself bound by the strictures of the Church. Dagmar loved another, and still did, and was that man's wife. And Pega must be dead for him to consider remarriage; he could never put so good a woman away. Now she was carrying his child. His thoughts turned in on themselves, relentless, painful, and without answer.

The woman who lay next him had given up hoping for him to speak. She whispered her good-night, and closed her brimming eyes. Hrald pulled her closer to him, and kissed the yellow hair where it fell upon her temple.

BROKEN SWORD

A month later five of Four Stones' outriders cantered up to the gates, two of whom had a second man clinging on behind the rider. The Sun had just risen, lifting in the greyed sky of a day warm and misting. The guards on the palisade whistled out their approach, and all breaking their fast within the hall gathered to meet them. The horses reined up, heads tossing, and one of the riders called out to Hrald as he stood with Jari.

"Attack on Geornaham last night. Danes of some kind have taken the hall."

The outcry was general, and the two clinging on slid off to stand before the crowd. They were gamesmen from this neighbouring keep to the east, a Saxon hall from which Yrling's first wife had hailed. It had been left in the hands of a steward, Tilbert, who ran it still. It was Tilbert's daughter who Hrald's neighbour Haward had been riding to court the day Hrald brought Pega to Four Stones.

Water was hastily brought for those arriving; all were breathless from the ride. Mul and his boys and Bork took the winded horses in hand, to cool them in the paddock. The gamesmen had run a long distance toward Four Stones before being intercepted by the first of its guards.

The two had escaped the mayhem by their returning from the wood to the hall to witness it. They gulped down dippersful of water and began.

Geornaham had indeed been overrun and taken by Danes, who they knew not, but they described the sudden violence of its taking. The attackers appeared at dusk, moving on foot from the cover of the near wood to the south of the keep. The gates were hastily closed, which availed nothing. They swarmed the place with makeshift ladders fashioned from tree trunks, their branches lopped off short to serve as rungs. Iron grappling hooks tied to hempen lines were heaved over the part of the wooden wall which housed the ramparts, catching there and giving purchase for men to walk up and over it. All this went on during a steady barrage of Danish arrows, raining down on those attempting to rally in the hall's yard. This ceased as soon as the first Danes were over. It did not take long for the gates to be opened from within.

"Send to Haward with this news," was Hrald's first order. "Tell him to come at once with twenty men, ready to fight."

He did not know how stood the man's suit of the steward Tilbert's daughter, but Geornaham, though free, was under the protection of Four Stones, and paid tribute to it. Haward as seeming ally to both must be ready to fight for its return.

Hrald next turned to Kjeld. "Send to Asberg at Turcesig, that he knows of this, so he might be on the alert. Double the watch to every approach to Four Stones."

Yrling was right there and piped up. "Let me go and tell him."

These riders would push their horses and themselves to the limit. Hrald would not allow his young brother to endanger himself this way. He shook his head.

While Kjeld was selecting the riders for these tasks, Ælfwyn and Pega stepped forward from the throng. Burginde, at Ælfwyn's side, had charge of Cerd, and a wide-eyed Ealhswith stood between her and Mealla. The maid from Éireann only stood the straighter under this news, defiance flashing in her eyes.

Hrald looked at the women; he must give them as much time as possible to make preparation. "I will be riding with – forty men. Provisions for two days. Packs only."

Much information was contained in this terse order. The hall of Geornaham was but three hours away by horse, yet Hrald assumed a stay of two nights. They must move as quickly as possible. No supply waggons would be taken, the provender carried would be only that which could be tied to each man's saddle rings. This meant no cooking kit; everything the kitchen supplied must be fit to eat with no fire.

"When?" was Ælfwyn's only question, as this was most needful for the cooks to know.

"As soon as Haward arrives."

This would give them only two or three hours. Ælfwyn asked no more; she and Pega would hear the rest soon, and the provisioning of the force was most important. Burginde placed Cerd in Ealhswith's care and instructed her to go to the bower house garden and keep the boy out from underfoot. She and Mealla and their two mistresses would have their hands full. The bakers made their many score of loaves once a day, beginning before cock-crow.

Now they would have to surrender every loaf they had set aside for the evening meal, and start afresh for the hall's needs. Others in the kitchen yard must pack pots of cheeses, nut meats, and any dried fruit remaining in the store houses from last year's harvest. The hens could be robbed of every egg and those boiled up. Brined and smoked hams from the smokehouse would be carved into slices and wrapped in waxed linen to fit into saddle bags.

As they turned to the kitchen yard Pega's fear was full upon her face. Ælfwyn placed her arm about her. Kjeld was coming by from the paddock, where he had been talking to the three riders he was sending to Turcesig. His long look at Mealla as she passed was briefly returned. Then she stopped and spoke aloud, causing him to turn.

"Will you go and fight?' Her voice was nearly a command, a sharp one, and left Kjeld uncertain of what her response might be at any answer he might give.

He could only tell the truth.

"I do not know yet. I want to go." He glanced at Hrald, deep in converse with Jari.

Mealla gave a toss of her head, but her mouth had softened. Still, she turned her back on him to catch up to the two Ladies of the hall.

Kjeld stepped into that low and urgent discussion, as Hrald and Jari considered their options. Yrling had shadowed Kjeld to the paddock and back, and entered that circle as he did. Kjeld held silence as Hrald and Jari recounted what they knew, and what they might do. Geornaham had been overrun by invaders. A siege was the simplest path to resolution, but oftentimes the most costly to both sides. It was also the slowest and cruellest path for the innocent; as stores were exhausted and hunger took hold not a beast would be left alive within the walls. All the folk of the hall were captive, at least those who had not perished in the taking, and folk had gone mad from hunger and turned on each other under such duress. It would demand constant watch, surrounding the entire perimeter of Geornaham, to make certain none of the enemy made foray under cover of dark to forage in the woods, or attempt to snare small game. This would stress the resources of Four Stones and could split their defences for weeks. Jari for one was not inclined to wait.

"Better to pay these invaders out with our steel," he offered. "Those left alive within will turn on their captors when they hear our attack."

Hrald must nod consent. Such a taking would be bloody, but could not be helped.

Hrald and Jari then made choice of men. Of those considered their most able fighters, they chose a score, rounding them out with younger men eager to make their mark. Hrald would send twenty men to Oundle to help secure it, and another ten men to the valley of horses to guard that portable treasure. The rest would be left to defend Four Stones.

"Full war-kit," he told those selected for the ride. "We leave wearing it. They might be on the road against us now. Ready yourselves."

Those chosen left to do so. Hrald called Mul over. "Take your boys, and Bork, to the valley. Bring back thirty head." Such numbers of horses were rarely moved at one time, but Hrald must give Haward's troop fresh mounts when they arrived. Yrling's face lit; he too wanted to be part of this drive. His older brother raised his hand to stay his plea.

Hrald must now look to Kjeld, of whom he had made no mention.

"You will stay, Kjeld," he told the man. Kjeld worked without success to hide his disappointment.

"I need you here more than with me," Hrald went on. "If there is booty you will have your share from my own take."

Kjeld must content himself with that. Hrald glanced at his brother at his side and thought of something more. "If word comes of the enemy nearing to attack, send my wife and mother, Cerd and Yrling, to the valley of horses. They will be safer there; the woods are dense and they can shelter within."

"I am coming, Hrald," Yrling proclaimed. "Let me carry a banner of yours."

The boy could not know what feelings his words awakened in his older brother.

Hrald must brush this off. There was Ashild's white stallion in the paddock, as he always was, that horse which had carried her to the place of her death.

"Nej, Yrling, you are not coming." Though the boy had addressed him in the speech of Angle-land in which they had all been speaking, Hrald answered in the tongue of the Danes, that first language of warfare. It signalled a change within him. Hrald would not treat the boy in the same way as Cerd; he must not.

"You have your spear," he told Yrling. "You will stay here with Kjeld, and defend Four Stones. The fortress your grand-uncle conquered."

When Haward arrived Hrald questioned him over a cup of ale. "You and Tilbert's daughter. How does it stand?"

"It does not," Haward admitted. "I was refused."

Hrald gave a nod. It was no easy thing to confess. "Well," he posed. "Now you can make both father and daughter regret that."

Hrald left unspoken the condition that only if both were still alive could they regret their rashness in rejecting Haward. Mul had returned with the horses, and Haward's men were at work transferring their saddles and kit to the new beasts.

Within the treasure room Ælfwyn and Pega were packing Hrald's kit. It was a task Pega had never done. She moved in a kind of fitful haze, while Ælfwyn drew forth from Hrald's belongings clothing and personal items needful for the coming foray.

"Will he want silver?" Pega asked. Some men, she knew, had been able to ransom their own life after enemy capture.

Ælfwyn shook her head. Hrald carried scant silver about the hall and its lands; there was no need. She was careful with her answer. "He takes very little, no more than what he carries here." Left unsaid was the hard fact it left less to be plundered from one's body. She could not say such a thing to this sweet young woman carrying her son's child.

Hrald walked in. He had already gathered all his weaponry, and was wearing his ring shirt.

Both women lifted their heads to him; the hour of departure was upon them all. Ælfwyn prepared to leave the two alone. But she went to Pega and wrapped her arms about her, whispering close to the girl's ear the only counsel she could give.

"Pega, think only of the babe. Nothing more."

As the door closed behind her Hrald went to his young wife, who seemed rooted to the floor.

She clung to him, swallowing hard so she might speak. The iron links of his ring-shirt felt a cruel barrier between them. "Hrald – to lose you now . . ." she could not complete the thought.

He answered with all the resolve he could summon.

"You will not lose me," he told her. "Certain Danes will lose their lives. I will not be one of them. Not unless God wills it."

Now he placed his hand upon the roundness of her belly. "You will not lose me," he said again. She fought not to break down; fought and lost.

He held her troubled face in his hands. Tears streamed from her eyes as he looked at her. He spoke as gently as he could. "Stay here, Pega. I must speak to my mother. Then both of you can see us off." He kissed her brow, and then her lips.

His mother stood awaiting him in the mouth of the kitchen passageway. He opened his arms to her. He kept her there in his embrace as he spoke. He did not wish to see her face as she reacted to his words. "I am likely to attack Geornaham. A siege is too costly in time and resources. If I do not return, give Ashild's gold filet to Sigewif, along with any offering you see fit for her soul. And for mine."

Her arms tightened about him, and he felt the heave of a repressed sob. No mother, regardless of her courage and her faith, could do otherwise. But she mastered her tears enough to smile at him when he released her.

"Kjeld will serve you well," he promised. "And there is Yrling," he said, in attempt to make her smile broaden.

Burginde was come, hastening towards them through the passage, to take his mother in her arms.

Hrald turned to see the priest Wilgot, ready with a drop of sacred chrism to anoint his brow.

The troop of sixty men approached Geornaham before noon. The gates were open. Men moved outside the palisade, knocking down the makeshift ladders where they still stood against the wall. One of the men was clearly Tilbert, moving slowly as he looked down at the ground. By his presence and action those who approached knew the Danes were gone. When he and his men walking before the wall turned and saw the coming horsemen, they fled within, and the gates were swung shut. As heavily armed as Hrald's troop was, they presented a fearsome aspect to a folk who had just suffered attack.

Hrald reined up just out of range of any answering arrow.

"I am Hrald of Four Stones," he called out. The gamesmen too called out in assurance, and the gates opened to them.

They rode by, eyeing several Danes still lying, contorted in death outside the wall.

Tilbert stood there to meet them, a man of some fifty years, with long and drooping moustaches of greying brown. He was surrounded by his warriors and folk. The shock of the attack still shadowed the man's face. Haward spoke first, calling down from his horse.

"Werburgh – does she live?"

"She is unhurt, away with her women, and weeping with fright. But they snatched every gem and bauble of silver she owned."

Within was a mournful scene. A few arrows stood lodged in the upper reaches of timber walls, or bristled from roofs. Serving folk worked setting to rights overturned fowl houses from which feathers of plundered birds wafted. Others gathered fragments of splintered doors and smashed casks. The invaders had laid waste in their rapaciousness, having snatched everything they could carry. The war-band took every waggon, every animal large or small, ransacked granaries and brewing sheds, rampaged through the hall, despoiling it of everything of value. Tilbert had literally nothing to offer, save water from the well.

"Who were they?" Hrald asked.

Tilbert shook his head. "They spoke little, and in the tongue of the Danes. They crammed food, bolting it like wild beasts. At dawn they left. I know only that we looked an easy mark."

He scanned the walls which had been so readily scaled. In truth, they were far lower than those of Four Stones or Turcesig, built in a more peaceful time, and never replaced or extended.

"And their numbers?" Jari asked.

Tilbert paused to reckon. "Two or three score. Once they gained entry, we were driven into the barn, and locked there. We heard them, but see them we could not. After they left we broke out."

Hrald and Jari looked at the other. The difference in facing forty men, rather than sixty, was great.

The steward thought of what more he could relate.

"They were a rag-tag lot, long on the road I should think. And they had a few women with them, also children. Danes, not captives."

He gave a helpless shrug of defeat.

As great as this misfortune was to Tilbert, he and his daughter had been left unhurt. And Hrald had no need to throw his men against the small fortress. The attacking war-band had been intent on food and anything else of value.

Tilbert then took them to the storehouse where the dead were laid out, killed in the barrage of arrows, or in direct fighting. Hrald and Haward saw the grim story their bodies told.

"Seven of my men," Tilbert told them, lifting his hand in the dim light towards the benches which had been carried there. Each held a body. "Four of the serving folk, including two women."

When they returned to the yard Hrald made offer.

"We have rye and barley to send you. Haward too," Hrald prompted, glancing at the man.

"Yes," Haward answered. After a moment he went on. "And the pigs have done well. I will bring some to you. Myself."

"Good neighbours make good allies," Hrald noted, with a meaningful look to Tilbert. The man could do nothing but nod in accord. Later he might look with renewed interest at his daughter's erstwhile suitor.

They readied to set off. Laden as they were, the attackers would be moving slowly. It enabled Hrald to make generous offer to the bereft keep. "I have two days' rations. We will catch up to them today, and end this.

I will give you half our food. Send two of your men to Four Stones, telling of what happened, and asking the Lady thereof for grain." Hrald thought instinctively of his mother here, but then remembered it would be Pega the men would be addressing. He hoped the news that no assault on Tilbert's hall had been necessary would cheer her.

The steward wished to ride with them, but conceded to the wisdom of his remaining to defend the keep from further attack.

Hrald set off. With the great number of waggons, wains, oxen and horses the Danes had stolen, it took no special skill to follow the train through tall grasses and rain-dampened soil.

Their passage took them through meadowland skirting forest, and then by way of a well worn track, into the trees themselves. The Sun was lowering and the heavy growth made it darker than the hour warranted. They had the advantage of cover, but so too did those they trailed. Hrald sent a man ahead to scout; their quarry must be ready to set camp for the night.

Sure enough, the man cantered back with news. He had ridden ahead until he heard the sounds of men and beasts. He tied his horse and went on foot, creeping through the trees alongside the track. In a natural clearing which opened on one side of the track, the Danes were setting camp. The waggons and wains had been pulled to one side, freed horses and oxen corralled with line, and the men themselves were busy with the plucking of dead wood with which to build their cook-fire.

"Nothing better," Jari grinned. "We will go up; surround them. Then wait until the food is ready to be ladled out." The Tyr-hand well remembered similar attacks from his youth. "A man with his hands on his bowl has not one on his blade," he counselled. "When they line up, bellies grumbling, we will appear. Our hunger for victory will be made the keener."

They gathered all about them to share the plan. From here on they must keep silence.

"We will give them the chance to throw down their weapons," Hrald ended.

He said this, not certain of what he would do if they accepted. Here in Lindisse there was no general hall-moot at which they could be tried. If the invaders took Hrald up on this, he must be the law. Even Ælfred of Wessex would hang their leader; Hrald knew this; but men begging quarter could not be denied. Parcelled out and separated from their war-chief, the culprits could make amends through labour at Geornaham, Haward's hall, and Four Stones.

Hrald then remembered Tilbert's words. "The women and children. Disarm them only, unless they are intent on blood. Then do what you must."

They made themselves ready. Helmets and war-caps stowed in saddle bags were drawn forth and lowered over heads. They walked their horses up the track until the scout raised his arm; this was where they must leave their beasts. Four men would stay behind to guard them. They swung down and tied the horses. Hrald was not alone in giving the neck of his mount a pat. His bay stallion had carried him to much action, and faithfully carried him back again. Jari rode a heavy-boned grey, well suited to his heft, and a particular favourite of his. The grey had a few words whispered into his furred ear by the big man. Haward and many other men could be seen doing the same, taking leave of their horses. Their animals were prized, and of home, and the last living thing of that place they must separate themselves from before entering the fray.

All slipped their shields from their backs, slid their arm through the strap and grasped the grip behind the boss. Hrald let his eyes fall on the cross he had painted inside his own protective disc. Wilgot had anointed him; he was ready.

Even before they slipped into the wood they began to smell both cooking-fire and the browis bubbling above it. Voices too were heard, snatches of laughter, men calling out in the tongue of Dane-mark. They fanned out, well back from the clearing, to encircle the camp. The signal would be the distinctive whistle of Four Stones, which Hrald himself would give. The lengthening shadows cast by the lowering Sun made the forest greens more brilliant, and its browns nearly black.

Haward had moved off ahead with his own men, leaving Hrald and Jari to anchor their two arms of warriors. Hrald had crept close enough to peer through the trees at the clearing. Sure enough, men were beginning to line up, wooden bowls in hand, to reach the centre of the camp and the cook-fire with its steaming cauldrons. Nearly all were on their feet, making it harder to see beyond them, but as most were now parted from their packs, he need not wait longer. The Danes' spears were left behind, and many who owned them might have also unbuckled their sword belts.

Hrald lifted two fingers to his mouth. His whistle shrilled out. It led all of Hrald's combined men to step forward and show themselves.

"You are surrounded," Hrald called in their native tongue. He had his sword in his hand. "Give up now, and live."

The heads of the encircled Danes snapped from right to left, learning this truth for themselves.

A voice bellowed out from near the fire-pit.

"You will not take me alive!"

Jari, at Hrald's left, was quick to yell back. "That is your choice!"

Hrald could not see who of the Danes had spoken, but knew that some had closed ranks about him. Looking out on the worn faces of the men and few women this chief led, he must speak.

"Do not doom your men to your own end," Hrald warned.

The retort was harsh and quick. "Pay for those words in your own blood!"

There was no choice but to fight. Their numbers may have been more or less equal, but the troop Hrald led was far better-fed, rested, and heavily armed. It was also fuelled by the insult of recent attack on an innocent folk.

How this man throws away the lives of his warriors, Hrald thought.

The first move came from those surrounded, a general howl of angered protest. Bowls were tossed down, any nearby spear snatched at, and some made move to where their weapons rested. Hrald's force, weapons in hand and brothers at their sides, leapt forward with answering oaths.

It was toilsome fighting. Though the stolen waggons had been pulled mostly to one side, some of the Danes had slipped between them, and used their bulk to advantage. The ground was littered with men's packs, and the saddles they had pilfered when they took the horses. A few women and children scrambled, dodging the lifted spears and drawn swords.

Hrald and Jari leapt forward with the others, taking on those Danes nearest to them. Each had picked up spears, and came at them with the rancour of trapped animals. Jari had his spear in hand, Hrald his sword. With weapons of unequal length, a spear had always advantage. Yet this vanished if a swordsman could advance to penetrate the space beyond the spear-point. Jari, with shield in his right hand, its pointed iron boss a lethal weapon on its own, kept the two weapons of the Danes fully involved with his own spear, harrying them high and low, giving Hrald leave to leap back in and slash a fatal blow against the second man's torso. As he toppled, his shield dropped, tripping the other Dane. While catching himself the man lowered his own shield, making him quick work for Jari's thrust to the belly.

The horses and oxen, scarcely confined with lines of hemp between trees, whinnied and chaffed, stamping their hooves and shaking their heads at the near conflict. The screams of men as blade bit bone rose over the grunts of exertion and shouted oaths of those fighting. Hrald caught sight of Haward, across the cook-fire from him, fighting his way forward, and saw from the tail of his eye two women and several children crawl under one of the waggons and out of harm's way.

Advancing steadily inward, Hrald picked out men armed with swords, freeing Jari from providing cover. He met some skill amongst the two he felled, but Hrald's youthful quickness and long reach gave him ever an edge. He overcame the first with a feinting thrust at the head, then as the Dane raised his own sword to parry, struck at his forward thigh. The crippled man yowled and dropped, allowing Hrald to end it with his blade to the chest. The second man was wiry and fast, and Hrald himself was feeling the effects of his efforts. He kept the Dane at bay and himself out of reach with the play of his shield, then lunged forward on one knee, driving the man back with the disc of alder. The Dane's sword tip caught just long enough to pull him forward, letting Hrald bring his own blade to bear in his foe's left shoulder. The shield arm dropped, and a moment later the man as well.

As Hrald turned from these opponents to scan the remaining foe he was struck by their look. There was a sameness to these Danes. Every war-band of any size had raw youths and greybeards, and every age between. These warriors were of similar age, in their third decade, seasoned and tough. They were also ground down from ceaseless exposure, short rations, and from the look of their clothing, little recent success in their raiding. They must be long-term followers of their war-chief to remain so loyal.

Hrald's men were a tightening cordon around the Danes. They drove them steadily to the increasingly packed middle of their campsite, where the contents of the unattended cauldrons still boiled.

Of a sudden a name rang out.

"Haesten!" a Dane called, as he tossed a spear to another, who was sorely beset.

Hrald's head whirled. Haesten. He was here, before him. Hrald stood, breathing hard, staring at the great war-chief. He saw a man well past mid-life, powerfully built, grey-haired, with a beard just as grey, plaited into a single plait. His eyes were almost unnaturally bright, light and flashing. His clenched jaw belied the sweat running from his brow.

Hrald did not speak.

He would face this man, with no taunts, no oaths. He needed none such. The words in his mind were enough.

Ashild. It was the actions of this man that had placed Ashild on that field of battle.

It was due to this man and his extended predation that Ceric had been on that field as well.

More followed, rising in Hrald's thought, the many struck down, directly or indirectly, by the hand of Haesten. The litany of loss stretched years into the past.

Thorfast threatened Four Stones at the urging of Haesten, which led to that duel in which Hrald must risk his life, and his friend Gunnulf lost his own.

Hrald's men at Saltfleet. His watch-guards killed by confederates of this man. Pega's father, a man he must regret not knowing, and whom she would grieve for the rest of her life. Even that cousin of the King she had been given to wed, and then was killed by this man's rapacity. His victims since arriving here were numberless.

If Hrald could rid this land once and for all of this scourge, he would do so, even at the price of his own blood. There would be no bargaining, no accommodation, no offer of silver for the old wolf to leave them alone. Hrald would settle this now, with his own life if need be.

"Clear! Clear!" Hrald shouted, ordering all make way for their unimpeded contest.

Perhaps a score of the Danes were left. Hrald prepared to face Haesten as his men were fighting the rest, cutting them down as surely as a reaper scythes grain.

Hrald drew himself up and looked at his foe. It mattered not that Haesten had more than twice Hrald's years. Hrald could see that in his opponent's steely gaze. The man was hard as iron, tested by decades of war, and had overcome numberless adversaries. It may have been a while since he had been called out in single combat, but he accepted it, and a man would only do such if he were confident of victory. Hrald would have more speed and greater reach, but Haesten knew and had successfully employed every trick in the warrior's arsenal.

Hrald had called him out, and would take the upper hand. He did so in an unexpected manner. Haesten had no helmet. In answer Hrald pulled off his own. He would fight better without its weight. He let his helmet drop to the ground, off to one side. There was more he would free himself from.

Hrald let drop his hatred of this man. He let drop even the face of his sister, and the remembrance of her weight in his arms when Ceric handed her body down to him. He thought of one thing only. It was something his father had taught him as a boy on Gotland, a lesson repeated by Asberg and Jari and every other man he had faced in training: any warrior will repeat what has worked in the past to keep him alive. Your task is to learn this quickly and make an end of his success.

The fighting about them had paused as men made way for the combat of the two leaders. They faced off fast by the cooking-ring, the heat of the fire and the smoking contents of the pots adding to the danger.

Hrald saw the sword then, one with hammered silver cut into its grip. It must be Haesten's, dropped from his hand by another opponent. Hrald gestured to it with his own sword, inviting the war-chief to choose it rather than the spear his man had tossed to him. Without taking his eyes from Hrald, Haesten bent for the blade, his spear lifted against attack. Hrald held his ground.

Haesten straightened, kicked away the spear he had dropped as he retrieved his sword, and gripped his shield more firmly. The shield face was plain unpainted leather, but the dark iron boss was broad and as sharply pointed as an awl. Hrald's shield was painted in those four quadrant wedges of red and black he had used since boyhood.

They began. Haesten was in movement at once, attempting to circle Hrald, get him to give ground. Haesten wanted Hrald's back to the fire and its suffocating heat. Hrald would not oblige. They would both stand here, their sword arm and shield arm respectively exposed to its heat.

Aggression backed with power had won Haesten many a victory with his sword. He attacked with almost wanton passion, and could back his speed with a strength usually found in far slower men. He blocked and parried every swing from Hrald with practised skill. The older man even wore a sneer upon his face as he did so, one Hrald determined to expunge.

Hrald would give him what he wanted. He stepped to the side, allowing Haesten to move from the fire, and placing Hrald's back more fully to it. The ring-shirt Hrald wore was warm, but that one of leather beneath it protected him. More swings and thrusts were exchanged, both the steel of their blades and the clang of their metal bosses colliding as they met. Forward and back from the fire-line they edged, their eyes locked, watching for a telltale shift to betray the next swing. Then Hrald paused in his actions.

He held his sword steady and at almost eye level to his opponent, and gently circled its tip before him. Haesten watched this silent taunt for a long moment, poised, and other than his breathing, still. Then the war-chief sprang, shield abruptly lifted, knocking Hrald's blade up.

Hrald was quicker. He stepped aside, allowing the full force of Haesten's weight to carry him forward. Down came Hrald's shield upon Haesten's shoulder, his boss punching into the leathern tunic the man wore. Haesten staggered and fell into the cook-fire. One of the smaller cauldrons tipped, splashing his hand with the boiling browis. The man screamed and scrambled forward, thrashing in the hot coals. He flung himself out, to meet Hrald's raised sword, which missed the neck but sliced down across his shoulders, cutting with force through both leather and flesh.

The old war-chief turned on that bloodied back, which now arched in agony. His staring eyes looked up, and the air he sucked grated through his open lips.

Hrald looked down at him, and took a needed gulp of air. Now he would speak.

"You came seeking land. You lie upon it now."

A woman was shrieking in the background, rising above the cheering clamour of his own men. Hrald lifted his blade to deliver the death-blow, that misericord this suffering man did not deserve. Hrald could not speak aloud the name in his mind as he plunged his sword through Haesten's windpipe; he would not allow it to fill the ears of this wretch. But his lips moved with a name as he drove home his sword: Ashild.

Hrald looked up to face those watching. The vehemence he felt came out in full force at his next words.

"His body will not be touched. The ravens will eat him. Blood to blood."

All fighting had ceased. Ten or eleven of the invaders still lived, and had thrown down their weapons. Hrald saw three women and a few children. One of the women was flanked by two boys, an arm around each. She was well into in her third decade, fairly tall, lean, her face marked by recent privation. The two boys were of perhaps ten and twelve years, and were now their mother's body-guard. Both clutched drawn knives. There was pride in this woman's countenance, a bitter pride which even her tears did not soften. She kept her eyes on the body of Haesten, then finally lifted them to his killer.

Hrald would not ask her if she was Haesten's wife; she would deny it, to try and save the lives of her boys. Those boys were this moment glaring at Hrald, as if burning his face into their memories. He could do nothing for this, save treat their mother with respect.

Hrald ran his sword back into its scabbard and addressed her. She was dressed in the way of Danish women, but even if she hailed from Frankland, she must understand the tongue of the Danes.

"I can send you and your children to Ælfred, King of Wessex," he told her. "He released you once, and sent you away with gifts. This time I think he will offer you shelter at Witanceaster. You can live in safety there."

The contortion of the woman's face told Hrald this was the last thing she looked for. He had another option to offer.

"Or I can send you to Saltfleet and put you on the first trading ship that calls there, to Frankland or Dane-mark."

He studied her more closely. She was wearing silver; she could sell that and make her way with these tattered remnants of Haesten's band.

"It is your choice," he ended.

"Frankland," she spoke, at last answering him in words.

Hrald looked again at the array of silver hanging from the woman's neck. "Do you wear treasure taken from the hall you attacked last night?"

She shook her head quickly, firmly. She pointed at the waggon nearest them.

Hrald went on. She had silver enough for a new start. "I will send you to Saltfleet."

She looked down at her boys, still holding their knives, knuckles white with their grip. She spoke too softly for Hrald to hear, but her words had effect, for they slid their blades into the sheaths at their waists.

Jari moved to the waggon Haesten's wife had pointed to. It did indeed yield much treasure. Other than the lost food, Tilbert would receive back nearly all stolen from him. Weaponry taken from Geornaham filled two entire waggons. Horses, oxen, wains filled with complaining fowl, sacks of grain and casks of ale, all could be returned.

Hrald and Haward had together lost only two men. Six had taken injury, none grievously, and were deemed able to rest the night with them here and be carried by the waggons in the morning.

The victors stripped the bodies of the dead. Their purses yielded almost nothing, and few had even amulets or bracelets of silver left to them. The gain for the warriors who had triumphed was in the weapons; all else was plunder Hrald would return to Tilbert.

Hrald took weapons from the three men he had killed, then knelt by Haesten's side. He had promised he would share any battle-gain with Kjeld. Well, Kjeld would have all he had taken from the first three. Hrald looked at Haesten's sword where it dropped from his hand on the trampled grass. This he would claim, this blade and the good Danish knife from the man's side. He picked up the sword, and felt it ringing in his hand. It would not be placed in the treasure room with the rest of his armaments, nor be displayed as a trophy wrenched from a most formidable foe. He knew its end.

They could ride no farther; dusk was upon them. The camp and even the meal was ready for them. They tied the captive Danes ankle to ankle, then to a wheel of a waggon. Those men of Four Stones who had stayed to guard their horses had already brought them forward, alerted by the cheers of victory.

The men dragged the bodies by the heels into the trees. Haesten's alone remained untouched. It would rot where it fell, on the grass by that fire-ring, grass which had already been watered by his blood. The bodies of the two men lost from Hrald and Haward's troop were set aside to be carried back to their respective halls.

The women and children were shooed into a waggon and placed under guard. In the morning Hrald would send all the remaining Danes to Saltfleet with a guard of ten men. There they would remain until the first ship heading for Frankland oared up. On it they would be sent off to their uncertain future.

All ate. Hrald could hardly do so. After the first full mouthfuls he let drop his spoon in the bowl he held. As the dusk deepened, his eyes kept returning to the body of Haesten. At last he stood and walked out of the light of the fire, and a little way down the track to where the horses stood. He stood there amongst the large and dark forms, listening to their snorting as they moved, pulling at the leaves on the trees.

Hrald slept that night as if he were himself dead; a slumber profound and yet without refreshment. All were up at first light, readying for the road. Once again rations were divided, so that those sent to Saltfleet might have sustenance. The waggon destined for that port left first, Haesten's captive warriors, wrists tied, walking behind.

Before Hrald went to his horse he shed a final look at the war-chief he had downed. You have met with Kings, he thought, and killed one too in Frankland, I have heard. Now your bones will moulder in this empty wood.

When they arrived at Geornaham it was at the head of a long train of returned waggons, horses, and cattle.

"Haesten is dead, by my hand," Hrald told the waiting Tilbert. "Much of what he robbed from you will be here, save for the foodstuffs eaten."

"My hall is yours," Tilbert said in gratitude. "Stay, rest, before you head back."

"No. I thank you. This news cannot wait. I must return to Four Stones with it."

Yet when the Sun was overhead and they approached Four Stones, Hrald scanned the mass of folk awaiting them. He turned to Jari. "You tell them," he said.

Bork ran forward to take his bay, but Hrald's eyes were fixed on the two women on the threshold of the hall itself. He went to them.

They walked through the empty hall to the treasure room, where a trembling Pega unlocked the door. Both women yearned to embrace him, but there was about Hrald that which kept them from doing so. Wife and mother had spent terrible hours together in this room, awaiting word. Now he was here, and seemingly unhurt, before them.

Hrald closed the door and spoke.

"I have killed Haesten." He tipped his head back, as if the grief the dead man had caused them washed over him anew, a sorrow overwhelmed by the knowledge that the man's wrongdoing had come to an end. "I have killed Haesten."

The back of Pega's hand had lifted to her mouth. Ælfwyn too was beyond words.

Both women, roused from their shock, came to embrace him, their arms surrounding this man they so loved. It was Pega who was first to speak.

"This unborn child, who my own father will never hold, thanks you."

In the hall Inga, Jari's wife, stood by with Burginde to meet the wounded, who were laid on hastily set up trestles, so that they might wash and bind their wounds. Ælfwyn would join them by and by, and Pega too asked to be of aid. "I will help. I must learn more of these things," she said.

Ælfwyn could only lay her hand on her wrist to stay her. "No, Pega, not now. There will be other times." She did not want the mother-to-be made ill by the gruesomeness of what she might see as the wounds were dressed, and sometimes searched. "Stay here with Hrald."

But Hrald gave a sign with his hand she must wait. He knew Bork would have unsaddled his bay and brought in his pack by now. He saw it, upon the high table, just outside the door. Haward was waiting for him there. He had another further distance to travel, and like Hrald, must return with the body of one dead. They studied each other. They were nearly the same age, both heading halls. Haward had never much to recommend himself in Hrald's eyes. His older brother had tried to kill Hrald, and he and Haward had once been kin through Hrald's annulled marriage. Haward had never given Hrald reason to trust him, but he had acquitted himself manfully on this mission.

"Return to Tilbert with those pigs as soon as you can," he counselled him.

Haward gave an uncertain smile at this seeming word of approval.

"I will bring every piglet I own, in hope it leads to Werburgh's hand," he answered.

"May you be wed before they are ready for the smokehouse," Hrald ended.

Haward accepted this blessing with a nod, and took his leave.

Hrald turned to his saddle bag, and removed something from it. Jari was still outside in the yard, telling Kjeld and those who had remained, of the recent action. He watched Hrald emerge from the hall holding what could only be a sword, wrapped in a piece of plain linen. Jari saw Hrald speak to one of the smiths, watched as the man handed him a heavy hammer. Jari waved off further questions, and began to trail Hrald at a distance as he made his way through the kitchen yard and out the rear door.

It was the old Place of Offering Hrald sought. When he reached there he set down the hammer and shook off the linen in which he had wrapped the other piece of steel. Hrald held Haesten's sword in his bare hand a final time, then wedged it between the heavy stones spanning the trench where of old, weapons had been sacrificed. He took the hammer in his right hand, drew it back, and with all the strength that arm knew, brought it down, ringing, on the blade. It snapped in two, killing it. It was no Offering, but sheer destruction, to render impotent this weapon that had wreaked so much havoc.

As the hammer rang down, it carried with it the force of his own guilt for allowing Ashild on that field.

Hrald straightened up, and kicked the two pieces of the shattered blade into the weed-filled trench. He turned and saw Jari there. Few men possessed a keener sense of justice than the old Tyr-hand.

"You have paid him in his own coin," Jari summed.

I WILL DO MY PART

RAEDWULF arrived at Four Stones just after Yule. He travelled with a single man, one of Ælfred's thegns, and was escorted to the hall unannounced save for the whistles of those ward-men who had found them on the road. A light snow had fallen and then melted, leaving all sodden yet glistening under a Sun trying mightily to shine.

The bailiff's arrival was entirely unlooked-for, and as the men rode up Hrald steeled himself as he stood inside the gates. Ælfwyn had no time to even change her head-wrap, but swathed as she was in her woollen mantle her face was framed by the soft brown marten fur trimming its hood. Burginde reached up to smooth Ælfwyn's hair, tucking a few errant strands in under the hood as if she were a child. Then the nurse slipped her hand in that of her mistress, and gave it a quick squeeze. They were greeting the bailiff without Pega, who, being great with child, was resting in the bower house, away from the near-constant bustle of the hall yard.

Yrling appeared, fresh from his sparring practice with Jari, and stood at his brother's side. He watched two warriors arrive and quit their horses. The elder was dark haired, and, Yrling saw from his kit, rich. His mantle was trimmed with red fox, and his boots, though muddy, had square toggles of silver. The warrior belted his knife across his belly, as his father did, telling Yrling he was likely of Wessex. The boy was introduced to the man, but then with a look from his brother, dismissed. Yrling was sorry to go, because the way Hrald and his mother looked at the bailiff, he felt something of value could be learnt.

As the guests entered the hall, a small boy scampered down the stairs from the weaving room, his aunt Ealhswith in tow. The boy ran to Hrald and roared out his name, then threw his arms around his uncle's leg.

Hrald must make another introduction, this one far quieter. "This is Cerd. The child of Ashild and Ceric."

The bailiff crouched down to greet the boy. "I am Raedwulf," the bailiff said, and held out his hand in welcome to the child.

"Raedwulf!" crowed Cerd in delight. He seized the offered hand in both of his. "My – name – is – Cerd!" he cried out, with only a trace of a childish lisp.

The bailiff studied him. Save for the green-flecked blue eyes he was a minikin of the elder son of Kilton. "You are like your father," is what he said. He turned his head and looked up at those watching.

"Away with you now," Burginde ordered. "Take Cerd to the garden, Ealhswith; Frost is there. Mind Cerd does not wake Lady Pega, if she be asleep." The garden with its gravel paths was never muddy, and boy and hound could romp there.

Hrald led the way to the treasure room; Burginde vanished down the kitchen passage with the young thegn, returning alone with ale. She closed the door behind her and took her customary stool by the bed.

The three at the table lifted their cups, took a sip. The gaze of the bailiff rested a moment on that right hand of Ælfwyn, bearing his ring with its blue stone of lapis. The eyes of both mother and son were turned upon him.

From the bailiff's demeanour it was clear there was no pressing message to deliver, no urgent call to answer, but the faces looking at him did so with fixed expectation.

"Ælfred is not well," Raedwulf began. "He grows, I think, weaker by the month. It will be a year, perhaps two, before Eadward is King."

This last was important for the Bailiff to state; he wished no doubt to take root in the minds of those in whom he confided that direct succession was in any danger. Challengers to the throne there were always, but that threat had never been so slight as it was now, in the waning days of Ælfred's reign. His successes, and the ability of his son Eadward, had seen to that.

Hrald did not like to ask the next, but would never have a better chance to do so.

"What will it mean, when Ælfred dies?"

Raedwulf took a deep breath.

"We can expect Eadward to continue on in the defence of the borders of Wessex. Continue on, and even expand his efforts."

This was of great moment, and Raedwulf must go on. "We may see the new King attempt to retake certain lands which have been lost during Ælfred's lifetime. Both in Wessex, and Mercia. And beyond."

This meant nothing less than the dissolution of the Treaty of Wedmore, which had formed the Danelaw. It was true the treaty had been upended, even abrogated, by Danes many times since the death of Guthrum. But the bailiff seemed to suggest that Eadward would be prepared to fight for the restoration of much which had been lost, consolidating lands once under the banners of many Kingdoms under the golden dragon of Wessex.

"This, however, is not why I have come," Raedwulf continued. The pause that followed was so long that mother and son found themselves sitting up even straighter in their chairs, as if this might make it easier to bear the coming news. At last the bailiff spoke.

"I have the King's leave to make my request, and ask for the hand of Ælfwyn of Cirenceaster, Lady of Four Stones."

Hrald's astonishment could be no greater. The bailiff had expected this, and went on.

"Life is fragile, and hangs by but a thread. I have more than twice your years, Hrald, but yet am greedy for more. The preciousness of each day is ever with me. This spurs me to ask for the hand of your mother as my wife."

Hrald was looking from Raedwulf to his mother. In the face of the latter he saw only the glow of pure happiness. The bailiff's countenance was one of steady and hopeful resolve. Raedwulf went on.

"My hall in Defenas is not large, neither are my holdings there, but hall and holdings both are choice. My coffers are not deep ones, but enough to provide for my wife in equal comfort to that she has always known. For her bride-price I offer you this."

Raedwulf reached for his belt, and removed a small white pouch from his purse. He lay the pouch on the table, and placed what it held upon it.

It was a gemstone, cut but unmounted, an oval dome of blue the size of a quail's egg. The richness of its hue was like unto lapis, but had subtle clarity to it. Such was its magnificence that Ælfwyn gasped.

"It is called sapphire," Raedwulf said. "They come from the furthest reaches of the east, and travel the same routes from Samarkand and like places as does silk.

"It is booty I won long ago, from a Dane."

It was Ælfwyn who made answer. She began by placing a hand on each of the hands of the two men who flanked her. Her smile seemed to light her face from within.

"This treasure room is rightly named," she told them. "It is filled with silver, and some gold as well. In weaponry it is rich. We have also our horses.

"At this age," she went on, her smile deepening, "I shall set my own bride-price. It is this, Raedwulf of Defenas, that you love me, and my children, and care for us as I know you are capable of."

It took much for Raedwulf not to rise and clasp his intended to him. But Hrald had yet to speak. The prospect of his mother leaving, of her wedding and moving to another Kingdom, had never crossed his mind. He thought that one day she might go to Oundle and profess as a nun, but that would be years hence. Now though, she would leave Four Stones, and soon. Her absence would wreak a profound change upon the hall. Yet looking at her, and how she clasped the bailiff's hand, he saw for the first time a woman in love, a woman deserving of love. And there was no more worthy man than Raedwulf.

"Yes, yes," Hrald finally answered. He looked at his mother and almost laughed. "She has given herself; I cannot say no."

He reached for the stone, then extended it to his mother. "A wedding gift," he told her.

"Hrald," she breathed.

"No, you must take it. If it were in my treasury it would be what I chose to give you."

She did so, curling it in her hand and holding it close to her breast. Raedwulf took that hand and lifted it to his lips.

Burginde, on her stool, was near to bursting. She jumped up. "I will bring mead," she said, wiping her tears with a corner of her apron.

"When can we wed," was what the bailiff asked. "I must return to Wessex within the fortnight."

"Then we wed three days hence," Ælfwyn told him. "Wilgot can say the banns beginning tomorrow, and we will wed after the third reading of them."

Her face clouded for the first time since they had entered the room. "I cannot leave until Pega's child is born," she told both men. "It will be another month perhaps."

"I will be back for you before St Helen's," Raedwulf promised. That saint's day fell a month before the coming of Summer; if all went well, Pega's babe would be baptised and nearly four months old by then.

They took a cup of mead. The couple looked over the rim of their cups at each other, in a toast as meaningful as it was silent.

Ælfwyn excused herself; she and Burginde had much they must attend.

Hrald and Raedwulf remained in the treasure room. "I have news for you, of a much different nature," Hrald said.

The bailiff was at once on the alert; even the warming mead had not dulled his senses. The sudden gravity of Hrald's face was sobering in itself.

"Haesten is dead," Hrald reported. "By my own hand."

The older man started; it was impossible to do other.

"Haesten! Are you certain?"

"His own man called him so, before our duel. Grey-haired, broad in the chest, a formidable fighter."

"Yes," came the bailiff's slow agreement. "Yes. That is the man."

"He attacked and overtook a small Saxon hall to the east, one in my care. We tracked him easily enough, killing nearly all his men. His wife and boys I sent to Frankland with what remained of his men."

"What tidings," Raedwulf answered, taking this in.

"Where – where is his body," the bailiff asked next.

"Rotting in a forest clearing, north of Geornaham."

Raedwulf took this in. "You say his sons still live," he said. The bailiff had met the boys, years ago when they had been baptised in their father's stolen camp at Middeltun. Raedwulf had never killed a child, and could never sanction doing so. Yet it was true that vengeance was the most powerful of motivators.

"Did the boys see your contest?"

Hrald nodded. "Yes. His wife as well. I sent them all to Frankland."

"We will hope they remain there," Raedwulf ended, in a lower tone.

Burginde was the bearer of Ælfwyn's good news, and made for the kitchen yard to deliver it. It took the form of instructions to the cooks for a special meal three days hence – one of modest proportion, given Winter – but one at which care should be taken. Reserved eggs, dug out of the hardwood ashes in which they had spent long weeks, would be beaten and baked in cheese pies, and whatever slight delicacies they could provide should appear on the table, for Lady Ælfwyn was to wed the rich thegn and bailiff of Defenas, Raedwulf, and this would be her nuptial feast.

Ælfwyn felt she must tell her daughter Ealhswith at once. She met the girl as she was coming in the door leading from the kitchen yard. Cerd was with her, and ran to Ælfwyn and flung his arms upon her skirts. She held his reaching hands as they stood together.

"My darling girl, I have happy news, the happiest for me. The Bailiff of Defenas has proved a good friend to us all, for long and troubled years. And now, I shall wed him. I will remain here until the Feast of St Helen, then he will return for me, and take me to his home in Defenas. It is there I shall live."

Ealhswith's thin face had paled. "Defenas," she repeated. She gave her head a shake as if to aid her understanding. She knew that part of Wessex to be nearly farthest from Four Stones as was possible.

"You need not decide now if you will come with me, or stay here with Hrald. There is much time for that." Ælfwyn dropped the boy's hands and reached to her daughter. "But I hope you will be happy for me, for knowing you are will add to my own happiness."

"Of course – of course I am happy," Ealhswith answered, though her voice faltered.

"There is much to be decided, but you yourself will decide if you stay, or come," her mother assured her.

The girl looked around, uncertain at what more to say. The door opened behind them, and Pega appeared, her dog at her heels.

"I will go up to the weaving room," Ealhswith said. "Mealla is there." And she left.

Cerd had taken a handful of Ælfwyn's skirts in his hand, and they led the way to the treasure room, where Hrald and Raedwulf stood talking. Burginde slipped in, her face telling of her satisfaction in how her message had been both delivered and received. Pega was surprised to see Raedwulf, but greeted the bailiff with true warmth. He had been the instrument of her marriage to Hrald, a man known to her father, and one trusted by both Æthelflaed and Æthelred. As Pega spoke to him Frost came frisking from her side, and made his own bow, as he sometimes did, stretching his long legs before him and dropping his narrow head nearly to the floor. He then rose, tail lashing, to circle Raedwulf where he stood.

After their shared laughter came silence. Ælfwyn and Raedwulf faced Pega, with expressions she could not quite discern. Raedwulf took the lead.

"I have been granted the privilege to make Lady Ælfwyn my wife," he said.

Pega's small gasp of surprise was answered by Ælfwyn. "It is true, Pega; we shall be married quite soon, in three days. And before Mid-Summer I shall go to Defenas."

Ælfwyn went on. "You have Mealla, who has impressed us all with her resourcefulness. And Jari's wife Inga is capable and knows well the ways of both hall and yards. I will be glad to ask my sister Æthelthryth to come from Turcesig before I leave, that she might spend the Summer here, while your babe is still so tenderly young."

It was much to take in. Pega stood, nodding her head in wonder, unable yet to gauge the vastness of this change, and the coming expansion of her own duties. These she let fall aside in her happiness for that joy which so clearly shown upon Ælfwyn's face.

She went to Hrald, who placed his arm around her. Pega had counted herself blest in the kindness of her mother-in-law, and now in a few months, would lose her. But Hrald would lose his mother.

There was much to consider, much to discuss, for those who stood in that room, save for boy and dog, who played amongst the treasure-bearing chests and casks.

Of his hall in Defenas Raedwulf had more to tell his intended, which he wished all to hear. Ælfred had granted him the place more than a decade ago, but Raedwulf, always in Witanceaster or on the move with the King, had known little time to improve or develop it.

"The lands are extensive, and my demands upon it, few. There is good pasture land for coming sheep. A steward and his wife keep all in order. Of men I keep but few of my own. When I am there, the King ofttimes sends me an escort, but I have had no real need to maintain warriors on my own account. Until now, that is," he added, alluding to the fact that now the place would hold something worth protecting.

"The garden –" he shook his head "– is but a kitchen garden, but there is much near ground for you to create something of your own. Also, I will build you a bower, should you like. It would provide you with some quiet, which I know you have enjoyed here."

It sounded, in short, a place with much potential to be an idyll, a haven of peace and beauty. Ælfwyn knew she would find happiness there. But her thoughts strayed to her daughter, and how she had received the news. Her going would change the lives of all.

"Ealhswith," she offered. "She is of marrying age." Ælfwyn could scarce go on beyond this, but Hrald saw it.

He did not speak, tracing in his mind what his mother may have already considered of the matter. She spoke again.

"I will not ask her to either come with me, or stay."

The onus was on Hrald. His sister was a valuable asset, and could serve as a vital peace-weaver here in Anglia, between him and another hall of Danes. As of yet he knew of no such alliance to be made, and after hearing Raedwulf speak on Prince Eadward's plans once he was named King, felt his sister's future better assured in Wessex.

"Nor will I ask her to stay, or to go," he said.

The Bailiff of Defenas felt moved to speak, renewing a promise he had already made to Hrald. "If she comes with her mother to Defenas, she could wed into the highest ranks of either Wessex or Mercia. I, and the King himself, would spare no pains to procure a match to ensure her safety, and happiness."

Hrald's mother took this up. The words of Raedwulf had spurred another possibility of her own. "If this should happen, Hrald, I will send you her bride-price, to make up that which you would have gained by her marrying here. I have no need of it."

The open-handedness of this offer might have stunned other men. These two, who knew her well, only nodded at the amplitude of the gesture.

"There is another choice for her," her mother cautioned. "Oundle. Mother is there. Sigewif as well. And of course, Ashild."

A moment passed before she continued with her thought. "Ealhswith may wish to spend time there, as she makes her decision." Ælfwyn did not know if her daughter had ever felt called to a true vocation; she had never mentioned such to her, but many well-born maids retired to convents to aid them in uncertain times.

Ælfwyn ended by looking at Hrald. The best she could do was repeat what she had just told her daughter. "There is no need for decision now; it will be five months before I leave."

"My sister Eanflad will want to stay here, I am sure," she went on, "though we shall abide by her choice." Indeed, it was hard to imagine the quietly industrious Eanflad any place but at her loom up in the weaving room, where she had ever seemed most content.

Cerd now scrambled out from behind the chests he had been hiding behind, and ran first to Burginde, then to Ælfwyn. He dropped down in a tumbled heap upon the edge of her skirts, and began playing with the round toggle of one of her shoes. Every eye fell upon him, though he saw them not.

Of a sudden Burginde stood up from her stool. All heads turned to her. She swallowed.

"'Tis rarely I am asked, but at times I must tell. And tell you I must, Master Hrald, and your dear lamb of a mother. The pup – he must stay with her. Do not let my Lady be taken from Cerd, nor he from her."

She sat down so quickly her skirt billowed around her knees. But she looked up, and into the face of Ælfwyn, one with whom her own life had been lived. It was the bed of Ælfwyn, and the alcove of Burginde, the boy had cried to be let into, in the nights following his mother's death. They had been his deepest comfort, and the arms to which he had clung.

"Yes, Burginde," Ælfwyn murmured. "I feel you are right. He is too young to make the choice; he knows not what we will be taking him to." She looked at her son. "His parting from you will be hard. But his parting from me – and mine from Cerd – " She could not continue.

She went on, in stronger voice. "It was always my plan, that Cerd should see Wessex. He must know his father."

She turned again to Hrald. She knew he would sorely miss the boy, though a child of his own was on the way.

"He is also of Wessex," she reminded Hrald. "He has a foot planted in both Kingdoms. And he is so like his mother; I think in a few years he will know where he most belongs. I do not feel I can keep him longer from Kilton. He must know his father and see his people." She stopped, and invoked the boy's mother.

"And none of us forget how Ashild named him."

The next day Ælfwyn went to Oundle. She took only Burginde with her, meaning to spend nought but a hour or two. During the long and restless night doubts had begun to creep into her mind; not of her love for Raedwulf, but of the seeming abandonment of her duty. She felt a powerful need to speak to Abbess Sigewif; a need nearly as strong as was that yearning for the man she loved. A steady drizzle fell the entire way, and the waggon they rode in slogged through mud, slowing their journey,

Sigewif received them in her writing room. After listening to all, the Abbess was decisive.

"Of Four Stones and its environs you need no dispensation. You have given your youth to this place, as I am giving my prime. Go with Raedwulf to Wessex, and know happiness once more." The Abbess paused, mindful of who lay within the church. "Or if happiness is beyond your ken, to the contentment God will surely grant you in such a union."

Ælfwyn lifted her hands, in both thanks and supplication.

"I am grateful indeed for your counsel. I was fully willing to leave with so noble a man. Yet, today . . ." Her words ended, and she looked fully at Sigewif. "You do not forsake your duty here."

This was met by Sigewif's smile. "I am a bride of Christ. My task is a light one; the lightest."

Ælfwyn turned from the penetrating grey eyes of the Abbess to settle on the gemmed cover of a book upon that woman's desk. Her thoughts ran over the entirety of her life. All that she had was at Four Stones. Her home at Cirenceaster was destroyed, all its treasures, save what she had brought with her as a bride, dispersed. The vast dowry she was sent to Four Stones with turned out to be the safe-guarding of it. Her sisters lived with her, one married to a Dane; her mother, a professed nun, was here at Oundle. Four Stones and Oundle were her life. For long years her whole duty was here, to run the hall, extend the work of the Abbey, see her children grow and become settled in lives of their own. Until they were, leaving had been unthinkable. Now her son was wed, and to a good woman, who would soon make of him a father. And Ashild – she was beyond any Earthly concerns, and in Heaven, Ælfwyn hoped.

"Go, with my blessing," Sigewif told her. "Pega is a worthy successor as Lady. And in Hrald Oundle could have no better protector." She smiled then. "Who knows what work God leads you to, in Defenas. Whatever it may be, you will rise to it."

On the slow ride home Ælfwyn took thought of another she must tell of her changed estate, someone far from her embrace. This was Ceridwen. Before Raedwulf returned to take her to her new home, she would write to her friend, trusting that Yrling would return to Gotland to carry her missive.

Ælfwyn determined to spare all the long ride on muddy tracks, and hold the ceremony at Four Stones, and in the bower house. The small round house had ever been her refuge and comfort. It is wholly mine, she thought, and I would wed Raedwulf here, in the house where I first gave my body to him.

She had known a hand-fast by force, up in the weaving room, where she had trembled as Ceridwen bound her wrist to the man she had been sent to wed. She had conceded consent to Sidroc, and after the birth of Ashild had made vow to him as wife. This coming union, simple as it was, would be the sole true ceremony she had of the three. She would at last come to a man not out of fear or sorrow or duty, but joy. That day was now upon her.

Raedwulf had spent the past nights sleeping in the hall with Hrald's men; he had not wanted to disrupt the weaving room with his presence there. Nor, knowing that Ælfwyn was so soon to be his in the eyes of the Church did he ask to come to her bower house. He had waited long to name her as wife, and three more nights would make that attainment the sweeter.

Late in the post noon of the third day came those Ælfwyn had invited. She had donned that gown of pale rose hue, long sleeved and gracefully draping, she had set aside for this day. Upon her pale hair was laid a sheer veil of cream linen, light almost as gossamer.

To witness she had her son and his wife, and her daughter before her. Wilgot her priest would say the benediction. Her sister Eanflad left her loom, and stood apart in meek attendance, her gentle smile a blessing in itself. Burginde and Mealla both took charge of Cerd. Ælfwyn would not pretend the boy would have any memory of his witnessing, but wanted him there just the same, as Ashild's beloved son. And Ælfwyn had asked Kjeld to be present, a man who had won her admiration and respect. As the party fanned out before the nuptial couple, neither the bride nor Pega's companion failed to notice the quick way in which Kjeld had come to stand at the black-haired girl's side, as if he himself were professing vows. Mealla's eyes rolled to the right to glance at him, but then returned to the nuptial pair.

A hush fell in that small room. Even Cerd was silent, looking up at those encircling the pair in the centre.

Raedwulf faced Ælfwyn. He extended his right hand, palm down, and Ælfwyn placed her left hand atop it, which he then enfolded with his own left.

"I, Raedwulf of Defenas, take you Ælfwyn of Cirenceaster, to wife. With my body will I honour you. My worldly goods I endow to you, and pledge to protect you and yours to the end of my days."

She drew breath and vowed to this man who stood looking into her eyes.

"I, Ælfwyn of Cirenceaster and of Four Stones, take you to husband, Raedwulf of Defenas. With my body will I honour you. I pledge to ever care for you, and bring you no cause for sorrow."

Raedwulf felt the gentle pressure of the hand he held. She smiled at him. He let go that hand, and took up her right. He slipped off the gold ring with its blue lapis stone, and placed it on the fourth finger of her left hand. She held his hand in hers as Wilgot made blessing over them.

"Two hands clasped in the eyes of God shall not be sundered," he pronounced.

A cry of joy went up from those surrounding them, and Ælfwyn, at last able to hold her hand in that of the bailiff before others, did not let it slip from her grasp. Entering the hall the party was met with cheers which, even at her age, coloured her cheek. Pega took up the silver bird ewer. With the help of Mealla, she poured mead into the cups before her mother-in-law and her new husband, and then into that of Hrald, and all the rest who sat at the high table.

They dined on the finest meal the kitchen could provide, though the newly joined pair ate but sparingly from their silver salver. To share food in this way seemed an intimate act after the guardedness under which they had lived their attraction.

Excusing themselves as soon as was seemly, they were cheered out of the hall, bringing a flush of pride to even Raedwulf's cheek. A drizzle was falling, and he lifted his cloak over their heads as they made their way to her bower. Approaching, they saw a welcoming light flicker.

Burginde was within, having herself slipped from the hall. She finished lighting the second of two cressets flanking the bed, gave her curtsy, and fled, grinning from ear to ear.

They turned to see that the nurse had sprinkled her coverlet with dried rose petals plucked from her garden in Summer, fragrant reminder of warmth to come.

He began to undress her. Her veil he removed first, letting it drape over the end of her bed. His hands went to her hair, and he kissed her lips.

"All is before us," he whispered. He took up her hands and pressed them to his lips.

She answered him with a fervent desire for their future.

"Seeing Pega," she whispered, "knowing of the child soon to come . . . you do not know how I wish this for myself, with you.

"I pray as devoutly as I know how to Mother Mary, that this might become so."

He looked ready to speak, but she went on.

"I have entered my fourth decade of life. Still, I might be as Sarai, wife to Abram in the Bible, and my womb made fruitful."

He would counter her fears. "You are yet young," he insisted.

She must nod in accord; her Moon-flow was still with her. Women years older had brought forth babes.

Raedwulf spoke again.

"And – I will do my part." He could not keep the smile from his face.

A CIRCLE OF GOLD

ÆLFWYN did not weep before her husband as he rode away, but swallowed down her tears in trust of their coming reunion some four months hence. Burginde and Pega flanked her at the palisade gate, and it was Pega who led her mother-in-law to the treasure room. Burginde and Mealla went to fetch refreshment, and left them at the door. Within its private confines the two Ladies of Four Stones held each other, and with Pega's coming babe aslant in that embrace, kissed. They must smile at the other. The younger Lady of Four Stones had before remarked that Ælfwyn's new happiness made her look almost as a woman of five-and-twenty.

"I am truly happy for you," she told Ælfwyn. "Yet in just a few months we must say fare-well, as you leave with this good man you have wed. I will miss you, dearly, and I cannot begin to think what your absence will mean to Hrald. But you know he is happy for you."

"Thank you, my dear Pega," Ælfwyn answered. She took a moment to look about at the treasure room. Pega had added many small touches of wealth and beauty to this room, which had before been always more armoury than chamber. "How I shall miss you, and all at Four Stones.

Coming peace may make it easier for us to see each other. I am only happy you have Mealla here." Ælfwyn had grown fond of that young woman, and Burginde was taking great pride in her ability. Soon they must leave Pega and Mealla alone with the hall and its demands. Ælfwyn took her daughter-in-law's hand. "In the meantime remember that I have given thanks every day to God that you were sent to Hrald. He could not have a more worthy wife. Nor one more loving.

"And you bring the blessing of your child, so soon to come," Ælfwyn went on, for it could not be many days before Pega was brought to her confinement.

Pega's eyes cast downward to the floor. The shadow about them grew the deeper. "I will hope the babe . . . will make Hrald love me," she said.

Ælfwyn drew a short breath. Pega, so caring, so giving, did not feel loved by her son. She almost could not speak, for fear of saying the wrong thing.

Pega eased the way. "He is kind to me, always. But – he does not love me. I have told him I love him. He cannot say it in return."

There were perhaps few other women who could understand this as well as Ælfwyn. No man had ever told her he loved her, save he who had just left her bed; nor had Ælfwyn said it to any other man. Not even Gyric, to whom she gave her youthful heart, heard those words from her lips; he would not allow her to speak them, so protective he was of her as he rode off to war.

All Ælfwyn could do was to hold the small hand in her own.

"I only hope one day his affection for me, will equal mine, for him," Pega ended, with a brave smile.

Ælfwyn was troubled enough by this that next day she sought her son out. Pega had again gone to rest in the bower house, leaving the treasure room free. Hrald could read the concern on his mother's face as he closed the door after them.

"It is Pega," she said, which caused her son's face to cloud.

Ælfwyn raised her hand. "There is nothing amiss with the babe," she assured him. "Though her time is near. It will not be long now; perhaps tomorrow, or the next day."

Hrald's uncertainty shifted as they regarded the other. She must say it, and alone as they were, had rare freedom to do so. Ælfwyn remembered something she had told Raedwulf, and expanded upon it now to her son.

"As I have grown older I have thought the heart is a large hall, capable of holding more than one love at a time. Once one becomes beloved, they may long linger there, even when we wish they did not. We cannot, I think, expel those we have loved from our hearts. Such regard may burn itself out; our feelings for them, due to lack of tending, may wither and die, like a blossom fallen into decay, and then dust.

"Your first marriage – the pain of its ending may have closed your heart, snapped it shut. But know that there is much room within to allow another."

"What . . . what has she told you?" Hrald finally asked.

"Only that she hoped that one day you might love her. That the child will allow you to love her. And tell her so."

Hrald looked up into the rafters of the room. In this room he had told Dagmar many times he loved her. They were words she could not repeat, but seemed close to doing so. Yet in her dealings with him, she made him feel loved; that counted for much.

He found himself shaking his head at the contrast between the two women. Pega was a woman to cherish and protect. Dagmar was one who inspired him, who he felt he need live up to. He thought of Dagmar still as his first wife, and must remind himself that the union had been annulled; it was as if it had never happened. Nothing could tell his body that. His attraction to her remained as powerful as ever.

He felt shame at this, here in his mother's presence, shame for thinking on that woman who had wounded all of them. And greater shame to think of Dagmar like this while his lawful wife stood on the threshold of a great travail, one which would cause her suffering and might even take her life.

He had no defence. He wanted his actions to Pega to say what his lips could not.

His mother, met with this silence, could do no more than utter a silent prayer that Hrald's heart might open.

Four days later Mealla came running to the bower house in the middle of the night. Ælfwyn and Burginde hurriedly dressed; Burginde went first to the kitchen yard and roused one of the boys there, bidding him heat water and broth. When Ælfwyn entered the treasure room, Pega, dressed in a shift, was white faced and panting, holding on to a post, while the faithful Frost stood whining at her feet in distress. Ælfwyn took the hound upstairs and to the weaving room, where she put him into the care of Ealhswith, that the animal might not be alarmed at the cries of his mistress. Then she sent both daughter and hound to the bower house, where Cerd lay asleep in his alcove.

Mealla was almost as white-faced as was Pega. Hrald stood, fully dressed, at his young wife's side, his arm about her, his face in high alert, as if he rode to fight. Ælfwyn was murmuring words of encouragement to them all when the door opened and Burginde bustled in. A blear-eyed and half-dressed Bork was just behind her, his arms full of clean straw. After him came a kitchen-woman, with basins and a jug. Outside the half-closed doors sounds of men, roused by all the activity, could be heard. Burginde shut the door and began ordering all about. Hrald she sent to Jari's house, to await word there, and to return to sleep if that were possible; Bork was shown where upon the floor to deposit the straw and told to return with as much again, and Mealla was set to digging through a certain chest for needed linens.

Pega's travail lasted as long as that of first mothers' often did. She bore it with courage, regretting her cries but heeding Burginde's many prompts to yell as loudly as she liked. The Sun rose up into a day cold and clear, short as Winter days are; and after that orb had set and the Moon rose the young Lady of Four Stones was delivered of her child. As Pega squatted over the birthing straw, Mealla holding her at one shoulder and Ælfwyn at the other, Burginde caught the red and slippery babe. Pega was allowed to fall back upon the linen draped for her, and the child laid upon her breast.

Outside that room Hrald had sat for many hours, Jari at his side. The high table had seen food and drink come and go, but Hrald hardly left his chair. The new silence of the treasure room told him of some critical juncture in his wife's travail. He stood up, hardly able to draw breath. He was aware of Jari standing behind him, that felt but unseen presence of reassurance following Hrald nearly all his life.

The door opened. Mealla looked out, her pointed face wreathed in smiles. Jari clapped him on the shoulder, and Hrald walked in.

Pega rested upon the floor on a heap of linen-covered straw, bolsters beneath her head. A sheet was pulled up past her waist, but upon her bare breast lay a tiny red babe, with wet dark hair.

Pega was looking down at the damp head, her hand covering nearly the whole of the babe's back. She lifted her eyes to her husband.

"It is a girl," she told him. Tears were in her eyes. She wanted a daughter, but wished a boy had been born first.

"A perfect and beautiful girl," Ælfwyn added.

Hrald crouched down at the new mother's side. The babe was moving, wriggling like a blind swimmer. The tiny mouth opened and closed, and chuffing sounds mingled with mewling cries. Pega shifted, and the babe found her breast. Hrald's finger reached and touched the wrinkled brow, now relaxing as it drew its first milk.

"I thank you," he breathed, looking at Pega. "She is beautiful. And perfect."

Later Hrald returned to the treasure room. Pega was sitting up in their bed. The babe had been washed and swaddled, and was again upon her mother's breast, fast asleep. Hrald bent down and kissed Pega on her forehead. He pulled a chair from the table and brought it close to her head. He sat down, and Mealla came to Pega, and gently lifted the swaddled bundle to his hands. Hrald held his daughter, marvelling at her smallness, and the solid if slight weight of her. He lowered her so she touched his knee, and spoke.

"This is my lawful daughter who I claim as my own, witnessed by all within this room at her birth."

With these words Hrald acknowledged the girl in law; no man might claim otherwise.

Tears of happiness were in Pega's eyes as he handed their daughter back to her.

Her voice was full of tenderness as she asked the next.

"Shall we name her Ashild?"

He closed his eyes at this. It would not be tribute, but a kind of theft, to use that name. He need not say so; she saw it there on his face.

"I understand," she whispered back, and just as kindly. "There is no need. Ashild lives on, as it is."

He must kiss her again for this, and did so. Then he took something from his belt, and before them all, presented it. Neither Pega nor Mealla had seen it before, but Ælfwyn and Burginde knew it at once. It was a ring of twisted gold, perfect and unblemished.

He lifted Pega's left hand where it rested upon their babe's back, and slipped the ring on the fourth finger. It fit perfectly, and Pega took a moment, blinking at it as it circled that finger.

"My gift to you," he told her. "But it cannot match what you have given me, this day."

That night when Hrald lay next to Pega, their babe still upon her breast, he spoke to her in the dark.

"I love you, Pega. You are my dear wife. And I love you."

He could not see the tears streaming from her eyes, tears welling from her own love of this man, and the child they had made.

The babe's naming feast was set for a month after her birth. The girl, having survived the hazardous first weeks of life, would be baptised, her god-parents named, and a feast held. Asberg and Æthelthryth had arrived from Turcesig to attend, so that the larger family of Four Stones might all be present.

Yrling was glad to see Asberg, who had brought his sons Ulf and Abi. Yrling would have the chance to spar with them, before the eyes of the old spear-man, and those of his brother. Yrling had put on height in the year he had been here in Lindisse, and was much the young stripling. His contest with the older boys would be the fairer for it.

"You are an uncle now," Asberg greeted him, grinning. Yrling had not quite thought of the puling babe, or himself, in that light. He knew he was somehow glad Hrald's child had been a girl. He had no real answer for Asberg's good humoured ribbing, and tried not to be bothered that Asberg had also greeted Bork, and asked the stable-boy about his own spear-work.

Within the treasure room the swaddled child slept, tucked in her cradle. The new mother moved about the room, making final preparation to greet their guests. Pega wore a gown of green, one now snug over her breasts.

Hrald too was there, dressing for the ceremony. Pega took a small pouch of red silk from her gem casket. The silver webbing he had given her as part of her morgen-gyfu came cascading out. She caught it up and fastened two of the clasps behind her head. Hrald saw what she was doing, and came to help her with the one at the waist, fastening it at the small of the back. She turned to him when he had done so.

"It looks well," he told her. The delicate silver links spilled from neck to hips.

She smiled, and dropped her voice. "One day I will wear it for you as you requested. For now, this will do, to show how much I like it."

This piece of rare jewellery had been given after the fulfilment of their union. The birth of their first child was another benchmark, and a worthy moment for her to don it.

The door was now opened to those who would stand for the babe, and bear witness. All had attired themselves with care, and even Yrling's unruly locks had seen a comb. Ealhswith wore a new gown she had just completed sewing, of wool dyed yellow with the round blossoms of tansy. She took charge of Cerd, who liked nothing better than to be within the treasure room and its many chests and casks, the stacks of shields and barbed spears against the walls, and the broad furred bed to climb upon. Kjeld appeared, clad in a new tunic and leggings. Burginde had taken pity on the man in his pursuit of Mealla, and made them up herself. She had as well made him sit before her on a stool that she might trim his light brown hair. Burginde saw the eyes of the maid from Éireann widen as he walked in so carefully dressed and groomed, and had to smile to herself. Mealla was in her best gown, the red one she had arrived in, but had a new ornament at her throat, a silver pin touched with gold, given by Pega. It was of curious design, two animals so intertwined one could not tell if they were one beast or two. Burginde's own gown was of soft blue, with a dark blue head-wrap that sat well with her grey hair. She had a strikingly large silver pin at her neckline, a circle set with three garnets. Ælfwyn had given it to her following the birth of Hrald, and to wear it now at the christening of his own child seemed more than meet.

For the second time in recent years Wilgot entered the treasure room bearing a tray. On it sat a fine basin of white bronze, a beaker of silver holding consecrated water, a linen towel, and a glass vial of holy chrism. Ælfwyn's sister Æthelthryth, firm in her faith, had been asked to stand as god-mother, and in light of his role in the couple's union, Hrald asked that the bailiff of Defenas be named as god-father, certain the man would agree.

Pega took the babe from her cradle and passed her to Æthelthryth, who with a deep smile, held the tiny head over the basin as Wilgot dribbled water from the beaker upon her brow. The babe laughed, chortling so that all must smile with her. Pega had selected the name Ælfgiva for their little daughter, and this is the name Wilgot chanted as he anointed her. In its opening letters it gave honour both to Ælfwyn and to Pega's former protectors, Lady Æthelflaed and Lord Æthelred.

Yrling, having himself been baptised into the Church not long ago, had been asked by Ælfwyn to present a gift to the babe. It was a silver spoon, that emblem of abundance which was common to the christenings of the high born. This one was sized for a babe's mouth, small enough so that when she began to take other than her mother's milk it might be conveyed to her mouth in its dainty bowl. All eyes were upon him as Yrling held it out to his brother's wife and grinned. Pega thanked him most prettily, promising that no other spoon would be used for the first meals of his niece.

They made ready to quit the room. From the gathering noise without they knew the hall was filling with folk eager for the feast. One more thing Pega would do. Upon the shelf by their bed was laid the golden browband set with coloured gems she had worn at their wedding. Pega placed it upon her head now, as an occasion worthy of her greatest treasure. Mealla, who had the babe in her arms, handed her back, and the Lady and Jarl of Four Stones passed through the door.

When Hrald emerged his men saw glinting against his chest the huge gold torc his wife had bestowed upon him. A roar went up, one of pride and approval. That gold about his neck was reminder of the power of the union between two Kingdoms, and reminder also of the riches this tiny babe would be part heir to.

THE HAND-FAST BOWL

The Forests of Kilton The Year 896

EARLY Spring found Ceric building a weir. The streams and brooks which etched the landscape wherein he roamed rushed with waters icy from snow melt. Ever-forming clouds roiled over his head and dropped pelting rain on the soaked woodland. The swollen waterways brought fish with them, newly spawned and those much larger.

Ceric had subsisted on scavenged verdure, nuts, wild fruit he plucked, and foodstuffs left him by Worr. Hunger-bitten as he was, he had steadily lost flesh. His hipbones became two sharp knobs, and under the fair beard the hollows of his cheeks swore testimony to the austerity of his life. His coppery hair, tangled and knotted, streamed about his thin shoulders.

One morning, sitting in the mouth of his cave, a good fire warming him against the sharp wind of a chill but bright day, he looked at the excess of hempen line he had taken from the supply point. It sat coiled on a kind of shelf formed by a projecting ledge of rock, above any creeping damp darkening the cave floor. He had as well several barbed iron fishhooks, also carried in by Worr to the fallen ash. Looking on the line, Ceric thought to make a trap to capture fish, and so expand his provender. He had never built one, but had seen enough to guide his hand.

The rill of water from which he had drunk on the first day of his forest habitation fed into a stream deep and broad enough for fish. Walking its meandering course, it took him a morning's labour to scout a likely place to build his weir, prodding the stream bed as he went with a long staff he had cut. There at a narrow spot he might divert the larger fish in the rushing water into his trap, for the smaller ones would swim through the webbing he would weave. He began with his axe. He used the straightest of the branches he could find as upright supports with which to hold his webbing. Using a flat-bottomed rock he pounded these into the sandy bottom, a knuckle's length apart. The water was still frigid, yet he took off leggings and boots to enter it, and drove the stakes into the soft stream bed. The weir described an almost closed circle, one with its opening facing the onrushing current of the stream. The final stakes he drove tapered like an ever-narrowing funnel into the centre of the circle. When all the uprights were placed he began the even more chilling task of tying the hempen line to the base of the first stake, then crouching in the water, weaving it in and out of each succeeding stake, building up a coarse webbing.

Almost blue from cold he climbed upon the muddy bank, rubbing his freezing thighs with his balled-up woollen leggings, for he had neglected to bring any towelling. He gazed upon his handiwork, at the blunted ends of the pounded stakes rising above the water line. The weir was striking in his wild landscape simply in that it had been made by the hand of man. He had built this, crude as it was, and after he drew on his damp leggings, pulled on stockings, tied the tatters of his leg wrappings over his calves, and fastened the toggles of his worn shoes he spent some little time studying the weir. He could do no more now, and must return to his cave where a few coals might be left of his morning's fire. He felt aware of his hunger, his need for warmth, and more than that, a glimmering satisfaction of having wrought something. He would return next day and see what, if anything, his labours had yielded.

He was back next noon. Weir-trapped fish could be dipped up in nets, but the making of such was beyond his scant resources. And cold as it was, he did not relish the thought of wading into the stream water to do so. But fishhooks he had, ready to be tied to the sturdy line of animal sinew Worr had also supplied. Worms and grubs were easily dug. He arrived at the weir with two hooks already threaded with the strong sinew. He cut himself a long and flexible pole, twitched a baited hook into the circle of his weir, and stood upon the bank, leaning against a tree, as if he were a boy again. It did not take long for the line to tighten. He snagged a large and fat grayling, shimmering almost silver as it splashed, tail thrashing against its capture. Lifted into the air there was a beauty to it, so much so that Ceric paused as it struggled for its freedom. One animal must die so that the other could live. He stunned the grayling with the back of his axe, and carried it away. Gutted, and threaded on a green skewer of wood he roasted it over the fire at the mouth of his cave. The smoky char of the fish flaked in his mouth, an unaccustomed and welcome feel and taste after so many months. From then on he returned to the weir every other day. He caught more grayling, and many slender dace as well, grateful for each and every time the sinew line grew taut. What he could not eat at once he dried, gutting and splitting the fish, keeping the tail intact so he might drape it over a framework above a smoking fire of green wood.

His success with the weir led him later to build snares. In this he was not wholly alone; he was companioned by memory. The act of finding a slightly-worn trail, forming the loops, and setting the snare took him back to Hrald's side, when Tindr patiently crouched beside them. That hunter would silently and with deft fingers work the sinew into something which in the morning might hold a hare for Gunnvor's pot, or that as a special treat, Tindr might gut and skin and roast for them on the spot. He found himself smiling at these memories, felt the corners of his mouth turn upwards, and the slight crinkle of his eyes, in an unfamiliar expression of pleasure and dearly-held remembrance. The flesh of both fish and hare brought him back to his own wasted body.

When the hens began laying again, Worr carried many boiled eggs to the supply point, which Ceric took with gratitude. These helped feed his starved muscles. When sheep and cows had dropped their young, and were beginning their weaning, milk-maids and cheese makers betook both ewe and cow of their rich milk. Soon after this their produce appeared in the food packs left for Ceric, soft cheeses packed in small crocks, and aged ones leaf-wrapped.

Though his body was now better nourished, the return of warming weather had done little for the state of his mind. He was tormented still by the visits of the galloping night-mare. It was ever the same vision, of him running on the field of battle, then picking up the spear. As soon it left his hand towards its target, Ashild turned round, horror in her face as she watched its approach.

He could not stop the unfolding image, certain as he was of the end; could not wake himself and thus spare the outburst of draining tears which brought no relief.

As Spring ripened Worr determined he must find Ceric, must at least look at him to allay the fears of all at Kilton. Worr knew Ceric had taken up one of the caves to the east; he had already tracked him there and seen the scant signs of habitation at its mouth. But he had never lingered long enough to catch the elder son of the hall either leaving or returning to the recess. An unspoken pact had formed, in the mind of the horse-thegn at least, that he would supply Ceric with those necessities of life to ensure his continuance, and in return would demand no more than he take what he would. But now with warming weather Ceric might abandon the cave which had been his Winter dwelling. The thought that he might betake himself deeper into the wood, or that he might at this point be weakened, or deranged beyond reclamation spurred Worr in his action.

One morning when Worr carried in the food pack, he did not stop at the fallen ash longer than to see if Ceric had lately visited there. He had; the bag of wheat kernels was gone. Worr went on, shouldering the pack, and pressed ahead along the now well-defined path leading to Ceric's first camping ground by the rill, then across it to the hollowed-out oak which had sheltered him, and beyond, on an easterly track to the rising ground pocked with caves.

It was not long after dawn, the Sun splitting through dark trunks whose greening leaves were half unfolded. Worr trusted that his early arrival would find Ceric still within the hollow he had claimed. The smell of a wood fire was the first sign that Ceric lived and was well. It led Worr where he hoped, the cave opening. A downed pine provided on its trunk a surface on which one might place things, or sit. Off to one side was a wooden framework hung with a few flayed fish, a low fire glowing beneath the drying flesh. The fire-ring of stone Worr had earlier noted was there as well, with the small tripod and cauldron Ceric used for cooking.

Ceric was catching fish. This fact alone heartened Worr. He drew a breath and addressed the dark void of the cave mouth.

"Ceric. It is Worr."

He paused then, judging what was most important to convey.

"I will not harm you. I will not force you back. I only want to see you. If you are there, step out, so I may do so."

Worr said this only once. He could not repeat his words if they flowed into an abyss. He stood still, well back from the darkness of the cave entrance, and waited.

He heard a scraping sound, a shuffling, and then a man appeared. Worr worked hard not to allow his shock to show on his face. Here was Ceric, in near rags, tangled and matted hair spilling down over his shoulders, his handsome young face obscured by a ragged, reddish beard. He was not only thin, he was gaunt.

Ceric pursed his lips and looked at Worr, then blinked. The horse-thegn spoke again.

"Ceric. I have brought you food today. You need not walk down to the fallen ash."

Ceric was still, studying him, yet with unmoving eyes, which burned a bright greenish gold from under his smudged brow.

"Worr," he finally said.

Those eyes were glistening; Worr could see this.

Ceric lifted both hands to his eyes, and brushed them with the backs of his thumbs as they blurred from tears.

"The Lady Edgyth prays for you," Worr said next. "Your brother Edwin needs you."

"Lady Modwynn?" Ceric questioned, as if unaware of his grandmother's death.

Worr's eyes lifted skyward. "She is in Heaven, as you will recall," he answered, in a tone low and soft.

Ceric's shoulders began to shake, but his head nodded agreement. "Yes, yes," he muttered.

"May I come closer," Worr asked, already beginning to take the smallest step nearer.

Ceric jumped back. "No, no," he breathed, a note of panic in this simple denial. Ceric stared at the horse-thegn, then gave a single nod. He turned his back, and vanished into the cave.

Worr took a further step, and dropped the food bag. Then he turned and himself left.

When Worr had gained the palisade he was glad not to have been spotted by Edwin. He went to Lady Edgyth, who he knew would be in the stone chantry, following the morning Mass she always attended. Finding her in private devotion would be the best way to speak to her alone.

She was there in the empty church, kneeling on a small cushion set upon the stone floor. Just before her was the slab under which Modwynn and Godwulf lay. Edgyth's head was bowed in prayer, but it lifted when she heard the door close. She rose and turned to Worr as he crossed himself and approached her. They moved to the near wall, and stood at the painted statue of Saint Ninnoc.

Worr saw by the Lady's face she knew he had seen Ceric. The soft grey eyes were brighter, even hopeful. Her delicate hands, still pressed as if in prayer, made a move towards him in supplication.

"Yes. I have seen him," he confirmed.

In response Edgyth crossed herself, in thanksgiving.

"He is indeed living in one of the caves. He has been fishing; I saw the dried fish upon a rack he fashioned. But he is pitifully thin."

Worr need not tell her that Ceric took little of all that was brought to him. No one could help that.

"I spoke of you, and of Edwin."

Edgyth's pale lips formed a question.

"Did he speak back?"

Worr had scant answer.

"Only to say my name." He thought a moment. "And to forbid me to near him."

Edgyth's chin dropped.

"So he lives, but as distressed as ever."

"I fear so, my Lady. Yes."

The silence between them extended, until Worr broke it.

"And I fear we will lose him forever, to death, or utter madness."

The gentle release of breath from Edgyth revealed she had also dealt with this fear.

"We must reclaim him," she murmured. She looked about the place, at the stone walls, the brightly painted statues, the crisp and snowy linen draped upon the altar. But she was seeing beyond, to an entirely Earthly realm.

"Please to come with me, Worr," she invited.

They left the stillness of the church and walked past Dunnere's house, her own bower house, and then towards the kitchen yard. A small garden grew on its border, one filled with pot herbs. Along its fence of woven wattles grew a riot of sweet pea vines; some green and reaching with spidery tendrils, others already in bloom. She stopped at them, her hands opening at their flourishing growth.

"Tomorrow will you take him some pea plants, Worr. They are still young and will grow well, if given light. They demand little else."

All Worr could do was nod. He recalled the Lady telling of her time at Glastunburh, and how men wounded in mind from war had found solace in the small rituals of caring for herbs, vines, and fruit trees in that abbey's capacious gardens.

A smile was forming on Edgyth's pale lips. "And he so loves peas," she remembered. "Now he can grow his own. If he can begin to care for them, to tend them, he may be able to care more for himself."

The next morning found the horse-thegn repeating his trek to the mouth of the forest cave. He did not summon Ceric, and the act of depositing the oiled bag that held the pea plants and the hand trowel was quickly accomplished.

When Ceric emerged, the slumping bag was there before him, the iron trowel laid out by its side. He opened the bag more fully to see what it held. Instead of the wild foraging he subsisted upon, here was something familiar from boyhood, and a favoured treat. The peas were part of Kilton's garden, and a cultivated life. The trowel seemed a command to participate, in however small a way, in that life.

He planted the pea plants by the shelter of the rock face, where the Sun's warmth would reflect upon the young vines. The stony ground there was of a paucity that he must travel to the rill bank and fill the oiled bag with damp brown soil to enrich it. He used sticks to give the peas support, and when he was done, spent some time fingering the winged white and green blossoms already unfolding there.

The warming weather increased his larder in other ways. As soon as they emerged he plucked bright green and tonic birch leaves to add to his broth and browis, pinched off the unfurling coiled heads of ferns, and when the dark red buds of butterbur sprang from the moist soil, gathered them, boiling out their bitterness to eat them with salt. Forest and open meadowland yielded borage, cresses, rosemary, dandelions, and mallow leaves to eat fresh, and the ever-present dried rose hips to give tang to the pot, or to chew whole when his mouth was dry.

These outward things he could do. One day Ceric went to the fallen ash tree to find a small wooden box sitting upon its trunk. He untied the leathern cord which held fast the two sides. Inside was a heavy metal circle, the size of the palm of his hand, with a small handle. He took it out, and turned it in his hand. It was his silver looking-disc, the polished face of it casting back to him a true reflection of his face.

His intake of breath was as sudden as the action of dropping the looking-disc back into its box. When Worr returned two days hence he saw the glint of the disc before he had fully entered the clearing; the Sun was shining on it. He saw Ceric had opened, and then left it behind. So unmoored was the man, he did not wish to be reminded of who he was.

Dunnere's letter to the Welsh Kingdom of Ceredigion had been carried off by a thegn of Kilton. To avoid ready detection he had ridden minor tracks, but riding alone gave him speed, so that the man was gone little more than two weeks. He returned late one misty forenoon bearing a rolled parchment in a short tube of hardened leather. His approach had been signalled from the parapet, and Edwin and Edgyth came from their respective tasks, he from the training ground where he had been sparring with Alwin, and she from the head cook in the kitchen yard. Edwin took off his war-kit and left it with his body-guards, saying he would shortly return, and Edgyth shook out the apron she had donned to protect her gown from the kitchen yard's spatter. They followed in the foot-steps of the thegn to Dunnere; the priest was as usual in his small house fast by the stone church. The missive delivered, mother and son watched the priest unwind the cord circling the toggle upon the round top of the tube. Dunnere tapped the parchment out, and as it was unrolled Edwin saw enough to glimpse a surface nearly covered with writing.

Dunnere cleared his voice and read aloud. The salutation was long enough.

"MY DEAR BROTHER IN CHRIST, DUNNERE, IN ANSWER TO YOUR LETTER INQUIRING AFTER A WIFE FOR THE LORD OF KILTON: May God in His infinite mercy grant you health to read this. As you well remember, King Elidon had only sons, two of the four now sadly deceased, the other two installed in their own princely holdings. Yet the King and his Lady have fostered the daughter of his younger brother, Dunwyd, dead these eight years, and his only get. The young woman –Dwynwen is her name – is of fourteen or fifteen years, healthy in body and sound of mind; a mind I might add, of decided bent. Dunwyd's widow – not the girl's mother but one he wed after that good woman's death – has made great impress on the girl; her connection to Ceredigion is intense. Dwynwen is of unblemished character, but like many of we Cymry looks upon those east of the Dyke as interlopers, barbarous ones at that. Needless to say I have spoken to the King and he welcomes the arrival of the Lord of Kilton and my beloved brother. Send word of your coming and the girl will be made ready for the Lord and you to see.

Yours in the Blood of Christ,
GWYDDEN, SERVANT OF GOD

Dunnere read it all, sparing his listeners nothing. Edwin was left shaking his head.

"Barbarous interlopers?" he asked, half laughing at this epithet. "Such a maid will not be happy to cross Offa's Dyke, and wed one."

The priest put the best face on it. "Gwydden is candid by nature," he said, "and our friendship is such that he could hardly be less than that. Not when the subject is a fitting wife for you." He let his eyes scan the parchment again. "But the young woman – Dwynwen – is devout, that is what matters. And she is the daughter of a Prince. Her uncle, Elidon, is King. Ceredigion has never in his reign sided with the heathen horde against either Wessex or Mercia."

This mattered greatly; unlike many Kings and Princelings of Wales, Elidon had never joined forces with the Danes.

The priest went on. "King Elidon is bound to provide handsomely for the girl, to make her attractive to you. Gwydden nearly says as much, that he welcomes your arrival."

Edwin considered. "Her name, Dwynwen – what does it mean?" Saying it for the first time, he was aware it had a certain strength to it, despite the softness of its sound.

"Wave. It means wave." Dunnere also gave thought. "A fitting name for the daughter of a sea-side Kingdom."

"May I see the name?" Edwin made gesture to the parchment which Dunnere still held. He wished to see it spelled out, to better understand it.

The priest lifted the creamy sheet, and made a subtle movement with his other hand. There it was, in the tight and well-formed hand of the far-away cleric: Dwynwen. Seeing how it was written gave needed shape to how Edwin thought about the name, and perhaps of she who bore it.

"I too can offer her the sea," Edwin pointed out, extending his hand to the priest's window. Indeed, the surf from the cliffs below could be heard even within Dunnere's house.

His mother Edgyth smiled at him. "That you can," she confirmed.

Her next words were what Edwin was thinking as well; the age of the proposed bride. "She is so young," Edgyth murmured.

Edgyth knew she would need to stay on here at Kilton a year or two with nearly any bride, until she felt established as Lady. Only if Edwin should wed a young widow, one already skilled in running a household, would she be able to shortly leave for a new life at Glastunburh. With a bride still a girl, she might need to remain at Kilton for years, to guide her.

Edwin echoed this concern to Dunnere. "Yes, if she is but fourteen, she is little more than a child."

The priest shrugged. Some maids destined for high-born unions wed at thirteen, as soon as they had known their first Moon-flow.

Edgyth answered, with her ever-gentle smile. "She will grow up here," she summed.

She looked now to Dunnere. "Dunwyd's widow appears to have great influence over the maid, which makes sense; her mother may have died years earlier, and Dunwyd himself has been dead since Dwynwen was but six or seven."

Edgyth looked now to her son. The nameless widow might be the one Edwin must persuade. Her, and King Elidon himself. Edgyth felt confident her son was up to the task, and said as much in the quiet assurance of her next words. “They welcome you,” she repeated.

Edwin looked back at his mother, then to Dunnere. It was he who must accompany him to Wales, and there vouch for him.

“Then let us go to Elidon,” the Lord of Kilton decided.

Having heard tell of Dwynwen, the young Lord of Kilton made decision to leave for Ceredigion as soon as preparation would allow. He had missed out on the chance to pursue a noble maid of Mercia; he would act at once on this maid of Wales. Indeed, it seemed as though King Elidon was now holding her in reserve, just for him. Not to appear in timely fashion would slight that monarch’s gesture. Still, he made clear to himself and his mother that his was merely a foray in which to look.

“I will take no bride-price, no treasure with me,” he told the Lady of Kilton that same day Gwydden’s letter had been read to them.

This gave Edgyth pause. “And if she pleases you, and the King and her step-mother consent?”

Edwin had answer, one that surprised his mother in the confidence in which it was rooted. “Elidon will hold her for me, until my return.” Edwin cocked his head. “To arrive with treasure – when I have not even seen her – that is to place too many cubes of lead in their scale-bowl.”

Edgyth dropped her eyelids a moment. Her son sought not only to appear on an equal footing before this King, but with the advantage of a mere casual interest in the girl. She knew he had been disturbed by the loss of the Mercian maid, who he had at least glimpsed and found attractive. His desire to protect himself now must be springing from that disappointment. And she must allow Edwin to make his own decisions.

It seemed to Edgyth a great distance to travel, but then if the girl was as young as fourteen, it was likely her guardians would hold her back another year, until her body could better withstand child-bearing, even if the agreement was struck when Edwin was there.

Still, she made a single suggestion, one to which he agreed. "Perhaps a modest store of treasure might be carried with you, enough to secure the girl until you return for her."

Together they went through his caskets of gemstones and silver, looking for something small yet substantial. "This," he decided, pulling out a bowl of gleaming metal. It was shallow, and of a size to nestle within the cupped hands of he or she who lifted it to their mouth. It was in fact a hand-fast bowl, one from which a newly wedded couple might share their first sip of mead or wine. It was shaped from silver, with a narrow border of gold encircling its rim.

Perhaps Dwynwen and I shall indeed toast each other with this, he thought.

The young Lord of Kilton set out three days later, leaving Worr in command of Kilton. Edwin took a supply waggon and five-and-twenty thegns with him. The priest Dunnere rode at Edwin's side, the two of them flanked by the captains of Edwin's body-guard. Alwin was now made first captain, and the thegn Wystan elevated to second. Springing from the saddle cantles of these last were two embroidered banners, each sporting the golden dragon of Wessex. One was that made for Edwin by his mother Edgyth, which he had carried to his first engagement with Eadward. The second was a banner made by his birth mother, Ceridwen. The golden dragon she had stitched was as different from that wrought by Edgyth as were the two women, he wagered. That which had fluttered from Eorconbeald's saddle on the Fateful day featured a dragon with a coiled tail, all pent-up energy and drive. The dragon Ceridwen had stitched was almost cat-like; a cat with extended claws, barbed wings, and a plume of blue fire spouting from its open mouth. He had grown up being told she had made it for his father, Gyric, of whom he had no memory. And now that he knew that Gyric was not his blood-father, the man receded even further in his mental landscape. The fact that his birth mother had made a battle-flag for a blinded man, said something; Edgyth had suggested to him that she did much to make her husband feel more whole.

Out of humility most clerics rode asses; but as walking speed was vital, Worr selected a settled and well-mannered gelding for Dunnere, that he might not impede the progress of the party. From the saddle of this beast rose a white banner with the Christian cross laid on in fabric of red, to mark the rider as a man of God. Edwin told his mother he expected to return in no more than three weeks. He would stay three or four nights at the court of Elidon, less if the girl was wholly unsuitable. They set off, well armed, and in so great a number they might ride far more openly than the thegn who served as courier.

Preparations were such that Edwin had not time to ride out to the hamlet wherein lived Begu. He could not send a line on a scrap of parchment; she could not read. And to entrust a messenger to carry the news he would be gone nearly a month, to Wales . . . He could imagine her fearful question, "Is there then war?" And the answer, which even Edwin could imagine would bring little comfort, "No, he seeks a bride . . ."

He shook his head at that image. He would see her on his return.

Begu had four families as neighbours in her hamlet. She and her husband had formed the fifth pair, one that never grew beyond the two of them. Her husband was native to Kilton, but she hailed from a village two days' journey to the north. They had met when he travelled thence to sell the treen ware he was skilled at crafting in his spare time. He had arrived with a basket on his back, stuffed with finely carved wooden platters, ladles, and fancy cups to rival those of bronze in their handsomeness. Each was taken with the other, and Begu, one of many in her widowed father's cramped house, happy to accept the smiling stranger. He had been left a small house in the hamlet, gift of his now-dead grandfather. On the way back to Kilton they had stopped there, and found it and the hamlet much to their taste. The young couple never dwelt in the crowded croft outside the palisade walls where Begu's husband was raised, but began their life together in the hamlet. Within a year he was dead, sickened by the slash to his calf he had given himself with his own scythe. Begu had remained.

She had never the opportunity to return to visit her own village. She had liked the hamlet and the start they had made of it, and wanted to continue on. Now a neighbouring family were themselves travelling near to her childhood home. She might walk with them, stay a week or so with her kin, and then return in their company when they did. She felt strangely moved to do so. Telling Edwin of her going was paramount, so that he would not appear at her door one night and find her gone. But night after night the Lord of Kilton did not appear. A fortnight passed without his coming. She was forced to leave, asking only of her nearest neighbour that if he saw the Lord, please to tell him of her soon return.

Chapter the Twentieth

TWO WOMEN OF CYMRU

EDWIN and his party travelled north up the coast, rounding the bend west and into Wales. There by the River Wye lay the southern-most point of the great earthworks built by Offa, King of Mercia. The Dyke was mounded soil, grass covered, and taller than a man. The other side was deeply trenched, to keep the Welsh at the disadvantage during attack. A man crossing from east to west might ride his horse up, and then lead it aslant down. Though undefended at this point, no waggon could cross it unaided, but folk there were ready, for a fee, to lay down a portable timber bridge that the supply waggon might be safely hauled over. The barrier crossed, Edwin found himself looking at a new land. From the top of the Dyke he had seen the range of rugged mountains awaiting them, and also the expanse of forest. There was mist and rain much of the way, but nothing impeding their progress. They skirted the foothills on their way north, hewing to the coast. This vast bay, sandy and broad, teemed with sea life, and riding along they spotted blowing whales, dolphins which broke the water as they leapt, and on spits of sand, fat seals basking in the warmth. There were mounds, too, graves of lost warriors and Kings, the ruins of hill-forts, and all that tells of a land long settled, and contested. Yet settlements seemed few. Keeping to the coast as they did, they saw signs of inland villages; worn tracks into the forest betrayed their existence. Along foggy beaches and tidal marshes were sometimes women and children out picking whelks, digging cockles, or cutting mussels from dense tufts of seaweed, or with framed nets scooping shrimp from the incoming water.

Mostly they marvelled over how sparsely peopled was this land. No one challenged them, no guards sprang out demanding what their business was, though they passed two Kingdoms before they entered the third of Ceredigion. They kept to themselves, threatened no one, and when they had occasion to meet up with folk, Dunnere addressed them in his native tongue. This placableness seemed near to indifference, and Edwin wondered at it. Was it instead mere confidence that his troop of less than thirty men, headed by himself and a cassock-wearing priest, posed no real threat?

On the eighth day out, while the party finished fording a shallow stream running through the sand to the sea, two riders approached at a canter. On Edwin's right was the thickest of forests, dense with pine, hazels and willows, clumps of bright birch and stands of oak. It was from this wood that the two riders turned and came at speed towards them. They were warriors, on horses of which no man need be ashamed. Each rider bore a brass horn at their waist. Edwin reined up to await them.

It was clear the men expected them, and one lifted his hand in welcome. The words issuing from his mouth were to Edwin unintelligible. The priest took over, gesturing to Edwin, to whom the men nodded their heads.

"Elidon's fortress is just ahead," Dunnere said.

One of that King's two riders now turned up the coast and held his horn to his lips. He blew out a steady blast, followed by three short. Those at Elidon's keep would know they had arrived.

After some steady pacing the forest thinned enough to reveal the King's dwelling, set well back from tidal waters. A broad river flowed north of Elidon's fortress, emptying into the sea, as had every other they had forded. The track leading to the palisade was well worn, and a cluster of small boats told that fisher folk from within the confines of Elidon's camp often launched from here.

The day was clear and warm, the sky a promising blue. Elidon's gates were open in welcome, and on the palisade above flew a large banner, snapping in the shore wind. The device thereon was a dragon, one of red. The eyes of all of Edwin's men fastened on it. They rode through with the golden dragons of Wessex trailing behind his flanking body-guards.

The folk within looked much like Edwin's own, though not perhaps as tall in stature. They were dressed in the way of the Saxons, with light skin, hair, and eyes much in evidence. Many slaves were evident as well, easy to mark from the poverty of their clothing and the work they were at.

Elidon was there to greet them: the gold at neck and wrist proclaimed it to be him. He stood before the open door of the largest of the halls within his gates. Edwin and Dunnere came within a few horse-lengths of the man, reined in, and swung down from their horses, to meet the man on his own footing. To Edwin's eyes the King looked a man in his fifth decade, stern, and with an old healed gash across his forehead. No woman stood at his side. Instead was a man clearly the priest Gwydden, much younger than Dunnere.

Edwin and Dunnere stopped before them. From behind him Edwin was aware of the gates being swung closed. Dunnere spoke first, a stream of unaccountable sound addressed to the King, continuing long enough to increase Edwin's wariness about a foreign bride. Then Dunnere ended, almost abruptly. The King addressed them both, and, to Edwin's gratitude, in the speech of Angle-land.

"You are welcome to Ceredigion, and to my hall," Elidon told them. The King's greeting was carefully spoken. It was rehearsed, and had taken effort to bring out. The Lord of Kilton was grateful for this sign of respect. He returned it with a bow, of a sudden abashed that he had not asked Dunnere to tutor him in a few words of this monarch's own strange tongue. His priest answered for him.

This welcome stated, Dunnere moved to embrace Gwydden.

Edwin's first impression of the compound was of one much like any common fortified burh in Wessex, one of no great size. The timber buildings within were round, square, and oblong, with roofs of thatch or timber planks. One distinction was a small timber church, set back from the work yards, and near what might be a pleasure garden of sorts; at least Edwin thought he glimpsed fruiting trees. The men and women of the place had stopped in their tasks to watch, and a score or so of Elidon's fighting men stood off to one side, bearing witness to the arrival of the men of Wessex. The eyes of these swept over Edwin and his body-guard, in that familiar gauging of worth all warriors practised. Edwin was aware of this, and kept his own eyes respectfully upon their King.

A movement at a high casement distracted him. The timber building holding the window looked a tall store-house of some kind, a granary perhaps, and had a window near its peak giving out upon the keep yard. A face seemed to be there, and then was gone. Was that the girl herself, Edwin wondered, eager to have a first glance of him.

The Lord of Kilton returned his attention to the King. He gestured to his men waiting at the supply waggon, and in response two of them hauled forth a narrow but tall pottery jug, which when set down, rose nearly to the height of a man's knee.

"Wine from red grapes," Edwin told the King.

Elidon knew these words, and his thin lips cracked into a semblance of a smile. He looked to his priest and spoke, and Gwydden, with a smile, gave report. "For a wedding feast, perhaps, the King says. It will fill our cups tonight."

Elidon's mention of a wedding feast pricked Edwin's thoughts. He had travelled so far; he should have listened to the Lady Edgyth and come ready to settle the matter here. Still, he had brought the silver cup as token, should he need it.

The rest of Edwin's men now dismounted, and stable-men and boys came forth to relieve them of their mounts. Elidon turned to his hall, and all followed him within.

The day was a bright one; the interior of the hall, though lightened by an open door at the far end, dim by contrast. The encampment itself had looked rude to Edwin's eye; the King's timber hall, though long, of no distinction. Yet entering he saw the area behind the high table festooned with treasure; an eye-opening display of battle-gain adorning the back wall. Shields hung there, knives and swords too, in scabbards and naked-bladed, along with clusters of spears in iron holders holding them upright. Edwin saw two helmets as well, surely of the Danes to judge by their make. This was not locked away, but fixed upon the wall as trophies.

It took a moment for Edwin to notice the woman there at the table. Dunnere murmured to him that this was Elidon's wife. She was considerably younger than her Lord, plump, and faded. Pale lips sat in a face of pallid skin. The hair which showed from beneath the veil upon her head was of a light but undetermined hue. Where Elidon was stern, his consort was meek. The lips formed a smile though as she spoke a few words in the tongue of the Cymry, words which Edwin responded to with a bow. It was mead she and her serving women then poured, of a sweetness and potency that helped one forget the long days in the saddle.

Edwin's eyes had made a circuit of the hall, looking for any maiden who might be she he had come to meet. Few women were there, and none who could be Dwynwen.

"You seek Dwynwen," Elidon said.

Edwin had to repress his smile at this abruptness. She was in fact what he had journeyed for. He nodded, cup in hand, awaiting the King's pleasure.

"I have no daughter of my own," Elidon managed, before continuing in Welsh to his priest.

"She is the King's brother Dunwyd's child," Gwydden picked up. "Dwynwen's mother died first, and he wed again. Dwynwen has been raised largely by her step-mother, first at Dunwyd's hall, then here since her widowhood. The bridal goods will be furnished by her."

Edwin could now ask. "When may I meet the Lady?"

The King must have anticipated this question, for he answered Edwin directly.

"Today. Luned you will see first. Then you may see Dwynwen."

Edwin bowed his head in response.

Luned, thought the Lord of Kilton. A name with a strange beauty to it. Its two syllables reminded him of the girl's own name, conjuring both softness and strength. This Lady was the girl's protector, and it was she, not Elidon, who would provide the dowry. Gwydden's letter to Dunnere had mentioned the influence the Lady had on the girl, and this was proof.

"I look forward to it," Edwin answered. He made a gesture to his dust-stained clothes, one easily read. The washing shed was needed, and a change of clothes.

Given the number of Edwin's troop they were assigned their own hall, though Dunnere would stay with Gwydden in the priest's small house. Little more than an hour later, a clean and freshly dressed Edwin emerged to see Dunnere awaiting him.

"We will go to Gwydden, who will take us to the Lady Luned," he said.

"The Lady – does she speak our tongue?" was what Edwin asked.

Dunnere paused. "She does. What is not clear is whether she will, to us. Gwydden could make no promise.

Thus it is perhaps best for both he and I to accompany you to her."

This instilled no confidence in Edwin. Dunnere led him past the timber church to a small and enclosed orchard of apple and plum trees, upon which fruit was growing large. Wattle fencing kept any stray animal out, save for a few hens from the kitchen yard which had flown over, and were scratching at the growth beneath the trees. Edwin did not see the figure beyond the gate until she moved.

It was a young maid, little more than a child, seemingly quite alone within the enclosure. The fineness of her dress suggested she was the maid Edwin had come to meet. Her gown of deepest red was enlivened with elaborate stitching in blue and green at throat, wrists, and hem, coloured thread-work that even Edwin knew had taken weeks of effort by a skilled needle-woman to create. Beyond this, a necklace of gold glinted about her neck when she moved. She was looking down at a black-speckled hen which had dropped, wings tucked, on the short grass, as if to nest. The maid did not glance towards the men, and indeed seemed not to know they were there. Both Edwin and priest stopped to regard her.

Edwin spoke in a low tone to Dunnere. "She is pretty enough. But she is a child."

The object of their conjecture was not only listening, but understanding. She had caught only the word "child" but guessed what its use referred to. She startled Edwin by looking up and answering in his own tongue.

"Yet I am old enough to wed," she returned. Though her voice was soft, her words conveyed a decided tone nonetheless.

It made both priest and Lord move forward.

"Forgive me, Lady. I meant no disrespect." Far from it, Edwin was full of admiration, not only for the maid's look, but her composure.

"I am Dwynwen," she told them, with the slightest of smiles. Her speech was perfectly clear to Edwin, with only the stress placed on certain words marking her as from Cymru.

Her words prompted the priest. "My Lady. This is Edwin, Lord of Kilton and Ealdorman in Wessex. I believe Father Gwydden has spoken of his coming."

Edwin offered a hurried greeting, while Dwynwen studied him. Her wide eyes were as inquiring as any child's. It gave him a chance to do the same.

Her colour was fresh; her cheeks and lips as brightly rosy as a child of six; the eyes appearing just as large in her face, as a young child's are wont to do. Those eyes were blue, streaked with golden brown. The face of oval shape was marked by the graceful proportion of brow line, nose, and chin. Her hair was of a shade which eluded Edwin's ability to name; a soft brown between dry and wet sand, and with just as much variation. It was completely straight, without any suggestion of wave or curl, and had evidently never been cut. It trailed down her back well past her waist.

In her rich garb, and framed in this enclosed grove, she looked a figure from some ballad Garrulf, the scop of Kilton, might sing of. And her youth – she seemed at the very cusp of turning from girl to woman, with untouched freshness, and the promise of every womanly possibility ahead.

At once Edwin regretted he had no bride-price with him. What if, after speaking with her, he wanted to marry her now, tonight? She was entrancing enough to think he might. Both the King and the girl's step-mother thought her ready to wed. The thought of the golden-haired maid of Mercia rose in his mind. He would not be the only one pursuing the hand of this Welsh maid.

"I saw your fire-drakes," she said next. It made him smile, both in its unexpectedness, and in proving his earlier guess to be correct. It had been her, spying from that high window.

He thought of what best to say. "We both use dragons. Ours is golden, and yours is red."

She gave a nod. "I prefer red." She gave a sly smile then, and gestured to the full skirts of her gown.

He was about to speak again when a second figure appeared from behind Dwynwen. She moved towards them from a vine-entangled trellis, garbed in a gown of near-white. Before she reached them she called out. Edwin heard her voice Dwynwen's name, but could make out nothing more of her speech. The girl bobbed her head to them, went to she who called, and vanished behind the same cluster of vines. Edwin and Dunnere were left facing the approaching woman. They saw her eyes lift to one side, and turning their heads, saw Gwydden in his dark cassock, come from his house.

Gwydden stopped before the gate, bowed his head, and spoke to the woman in Welsh, gesturing to both men. Dunnere spoke as well, addressing the woman with the same respect his brother priest had shown. Edwin allowed his eyes to rest on she to whom they spoke. He saw an old woman, not tall, and of curious countenance. This must be Dwynwen's step-mother. She was a handsome woman; he was aware she would be called this, but odd in a way he could not name. Her voice was low-pitched, almost sonorous, but even in the few words he had heard, capable of conveying command.

Dunnere was also considering her. He noted a face delicately boned, eyes bright and even searching, her person slight, yet with that slender strength of a forged blade. Her hair of an almost snowy white was caught up in loops by a length of some gossamer stuff. It added, despite its colour, a youthful air to the face by virtue of its very brightness. He thought it must have been quite dark in her youth; in his experience only the dark-haired attained this whiteness. Those of fairer sort had hair which paled to silver, or stopped at steel-grey. The choice of gown for an older woman was unusual; indeed few woman of any years wore white. Hers was that luminous shade of walrus ivory, a perfect complement to her hair.

Luned nodded to both priests, and turned her eyes to the Lord of Kilton. Her eyes swept over him, lightly, only as long as was needful. She found him full of manly beauty and arrogance. There was no way under star-light Dwynwen was going to this Saxon.

She then addressed Gwydden and Dunnere, briefly, and in Welsh. What she said made them look to Edwin, nod, then leave him there alone.

Luned moved to the gate, unlatched it, and allowed Edwin entrance into the grove. She must go through the formality of speaking to him; a few words would suffice.

"Lady Luned," he said, in way of greeting. "I am Edwin of Kilton."

Her response to him was a simple demand.

"Who are your people?"

He had somehow thought this preliminary information had been before conveyed. But no; or this woman wanted to hear answers from his own mouth. And at least she spoke to him so he could understand.

He had to pause. He had vowed to tell no one of his true parentage. How much more impressive it was to be the son of the Lord of Kilton, rather than that of his younger brother. He struggled with himself, then honoured his pledge to Worr.

"My father, long dead, was Gyric, second son of Kilton. At my birth I was adopted by his older brother, Godwin, Lord of Kilton, to be his heir."

"Why is he not here?"

The sharpness of her tone caught him up, just as much as the directness of her query. He felt his heart race, and took a breath to steady himself. He would tell in essence his blood father's Fate.

"He fell in battle, long ago."

She gave a toss of her head. Like that, this woman dismissed his lost father, that was clear. Utter disinterest was all that shown upon her face.

"And your mother?"

"Ceridwen, daughter of Cerd, from the River Dee."

At this the woman twitched, a small but abrupt movement of her head. Her body froze. Her eyes flicked up to the flight of a distant bird. They rested there before she lowered her gaze, her eyes shrouded by dropped eyelids.

Her grandson stood here, before her.

She took a long moment before lifting her eyes to the young Lord. The tone of her next question changed. It was again a challenge, but held perceptible interest.

"Your mother – does she still live?"

"She does. But far from here, away to the east, on an island in the Baltic."

The Lady Luned drew breath. Her eyes were now fixed on Edwin, so that it was all he could do not to flinch under their stare.

Her following question was much more quietly posed.

"Do you favour her?"

Edwin felt the confused movement of his own face. She cared nothing of his sire, and now this concern about his mother. Yet by her name he had identified her as being of Welsh blood; that must be it. It was an easy query to answer, and he did so.

"Lady Edgyth, the widow of Lord Godwin, has told me that it is my brother who most favours her. I look more like – my father." He was taken back in memory to his symbel, when Ælfred formally presented him with Godwin's weapons. "Even the King has said so."

She nodded, and spoke again.

"What manner of woman is your mother?"

Edwin blinked. It was not a question he had heard asked of any woman. He thought of what Ceric had told of his time on Gotland, and thought too of her life before the abduction which took her there at last.

"In truth, Lady, I know little of her, in direct manner. At her father's death she was taken to a priory and raised. When older she left that place, met with a young woman, and ended in Anglia in a burh captured by Danes. Gyric of Kilton –" he could not in honesty to himself again call this man by the name father – "was prisoner there, and gravely wounded. My mother was young, of fifteen years I think, but out of pity escaped with him, and returned him to Kilton."

"It sounds a stunning feat."

"She was greatly honoured for it, I know." He had so little memory of the woman herself; the stories of others were all he could relate. "She and Gyric wed."

Luned paused, taking this in, and though he could not read the workings of her face, felt she was deep in thought.

"And of your siblings?"

"My older brother Ceric – "

"Older, yet you are Lord?"

"Yes, I was adopted by the Lord and Ealdorman of Kilton, Godwin, to be his heir." There was subtle weight behind Edwin's naming of the man. He went on.

"There was a girl as well, younger than me, who died an infant of fever, which took also the life of Gyric. After his death my mother and brother Ceric went to visit the fortress in Anglia where she had rescued him. My mother left Ceric there with her friend, meaning to return in a year for him. Before she began her journey home, she and the Jarl of that place were captured by slavers. They were carried away east, past the North Sea, but won their freedom and settled on Gotland. My brother visited them there on the island while still a boy, joined by a son of the Jarl. The former Jarl, Sidroc, is a rich trader there, and our mother has children with him."

"And a full life," the Lady added to this account.

He nodded. He had not seen it himself. He did not know how he could stand before the man who had killed his father.

Luned stood, seemingly lost in thought. He could only think that given her imperious manner, it was a stroke of Fortune that his own mother was half-Welsh.

"I have no love for you Saxons," she proclaimed. "But neither do I wish war with them, nor any folk. And you have the blood of Cymru in you."

The silence that followed was not one Edwin felt he should break. She looked not at him, but away, deep into the fruiting trees.

At last he felt he must return the discourse to its purpose. "I know I was not meant to see the Lady Dwynwen before I had the honour to meet you," he said next, in way of apology.

She gave her head a shake. "My step-daughter finds her own way in most things," she conceded.

Edwin wondered if Luned knew the girl had earlier espied him, on his arrival, or even if her step-mother had been at her side as she did so. At any rate he would forge ahead.

"She pleases me greatly," he offered.

The Lady said nothing to this, and her seeming distraction made him think his words had not been heard. He would assume being approved of, and said the next.

"When may I speak to her?"

This roused her. She looked about, into the green coolness of the tree cover, where fruit of red hung ripening.

"Return here before the evening meal," was her instruction. "Dwynwen will be ready to hear you."

She moved to the gate, his signal that he take his leave.

After this meeting Luned went to her bower, which sat beyond the far end of the church, well away from the footfall of others. She lifted the key from her waist and unlocked the stout door. Closing it behind her, she turned to the inside lock, and with a second key, locked it from the inside, as was her custom.

No one entered this bower house, save for Luned, her serving woman of many years, and Dwynwen. Elidon had built it for her upon his brother's death when she had arrived with Dwynwen and all of their goods and taken up residence with him. They had come from Dunwyd's hall in the mountains; a property which Elidon had then given to one of his sons. He had never stepped foot within Luned's bower house. If Elidon had not understood his brother's taste in women, he could at least appreciate the forthrightness and silent strength of his widow. The house he had raised for her was round, of good size, and as well built as his own hall.

Luned had richly filled it. Metal glinted and gleamed, its harsh strength muffled amidst layers of woollens, linens, and furs draping walls and set upon bed and benches. Any wall space not swathed in rich stuff carried designs painted from the Lady's own hand; glyphs of which only she knew the meaning, but which Dwynwen's eye never tired of tracing. The greatest surprise was overhead. From the rafters were hung the single stems of Summer flowers, hundreds of them, suspended on long poles which ran from wall to wall, so that looking up one stood under a cover of dried blossoms of soft yellow, pink, and white which seemed to rain ever down.

Today Luned took a few steps within the room, stopping beneath the very apex of its peaked roof. She stood with perfect stillness, though she was aware of the quick beating of her heart.

She had not seen this coming in her dreams, her scrying, nor in all the patterns she had allowed her fingers to trace in the shallow dish of sand in which she drew. Nothing had emerged to warn her of this.

All things work in circles, Luned thought. We dance on the rim of a cauldron, round and round.

She went to the wall opposite her bed, to a shelf affixed thereupon. Two silver cups were there, never used, but preserved in sight. One was that set with white crystals she used to drink from in her mill house at the River Dee. The second was that lifted by her guests. One of these had been a girl – her own girl, who had drunk from this cup many times. She took this second cup down and held it in her hand. Here again was the rim her daughter's lip had touched. Another circle. No beginning, no end, but enclosing the workings of us all.

Luned stood staring into the depths of that silver cup. The inside of it had grown dark with tarnish. A tumble of memories came flowing back, like the rush-choked stream at the broken mill house she fled to. The rushes could not hold the water; flow it must, as did her stream of thoughts. They carried her further back.

She saw again the two warriors from the River Dee who had appeared, fronting their war-pack, at her Cymru home. The brothers, with red-gold hair, stood in triumph before her hapless and defeated kinsmen, accepting their tribute. Cerd and Cedd, these victors named themselves. She was there, with all her surviving kin, compelled by force to witness it. One of the brothers then waved away a fine piece of war-kit, and instead pointed to her.

THE LIFE OF A MAN

DUNNERE was anticipating Edwin's return, and had lingered not far from the door of the church. Edwin approached, his eyes fixed on the priest, his eagerness in his voice.

"Yes," he told him. "I want her."

"If she will come," Dunnere cautioned. Gwydden had warned him this would be no simple granting of the girl by her protectors.

"Yes. Of course." Edwin said this readily enough, yet knew himself reluctant to consider any bar to the consent of all.

"How many years has she," Edwin asked. "Has Gwydden mentioned this?"

"She is but fourteen," came the unadorned answer.

Edwin's face fell, but the priest went on. "The Lady Luned would not offer the girl, if she were not yet fit to be a wife."

Edwin must take this into account. Frosty as she had at first been to him, the older Lady was allowing him access to the girl, who must be woman enough to wed. Of what Lady Edgyth might adjudge he could not guess, but he would wait a year for her, as long as she were there at Kilton, and his in reserve.

The priest read the confused thoughts of Edwin and said the next.

"Of Elidon I think there is no cause for concern."

Edwin agreed, and went on. "The Lady Luned – she asked me to return before our meal tonight, so I might speak to Dwynwen."

Dunnere nodded. It was in fact now largely up to the girl. "Which means she and Lady Dwynwen are conferring now. We must await their verdict."

Edwin and Dunnere spent two of the ensuing hours in the company of Elidon and his priest. First they were taken inside the modest timber church, where the King and Gwydden outlined plans for its replacement in sandstone from the eastern reaches of Wales. They then went to Gwydden's house, where the priest displayed three bound books, a Gospel and Old Testament in Latin, and a book of history he had himself compiled, in Welsh. Though able to sign his name, the King could not himself read. Through Gwydden he explained. "A man past a score of years will be hard pressed to remember it all," the priest repeated, as the King flexed his fingers as if the trials of quill and ink still lingered there. Yet Elidon's approval and even pride in these objects was evident. Stacks and rolls of parchment also gave proof of the many letters Gwydden exchanged with clerics in other lands, some even as far as Rome itself.

Edwin was grateful for the distraction at the same time he was impatient at it. He was dressed in the same fine clothes he had donned after bathing, the best he had with him, and eager to see Dwynwen again, to confirm his first impression of her. The topic of his potential bride was never raised by the other men, sparing him the discomfort of speculation.

At last it was time for him to return to the grove; the activity of the kitchen yard proclaimed it. He went to the alcove in the hall given him and unlaced one of his leathern packs. The silver bowl was there, that bridal-cup he had brought if needed. It was housed in a soft pouch of linen, and he took it with him now. He wanted to arrive at the grove first, and await Dwynwen.

He was not first. When he approached the gate he saw beyond it Dwynwen in her gown of red, and next her, the white-robed Lady Luned. They stood between two gnarled apples, whose boughs were lowering with ruddy-cheeked fruit. The speckled hens Edwin had noted this morning were still there, strutting about, pecking at the soil, and in some instances, roosting at the base of trees. Dwynwen came herself to the gate and unlatched it for him, the same small and private smile on her lips he had seen before. He greeted both ladies, and paused, expecting the elder to now excuse herself. She did not. Lady Luned made it clear by her remaining that what he wished to say, must be said before her. Was this a test of his nerve, or just her new interest in him? He could not know. But this was his chance, and he must take it.

The three moved to a rustic table encircled with short benches, set under one of the trees. Luned and Dwynwen sat, and he did also, placing the pouch of linen on the bench next him. He watched the girl's eyes rest upon the pouch, and the pretty lips purse a moment. She would guess it was for her, and wonder what lay within.

He turned to Dwynwen as if she alone were before him.

"Our folk are not known to the other," he began, "but Dunnere and Gwydden have a friendship of long duration. Dunnere is our priest at Kilton," he went on, not certain where he was heading with this line of reasoning, but grasping at it nonetheless, "and as such I trust him. I trust his judgement," he continued, "just as I know you must trust that of Gwydden."

He had no way to know if the priest had actually endorsed him or not, but forged ahead. Dwynwen was listening, to his eyes with true intent, which made it easier.

"My hall, Kilton, sits on a bluff, with the sea below. You – you could perhaps see Cymru from there," he added, and at once regretted it, lest it prompt the girl to think of future longing for her home.

"The Lady of Kilton is Edgyth, my mother by adoption. She is kind and generous, and skilled in herb-craft and all healing arts. She is eager to welcome you."

He must now look to Luned. The point was a delicate one, and he lowered his voice to convey it. "She made it clear that if Dwynwen feels too young to wed, we might wait a year, until she is more grown."

The older Lady looked surprised at this offer, and perhaps a little gratified. Dwynwen's round eyes grew rounder, but Edwin could not tell if from her own surprise, or a budding indignation in being judged too young to be made a wife. He wished to move on from this, and did so.

"Kilton has ever been close to the royal house of Wessex, and has known special favour from it." Edwin could in truth not offer that Ælfred would stand as god-father to any coming babe, but wished he could, as a sign of that favour. Still, there were many proofs of the bonds between the grand-sons of Æthelwulf and of Godwulf.

"Today Father Gwydden showed us fine books, which I was pleased to see. At Kilton we too have books, several given us by the King, who himself has turned books of Latin into our own tongue.

"Our scop is renowned for his tales and singing. There is no better harp-player than he.

"Our church is of stone, with windows of glass from Frankland. There is a fine garden within the palisade," he remembered, "and a pavilion from which to enjoy it. The village prospers, and each year produces excess of rye and barley . . ."

Edwin went on, until he ran short of attributes. At last he was silent, and sat looking at the maid before him.

He then took out the bowl. It was meant as a pledge-gift. Edwin was entirely uncertain how to present it now. It felt almost an oblation. He took it in both his hands. He held it to Dwynwen, as a man would offer the first cup of ale or mead to his new wife.

"I brought this for you," he said. "Perhaps we might drink from it. At our wedding."

The girl started. It was the suddenness of it, Edwin thought; but her hands did not raise to take it from his.

Luned's did. She took it in both hands.

"We thank you," the old woman answered.

Her step-daughter sat looking at Edwin, Lord of Kilton. You did not ask for me, Dwynwen thought. You have told me of your hall and King and much else but you have not asked for me. And you have everything – why should you need me.

She shifted her eyes to her step-mother. Before his arrival, Luned had told her a foreigner was coming to woo her, and that she might dismiss him out of hand, as she herself had already done. Then when Luned and Edwin of Kilton met, her step-mother told her that if she wanted this man she would not object. Dwynwen did not know why her step-mother was of a sudden responsive to this Saxon's pursuit, but she had her own stipulation to present. She turned to Edwin and revealed it.

"You have travelled far. So must I, to go with you. But I will not wed until I have seen the home offered me."

Edwin had no time to be stunned. It was not a reversal, but she had somehow seized the tiller on the small ship he had sailed into her life. She set a condition, and he must meet it. There was decision in her words, reflecting the sureness of her nature. Child or no, it made him want her the more.

He must restate the terms before them all, to make certain they were understood. "You will leave with me, now, see Kilton, and then decide?"

"I will." It was said as calmly as one consenting to take a walk by the sea.

Luned looked to Dwynwen, and then to Edwin. Her voice was cool, but not without a note of command.

"Before you leave," the elder Lady said, "you men will decide as to the treasure exchanged."

Indeed, having been herself sold, Luned would have nothing to do with the bride-price. "I will send Dwynwen suitably equipped. And should she decide to remain, all she carries with her remains in her own possession."

"Of course," he agreed. "That is the custom of my folk. A bride's personal goods remain always hers."

"I speak also of her dower," Luned stressed. "Her goods are her dower. And they must remain hers, to use as she sees fit."

This condition was unexpected; indeed, to most men it would have been unacceptable. A bride's household furnishings, clothing and jewellery remained always hers following her marriage, but a separate sum of treasure, her dowry, was handed to her husband. Luned was telling him his bride would retain all.

Edwin realised now at what a disadvantage he stood. He had no father nor uncle nor counsellor to bargain for him. Was this then the custom of Dwynwen's folk? He could not know.

He moved his eyes to Dwynwen. Her face betrayed no emotion. She is like her name, he thought; a wave has force, yet is hard to capture . . .

Still, rich brides could be open-handed with their new kin, endowing them with much from their own store as gifts. And – he had immense wealth, in his own right. His grandmother had greatly added to it upon her death, for other than sums awarded to distant kin and faithful serving folk, she had divided her vast fortune in half between him and Ceric. He was not seeking a wife for her silver, but rather to give him sons.

Beyond this, Dwynwen as his bride would forge a worthy bond with the King of Ceredigion, both rewarding Elidon for his past loyalty to Wessex, and ensuring that other of the Welsh Kingdoms saw that if they joined with the Danes, they did so with an ally of Wessex squeezing them from their western coast. The Lord of Kilton could well imagine with what favour Ælfred would look upon this union.

Edwin found himself nodding in concession.

"Would you escort the Lady Dwynwen to Kilton," was his next, and tentative question to Luned.

"I have travelled once before beyond Cymru," she stated. "I will not do so again."

The silence that followed was one that Edwin did not wish to break.

Luned bridged the gap, moving them all forward.

"On her travels, and while there at your hall as maiden, she will be placed under the protection of your priest. And your own honour."

"I thank you, Lady Luned."

"You may return to Elidon now," she said, in way of dismissal.

Edwin told the priests of his meeting with Dwynwen and Luned, and asked what bride-price Elidon might expect for his niece's hand.

The King was ready with his answer. Elidon gestured to the jug of wine, which had been hauled upon a table. He spoke to Gwydden in a steady stream of Welsh, glancing twice at Edwin.

"This jug," the priest began. "The King says that what we do not drink during your stay, he will pour out and keep. You will return to Wessex with it. If Dwynwen remains with you as your wife, return the jug to him, filled with silver. In coins."

Edwin blinked, looking at the vessel. He had no idea what it would take to fill it, perhaps as much as thirty or forty pounds of the metal. Coins would fill the jug most completely; larger pieces of silver would create gaps. It was a canny detail of the request.

While he gauged this, Dunnere spoke up. "The Roman Caesars stripped both silver and gold from Cymru, using our folk as slaves to dig it for them. Gold is ever hard to come by, but the King is seeking to return silver to Ceredigion."

Edwin nodded. Of all possible demands, this was the easiest to meet. It was a single payment, then done. Rents from lands granted, if far from the bride's new home, must be collected and sent off. Weaponry demanded must be forged at the expense of the time and effort of skilled smiths. Silver Edwin had, and in abundance.

"And of her dowry," Edwin asked. Gwydden restated this point to the King, and after listening, spoke.

"The dowry of the King's niece is presented by her step-mother. It represents a generous share of the wealth of his late brother, the silver and weapons thereof having been converted into goods as the Lady Luned has seen fit."

The woman had absolute freedom in her choices, that was clear. Edwin wondered what goods she had selected to accompany so covetable a bride as seemed Dwynwen.

After Luned had dismissed Edwin, she and Dwynwen walked side by side to the elder woman's bower house. Dwynwen did not live with her there, but the girl spent much time within. Luned was not tall of stature, and despite her youth Dwynwen was near her in height. Their footfall matched in almost perfect rhythm.

Dwynwen was looking down, and could see the tips of her red-dyed shoes emerge from her swirling skirts with each step. But she scarce felt her feet upon the ground. She had just said that which might change her own life, and forever. She had awaited a sign. It had been two years since her body had taken on the ways of a woman. At her first blood-Moon Luned had anointed her brow with nard, and made the prophecy. It had come forth from the symbols her step-mother traced in her bronze dish of sand.

"You will hold the life of a man in your hands," she predicted.

She, Dwynwen, would do this. She would determine if a man would live or die.

When this fell in Dwynwen's ear, she thought of a certain tale chanted by Elidon's bard. Of all his offerings it was that she favoured most. It told of Trystan and Esyllt, and how, through misadventure, they held each other's lives in their hands. And Luned was telling her she, a budding girl, would be such a one as Esyllt? Every fibre in her tender body had thrilled to that possibility. Now perhaps she stood on that threshold.

Both she and her step-mother kept silence on their way to the bower, one purposeful and pregnant with meaning. Luned unlocked the door and let them in.

Within the bower were two narrow windows. Sunlight streamed through one of them, a shaft as sharp as a naked blade. It fell upon a small table, holding a bowl, filled with water. The bowl was large, and of glass, precious beyond counting, and had melded to it three short legs of glass, to hold it steady above the dark cloth which shrouded the table's wood surface. Dwynwen went to this table, and touched the tip of her left pointing finger into the middle of the bowl, a light touch at the surface of the clear water. The tiniest of ripples issued forth.

One other object was upon the table, a minute round pin-cushion covered in coloured thread work. Into it was stuck a single needle, one of pure gold. Dwynwen took a breath, then pulled the golden needle out and held it above the surface of the rippling water. She laid the golden thing at the apex of the ripples, and watched.

Both females had their eyes fixed upon the movement of the needle.

The needle quivered, shifted, and then stopped. It pointed almost due south. The land from which this Saxon hailed.

"Metal and sea confirm it," Luned announced. "Yours is a good choice."

Dwynwen lifted her eyes for a moment to those of her step-mother, then let them fall again to the needle. What of air and fire, she wondered. Gazing into this well of truth we see only half the elements that rule us.

She would not ask for a test thereof; it was clear Luned favoured this trial, wished her to go with this young Lord. She would learn later if he be the one she awaited. If he was, she would begin to fulfill that Fate which had turned in her head ever since her step-mother's prophecy had first filled her ears.

Edwin and Dwynwen sat together at the welcome feast that night. Elidon and his wife were at the centre of the high table, the King's chief body-guard to his right. To the left of his consort sat Luned. Her step-daughter and their guest from Wessex came next, and then Dunnere and Gwydden. Edwin's red wine filled a silver beaker from which Elidon's wife poured. Edwin knew the wine to be good; it was some of that freshly bought by Lady Edgyth from a vineyard to the south in Scireburne, and carried to her by the steward thereof. When his cup was filled and he lifted it to his face, the fumes of it rose strong and raisin-like, to his nose. It had scarcely been watered, and he knew to be careful of it. He noted with satisfaction that Elidon drained his cup almost at once, and gave a nod to the giver of the ruby stuff.

Edwin looked to Dwynwen at his side, her cup in hand. He watched her take a delicate sip, saw how her face changed. "Does it please you?" he was forced to ask, as he could not gauge her response.

"I do – I do not know," she answered, with her half-smile. She may have been speaking of the man who had brought it, as well. Her eyes dropped to look within the vessel she held. "It has beauty in the cup," she added.

The food was of unusual savour, with sea trout, poached in milk with fresh thyme, carried in. This was presented to Edwin and all else at the high table on salvers of silver. Torches flared from the wall, hitting the steel hanging behind those seated there, and casting flickering reflections from over their shoulders, which danced also upon their salvers. The effect to Edwin was almost as if a second fire-pit lay burning behind them. All was heightened by the beguiling maid at his side. The heady wine and reflected fire-light made Lady Dwynwen's presence even more warming than he had expected. She said little to him during their meal, and indeed the wine had lifted the spirits of many of those drinking it, making it difficult to discern any but words spoken in one's ear. Yet he was aware of she and her step-mother in brief converse, and could not help but wonder if he was not their subject.

When the salvers were cleared away the hall quieted. Dunnere had spoken more than once of the excellence of Welsh bards, and now Elidon's came forward from the table at which he had supped. He was as well dressed and adorned with silver as the King's own body-guard, a testament to the rewards his songs had won him. His harp was curious, small, and of red-painted wood, but when he struck it the strings resonated from beneath his strong fingers and filled the hall to its gabled roof.

He sang in the tongue of Cymru, which, stretched into form by the melody of his harp, took on a mellifluous quality Edwin had not heard in common speech. All eyes rested upon him, and Edwin was aware of Dwynwen's straightening on the bench, and the slight inclination of her body towards the man.

Indeed, Dwynwen's lips parted when she heard what the man had chosen to play. He had at his finger-tips any number of songs to enchant the hall. Not only stories of the old Gods of Cymru, but of their great warrior heroes, and many songs too of the women thereof. This night, which looked almost near one of betrothal, he might have sung of the trials of King Arawn and his constant wife, the Lady of Annwn; or, in light of Dwynwen's youth, told of Elen of the Ways, that Goddess crowned with ren-deer antlers, who, like those deer of the distant north, might wander far but always find their way.

This night, he played without prompting, her favourite, that of Trystan and Esyllt.

Edwin could not know what was the subject, but his sidelong glances at Dwynwen, and the sober attention of all others as they fixed their eyes upon the bard told him of the solemn nature of the tale. Dunnere whispered a few words into his ear. The man sang of Trystan, young nephew of the noble King Marc, sent to Éireann to fetch Esyllt, the bride promised him. Of how the courier and the King's intended bride took ship together, much against Esyllt's desire, and yet how upon that stormy passage their eyes returned again and again to the other. Not bearing to lose Trystan, Esyllt cast a love-philtre into the wine they drank, which made both forsake their duty and give themselves in the act of love . . .

Dwynwen knew the story by heart. Yet tonight it washed over her as if new. She felt rather than saw the young man at her side. Yesternight I heard of your coming, she thought. Tonight I sit at your side. And overmorrow I shall travel away with you.

She could not guess what she would find at the end of those travels. This Lord who had come for her was favoured with high good looks, and was rich. He had made impress enough on her uncle the King, and on Lady Luned. And his folk honoured fire-drakes; that mattered.

Late the next morning the Lord of Kilton was invited to view Dwynwen's bridal goods. Gwydden escorted him, along with Dunnere, back to Elidon's hall. Much to Edwin's surprise, Dwynwen was there, standing between her step-mother and uncle. The three stood behind the high table. The side door of the hall was left open, and morning light flooded the space. Ranged along the table before the three sat Dwynwen's dowry.

It was silk, bolts of it. The fabric shone under the force of the slanting sunlight. It lay in neat folds, a watery blue, a verdant green, a red the bluish hue of ox blood.

"It totals fifty ells in length," Luned said in a low tone.

How she could have amassed this rare stuff was beyond Edwin's ken. But looking upon it, hearing its length, he knew it to be enough for the fashioning of gowns, tunics, and rich mantles, and for the celebratory vestments of bishops. He remembered the brilliant cope he had admired on that of Gleaweceaster.

Dwynwen too was looking down on the silk, and seeing the awed pleasure their guest took in it. Luned told her it was nought but the spittle of a lowly worm, and yet from it came a shimmer such as this. There was a lesson there, Dwynwen thought, of never misjudging the value of one that is small.

It was not all the Lady had to reveal. Off at one end of the table sat a small crockery jar, with a wooden stopper dipped in wax to seal it. Lady Luned lifted the knife from her sash and sliced at the thick brown wax. She gestured Edwin forward to open it. He did so, more than curious as to what this small crock could hold to match the fabric arrayed before him. The pungency of the black and mounded contents arose at once, a smell beguiling in its piercing keenness. Peppercorns, a vast number of them. Their trading value was immense, but how prized they would be in the kitchens of Kilton. This was a treasure unto itself.

Dunnere, looking on in respectful silence, took this in. He knew Edwin understood the value of silk, and of the rarity of peppercorns he was also aware. Rich folk who died possessing these tiny dark orbs assigned them in their wills to fortunate recipients, so highly regarded were they. But Dunnere was struck also by the feminine nature of this dowry. No weaponry, no horses, no war-kit of any kind, and no metals wrenched from the plundered soil of Middle Earth. This treasure was wholly sensual, of the senses. The shimmer of silk to adorn the body, the pleasing bite of pepper to excite the palate. He had not seen nor heard of such a dower, and would record it carefully in the annals of the family, as much for its unusual nature as for its value. A third aspect of note was that it belonged entirely to Dwynwen.

Dwynwen was familiar with this all. She had watched her step-mother take the motley hack-silver, weaponry and tenanted land her father Dunwyd had left her and transform it year by year into this singular treasure.

Luned, looking over the treasure of goods her step-daughter would travel with, had her own thoughts. She recalled a cold and wet Winter's morning, and the single coin of silver she had pressed into her blood-daughter's hand. Her Ceridwen had lost everything as a child. What spiraling of Fate was it, that Dwynwen was offered the chance to wed her grandson. If it was to be, the girl would indeed be suitably equipped.

The day was one of much activity, for upon the morrow Edwin's body of men would depart, along with Lady Dwynwen and her chattels. Elidon's hall was generous in provisioning them, and at one point Edwin himself was called out to the stable yard to witness this. He found Elidon there, and next to his supply waggon, a second waggon, spanned with wooden arches covered by waxed tarpaulins. A pair of tethered horses stood near.

The King lifted his hand. "Waggon and horses are my gift to you," he said. Edwin began his thanks as they approached the rear of the waggon. A line of serving folk were emerging from the hall, arms full of baskets. Others hauled chests and leathern packs, all carrying Dwynwen's goods, and all destined for this waggon. Peering within, Elidon gestured to the front of the waggon, just behind the waggon board. At one post of the arches supporting the tarpaulin stood lashed the large pottery jug his guest had brought. Elidon grinned, and Edwin was forced to smile in answer. If all went well and Kilton agreed with the girl, the King would see that jug soon, and much the heavier.

As for Dwynwen, Edwin scarce saw her that day, only meeting up with her as they approached the hall for the evening meal. She would travel in comparative comfort in her own waggon, which made him give thought to her life on the road. It was true he had Dunnere with him, but the close kin of a King must have a female with her as well.

"Is there a serving woman you would bring?" he asked.

Dwynwen cocked her head. Luned's aged woman was crabbed, and entirely devoted to her mistress. She could not think of one she would force to travel away from Ceredigion with her; not one she wanted at her side, at any rate.

"I will choose a slave," she said.

Such would serve as stop-gap, Edwin thought. "At Kilton Lady Edgyth will find you a suitable woman, well-trained," he promised.

It was her turn to nod agreement. "You said she is skilled in healing arts," Dwynwen posed.

"Yes. That she is." Of all he had told of Kilton, this had struck the girl, so he went on. "She has spent much time at Glastunburh, a great abbey where nuns and monks have compiled healing recipes from the known world."

She took this in, thoughtfully, he felt, from the look on her face.

Edwin's first feast in this hall had been one of welcome; this second was of fare-well. As sendoff to Dwynwen it was perhaps the richer, even as it was the more sombre. The red wine was again poured out, and fine dishes carried forth, echoing its hue, for red beetroot had been used to stain the browis, upon which sat boiled eggs, the whites of which had also been rubbed red. But this night the Welsh bard did not sing. It was Gwydden the priest who held forth, recounting the story of the widowed Ruth, who would follow her mother-in-law Naomi to Judah, even though as a Moabite Ruth would be placing herself amongst those who worshipped differently from she, and who were disdainful of Moab.

Edwin hardly knew what to make of this tale delivered thus, or whether it had any deeper meaning than a story of womanly loyalty and devotion. Was the Welsh priest encouraging Dwynwen to henceforth consider herself a woman of Wessex, and to remain always at Kilton should he, Edwin, be killed? His thought took a deeper turn. Dwynwen would in truth have two who were her mother-in-law, the Lady Edgyth, and his birth-mother, Ceridwen, once of Kilton . . .

In the morning all was in readiness for their departure. Final foodstuffs were carried to the waggons, horses harnessed, saddle bags affixed. The forecourt fronting Elidon's hall was alive with men and beasts.

The slave coming with Dwynwen was there as well, clutching a basket, eyes wide with uncertainty. Luned had the girl scrubbed, and dressed in a better gown. The girl, no older then Dwynwen herself, was plucked from the ranks of the scullery workers, and was affright. After donning the new gown, and wrapping her still-wet hair in a fresh head wrap of linen, she began to be less fearful. She was going with the King's niece to a foreign land.

Luned and her step-daughter had a private parting in the elder's bower. Dwynwen was dressed in travel clothes of dark blue, a shade that made the blue in her round eyes speak the louder.

"While you are there you will learn what you can of his mother," Luned told her. "And of his father," she added, almost as afterthought. "If you return, you will bring this knowledge back yourself."

The girl nodded, though she did not know what difference such findings would make, if she chose not to stay.

"If you remain, you will have Dunnere the priest write it all out, and send it to me in a letter."

Again Dwynwen nodded, for though, like Luned, she spoke the tongues of both Cymru and Angle-land, she could write but a few words of either.

They embraced. Dwynwen had been raised to leave, and she was doing so now. But she felt the shudder which ran through Luned as she held her. When they pulled back tears were welling in Dwynwen's eyes.

"Will I see you again," she must ask.

"All things circle," Luned told her, her voice husky as she answered. The lids dropped down over her own eyes, perhaps to hide the water gathering there. When she opened them her voice was clearer. "You will see my face, and I, yours."

After they had driven off to the cheers of the entire hall, Luned returned alone to her bower. She looked into the glass bowl of water, and wept.

RECLAMATION

KILTON awaited Edwin's return from Wales, with all in hopeful expectancy that he might bring a potential bride with him. Dunnere was off at his side, which meant those at the burh must conduct their own prayer services. And Ceric, eldest son of the hall, still lived a wild man in the forest.

One who had been away had returned: the woman Begu. She had gone to her home village, and now, in company with those of her neighbours with whom she had travelled, had returned to the hamlet. She was there but a day to rest when she set out on foot to the hall of Kilton. She arrived at late morning, walking from the trodden side track, and saw the expanse of palisade, the peaked gables of certain roofs beyond it, and the village before it, which seemed vast to her eyes. It was late Summer, all folk were about in field and croft, and the rows of hoed cabbages, beets, turnips, and onions stood high and green behind every cottar's wattle fence. Their life was like her own, unlike the forbidding wall before her, with its sentries poised on the ramparts, brass horns in hand. Yet the wide gates were open, and she braced herself and approached them.

She could not bring herself to step within, and raised her hand to a man passing by, surely a thegn from his dress. He came to her.

"My name is Begu," she told him. "If Worr the horse-thegn is within, I bid you ask him to come."

While she waited her eyes rested upon the hall itself, with its deeply carved end rafters rising above the gabled roof peaks. It was more splendid than any hall she had imagined. She kept her eyes upon it, not wishing to meet the gaze of the many workmen and women who passed by on their daily tasks, or the small groups of thegns who gathered by the armourer's work stalls, or stood saddling horses by the stable that they might ride out on their watches.

Worr approached, from beyond the stable, where sat a variety of smaller buildings. She stood the straighter as he neared, certain he would not recognise her.

He did, and spoke her name at once. "Begu," he said, with a smile of both recognition and acknowledgement. It had been years since he had seen her, and he was carried back to the day he had taken a young and restless Ceric out to meet her. Time had touched her but lightly, and she looked much the same, with only the slightest creases forming about her eyes and mouth as she smiled in answer.

The smile was brief, for what she must ask.

"Ceric of Kilton has not returned," she said, hoping he would correct her.

"He has not." Worr looked about him and went on. "Edwin too is gone, if it is he you seek."

"It is Ceric I came about," she admitted. She did not think this man would think she presumed too much by asking the next. Still, her voice was low and soft as she asked it. "But I would be happy to know the Lord is well."

Worr had to take a breath. He would tell her the truth, without dissembling or delay. She was ever a kind woman, and deserved nothing less in return. "We think he is well. He is off to Wales, to seek a bride. The niece of a King."

Begu took this in, nodding assent. Edwin was fulfilling one of those tasks he had been born to do – marry well.

She had come to speak of his brother, and returned to him.

"Ceric. Will you take me to him, Worr? I have heard that you go into the wood and leave him food. Let me go with you. I must speak to him."

Worr looked at this woman, one in whose bed he had also known a few nights of pleasure. She had been Ceric's woman for years, before he had considered himself wed to Ashild of Four Stones. After this Begu had been handed over to Edwin. She had, Worr thought, served both men well, at perhaps a cost so great that no silver taken to her was recompense enough. He could not say no to her now.

"Tomorrow is the day I would go and leave him food. You may come with me, if you like."

The breath she exhaled told him how great a granting this was to her.

"I will return tomorrow, then," she said. She squared her shoulders as if she meant to turn and leave him now. Worr stopped her.

"Let me take you back to your home. It is a long walk."

Her mouth opened in surprise at this offer. But she shook her head. "I cannot ride. I have never been on a horse."

Worr could smile at this.

"No matter. Just hold on. You will sit behind me. We will go slowly."

Walk slowly they did, but it nearly halved the tiresome trip, and gave Begu her first look at the world from the height of a horse's back. The hamlet folk were about when they arrived, and one man came even to help Begu down from the mare's back.

"I will come in the morning, to take you," Worr said, as he looked down at her standing by the door of her cottage. "The cave where he lives lies between the hall and your hamlet. Leaving from here will save time."

It was not far past first light when Worr appeared at Begu's hamlet. She heard the nicker of his mare, and was ready for him, stepping out almost at once with a leathern pack slung about her shoulder. She was wrapped warmly in a woollen cloak, for though the day would warm, the coolness of night still floated in the air.

They made their way overland until they left the mare, tying her at a second trail Worr had discovered. This also led to the rill of water they must pass to reach the cave Ceric had made his home. Since finding the cave Worr had abandoned the earlier supply point, and carried food directly to the rock face. He did not press Ceric to appear, and in fact, knew that the man was often out, gathering firewood, foraging for berries or nuts, or wandering the greenwood, for Worr had at times glimpsed him on his return from these outings.

Worr led the way through the brush and trees, carrying a food pack, while Begu followed, grasping her skirts to her to keep them from being snagged on the undergrowth.

The Sun was fully up, bright and warm over their heads, when they began the climb to the rocky face where sat the cave. The small cauldron and tripod were there, empty, the fire cold. The pea plants Edgyth had given him were withered away, though they had been plump with pods earlier; Worr had seen it. But today it looked that Ceric was not here.

To be certain, Worr called out, addressing the dark mouth of the cave.

"Ceric. It is me. If you are within, come out, so I may see you."

There was no response.

Begu made request. "Will you leave me, Worr, that I might sit here and wait? I have water, and bread, and my cloak if it grows cold."

Worr gave a sigh, but nodded. He recalled something he had with him, and drew it forth from the food pack. It was a little bird, carved of plain wood. Small marks were upon it, those of a teething child. Worr had taken it from the window sill of the bower Ceric had left, meaning to leave it for him now. He would entrust it to Begu.

"If you find him, give him this. His father carved it for him, when Ceric was little more than a babe. Ceric has a son of his own, away at Four Stones in Lindisse. This may remind him that he himself is now a father of a toddling boy."

She enfolded it in her hands, and lowered her head.

"I will come back for you as the Sun is lowering," Worr told her. He thought of what more he might say.

"Sometimes – many times – I never see him. If he will not show himself . . . do not take it amiss."

Begu nodded. Worr turned and made his way down the slope, and vanished into the waiting trees.

A pine had fallen not far from the cave opening, and looked a place where she might set her pack, and herself. She did so, and spent a long while at rest after the ride, the walk through the trees, and the final climb to this rock face. The grey rock looked forbidding, and the hollow of the cave made her think of what beasts might have once dwelt within. Yet the boughs from the near trees arched overhead, filtering the Sun which cut through the green leaves and slender needles. Birds sang, calling out, near and far, that twittering to announce their presence to others.

Begu listened. She opened her own throat, and sang. She did it in response to the blackbirds about her, and to keep herself company.

Ceric, walking through the trees, heard her song. He knew it to be that of Begu. A song was the first of her voice Ceric had ever heard. He stopped to listen, and then moved towards the singer.

He could see her now, sitting atop the fallen pine. He looked at her from the side, her curling yellow hair catching the Sun. Begu was the first woman whose body he had known; she who had given so generously of herself. He stepped nearer, until she noticed him.

She jumped up, out of startle. His red-gold hair, which she had taken delight in stroking, hung in dark and twisted hanks, falling far beyond his shoulders. Bits of leaves and twigs were stuck in it. His beard was ragged, as if cut away with the seax he wore. His frame, pitiably thin, was dressed in tatters, his leggings pulled tight around a shrunken waist.

She felt no fear of him, once her startle passed. He eyed her, in her gown of pale hue, as she stood before him, part of a hopeful past, now blasted beyond redemption.

Tears flooded his eyes.

"You can do nothing for me," he choked out. His voice was little more than a croak, rusty from disuse.

Begu had ready answer for this.

"I am not here for your sake, but for my own," she told him. Her words were steady, yet firm. Nothing would keep her from saying what she must.

"For the sake of what you have meant to me, I must speak to you. You are not alone in being robbed of that which you loved. My husband and I were happy. We had been wed just over a year when he cut himself, scything. The wound went green. He died a horrible death, in my arms, after days of suffering. I could do nothing to save him. I would have liked to have died myself, but I did not. He would have wished me to live, and so I did, as best I could. I went on living. You were a part of that life, Ceric. The part I will never forget."

She drew a long and steadying breath, and turned from past to present.

"I am leaving Kilton, forever. I have returned from a trip to my home village, inland. It had been long since I had seen it. I went on foot, with a small wicker pack over my shoulders, travelling with a neighbour family who were journeying nearby. At my village I met a man who had also just returned, for the death of his mother. We were children together. He has three young ones. His wife died in childbed with their fourth. We spoke together, and despite the years and what has befallen us, were able to laugh together, recalling our time as children. I told him all of my life. All. He knows I have whored."

Ceric winced, and shook his head.

"Yes," she corrected. "I have whored. The use of my body for silver or goods is just that. I have not walked the lanes of some great trading town, but I have sold myself, nonetheless."

Ceric was compelled to answer; he must refute such ugliness. His words were halting, but more resembled human speech. "What we had – what you have with Edwin – is far different."

"With your brother there was affection there, kindness, certainly," she allowed. "But what I felt for you, was something far more. Love."

He had no answer for this, but knew somehow how vital it was for her to name it. He found himself shaking his head again. "You – you did nothing wrong . . ."

"I did much wrong. As did you." She spoke here not of her whoring, but of allowing herself to love him, and on his part, being unable to see it.

"Did you not go to Dunnere, and confess your visits with me?"

He closed his eyes at the truth of this. "The sin was mine. Not yours."

It was her turn to shake her head. "It matters not. It is our past, nothing more nor less.

"You have been kind to me," she went on. "And I have been even kinder to you. I have forgiven you your thoughtlessness, forgiven you your selfishness. Forgiven you for thinking I had no greater life, and no hope of one, beyond what I gave you in my bed. I forgive you all this."

A new strength was come into her face and voice as she spoke these freeing truths.

"I have wed this man, from my childhood. I will at last have children to raise. It has been a great lack in my life. And I will be at the side, each day, of a good man. He is coming for me, soon, in an ox cart, so I might take my things away to his house. I have much silver, that which you gave me, and that also from Edwin. We will buy cattle. With cows we will have milk enough for cheese-making."

She paused here, overtaken by the promise of her own future. She went on, in the here and now. "My own house I have given to that neighbour-woman who was kindest to me. She was grateful for it, as it will serve her daughter when she weds. As I have done."

Begu had come to the end of her telling. She stood looking at Ceric, moved to the depths of her heart by his plight. Yet he said no more.

"Will you not take comfort in all I have said?" she asked, as plea.

"I am beyond comfort," he told her. "I have killed my wife."

"You could not know that. And . . . there are others, who need you."

She turned to her pack under the tree, and held out the tiny carved bird.

"Worr, your faithful Worr, gave me this, should I see you. He wants you to remember the little son you have left, a child who needs you."

His face changed, crumbling into despair. Tears ran from his eyes, yet he reached for the wooden bird. His fist closed around it and he pressed it to his chest.

Begu feared taxing him more; she could not, weak as he was. She drew a dark shawl, one from her bed, out of her bag, and draped it along the trunk of the pine.

"Come," she said, as gently as speaking to a frightened child. "Sit next me now."

He did so, and her first act was to place her arm about him. It allowed him to lower his head, first to her shoulder, and then, with a deep release of breath, fully into her lap. She took her free hand and began to gently stroke his face. Her fingers traced the furrowed brow, smoothing it under her touch, and ran down the line of his noble nose, to circle up to his cheek, and then his ear. She began to sing, a soft and low lullaby, a tune melancholy but not without sweetness.

His breathing began to slow, and the fingers which clutched the wooden bird gradually relaxed. It fell into her lap.

Begu sat a long time, her arm circling Ceric's shoulder as he slept there.

When Worr entered the clearing, he saw Ceric asleep, his head in Begu's lap, her arm around him.

He stopped. He had heard tales of how maids could sit in the forest, and savage beasts approach them, and harm them not, but find needed succour in their presence, enough to lay their heads in the maid's lap. Begu was no maid, but Worr saw she possessed power of her own.

Worr had suspected Begu's deep constancy to Ceric, despite his having forsworn her, and left her to his brother. If anyone alive could effect this on Ceric now, it would be the woman who was now before him, her arm protectively laid upon Ceric.

As if made aware of the presence of another, Ceric started up. Worr stood unmoving, afraid a single step would make him flee.

"Ceric," Worr said, his voice little more than breathing the name.

Ceric stood staring at Worr. Begu lifted her hand and placed it on Ceric's back, in support, and encouragement. He took a step nearer the horse-thegn. Worr closed the distance between them, his own arms raising to enfold him.

Ceric let himself be held, but began choking out words he had long had none to tell.

"I cannot forget . . . that moment she turned to look at me, and saw . . . the spear I had thrown . . . I cannot forget that."

Worr's head jerked back. He stared at Ceric, then grasped more tightly the shoulders of the anguished speaker.

"Ceric! What are you saying? She saw nothing. I was there; I saw the wound. The spear hit her back, between the shoulder blades. It struck the heart. It beat another beat – no more – and then was stilled.

"She knew nothing, felt the impact, nothing more. She was alive, and then she was dead."

Ceric stood, slack, with little more than Worr's hands keeping him upright. The horse-thegn went on, in quieter tone but just as much urgency.

"You must free yourself from this. It is not the truth. She died at once, without seeing who or what caused it."

Worr knew how battle stories could change in the minds of men, after long rumination. This was one, one which had so turned against the teller. Not only had Ceric unwittingly killed Ashild, he had begun to believe she saw him in the act.

Ceric stood, brow knitted as he absorbed this. His eyes shifted, tracing movement, as if he again were upon that field of war, and running for his target. Then he closed those seeing eyes.

His hands lifted within the arms of Worr. His fingers touched the arms of the horse-thegn, his friend.

"Yes," he breathed. "I recall it now. She was walking away from me. Holding the banner aloft, and walking away. She did not turn."

His head dropped low, at this truth. When he lifted his face to look at Worr, his eyes were clearer. He spoke again to his friend, and with new certainty.

"She did not turn."

He wept now, cleansing tears of relief.

When the three emerged from the wood, Worr had Ceric mount his mare. He and Begu walked alongside. They passed two cowherds heading home with their horned milkers, and the drovers looked at them in wonder. Worr nodded his head, granting one of them the task of running ahead to the palisade gates with the news.

When they reached the hall the Sun was dropping to the west. Edgyth stood there, outside the opened gates, her hands clasped at her breast as if in hopeful prayer. They stopped before her, and Ceric slid from the horse to her open arms.

"Forgive me, Lady," Ceric managed. Her tears of relief could not hide the question on her face, as she looked from Worr to the woman at his side.

Worr spoke. "It was not me Lady, but Begu, who worked this."

Begu made a deep curtsy, and spoke. She had never thought she would come face to face with a Lady of Kilton. She answered with the simple honesty of her nature.

"Dear Lady, yes, I am Begu. I am known to both brothers of your hall. I have served to comfort them."

Edgyth had heard of this woman, and now she stood before her. Modwynn had known of her as well, though the two Ladies of Kilton had never discussed her. Edgyth knew why. Modwynn held these matters were not theirs; they belonged to the young men in question. Worr had vouched for Begu, that was enough.

The Lady of Kilton looked between Begu and the returned Ceric. "Our thanks to you are endless," Edgyth whispered.

Begu refuted these thanks, as gently as possible.

"Do not thank me, sweet Lady, for doing that which was mine to do. I leave Kilton forever. I have wed a man I knew as a child. He is coming for me and will be here on the morrow, or the next.

"If I have aided your hall and folk, I leave untroubled in heart and mind," Begu ended.

Edgyth moved to the speaker, and lifting her arms, enfolded Begu. Of any thank-offering Begu could receive, this act was the most meaningful.

As the Lady of Kilton stood in embrace with Begu, her mind ranged over the roles each had played in the lives of Ceric and Edwin. Edgyth knew Begu was barren, just as she herself was. Each woman had found fruitfulness in caring for the brothers, helping to bring them to manhood, and now in the case of Ceric, reclaiming him from mad wandering in the greenwood.

Worr spoke now. "I will take you home," he told Begu. He untied the saddle bags holding those things of worth which had been with Ceric in the forest.

Ceric made gesture toward Begu, who in her answering look, granted him a parting embrace.

"Fare thee well, Ceric," she whispered, her arms about him for the final time.

He returned this wish, as sincere in his desire as was she. "Fare thee well, Begu."

Edgyth took Ceric to his bower house, and had food brought. A large salver was carried in, crowded with dishes offered by the cooks. Barley browis filled a small bowl. There were eggs, seethed in the fat of the bacon slab which accompanied them, loaves baked that morning, a scoop of yellow butter, pots of soft cheeses, a dish of newly-plucked raspberries. Drink was there as well, a pottery cup of warm broth, and a silver one of cool ale. Ceric might have his fill of all of this.

He took a sip of the ale first, something unknown to his mouth in these last twelve months of his removal. He ate, taking a little of all things before him, enough to make Edgyth glad. Beginning tomorrow she would mix him draughts using wild celery, to help build his appetite, and as an aid to sleep.

When Worr returned, Ceric allowed himself to be led by the horse-thegn to the bathing shed. The ragged clothing left behind was fit for nothing but burning. As Ceric re-entered the bower house to sit before Edgyth, clad in a white linen tunic and dark leggings, she thought how best to address the tangle of his long hair. Even softened with rain water her comb could not penetrate it more than a finger's length away from the scalp. She began to cut. Matted clumps of hair dropped about him, twisted and knotted strands which had formed about caught twigs. It was left shorter than Ceric had worn in many years, but the wave in it added fullness, showing golden highlights in his coppery curls. When Edgyth laid down the shears, she showed him his visage in the looking-disc of polished silver. He regarded the face reflected with seeming curiosity. He took the shears and with Edgyth holding the disc before him, trimmed his beard short.

They sat then, alone in this bower house which had once been Edgyth's. This small abode also was the place he was born. His eyes moved to the dragon bed, which had served as marriage bed for Edgyth and Godwin, for his own parents Ceridwen and Gyric, and which he had hoped would be his with Ashild. The thickening shadows in the room softened the outline of the dragon posts upon the plank floor.

"How do I begin," he asked. He spoke so slowly she knew every word was weighed and measured. "Begin to make my way back. Back from the deadly silence of my thoughts."

Edgyth drew a slow breath. She knew a great deal about silence, having craved it, and having at times the silence of the nunnery granted to her. She uttered four words which she believed to be true.

"God works through silence."

This rested in the air a long moment. "You need rest, rest and food," she went on. "As your body re-builds, your strength to meet that silence will grow."

Other than his father, Edgyth had never seen a man so transformed as was he before her. His heart had broken, and his mind too; but Ceric could mend. She believed this. She did not know what God had now in store for him, but trusted Divine Providence would send Ceric what was most needed for his fullest recovery. She wondered if he might be called to vows, and become a monk.

"I will leave you now," she told him. Soon the entire hall would gather for the evening meal, and she must be there. "Would you have a serving man outside your door?" she asked.

He shook his head. "I need nothing. Only to ask your pardon for the worry I have caused."

The smile on her pale lips was sincere. "You are restored to the hall. Nothing matters, beyond that."

When the day darkened, Worr came alone to the bower house. He found Ceric sitting at the table within, the cresset unlit. Worr struck a spark into the wood curls in the dish and blew breath upon it. He picked the tiny flame out with a straw and held it to the blackened wick. As the light flickered into yellow life, he asked Ceric a question.

"Can you stay alone tonight," he wished to know, with a nod to the single alcove in which he could sleep.

"I will sleep," Ceric said, more hope than promise.

Still, it gave Worr heart, though he was not certain the kind of deep rest Ceric needed could be found solely by sleep.

The elder son of the hall did fall asleep in the dragon bed. But he awoke in the dark. Whether it was the now-unaccustomed softness of the feather bed, or the deep quiet of the house, as opposed to his forest dwelling with its calls of night birds outside its opening, he did not know. But he arose, drawn to do so from the brightness of the Moon falling through the casement. He pulled on the same dark leggings and white linen tunic he had donned following his bathing, and stepped out into that light.

The Moon was at three-quarters, waning, marking another cycle spent. Even in its diminished state it was brilliant in the cloudless sky. He walked towards it, until he stood at the garden. Moonlight made a rippling stair of light across the sea, at this hour also calm. It drew him closer to the cliff edge. A few steps more and he was nigh the precipice. He looked down at the rocks below, but dimly outlined from the shadow cast by the projecting bluff to his right.

Though he could not see it, the bottom was there, rocky and sure. It lay, a great void before him, just as his life was now a void. He took a step nearer that darkness. He could step into that void at any moment. It awaited him; he could choose it at any time.

Instead he looked up, filling his eyes with the Moon. He stepped back, and turned. He saw at this distance the edge of the stone chantry. Moonlight was striking the face of the church, falling at a window. He went to it, opened the door and walked within.

A single light burnt inside, that sanctuary oil lamp always burning near the altar. He moved by its light. The Moon aided him too, and took him to the stone under which his grandparents lay. He could just make out the crisp lettering impressed there, naming Modwynn, Lady of Kilton. Her name was carved next to that of his grand-sire Godwulf, Lord. A small cushion was upon the stone, one he knew was used by Edgyth as she knelt in her daily prayer.

Ceric dropped on his knees to the unyielding stone. He knelt down upon the cold stone covering his grandmother and asked for help. He prayed. His head dropped forward over his hands, and he sank to the stone, and lay there on his back upon it, his head resting on that firm cushion.

He dreamt a freeing dream. Ceric was upon the battlefield again. He saw himself running, and picking up the spear, saw too his hand releasing it. The figure he aimed it at turned, and it was Ashild. But there was no horror upon her face. She was smiling at him, smiling and radiant. As the spear sailed towards her it dissolved into the glow of light emanating from her, a radiance which also obscured her from view. Though she was gone, the splendour remained.

He awoke at the dawning of the day, a beam of morning sunlight pouring through the window, and onto his face. He lifted himself to his knees over the bodies of those beloved dead, and resolved to try to live.

THE WELSH GIRL

DWYNWEN was soon to alight at Kilton. Edwin had sent a rider ahead on the last stage of the journey, that the hall might prepare. Even before his messenger had ridden off, as soon as the first horse trod on Kilton's soil, a horn rang out, signalling to those watch-guards ahead to sound the approach. Edwin's troop now passed through the palisade to find all assembled to meet them.

The rider who had been sent was Wystan, now Edwin's second captain of his body-guard, and he related to Lady Edgyth the nature of this return. Her son was arriving with a potential bride, and the condition of her staying was the agreeableness of Kilton to her taste. Wystan added that the bride was yet a child of fourteen, so that the Lady should not be taken aback at her small size and extreme youth.

This news, that her son was returning neither empty-handed nor with a wife, caught Edgyth somewhat by surprise. A maid was arriving, yes, but it would be unseemly to welcome the young woman as her daughter. She hurriedly scaled back the meal from that of a bridal-feast to one of abundant and hearty welcome.

Then she went to speak to Ceric. Since his return a week ago he had spent his time largely in his bower house, or in the garden. Today, on a clear Summer morning, she found him seated at the table there. The trellis work of the small pavilion, thick with roses at this season, provided shelter from the cross winds off the cliff face. From there one might look out and enjoy not only the flowers and vines of the garden, but the sea beyond.

She sat down in a chair across from him and began. "Edwin is returned," she said, her smile proof of her relief at his safe keeping. "He will be here shortly. He has brought not a wife, but a woman who might become so. As we had been warned, she is quite young, of only ten and four Summers."

As she said this aloud Edgyth realised that if the girl determined to stay at Kilton, surely she herself would be needed here for perhaps two years, or even more. The child might not be ready for the marriage-bed, and despite being raised in a royal hall, there would still be much of the managing of such a place she had not had time to absorb. Edgyth swept this from her mind. She must rise and leave the garden. Many tasks awaited, and she was glad for Edwin, that he had found a girl he liked so well as this one.

"There will be a feast tonight, one of welcome. If you would like to appear, it would I am sure, gladden all. But you need not attend, if doing so causes distress. You will meet the maid by-and-by. Edwin and I shall bring her to you."

He nodded. "I thank you," he told her.

Ceric had entered the hall a handful of times since his return, and broke his fast there some mornings. The raucousness of the evening meal was not something he could yet face.

A horn sounded; one from the parapet. They must be near.

"Edwin will be glad to see you," was what she left Ceric with, that, and a squeeze of his hand.

The Lady of Kilton took up her post by the front door of her hall, opened wide in a gesture of welcome. By her side was Worr, the horse-thegn of Kilton. Edgyth had changed her head-wrap for a fine veil, affixing it to her hair with long golden pins, mementos from Modwynn. How she wished that Lady at her side now.

The view from the open gates gave out past the village road to the orchards, and dark forest beyond. In due time the troop appeared on the road, now moving past the pear grove.

Edwin and the priest Dunnere fronted a waggon new to Edgyth, on the bench of which she saw the maid, garbed in a gown of red. Five-and-twenty riders followed, dusty from the road, and then came the supply waggon they had left with. Edwin was smiling, and he waved as the hall cheered him in.

As he led the girl to her, Edgyth had a chance to take her in. She was perhaps the most striking child she had ever seen. The face was notable for its round blue eyes, pointed chin, and rose-tinted mouth. Her poker-straight hair of light brown fell nearly to her knees. In her freshness and distinction there was something other-worldly about her. Edgyth found herself thinking of the lives of certain female saints, and of how in girlhood they must have been distinguishable from other children. Dwynwen had such a quality about her. Her person was made the more remarkable by the gravity of her demeanour. In height Dwynwen did not come even to her son's shoulder, yet there was no silly girlishness in her step; she moved with supple assurance. Yet as the girl looked on her, Edgyth sensed warmth behind the placid eyes, tinder waiting to flare, which might foretell strong attachment.

They stopped before her, so that Edwin might make formal introduction.

"Edgyth, Lady of Kilton, this is Dwynwen, daughter of Dunwyd. Niece to King Elidon of Ceredigion."

Both Ladies inclined their head to the other, and Dwynwen, being so youthful, also curtsied in respect.

This done, mother and son could embrace, and the Lady of Kilton extend a warm hand to the girl Edwin had brought with him.

A welcome-cup was taken, of clear and golden ale, and while within the hall both Edwin and Edgyth tried to gauge Dwynwen's reaction to it. The wide eyes opened no wider at the bright spaciousness they stood in, but neither did the slight smile fade. Having been safely delivered, Dwynwen was now in Edgyth's hands, and she next presented her to Worr and his wife Wilgyfu, and to those others of the hall the girl should know. Though her responses were short, Dwynwen had a pretty turn of phrase for all she met, and her careful way of speaking the tongue of Angle-land won admiring looks from those she addressed.

The Lady now looked back to Worr, who nodded in acknowledgment. She watched him move to Edwin, who was speaking with Dunnere. Worr had been charged with telling them both Ceric was returned.

This done, Edgyth led Dwynwen to her lodging. Following Modwynn's death, Edgyth had moved into that

Lady's bower house, and now assigned that which had been her own to her guest. The waggon bearing the girl's goods was drawn up before it.

After halting the horses, the driver came around and unlaced the tarpaulin protecting its contents. As he pulled it open, a scrabbling was heard. A niddering girl was within, clearly affright, silent, and cowering at her discovery.

Dwynwen called out to her, in the tongue of Wales, and the girl stilled.

"She is my slave," was what Dwynwen told Edgyth.

The girl was wild-haired, her clothing askew, and no older than Dwynwen herself. Her hair had been knotted up in a head wrap from which most of the brown curls had escaped.

Edgyth could do nothing but make a murmur of assent. Kilton had no more slaves, only freed-folk; following Godwin's death Lady Modwynn had made sure of that. Those enslaved were freed, and she had equipped them, as the law dictated, with the means from which to make their own living. Some farmed a tract of common land set apart for this purpose, others remained within the confines of the palisade of Kilton, doing much the same work as they had before, but with greater protections and freedoms. If Dwynwen stayed, Edgyth would encourage her to free this one, as well.

"I was wrong to bring her," Dwynwen admitted, which served to make Edgyth look even more kindly on her guest. "I took her from the scrub-kitchen, and she knows nothing but the cleaning of pots."

The Lady of Kilton considered this. With Dwynwen's consent, Edgyth could give the girl to the cooks, who would make good use of her. The kitchen yard was the most favoured of any labour given to such, as there they would not go hungry. But Dwynwen might want her near, untrained as she was, for at least the girl spoke her own tongue.

"I will give you a serving woman, that your own might benefit from her knowledge," Edyth suggested.

Dwynwen gave her small smile, and nodded. This is just how Edwin told me she would respond, she thought. How well these folk know each other. Elidon knows almost nothing of importance of Luned. Or of me.

Her goods were carried in by the driver and the slave, and soon the small house was crowded with packs, baskets, and chests.

"There is light enough to unpack later," Edgyth invited, "and our meal is hours away. Let me show you our chantry."

They entered the church together, Edgyth pointing out on the way which house was that of Dunnere. The church itself, empty, cool, and smelling of incense and stone, seemed to make impress on the girl; she bowed her head and stood quietly by Edgyth's side as the latter whispered to her of those who laid buried below. The painted statues on the walls caught Dwynwen's eye, and they moved to one dressed in red, as Dwynwen was.

"St Ninnoc," Edgyth murmured with a smile.

"Ninnoc." Dwynwen repeated the name in some wonder. "She is of Cymru."

"Yes, though she went to Frankland as a nun." Edgyth's face turned thoughtful. "It is a name held in dear remembrance here. Edwin and his brother had a tiny sister of that name, who died of fever." She turned to a grave slab she had earlier pointed out. "She is buried there, with their father." They looked back to the statue, and Dwynwen noticed the golden finger rings at the base. "They are those of Ceridwen" – Edgyth smiled at this additional Welsh name – "who is their mother, and of Gyric, their father."

Dwynwen took this all in. Now that she was here, it was not the barbaric land she had imagined.

While the Lady of Kilton was welcoming Dwynwen, Edwin went to see Ceric. He came straight away from the hall and the welcome ale, to find Ceric standing at the edge of the cliff. It stopped Edwin, the sight of this, and he remembered forcing himself to look over that rock face to see if his brother's broken body lay below. He wished he did not stand so near the edge now.

He did not like to call out, so came to the pavilion and moved a bench upon the paving stones there. Ceric turned at the scraping sound. Edwin smiled, at the same time trying to hide his dismay at the spareness of his brother's frame. All warriors lost flesh while on the road, and he had seen Ceric return from campaigns needing food and drink to restore him to full strength. Today he looked as starved as any roving beggar.

Neither spoke, but their embrace was long and firm. Edwin could feel his brother's ribs through his linen tunic.

They both sat down at the benches behind the table.

"How long have you been back," Edwin asked.

"Several days," Ceric answered. He seemed unsure of the exact passage of time.

There was much Edwin wished to know, but he feared asking any of it. Finally Ceric spoke.

"I will not be at the feast tonight," he told him.

Edwin began to object, and then took thought. Here he was, bringing his bride to Kilton, when his brother had lost his own. It would be hard. He ended by nodding his agreement.

"I will meet the maid soon," Ceric said in promise.

Edwin saw again how thin Ceric was. "You are eating," he asked.

"Yes, yes. Putting on flesh," Ceric answered, with no heartiness.

Worr appeared at the edge of the garden, waiting to be summoned within. If Ceric were alone, he would approach him directly, but with the Lord of Kilton there, he paused until Edwin gestured him to approach. The horse-thegn's appearance at this point was intentional. He had watched Edwin greet his brother, given them time to say a few things which might be needful, but then stepped in. He did not trust Edwin to honour the limits his older brother still must place on himself. Worr was the pledged man of Ceric, and would protect him, even from his own Lord and brother.

After a few words to both brothers Worr addressed Ceric. "We might ride out together this afternoon," he posed. "It is a fine day for it." Getting Ceric out and beyond the hall precincts was a goal with him; the man kept so much to himself, staying in the bower, or the confines of this garden.

Ceric nodded. "Let us do that," he said.

"I will ready the horses," Worr said. He looked to Edwin. "You are, I think, wanted by Lady Edgyth," he offered. This was not true, but he had news he must share with the Lord of Kilton. He and Edwin left the garden together, Ceric remaining at the table. As soon as they were outside its borders Worr spoke.

"Of the woman Begu," he said. The horse-thegn's tone was low, but hearing her named so abruptly pitched Edwin from his thoughts. He turned to Worr, fully attentive.

"She has left Kilton," Worr reported.

"Left Kilton?"

"She has wed a man from her home village. A widower, with children. It is what she ever wanted, she told us."

"Told us?"

"Yes. For it was Begu who reclaimed your brother."

Edwin stood open-mouthed.

"She came to me, asking to be taken to Ceric. I did so, and left her there all morning, never thinking he would appear to her. When I returned, he was lying, his head in her lap, asleep, and perhaps knowing some kind of peace after all the long months since the battle.

"He let me approach, for the first time. He began to tell of the night-mare he rode, of the death of Ashild of Four Stones. The story had twisted in his fevered brain, into a lie. He had come to believe she watched him throw the spear. I made him see that this was wrong. It has, I think, furthered his healing." Worr paused a moment. "The truth is hard enough."

Edwin was nodding his head to all this, his mind racing. His brother was back, but Begu had left.

"And Begu is gone – wed."

"Yes. She said at last she would awaken each morning with a man at her side."

Worr, when an unwed man, was one of many who had left her in the middle of the night. He felt pity that she had been deprived this simple comfort for so many years.

"Did she leave message for me?" was Edwin's plaintive question.

Worr must be truthful. "To me, no. Perhaps she said something to Ceric. Later, you might ask him."

Worr would continue with what he could tell.

"She came here to the hall, with Ceric. She spoke to Lady Edgyth with simple courtesy, and warmth. Such was Begu's nature," Worr ended.

Edwin could only nod. It was a blow, one he must not allow himself to feel.

Well, he would not need Begu now. He would wed soon. He felt certain of it.

In the morning, after the hall had gathered to break their fast, Dwynwen felt called to visit the stone chantry again. The fact that a saint of Cymru was honoured there held meaning. Dunnere was Cymry, and was here as well, but Ninnoc was different. The statue was an old one; Ninnoc had been revered here far longer than Dunnere's presence.

The church door, heavy as it was, yielded almost easily to her hand. It gave a further sense of welcome in doing so. She left it open behind her, though the sunlight pouring through the stone casements flooded the place with a soft glow. The cool whiteness of the stone, and the snowy linen trailing from the altar lent a chaste, even maidenly, air to the space. It was the first church of stone she had ever seen or entered; all others she had known were of timber, though she had heard from Gwydden of huge churches these Saxons used, made within temples of dressed stone the men of Caesar left behind.

I could be wed here, she thought. I could stand before that door that I opened so readily, and be wed.

She thought of Edwin. She was not certain what she felt towards him, but Luned's words returned to her: You will hold a man's life in your hand. He seemed to want her enough, perhaps that was what was meant. Wanting someone badly could lead to madness, treason, and death; she knew this from what had happened to Trystan and Esyllt.

Yet it felt no heartbreak to be carried from Cymru. It was the Fate of all women to leave their homes, of Esyllt as well, carried from Éireann to wed a foreign Lord in a distant land. Dwynwen had been raised for it. She had known from girlhood of this. After her mother died, and then her father, she knew she would lose her step-mother Luned as well, this woman who had schooled her in so many arts.

She walked to the painted statue of Ninnoc, standing there against the wall in her red gown. Today Dwynwen wore one of blue. She looked again at the two gold rings placed there at its base. One of them, the smaller, was set with a stone of green. That must have been worn by Ceridwen, Edwin's mother.

Her hand moved to it; she could not stay it. She let her finger rest a moment on that stone of green.

This came from your hand, she thought, and I touch it now with mine own . . .

A sigh escaped her lips, a deep emptying. She turned to the altar, made her genuflection, and left.

Outside the door, she lifted her head, and caught scent of that sea she had glimpsed on their approach.

Past Dunnere's house were a few smaller houses, bowers perhaps. Beyond them she saw a screen of trees. She walked to it, to find beyond the clipped beeches the broad expanse of sea. Between her and the rolling waves were carefully tended plots of herbs, flowers, and trained vines.

This then was the garden Edwin had spoken of. The burh was encircled by the tall palisade, all except here. The sheer cliff face was such no wall was needed.

The garden itself, deep within the private area of the burh, had no fencing save the beech hedge. Past them it began, with gravel paths wending their way between the beds. It was empty of all folk, and seemed to invite her in. As she passed a tangle of honeysuckle clinging to a framework, she saw a kind of pavilion. There flat stones had been laid upon the gravel, and a large table, some chairs, and a few short benches placed. It was protected by trellis work nearly smothered in blooming roses of pink and white. The sea breeze which had led her here was now scented by their sweetness.

She wished to come closer, and did so. The gravel crunched under her feet as her footfall moved it.

Of a sudden a figure rose, one who must have been seated at the table, sheltered from her view by the trellis.

It was a man, like Edwin in colouring, and yet strikingly unlike him.

Edwin had told Dwynwen little about his older brother. She knew that he fought in the train of the Prince of Wessex, and that now he was somewhere away. That was all. But this must be him.

Ceric had risen at the sound of someone's near approach. He turned to see a young maid, with a puzzled half-smile on her lips. She had no guardian with her.

You are the Welsh girl, Ceric knew.

Then he thought: And you are fey; you are of the world of faery.

In face and stature she looked a creature between girl and woman, between this world, and that spirit world said to still roam the mountains of Wales.

Dwynwen waited for him to speak. He did not.

She opened her own lips.

"I am Dwynwen, daughter of Dunwyd."

He kept regarding her, but gave a deep bow of his head, as if before a King or Queen.

His first act spurred him to further courtesy, and he spoke.

"I am Ceric."

That was all he said.

Dwynwen too was silent. He stood before her with an openness she had seen in no man. There was no posturing, no strutting vaunt; nothing to proclaim, or impress her with. Dwynwen felt she looked into him, even as he looked at her.

She saw a man worn nearly to the bone, yet with a warrior's uprightness, the cheeks under his fair beard hollow, but with a nose straight and finely formed beneath the fair brows. The eyes were slightly sunken, shadowed, as if they had seen too much. His Sun-touched copper hair was cut short, curling about face and neck. Around that neck she saw a thin chain of gold, holding, she thought, a talisman or amulet concealed upon his chest under his tunic.

He looked a man of youth and strength who had been grievously ill, and had just now planted his foot on the long road to recovery. His suffering had placed him in a crucible, from which all dross had been burnt away.

Given his age, his standing, and his handsomeness, he must be wed, even if no mention of this had been made. She made it hers to learn.

"I look forward to meeting your Lady-wife," she told him.

He stared at her, the eyes lifting upward a moment.

"Hers is a Heavenly abode," was what he answered. Dwynwen followed his gaze as he looked around at the garden on the bluff; one might feel this was Heaven on Earth, right here. His ending words were near a whisper. "But I thank you."

He stood, looking out to the white-tipped sea. Her own wide blue eyes remained on Ceric.

The utter rawness of him compelled her gaze; she could not look away. I was Fated to save a man, she thought . . .

He turned back to her, his gold-green eyes meeting hers, or somehow looking through her, she felt, and far deeper than she had seen into him. She felt herself ablaze under the force of those burning eyes.

He looked down of a sudden, as if aware of some violation in his so fixing his eyes upon her. He turned, walked the few steps back to the pavilion, and slumped down into the chair behind the table.

I was Fated to save a man, Dwynwen thought again. She inwardly repeated her step-mother's exact words: You will hold a man's life in your hands.

She had not known when told if it might be through some act of valour, or some healing art. Now a chilling thought welled in her mind, one she shook off as soon as it arose, that she might hold a man's life, only to destroy it.

Never, she thought. This man, ravaged as he looked, was not blighted. He was like a noble and sacred circle of stone, such as were worshipped by the followers of the Old Gods, which time and thoughtless waste had tried to ruin, but could not.

Wordlessly she turned on her heel and left, hastening back to the bower house. There was a single leathern pack she had not opened; Luned had told her to save it for that day when she knew if she would stay. She opened it now, plucking at the lacing. Inside lay the silver bridal-cup. She pulled it from its sack of linen. Lady Luned had packed this bag. They were her hands which had last encircled this bowl.

It was Dwynwen's cup; she had been given it, and she might do with it as she pleased. She did not need precious wine, or mead, or even ale; she would mix no philtre into the drink she prepared. She carried the bowl to the well by the kitchen yard. A barrel was there, filled, ready for dipping. She ignored it. It was living water she needed. She dropped the bucket down, and pulled up a fresh. She poured a dipperful into the bridal-cup. Then she carried it in both hands to where Ceric sat, chin lowered.

Ceric looked up. He saw the Welsh girl there, standing before him. She had a silver bowl in her hands, a large cup. Dwynwen looked at the man before her, his eyes questioning her. She warmed at the feel of those eyes upon her. Her lips formed a smile. She lifted the rim of the silver bowl to her mouth. This is the Water of Life, she thought. Dwynwen took a sip, and then passed the bowl to his waiting hands.

Here ends Book Nine of
The Circle of Ceridwen Saga.

FREE CIRCLE OF CERIDWEN COOKERY BOOK(LET)

You've read the books – now enjoy the food. Your free Circle of Ceridwen Cookery Book(let) is waiting for you at www.octavia.net.

Ten easy, delicious, and authentic recipes from the Saga, including Barley Browis, Roast Fowl, Baked Apples, Oat Griddle Cakes, Lavender-scented Pudding, and of course – Honey Cakes. Charmingly illustrated with medieval woodcuts and packed with fascinating facts about Anglo-Saxon and Viking cookery. Free when you join the Circle, my mailing list. Be the first to know of new novels, have the opportunity to become a First Reader, and more. Get your Cookery Book(let) now and get cooking!

THE WHEEL OF THE YEAR

Candlemas – 2 February

St Gregory's Day – 12 March

St Cuthbert's Day – The Spring Equinox, about 21 March

St Walpurga's (Walpurgisnacht) – 30 April

St Elgiva's Day – 18 May

St Helen's Day – 21 May

High Summer or Mid-Summer Day – 24 June

Sts Peter and Paul – 29 June

Hlafmesse (Lammas) – 1 August

St Mary's Day – 15 August

St Matthews' Day – The Fall Equinox, about 21 September

All Saints – 1 November

The month of Blót – November; the time of Offering for followers of the Old Religions; also time of slaughter of animals which could not be kept over the coming Winter

Martinmas (St Martin's) – 11 November

Yuletide – 25 December to Twelfthnight – 6 January

Winter's Nights – the Norse end of year rituals, ruled by women, marked by feasting and ceremony

LITURGICAL HOURS OF THE DAY

The Canonical Hours – special daily prayers, as practised by Oundle and other religious foundations, are as follows:

Matins, or night-watch, about 2 a.m.

Lauds at dawn

Prime (the "first hour") about 6 a.m.

Terce (the "third hour") about 9 a.m.

Sext (the "sixth hour") about noon

None (the "ninth hour") about 3 p.m.

Vespers, the lighting of the lamps, at sunset

Compline, or retiring to sleep

ANGLO-SAXON PLACE NAMES,

WITH MODERN EQUIVALENTS

Æscesdun = Ashdown

Æthelinga = Athelney

Apulder = Appledore

Basingas = Basing

Beamfleot = Benfleet

Beardan = Bardney

Bearruescir = Berkshire

Bryeg = Bridgenorth

Buttingtun = Buttington

Caeginesham = Keynsham

Cippenham = Chippenham

Cirenceaster = Cirencester

Colneceastre = Colchester

Cruland = Croyland

Defenas = Devon

Englafeld = Englefield

Ethandun = Edington

Exanceaster = Exeter

Fearnhamme = Farnham

Fullanham = Fulham

Geornaham = Irnham

Glastunburh = Glastonbury

Gleaweceaster = Gloucester

Hamtunscir = Hampshire

Headleage = Hadleigh

Hreopedun = Repton

Iglea = Leigh upon Mendip

Jorvik (Danish name for Eoforwic) = York

Legaceaster = Chester

Limenemutha = Lymington in Hampshire

Lindisse = Lindsey

Lundenwic = London

Meredune = Marton

Meresig = Mersea

Middeltun = Milton

Readingas = Reading

River Lyge = River Lea

Sceaftesburh = Shaftesbury

Scireburne = Sherborne

Snotingaham = Nottingham

Sumorsaet = Somerset

Swanawic = Swanage

Turcesig = Torksey

Wedmor = Wedmore

Welingaford = Wallingford

Weogornaceastre = Worcester

Witanceaster (where the Witan, the King's

advisors, met) = Winchester

Frankland = France

Haithabu = Hedeby

Norse Place Names:

Aros = Aarhus, Denmark

Laaland = the island of Lolland, Denmark

Land of the Svear = Sweden

Welsh Place Names:

Cymru = Wales

GLOSSARY OF TERMS

Althing, and Thing: a regular gathering of citizens to settle disputes, engage in trade, and socialize. Gotland was divided into three administrative districts, each with their own "thing" or meeting, but the great thing, the Althing, was held at Roma, in the geographical centre of the island.

alvar: nearly barren stretches of limestone rock, typically supporting only tiny lichens and moss.

Asgard: Heavenly realm of the Gods.

brewster: the female form of brewer (and, interestingly enough, the female form of baker is baxter . . . so many common names are rooted in professions and trades . . .).

browis: a cereal-based stew, often made with fowl or pork.

chaff: the husks of grain after being separated from the usable kernel.

ceorl: ("churl") a free man ranking directly below a thegn, able to bear arms, own property, and improve his rank.

cottar: free agricultural worker; in later eras, a peasant.

cresset: stone, bronze, or iron lamp fitted with a wick that burnt oil.

drekar: "dragon-ship," a war-ship of the Danes.

ealdorman: a nobleman with jurisdiction over given

lands; the rank was generally appointed by the King and not necessarily inherited from generation to generation. The modern derivative *alderman* in no way conveys the esteem and power of the Anglo-Saxon term.

fey: possessing magical or supernatural powers; one belonging to the Land of Faery.

fulltrúi: the Norse deity patron that one felt called to dedicate oneself to.

fylgja: a Norse guardian spirit, always female, unique to each family.

fyrd: the massed forces of Wessex, comprising thegns – professional soldiers – and ceorls, trained freeman.

hack silver: broken silver jewellery, coils of unworked silver bars, fragments of cast ingots and other silver parcelled out by weight alone during trade.

hamingja: the Norse "luck-spirit" which each person is born with.

leech-book: compilation of healing recipes and practices for the treatment of human and animal illness and injury. Such books were a compendium of healing herbs and spiritual and magical practices. The *Leech Book of Bald*, recorded during Ælfred's reign, is a famed, and extant, example.

lur: a vertical (or curved) sounding horn fashioned of wood or brass, dating from the Bronze Age, and used in Nordic countries to rally folk from afar.

morgen-gyfu: literally, "morning-gift"; a gift given by

a husband to his new wife the first morning they awake together.

nard: (also, spikenard) a rare and precious oil, highly aromatic, derived from the crushed rhizomes of a honeysuckle-like plant grown in the Himalayas, India, and China. Mary Magdalen was said to have anointed the feet of Christ with nard.

philtre: a potion to excite love or lust in another.

quern: a small hand-driven mill consisting of two grind stones, the top stone usually being domed and having a hole to insert a wooden handle for turning. The oats, wheat, or other grain is placed between the stones, and the handle turned until the desired fineness is attained.

rauk: the striking sea- and wind-formed limestone towers on the coast of Gotland.

seax: the angle-bladed dagger which gave its name to the Saxons; all freemen carried one.

scop: ("shope") a poet, saga-teller, or bard, responsible not only for entertainment but seen as a collective cultural historian. A talented scop would be greatly valued by his lord and receive land, gold and silver jewellery, costly clothing and other riches as his reward.

scrying: to divine the future by gazing into a looking glass, a crystal, or water.

shingle beach: a pebbly, rather than sandy, beach.

skeggox: steel battle-axe favoured by the Danes.

skirrets: a sweet root vegetable similar to carrots, but cream-coloured, and having several fingers on each plant.

skogkatt: "forest cat"; the ancestor of the modern Norwegian Forest Cat, known for its large size, climbing ability, and thick and water-shedding coat.

Skuld: the eldest of the three Norse Norns, determiners of men's destinies. Skuld cuts with shears the thread of life. See also Urd and Verdandi.

strakes: overlapping wooden planks, running horizontally, making up a ship's hull.

symbel: a ceremonial high occasion for the Angle-Saxons, marked by the giving of gifts, making of oaths, swearing of fidelity, and (of course) drinking ale.

tæfl or Cyningtæfl ("King's table"): a "capture the King" strategy board game.

thegn: ("thane") a freeborn warrior-retainer of a lord; thegns were housed, fed and armed in exchange for complete fidelity to their sworn lord. Booty won in battle by a thegn was generally offered to their lord, and in return the lord was expected to bestow handsome gifts of arms, horses, arm-rings, and so on to his best champions.

treen: domestic objects fashioned of wood, especially tableware.

Tyr: the God of war, law, and justice. He voluntarily forfeited his sword-hand to allow the Gods to deceive, and bind, the gigantic wolf Fenrir.

Tyr-hand: in this Saga, any left-handed person, named so in honour of Tyr's sacrifice.

Urd: the youngest of the three Norse Norns, determiners of men's destinies. Urd makes decision as to one's calling and station in life. See also Skuld and Verdandi.

Verdandi: the middle of the three Norse Norns, determiners of men's destinies. Verdandi draws out the thread of life to appropriate length. See also Skuld and Urd.

wadmal: the Norse name for the coarse and durable woven woollen fabric that was a chief export in the Viking age.

wergild: Literally, man-gold; the amount of money each man's life was valued at. The Laws of Æthelbert, a 7th century King of Kent, for example, valued the life of a nobleman at 300 shillings (equivalent to 300 oxen), and a ceorl was valued at 100 shillings. By Ælfred's time (reigned 871-899) a nobleman was held at 1200 shillings and a ceorl at 200.

NOTES

TO *TWO DRAGONS*

Chapter the Fifth

Ashild's hallowing. In the early middle ages, local heroes and wise women were often venerated, with many referred to as saints. Much of this was done outside the formal processes of canonization from Rome, a series of attribution and proofs which was ever-developing. Some of those venerated had religious vocations, as nuns, abbesses, monks, priests, bishops, hermits or anchorites; others were men and women renowned for healing, or warrior-kings for their courage and self-sacrifice. Remains of their influence can be found in many place names in Great Britain. Two useful references are *The Hallowing of England* by Fr. Andrew Phillips, Anglo-Saxon Books 1994; and *The Book of Welsh Saints* by T.D. Breverton, Glyndŵr Publishing, 2000.

Chapter the Twelfth

Heligo, King of Denmark (also recorded as Helge and Halge). The records of ninth century Denmark are appallingly slim. Without educated religious such as monks and nuns to record history, little was saved, and that sometimes only years later. Adam of Bremen in the 11th century notes a briefly-ruling late 9th century Danish King of this name. I have given this scrap of information the job of serving as the King to whom Vigmund is attached.

CHAPTER THE THIRTEENTH

Ivar, King of the Svear or "King in Uppsala". We know nothing of the 9th century Kings of Sweden. It is extraordinary but true that the King of the Svear the Gotlanders made a treaty with goes unnamed in the Gutasaga. Ivar is the name of a legendary early King, and I have re-purposed this name and bestowed it on the late 9th century monarch who Eskil represents on Gotland.

The Gutasaga. This foundation story is the Saga of the Gutes – the Gotlanders. This brief document describes the history of the island from the arrival of the first man, Tjelvar, who Prometheus-like, kindled fire and thus kept Gotland from sinking beneath the waves of the Baltic each night. It mentions the deal struck with the unnamed King of Uppsala, and describes the coming of Christianity to the island. The Gutasaga was composed in the Old Gutnish dialect of Old Norse possibly between 1220 and 1285, and committed to parchment later, surviving in a single manuscript, Codex Holmensis B64, dated to about 1350. The MS is housed at the National Library of Sweden in Stockholm.

CHAPTER THE SIXTEENTH

Haesten. As noted in Book Eight, *For Me Fate Wove This*, Haesten disappears from the annals of history in 894. This allows the novelist free rein in imagining a suitable end for a bedevilling foe, one in which Hrald, the young

Jarl of Four Stones, comes into full play, protecting his interests and those of his folk. He settles a score for many in his act of justice.

Chapter the Seventeenth

Raedwulf's sapphire: Sapphires were exceedingly rare in 9th century England. It is not likely that any living there had ever seen a sapphire, let alone possessed one. Raedwulf's stating that he had taken it as battle-gain from a Dane he had killed underscores that only a trader/raider in contact with the flow of luxury goods along the Silk Road would have access to such a gemstone. I like to think that Raedwulf's gift eventually ended up as the real sapphire, known as St Edward's sapphire, fronting the crown of Queen Victoria, on display in the Tower of London. This is the oldest gemstone in the vast array of stones in the royal collection, and believed to have been part of Edward's coronation ring in 1042.

Chapter the Twenty-first

Trystan and Esyllt. Welsh names for the legendary, and doomed, lovers Tristan and Iseult.

ACKNOWLEDGEMENTS

The flight of *Two Dragons* was made much surer through the attentions and discernment of Beth Altchek and Libby Williams. Their initial reading in the developmental stage of creation has become the sweetest and most anticipatory parting I make with a new novel. The unfailing encouragement, stalwart support, and unflagging enthusiasm they offer for the Saga Folk (and their creator), even through the darkest moments, is a gift I cherish.

This series continues to be blest by the affectionate yet scrupulous care of a highly dedicated, and skilled, group of First Readers. My thanks and boundless admiration are due to Judy Boxer, Lyndall Buxton, Shani Goode, Mary Kelly, Elaine MacDonald, Kristen McEnaney, Amanda Porath, Ellen Rudd, Linda Schultz, and Lorie Witt. Your passion for the Saga characters and their lives is a continuing inspiration to my work.

Janine Eitniear and Misi are Founder and Moderator respectively of The Circle of Ceridwen Discussion and Idea Group on Facebook. Their dedication to the Saga and the interests of its followers have led them to create a happy and engaged on-line community which never ceases to delight me. There members can discuss the novels, comment on new archeological findings about the Anglo-Saxon and Viking Age, explore period handcrafts, foodways and fashion, and find the kind of fellowship that springs from shared interests and mutual delight. Janine and Misi truly “grow the Circle” with me each and every day, and my thanks to them are sincere and deep.

ABOUT THE AUTHOR

Octavia Randolph has long been fascinated with the development, dominance, and decline of the Anglo-Saxon peoples. The path of her research has included disciplines as varied as the study of Anglo-Saxon and Norse runes, and learning to spin with a drop spindle. Her interests have led to extensive on-site research in England, Denmark, Sweden, and Gotland. In addition to the Circle Saga, she is the author of the novella *The Tale of Melkorka,* taken from the Icelandic Sagas; the novella *Ride,* a retelling of the story of Lady Godiva, first published in Narrative Magazine; and *Light, Descending,* a biographical novel about the great John Ruskin. She has been awarded Artistic Fellowships at the Ingmar Bergman Estate on Fårö, Sweden; MacDowell; Ledig House International; and Byrdcliffe.

She answers all fan mail and loves to stay in touch with her readers. Join her mailing list and read more on Anglo-Saxon and Viking life at www.octavia.net. Follow her on Facebook at Octavia Randolph Author, and for exclusive access and content join the spirited members of The Circle of Ceridwen Saga Discussion and Idea Group on Facebook.

Made in United States
North Haven, CT
12 March 2024